sotfee

Don Leask

Copyright © Donald Leask

First published 2024

All rights reserved. No part of this publication may be reproduced, stored or transmitted in any form or by any means without the prior permission in writing of the author, nor to be otherwise circulated in any form of e-publication, binding or cover other than that in which it is published without a similar condition, including this condition, being imposed on the subsequent publisher

This book is a work of fiction and any resemblance to actual names, persons either living or dead, characters, organisations, places, events, incidents or anything else is entirely coincidental and without any real or implied attribution of any kind

Contents

1.	Journeys and destinations	1
2.	A sandy mote in the galaxy's eye	9
3.	Trouble with the locals	19
4.	Friends and enemies	25
5.	Flivvers, flivvers everywhere	34
6.	Hab, hab on the range	45
7.	Off-planet, in a bad way	56
8.	Ring-ship	63
9.	More ring-ship	68
10.	Every jump is a leap of faith	75
11.	Alarums and excursions	80
12.	Jump back	85
13.	CS1 redux	92
14.	Nine years on	100
15.	The last hive	108

16.	First contact	115
17.	Good guys – 1, Bad guys - 0	120
18.	We are leaving	126
19.	First away	133
20.	It all goes a bit semi	138
21.	All away	146
22.	Every journey begins with a single step	151
23.	Step two	160
24.	Step three	166
25.	Step four	177
26.	Servcon – my kinda place	183
27.	Servcon – maybe not my kinda place	191
28.	Outstaying our welcome	203
29.	The other side of the galaxy	211
30.	Planetfall	216
31.	Second group away	227
32.	All down	233
33.	Just when you thought it was safe	242
34.	The second is never as good as the first	248
35.	Exploration	258
36.	Another of those aliens	268
37.	Ring-ship and Flivvers	278
38.	Franky, Alien, Subterranean	286

39.	And down they go	291
40.	Flivver planetfall	301
41.	All roads lead to yesterday	312
42.	More tunnels, only different	317
43.	Another planet, another junkyard	325
44.	Secure area	330
45.	Insecure area	334
46.	No Central Control	340
47.	Up and out	344
48.	Straight back down again	351
49.	The operation was a success, but the patient?	358
50.	Hestia	368
51.	Acknowledgements	372

1
Journeys and destinations

There's a certain something about your first steps on a new planet. You've been stuck in that ship for months. You've been fighting broken systems, all of them trying to kill you. You've been eating, drinking, breathing stuff that's been re-cycled far too many times to count.

Man, that first breath of new air extends out into the distance, promising great things to come.

Every bit of that promise was giving its very best salute to the foaming glassful placed right down there in front of me. Fitted my hand like a glove and after a quick tox-scan, that first swallow was good enough to cut your thirst off at the neck. An accompanying hot sandwich(?) followed right behind, plenty of 'real Terran cheese' as advertised and a price to match. That yellow ooze was an alien biology lesson but hey, three green lights. Not bad at all. Warm to the hand and a taste to die for, if definitely not of.

So, another knackered old planet to add to my list. This one was even further out in the big black than the last one, but hey, us space engineers have all the fun, right? That non-stop tour of the galaxy at other peoples' expense and all I had to do was make sure we got there.

The unspoken '...and no one dies' was the usual "Meh, whatever," and anyway, that's what I'd been doing all of those hundreds of light-years whilst the crew deep-slept their funny little heads off.

And that was the problem. This crew. Not that I'm picky or anything, but you know Shonats, right? They see anyone not Shonat-shaped as pretty much primordial slime, even if that same slime was the only thing keeping their ship going. Both the size of the sign-on bonus and state of the ship should have warned me this was going to be a bad one, but they didn't, and I'm an idiot.

At least they got straight off into deep sleep, but everyone's gotta wake up sometime. And sure enough, come journey's end, up they got and everything slid right down the pan. Our roller coaster ride to the planet's surface was just more of the same shouting and screaming, except that they'd now added specific abuse for the state of the orbital pod we were using. Which was theirs. And a bag of bolts. And I'd already warned them about it. Sigh...

Now, the ship's best thumbnail had said arid sun-scorched sandball. The wrecked buildings and piles of rubbish appearing out of the clouds of rocket exhaust didn't exactly improve things. The air was eighty C, the UV was off the scale and it beat me why anyone would come anywhere near here, let alone these Shonats. Still, for the first time since I'd met them they actually seemed happy about something, and off they scuttled straight across the sand and down the nearest tunnel.

I was happy to do much the same, but in a place like this? The pod's ID Friend or Foe protection up and running first, everything else very much second. Unless that is, we wanted to be greeted by no pod and clouds of rocket exhaust when we got back.

A dash across the sun-blasted sand told me exactly why the Shonats had gone so quickly. Scorching doesn't even begin to describe it. The tunnel, on the other hand, was much more civilised except that locals were gathering and the rapidly growing welcoming committee was a right motley crew. People from five different sentient species and everyone's faces saying that they couldn't wait to get our money into their pockets and as quickly as possible please. And oh yes, maybe they'd also like to have a quick chat about that pod of ours?

IFF first, last and every time, right?

Still, the Shonats started talking and negotiations duly proceeded much the way you might expect. Me? I was too busy keeping an eye on the pod's IFF feed streaming to my Head Up Display implant to listen. We'd only been here an hour and alarm flashes across my left eye told me that a collection of locals were trying to break into the pod. Still, the IFF was handling it all no problem so I just sat back and watched.

By day's end, Shonats vs. the locals seemed to be about evens, although the smoking piles of charred remains scattered around the pod only emphasised how little real progress they'd made. It was difficult to work out who or what the piles had been, but I guess the more energetic locals will always want to explore every possible way of expediting negotiations.

Next morning, the Shonats and I were up bright and early, being greeted by an even larger group of the less energetic locals whose smiles said that they hadn't even started yet.

Thing is, the Shonats were getting bored with that kind of conversation. Yer average Shonat - bathtub sized body covered in scales, large head, lots of teeth - usually runs around on all four legs. They'd now changed to standing upright on their solid back legs, with the weaponry hanging around them saying that they could, they would and anyone even farting in the wrong direction was gonna get the full benefit. So, discussions started up in a much more positive fashion and continued to improve throughout the day.

Come close of play, more piles of smoking remains showed there were still some locals who hadn't got bored playing the pod IFF's particularly lethal game of grandma's footsteps. I guess they just must have been slow learners. As for the set of unidentifiable tracks dragging one particularly juicy carcase out into the desert? Well, the IFF wasn't too concerned, so I guess we weren't either. In any case, after my busy day watching the locals staring at the Shonats and the Shonats staring straight back, I was too bored to care.

The never-ending grunting chatter lulled me off to sleep, and the next morning they were off before I'd even had breakfast.

"We don't need you today – just stay available," was tossed back over the boss's shoulder, almost as an afterthought.

And there I was. Money in my pocket, time on my hands and a world's worth of R&R to explore. Just what the doctor ordered.

Trouble was, any sort of R&R suitable for a Terran just didn't seem to be available. In fact, I'd not seen a single Terran anywhere. The universal language of thirsty customer with money to spend seemed to cause all sorts of problems, and once we'd got over that little hurdle there was still the game of finding something that wasn't going to kill me. Eventually, my inbuilt tox-screen did its usual best friend bit and I found myself in front of what I've already described, and thank bloody goodness for that.

I mean, strewth, it shouldn't be difficult. I've spent my life flitting around the galaxy, but this trip, and now all of this titting about just finding something to eat and drink? It felt like I'd aged a decade.

That 'real Terran' brunch looking up at me wasn't exactly improving things, but the 'real Terran' beer alongside? Now, there's a joke that goes something like this – A girl takes a bite out of her food then spits it out with a "Yeuck, that's the worst thing in the entire galaxy," to which her friend says "Ah, but you've only seen part of the galaxy."

Well, I've been to a lot more of the galaxy than they had, but a beer's a beer, right?

While I was contemplating both that and another interesting bite of the real Terran brunch special, I took a good look around. You know what? This whole place was rather like the beer. Definitely an acquired taste, but who cared? I had somewhere to sit, there was a nice rack of beverages behind the bar and it all looked pretty good to me. No one was in my face. No one was causing me any grief. They were serving, I was relaxing, and the only person keeping an eye was the barkeep, and that was just to make sure my glass stayed filled.

I tried another mouthful of brunch, and a slurp of beer nicely numbed my protesting taste buds. This staying available lark was looking pretty good and all I had to do was wait around while the Shonats finished whatever it was they were doing here. I could feel those thousand light-years' worth of aches and pains easing out of my shoulders and with a bit more time and effort I reckoned I might just be ready for the next thousand.

A few of the locals sloped in and we started catching up with what was going on in each of our interesting lives. They ate, we chatted, and the morning kept moving along very nicely. Several hours later the afternoon poked its head up over the horizon and with a new crop of locals plus stories, time continued to pass very pleasantly. The evening opened up a lazy eye, then another, and suddenly it seemed like the barkeep's eyes were drilling holes into my back as I was the last one here.

A leisurely amble back to the pod and the IFF tracked me right in across the sand before telling me that it hadn't seen the Shonats. In fact, they seemed to have disappeared off the face of the planet. Various comments from the locals about things in tunnels you didn't want to meet did make me wonder but hey, they were big boys and girls. They could look after themselves.

The next morning saw me slowly swimming awake to a silent and deserted pod. A bit of a thick head from yesterday's refreshments, but I knew where to get a cure for that. In fact, it would have been rude not to at least start the day where yesterday left off, even if strong coffee and lots of it was definitely required.

I'd have sworn there was something moving in this morning's 'New improved Terran brunch special with real cheese'. Also, the drink may have been warm and brown, but it was certainly not coffee. Still, three greens from the tox screen and all of that caffeine was definitely doing the trick. The same posse of locals moseyed in, the same banter started and it looked like another relaxing day staying available was very much on the cards.

That being said, you had to concede that this whole place was a complete dump. The planet - CS1 I think the ship called it - had been mined out long ago and the people still living here were doing that in a selection of handmade shacks, re-purposed mechanicals and the odd pre-fab, all scattered about in an extensive network of mining tunnels and caverns.

Slabs of concrete and metal panels seemed to be their preferred construction materials and even this bar wasn't anything other than a shanty. As for what they were serving? Well, I suppose it was pretty typical of what another species thought that a Terran might like, and where it all came from didn't bear investigation. At least not without a beer, and certainly only after I'd finished my coffee.

I was sitting there watching some odd-looking gal with an even odder-looking something pulling on the end of a chain when my nicely lubricated consciousness popped up an interesting question. So, this place was a dump and it had been for decades. However, if it that was the case, why were there still so many people here? And what were they all doing?

Sure, any inhabited planet has its own weird and wacky ways of doing things, and what with all of the different sentient species making up our galactic civilisation, what else would you expect? Still, and it's a pretty big still, every planet I'd ever visited stuck to the same general rules. The more prosperous the planet, the more people, the more money and in fact, the more everything. Planets at the other end of the scale were barren rock balls with no inhabitants and nothing else.

This place was pretty much at that other end of the scale and yet we had tens or even hundreds of people from most of the galaxy's sentient species. Those wannabe pirates' charred remains showed that at least some of them wanted to get away, so why were they still here? Also, now that I came to think about it, why the hell had the Shonats come here? It just didn't make any sense.

I was taking another slurp from my beaker of brown caffeine medicine when a pop-up from the pod AI interrupted any further contemplations. Something about prepping for launch. I immediately cancelled it as come on, I was in the middle of breakfast. Also, the Shonats had disappeared, so no one was launching anything anytime soon. I returned to my interrupted cogitations but up popped another advisory, this time saying something about tank pressurisation and passenger readiness.

Ummm, now that *was* odd. I'd left the pod on standby and there hadn't been a peep from the IFF. Back went a quick query, and I nearly choked on the reply. Very matter of fact, nothing to see here. All passengers were boarding and immediate launch had been requested to hit the current ascent window back to the ship.

Shit – that couldn't be right. Maybe some locals had managed to get past the pod's security, but if they had then why hadn't the IFF screamed? Another check of the launch status and all of the correct startup authorisations had been given. We had no red flags. We hadn't been boarded. We hadn't been hacked. Everything looked like it should do except that I was here and the pod was there, getting ready for launch.

I pinged another query, but "Command access denied" came straight back, together with the next launch status update.

More indications. The Shonats were shown as strapping in, but hold on a minute. There were other entities in there as well and these weren't even showing IDs.

I tried another command query. The same response: "Command access denied"

OK, don't panic. I knew what these Shonats were like and they'd probably forgotten to tell me. I'll ping the boss-man.

No answer.

OK, I'll ping him again and thank goodness, a response. Straight back, short, sharp and very much to the point.

"Terran, we no longer require your services. The termination payment as detailed in your contract has been left at the landing grid. We will leave you a five-star rating," and the link closed. Just like that.

Shit, shit, shit! This can't be happening.

I grabbed my sandwich - I mean, real Terran cheese is real Terran cheese right? – and raced out of the bar. Heads turned as I barged past the happy shoppers but their annoyed cries were just too bad. My life was dropping down a hole and with the pod AI's ever-decreasing countdown, that hole kept getting deeper and deeper.

One puffing, panting slog up the tunnel later and I staggered into the wide-open outside entrance. There was the pod, stood out there in the sun, looking at me as I stared back at it through the waves of heat.

This must be a mistake. Not even those Shonats would leave me here. My HUD tried another comm but not a peep. I jumped as someone pressed a package into my hand but she was gone, a blue winged figure flitting away down the tunnel as my gaze flicked back to the pod.

This was no mistake. It was really happening. Everything shutting up nice and tight, blast shields in place, fuel vapour venting away in the wind, all ready to go.

Fountains of sparks from the pre-igniters. A briefest heartbeat then the main engines lit up with a planet-shaking roar, everything disappearing into a maelstrom of rocket exhaust. The metal teardrop lifted out of those churning white clouds, powering upwards on a tower of flame that left only a deafening wall of noise behind. Faster and faster, getting smaller and smaller, shrinking into a sparkling dot at the tip of a smoke trail that was already blowing away in the blistering wind.

The pod's sparkling dot winked out as last wisps of rocket exhaust flickered across the pad. A slick of melted real Terran cheese dripped out of the sandwich still clasped in my nerveless fingers and plopped across my boot like a Shonat middle finger stuck up right there in my face.

My sweat-soaked shirt, now flapping flinty-dry in the blistering wind.

Endless sand stretching away, wind frothing the tops of the dunes.

Nothing but me, standing there, watching.

They were up there, I was down here and as sure as hell was hell, they weren't coming back.

2
A sandy mote in the galaxy's eye

Flocks of birds circled in the dawn's early light, soaring upwards as the sun's heated claws clamped down onto bleached desert sand. Larger birds tracked lazily after their smaller friends, the whole lot jellying away into a growing heat haze that left only unblemished copper-coloured sky horizon to horizon.

Animals had already hunkered down in the shadows cast by the scattered junk piles, hiding away from the blazing sun and rocketing temperatures. That sun and the scorching wind almost guaranteed spontaneous human combustion for anyone stupid enough to be out there.

My food unit's most annoyingly cheerful good morning chirp interrupted my contemplation as it spat out that first essential cuppa. The usual bleary-eyed face stared back at me from its mirrored front, and whether it was worse to wake up to that or the flaming sun outside was a very close thing indeed.

CS1 was still the same god-forsaken sand ball it had been yesterday and every one of the days I'd been stuck here. Those aerial denizens weren't even vaguely alive, just free-flying drones off to do something for someone, somewhere. The animals hiding in the shade were also drones, sitting there waiting to be told what to do or they'd died there waiting. You did occasionally see a real animal skulking about, but they generally stayed well away. Real and wild was just the job, but staying alive pretty much trumped everything.

A quick duck in and out of the shower, shaving gel, five minutes "Just catching up with the news..." as my dad used to say, essential squirts in those essential places and we're nearly there. So, it's through the main cabin to the front door and a quick pat down. Full coverage sand suit - check, knee-length sand boots - check, fold-down cap at just the right angle - check, tool belt - check, and we're good to go.

Final check from the hab's built-in IFF, a quick mental handshake with my own embedded systems and that reassuring 'Active' as I walked out into the same rock tunnel going left and right. Left for a walk into the underground wilderness and right for that ten-minute walk to work.

As per usual, right-hand tunnel it was and off I went, nose full of the flint-dry air and boots kicking up puffs of sand as they shush-shushed along in the rock-walled silence. This was definitely the best part of any day with just me disturbing the dimly lit silence, even if the cascades of sparkles from ancient burrower teeth marks across the walls gave me their daily reminder of just how far away I was from the open sky.

Around the corner and there was the Flivver hive, shut up nice and tight with its customary sentinel standing there. I walked past, raising a hand to the carved-in-stone figure as its eyes tracked me down the tunnel. More of the same rocky, artificial silence and then speckling across my footfalls came the sounds of people going about their business, together with the high-pitched whine of drones going about theirs. That final bend and there it was, the CS1 market area. Scruffy, decaying and the best my underground world ever got.

Inhabited caverns are generally a mixture of neat construction, scruffy remains and monster-took-bites-while-chasing-someone. This place was pretty much the monster-munch version, with clapboard stalls, shacks, dead mechanicals plus other assorted rubbish spread everywhere. Some of the lighting was pretty odd, but it was the rich cauldron of smells that told you all kinds of stories you didn't want to hear.

That fresh smell of a new planet? Not down here matey boy. Too many people from too many species, all stuck together for far too long and that all-pervasive extra from the bug tanks to really make your nose hairs curl. It sort of draped over you after a while, even if you definitely avoided certain corners if you wanted to keep your nose working.

I spent my days over on the far side, which involved a leisurely walk through the sheds and shacks of the various different species' areas. Most people were pretty friendly, even if it was the same old jokes, from the same old folks and all totally hilarious. If, that is, you were one of them. Still, when the joker's an orange furred, six-legged, four-armed brick shithouse weighing three-fifty plus kilos, you just kept smiling.

Round the final pile of dead machinery and there it was, 'CS1 Mining Corporation'. Mining? Hah! No one had done that for decades, maybe even longer, but the Smuts who ran it were a good bunch.

I like Smuts. Telepathic guys as high as your shoulder, everything covered in black fur, regular numbers of eyes, nose, mouth and other body parts. Oh yes, and they always come in pairs. How they'd managed to get themselves stuck out here was anybody's guess, but their ability to read most sentient organics' minds had truly saved my life.

You'll no doubt remember how those oh so friendly Shonats flew off, leaving me with just a tatty bundle of currency and the clothes I stood up in. Hollow laughs were the best I got with any of that money, so here I was stuck on a derelict planet with no funds, no stuff and no way off. That was only headed one way, and then I met the Smuts.

They were looking for an engineer. My stunned and very depressed engineering astral presence walked past. Many apologies for whatever they found when they looked between my ears, but they must have liked at least some of it. Out they came. Did I want a job? Yes I did, and the rest as they say, is history.

It really was the craziest luck. CS1 Mining Corporation was just one more wrecked old mechanical slumped in the sea of mechanical wreckage that made up so much of the market. If they hadn't come out to say hi, I'd have walked straight past and you probably wouldn't be hearing this story.

And actually, funnily enough that sea of junk was my second piece of luck. CS1 was stuck out in the middle of the big black, but the various sentient species living here were at least vaguely civilised. And what do civilised beings want? They want working stuff. And what do you need to get stuff working? You need an engineer. Like me for instance. Which was why the Smuts were looking for one. Ok, so it wasn't like I was keeping space ships flying, but making things work was what I did, and five years later that hadn't changed.

I walked up to be greeted by the usual selection of telepathic 'brain tickle' greetings which were mostly derisory at this time in the morning. They pointed me towards a mining burrower that was so large I could walk into the gearbox. Definitely a job for my biggest hammer. In I went, hammer in hand, and it was the start of another shitty day in paradise.

Four hours later and out I came, my HUD telling me it was time for lunch, and the Smuts asking me to keep the noise down. Highly amusing guys, but I needed a break even if lunch wasn't much to look forward to.

You've got to remember that this was a worked-out desert planet with nothing you'd recognise as food, anywhere. Everything we ate started with the bug tanks, and they just contained alien microbes and things that wriggled. So, first a food unit had to process all of that wriggly slurry into something that wouldn't kill you. Then it had to make whatever tweaks and twiddles were required to make something edible. Trouble was, tweaks and twiddles for one species could be very odd for another, so I generally stuck to the simple end of the menu.

Lunch today was pretty much what it had been yesterday, the day before, and the many days before that. A couple of my food unit's best portable energy bars. They were portable. They gave you energy. They were bars. Not exactly a nice cup of coffee and a pie, but they kept you going even if best not to think too hard about the ingredients. Or what the bars looked like.

After that little interlude, my afternoon's wrestling with knackered old mechanics was a repeat of the morning's entertainment. Eventually my HUD chirped that it was time to stop and thank bloody goodness for that. Another day done, and in fact one more on top of the one thousand, eight hundred and forty-two little beggars I'd already completed. Stuck underground. With no way off. Welcome to my world.

My aching body came out of the mechanical obstacle course with its usual clicking and cracking round of applause. A heartfelt 'Aaaah!' was joined by a chorus of Smuts pleasantries and that really was it for the day.

Back through the market, pursued by a collection of good-natured obscenities from the friendlier stallholders, mostly along the lines of how I should get a new partner/pair/concubine/whatever, if my current one(s) had left me in such a wrecked state. Highly amusing of course, but isn't it interesting how with all of these different sentient species down here, each having their own sometimes hair-raising version of the old in, out, shake it all about kinda malarkey, I'll give you one guess what most of the jokes are about. Yep, you've guessed it, every time.

And talking of which, I'd very quickly found that I was one of only a handful of Terrans on the planet. Going back every night to stare at the walls on my solitary lonesome was not a path I wanted to go down. I knew where that led. Instead, the sweet taste of liquid success was much more convivial and, let's face it, keeping adequately hydrated on a desert planet was pretty important. Also, you can have a drink with almost anyone.

Trouble was, welcome to CS1. Every species down here got their fun in so many different ways, but no one was going to make something if there wasn't anyone to buy it. That place I'd found when I first got here didn't serve anything specifically Terran. They just took other species' food and drink, gave them enough of a wiggle so they wouldn't kill me, changed the name and there we were - 'Brunch sandwich with real Terran cheese plus a beer.' Marvellous.

The Shitstorm, best translation I'd come across but more generally known as El Shitto, was still as good and as bad as it got. Good – I could eat and drink at least some of the stuff they served. Bad – it was the only place I'd found that served anything that wouldn't kill me.

They'd now moved from their original shack to a nicely refurbished mining control room up one of the tunnels, in the process adding pretensions plus door security. I'd tried complaining about the lack of real Terran food and drink, but as I've already said, they were the only place serving stuff I could eat and drink. I knew it, they knew it, so nothing was going to change any time soon.

The added door security couldn't possibly have been anything to do with me, but I was still impaled by suspicious squints from the big guy's three eyes as I walked up. He knew who I was of course, but that's the trouble with Grangels. Bigger than large, bone and muscle everywhere, a silent hillock of suppressed aggression that was just waiting for any excuse, or maybe no excuse at all.

Thing was, who was he trying to kid? People had to get in, otherwise what was the point? So, that glare, followed by the regulation pause to let me know just who was boss, then a final disinterested sweep of the arm to let me in.

"What a tool," was my only thought behind the thankful smile and in I dived, heading straight for my favourite spot around the bar's brightly-lit guiding star. The barkeep, a quadruped hybrid with contributions from several different species wandered over.

"Wha' de' ya wan'?" was her grunted best attempt as she simultaneously started to pour. OK, so I know it's not a good sign when the barkeep's already serving before you open your mouth, but this gal had never held the Shonats' kidnapping of all of those hybrids against me. In fact, the size of my bar bill probably made her a bit of a fan. Of me, that is, not the Shonats.

It was pretty quiet this early and as per usual, Silent Bob was sitting seemingly grafted into his favourite seat, that thousand klick stare piercing the wall. A few Flivvers were over in one corner, bouncing around on their bent back legs like a flock of shoulder-high Old-Earth crows. Black eyes flashed in their bird-like faces while multi-shade blue wings and feathered arms flapped about for added emphasis to their rapid chittering. So, usual evening, nothing new, same old, same old.

And then, a Terran appeared but my heart sank. It was Dougie, no one's friend but a friend to everyone especially if he even suspected you were buying.

The barkeep interrupted this unpleasant vision with my foaming glassful. Its refreshing smile made up for the odd colour and tonight's even stranger aroma and while I couldn't think of anything worth raising a toast to, that first slurp really hit the spot. It was only unfortunate that my descending glass revealed Dougie sidling in with an ingratiating, drink-pinching expression smeared all over his pasty face.

"Hey there Franky," he said, "'ow ya doin'?"

"You know what?" I said after another mouthful. "I'm OK. Another day knocking the hell out of knackered old metalwork and it's time to replenish the vital fluids. This is purely medicinal."

"Hey, you're talking my language," he said, plonking his fat, sweaty personage down right next to me. "Something medicinal sounds great."

With him came that smell of someone who's not best friends with soap and water, but when there's only a few Terrans on the whole planet even the scabbiest is probably a good mate. I gestured to the barkeep and Dougie's eyes never left the slow pour before he almost snatched the filled glass out of the barkeep's hands and tipped half of it straight down in one go.

"Aaaah," he breathed, "definitely the best medicine. You're a real pal. No one seems to want to drink with me anymore."

"Well, you could try sticking your hand in your pocket," I said. "That might work."

"You sadden me old friend," was his necessarily shortened response as the second half of his beer disappeared straight after the first. "My turn," raising his hand in that universal gesture.

My expression of surprise was mirrored by the barkeep's. She got herself busy, then plonked down two more beers before retreating back to whatever contemplation of the infinite was so much more interesting than us.

"Thing is, Franky my son," continued Dougie after his first eager swallow, "you and me are the only real space engineers on this planet. More than half a millennium ntime each, gone round the galaxy and only stuck here completely by accident. CS1's a shithole, but every single jump I've ever made had things you wouldn't believe, even if you'd been there."

Of course, I'd heard this standard BS so many times I'd almost stopped listening. There was an odd social thing here that you never asked people how they'd been marooned. I did ask one guy, but his reaction was like I'd asked him how he'd caught the sort of disease your Mum warned you about, from the sort of person your Mum also warned you about.

With Dougie, however, you didn't have to ask. He'd been planet-side for over a decade since a ship's crew had decided that they couldn't bear his presence a moment longer. What he did now was a bit of a mystery, although his own smiling description, "Dirty deeds done dirt cheap" seemed to consist of jobs that no one else would touch, and when he wasn't doing them, bumming drinks off anyone who couldn't run fast enough. Definitely the living, breathing, sweaty embodiment of someone who'd fall into a pile of plop, but come up smelling of roses every time.

A final happy slurp signalled his second beer's disappearance and I grudgingly lifted my hand for a refill. The drinks arrived, and with his third now getting the same loving attention as he'd given the first two, we started on Dougie's favourite topic of conversation - amazing things he'd seen and vast riches he could tell you about if he only had a mind to, all seasoned by surreptitious winks and requisite taps of his finger to the side of the nose.

I just let it sweep over me as we'd got to that stage of the evening where only the odd affirmative grunt was required to keep Dougie's verbal diarrhoea flowing. I was drifting off into contemplation of the great job I was doing on that mining burrower when something I'd not heard before jerked me straight back to the land of the listening.

"…and I'll tell you what, that was the oddest trip ever. Just as we jumped, the Navcom went tits-up and we sort of randomly ended up right across the other side of the galaxy. I mean, fifty thousand lights. Can you believe it, but wait 'til you hear what happened next," and this was obviously so exciting that Dougie required an extra large swallow before he could even think about continuing.

"Anyway," he said as he put down his glass, "once we'd fixed the Navcom we did another jump to the nearest system. I mean, we're half way across the galaxy so why not eh? And guess what? Just a single Goldilocks planet and the whole place is covered in buildings. Nice temperatures, breathable air, everything you need, but not a single person anywhere."

He looked at me with a raised eyebrow. "Whatcha think about that then?"

Well, every species has its own stories of mysterious, deserted, high-tech planets, but Dougie was the first storyteller I'd ever heard who'd actually been there, honest he had. Almost in spite of myself I couldn't wait to hear what happened next.

"So why didn't you stay and open it up?" I asked as an interruption to his next long swallow.

Dougie gave me a wink plus very definite tap of the nose.

"Well," he said, "we did a survey and everything kept getting better and better. The whole planet really was deserted, although," and he shuddered, "it was a real things-moving-in-the-corner of your eye kinda place. You didn't want to be anywhere on your own and that's a fact.

"Anyway, we did the mapping and decided to get back to Servcon for some serious help. Trouble was," and here he did look a bit sheepish, "when we jumped I guess the Navcom hadn't been fixed properly and the ship's power grid got slagged. Even the AIs were hosed."

He sighed. "Took us seven months drifting just to get back to Servcon, and when we did? Nothing retrievable except basic mapping stuff. Also, I sort of had to leave the ship 'cos they blamed me for not fixing the Navcom. Bloody cheek if you ask me, but what can you do?"

A final appreciative swallow finished the story.

Well, he could certainly tell 'em and this particular reason for a Treasure planet disappearing into the ether was a new one on me, even if just as unbelievable as the rest. Still, fun though a couple of beers and Dougie's crapola was, I needed to get back. Tomorrow beckoned. That burrower was looking no better than it had this morning and the longer I stayed, the worse it looked.

I paid up and managed to dodge his beery attempt at a man-hug before making a break for the door. His plaintive: "C'mon Franky, one more for the road, surely?" pursued me outside, with the doorman's firmly closed door cutting of any more of that nonsense very nicely.

3
Trouble with the locals

The wider tunnel systems stretched away from the market into a darkness where things and people you didn't want to meet lurked. I was therefore rather surprised to see a group of Minos along the tunnel, playing some sort of game with a couple of Flivvers. Minos are the Grangel side of large, massive heads, four legs, two enormous arms and totally lacking of a sense of humour. You generally stayed well away unless you welcomed whatever benefits might accrue from a face-to-face encounter with a brick shithouse-worth's of aggravation.

They were wearing heavy work gear and looked as pissed off as hell. Still, those glasses of El Shitto's finest were working their worst magic on my feelings of righteous indignation, and two forty kg feathered Flivvers versus half a dozen three hundred kg Minos was no kind of fair fight. In fact, it was no kind of fair fight at all and I reckoned I needed to do something about it. I needed to do something about it right now.

"What's happening guys?" was my rather feeble opener.

"We caught these feathery runts" <80% xlate confidence> - my translator implant doing its best and sort of succeeding - "stealing something," grunted the nearest irate lump of bone and muscle.

"We're just getting it back and they're going to get a smack they won't forget."

"We didn't steal anything," chittered one of the very worried looking Flivvers. "One of our cousins lost a comm unit and these Minos were trying to sell it. We just want it back."

"These Flivvers say this comm's theirs," I said to the first Mino, but you know how you can always tell when things aren't going well. Minos in general, and very obviously these Minos in particular, regarded possession as being nine tenths of any law you cared to mention and here, they were the law.

The Mino repeated what she'd said and the circle of anger started re-arranging itself to include me with the Flivvers. Now, you can't argue with a Mino, but there's a trick that sometimes works. Violence is their preferred solution to most problems, but if money's a possible option they like that even more.

"Look," I asked. "Can I buy it from you?"

The closing angry circle halted as that magic financial factor grabbed hold of their attention.

"Well OK," came the ponderous reply. "100 credits, but we're still going to give them a wallop."

"How about 150 credits?" I said, my lightning brain well out in front of her. "I get the comm unit and also the pleasure of taking it out of their feathery hides."

Silence, and I could see the effect that a hundred and fifty credits was having on wounded pride. The Mino pondered some more then stuck out her arm in a surprisingly Terran gesture.

"150 credits."

So, I'd won that argument, but did I even have 150 credits? Delving into my pockets' manky depths I scrabbled out everything I could find, and a quick tally gave me the grand total of one hundred and forty-seven.

"3 credits discount for cash," I stated.

The Minos started to close in again, but to my surprise: "3 credits discount for cash," was the main lady's response, before adding: "They wanna watch out as you won't be here next time."

I plonked the cash down into what passed for her hand, grabbed the two kids by the scruffs of their feathery necks and raced off down the tunnel before anyone changed their minds.

"What were you thinking?" I said as we hustled through the deserted market. "Piss off a Mino and you're going home in pieces."

Their indignant chitters came straight back, but I ignored them. I'd had more than enough for tonight and the sooner I got them back to their hive, the better.

The hive sentinel watched our rapid approach with a great deal of interest. I was about to call out a greeting when out of a concealed side door burst a strange looking Flivver kid, closely pursued by a loudly chittering adult.

Aha! Now that was something I recognised. The kid had obviously done something they shouldn't have, and a quick getaway was the best way of escaping any inevitable retribution. She was showing a fair turn of speed except that the first rule of running away states that the person chasing you can always cut corners. Our rapidly-moving escapee turned down the tunnel towards me, and as if to prove the continued application of rule one, her pursuer flipped out a hand and grabbed a trailing wing tip. The resulting squeal jerked off to one side and straight into me.

Down we went and the adult piled in on top. The child was fighting to get away, my two kids were doing their best to escape and as for me? Well, I was just trying to get out of the way as the child never stopped screaming her torrent of Flivver abuse.

"Get off me you dirty person with no hive and no children" <85% xlate confidence> "and you also, you featherless, pooh-skinned" <90% xlate confidence> "dirty Terran. Let go of me you horrible, sweaty, stinky, smooth skinned, wing-less..." at which point my translator gave up, substituting a line of angry face emojis for the continuing hosepipe of childish invective being sprayed in our faces.

Eventually the adult managed to struggle upright, holding the still wriggling and caterwauling bundle of fury in both hands. They were about the same height, but the girl child was an odd mixture of feathered Terran with wings growing out of her back. So, definitely not pure Flivver, but a Terran/Flivver hybrid? Here?

Hybrids generally kept a very low profile, although the stream of vitriol being shouted in this one's direction showed that she definitely hadn't got that memo. I left them to it as I had other things to worry about. Like both eyes being full of CS1's desert for one thing.

The chittered abuse slowed as the adult ran out of things to say, then she started dragging the hapless child towards the gaping door from whence they'd both sprung. An irate chitter at the two Flivver kids, a scorching glare for me and they disappeared behind the vigorously slammed door.

Sudden quiet. Yours truly standing there staring, my eyes still streaming from all of that sand.

"Nothing but trouble that one," piped up the previously silent sentinel. "No one wants either of them, but they're only kids. What can you do?"

Either of them, eh? So, she's not the only one? To my inquisitive expression he continued: "Some scientist left them here years ago. Who knows what they're made of but they don't belong here," and he paused, cocking his head. "You've had a busy day."

"Yeah," I said, "never a dull moment. Some Minos were about to rip those kids apart and it took 147 credits to convince them otherwise. I'll want those credits back by the way."

The sentinel listened but made no further comment. It had just said more than it had in the previous five years and I'd probably also had the next five's-worth on account. Still, as I finished dusting off the worst of the sand, I had to smile. I'd done some pretty stupid things when I was young and it was generally an understanding adult who'd pulled me out of the doodoo. I owed Karma big time and maybe those hundred and forty-seven credits were just one tiny bit of the massive back payment I still owed.

I left the sentinel to it and, as my hab appeared out of the gloom, yet again raised my grateful thanks to those Flivvers. Dumped on a planet with no friends and no stuff is definitely not the best of starts, but for some reason they'd been very helpful, and especially the one who'd handed me my final payment by the launch pad.

Before I managed to find the Smuts, they'd given me a bit of paid work and then they'd found me this knackered old Flivver command vehicle. Mucho time ripping out the insides, then adding the sorts of things that any self-respecting Terran might need, had left me with the home sweet home that was right there in front of me.

The hab IFF greeted me with its standard friendly Flivver chirp, opened the door and started up everything just for me. A homely mix of knackered old couch, table, chairs and several coats of cheap white paint to cover the stains. Absolutely perfect. And as for my stuff? Well, strategically placed all over the floor, just the way I liked it.

This was my haven from the whole CS1 craphole. Actually it was so much better than anything I'd ever had before, even on Old-Earth. There were six rooms and no one else was stinking up the place, although talking of which a shower definitely beckoned. The cleaning drones were already snapping up what I'd just tracked in and I wandered off to further disturb the cleanliness they'd been working on so hard all day.

Dinner went down nicely, and nightcap in hand I wandered through to the command cabin. As usual, there was nothing. Nothing in orbit, nothing further out and indeed, not a peep from anyone, anywhere.

I didn't miss Old-Earth, but I'd swapped that shithole for this shithole and where did that leave me? CS1 had been stripped bare, with only wilderness, tunnels, ancient mining tech and a liberal seasoning of toxic waste as the miners' enduring memorial. But you know what was worse? Getting stuck here was my own stupid fault.

I'd broken that first golden rule of space engineering. You know, the one that says you never, ever, fix everything, or even worse, make it look like you've fixed everything. And why don't you do that I hear you cry? Well, if everything's working then they don't need an engineer, and your average ship's captain promptly manages on-going costs and cashflow by leaving you on the next planet they come to. Like CS1. What was even worse, every single day was normal spacetime, not relativistic travel time.

Most people live on planets or stations their whole lives, growing old across whatever their own species' version of three score years and ten prevails. However, space travellers like me spend their time travelling up to and faster than the speed of light and OK, I know that a jump isn't faster than light 'cos you can't travel faster than light, blah, blah, blah, but the effect is the same. The faster you travel, the slower time passes for you relative to those not travelling as fast. We call this reltime and the clue is in the name.

When the Shonats and I jumped to CS1, we only aged a couple of months relative to everyone else living in the twenty years of normal spacetime, or ntime, that our journey actually took. And that's just fine for ntimers, but my reltimer life was hopping through space and time with every reltime jump. These last five years ntime on CS1 should have actually been five years of mostly reltime, during which I'd have travelled through centuries of ntime.

You'll remember me wondering why there were still so many people living here, and the sad answer was oh so very boring. This was just one more of those "used to have something, no longer has anything, still full of people from the good old days" places.

There was nothing here, so no ships came. In fact, the ship I was on was the first they'd seen for ten-ish local years ntime, and the only reason that the Shonats had come here was to find hybrids with fat bounties attached.

So who was going to be the next happy visitor to come along and give us a ride? Well, I'll tell you. No one at all, that's who.

Basically, I was so far up shit creek without a paddle, I didn't even have a creek.

4
Friends and enemies

One good night's sleep later and my Uuugh-it's-morning thoughts were replaced, for a change, by happier ones. Two kids rescued from those psycho Minos was a good job well done, and that essential first cuppa of the day seemed to have an added kick-start kind of something to it.

I walked out of the hab with half an ear cocked for the IFF's cheery chirp, but was stopped in my tracks by a blue streak that whipped around the side of the hab. However, there was a matching blue face that peeped out before ducking back in again, and I relaxed. A Flivver kid and there was obviously some sort of game going on. However, that wasn't the birdlike face of your average Flivver. It was actually more like what had concluded yesterday's rather interesting walk back from El Shitto.

Still, you know how it is, things to do, people to see. So, off I walked down the tunnel, but as I approached the Flivver hive, something was happening. The usual morning's deserted silence had been replaced by several adult Flivvers standing by the hive's massive main door, which should have been shut but was now wide open with light streaming out. The Flivvers' eyes never left mine and then, oh great. There was the sentinel walking out, energy weapon in hand. Shit! What had I done now?

A chittered greeting flew my way but all I heard was Flivver. I pulled out my translator plug and gave it a tap. The green tell-tale re-appeared. I really needed to fix that. Shoving it back in again the chitters resolved into: "...wondering whether you have seen her?"

"Sorry," I said, "missed that. What d'you say?"

A quick repetition and basically, a youngster had run off and they didn't know where she was. I told him I'd seen someone up by my hab, but then, a matching "Aha!" moment. If they went anywhere near, the IFF would undoubtedly do its job and that would be bad for everyone. In fact, it might have already zapped the child. A mental groan and I knew I was going to regret this.

"Look," I said, holding out my ID fob. "I'm off to work, but if you're going anywhere near the hab this will disarm the IFF. Flip it back when you've finished."

His eyes widened but he bowed his head. "Many thanks to you, trusted hive-friend." <85% xlate confidence>. Trusted hive-friend eh? What was that all about, but before I could ask he was off back to the group standing by the main door. A few quick chitters and they turned, bowing their heads before starting up the tunnel towards my hab.

Oh well, best of luck to 'em, and I hurried off to the Smuts and my waiting mechanical nemesis. The usual chorus of derisory greetings pursued me into its malevolent metalwork, but soon afterwards I got yet another demonstration of why you can run from a telepathic species but you sure as hell can't hide. Even deep within the guts of my tunnel-wide burrower, a Smut's thoughts unerringly tickled across the ether and squirted their goodies into my consciousness.

Apparently, the ancient airflow system which ventilated our system of tunnels had turned its toes up again, and a group of the locals wanted me to fix it, again. I lay back and sighed. The last time we'd had this particular piece of nonsense, beyond totally shagged-out was where everything started. Some miracle had eventually allowed me to get it working, but that was when my grateful customers had sort of forgotten to pay me.

I called back to the enquiring Smut that up-front cash was the only place this transaction started, and the usual negotiation ding-dong duly did the same. They first tried the "what helps us, helps you" argument. They then tried the "but you already work for us" argument, and so it went on. Eventually, after much rudery and insults on both sides we got down to guaranteed payment and, as a final sweetener, they'd fund the celebratory beers. I just ignored the concluding smartarse comments about Terrans and their desire for beer at any time of the day or night.

I wriggled my way out and scooted straight off. I mean, anything was better than that bloody burrower, and this time there was guaranteed cash and beers!

The busy market sounds filtered away as I walked down the tunnel past a long line of discarded mining mechanicals, drifts of sand slowly absorbing them into the wall. The silence of what was generally known as the Badlands started pressing down, but Badlands? Really? Sure, I'd heard the stories, but I'd never actually seen anything. I mean, those Minos were probably a lot scarier than anything native that might be down here.

Five minutes more and out of the gloom appeared a rank of ventilation louvres. I'd already felt the lack of airflow, but the matching quiet merely confirmed that we had a problem.

In through the main entrance and the cavernous machine hall was silent as the grave, as were the three massive fan units that should have been rotating merrily, sucking air down from the surface and blowing it out through the louvres in the tunnel. Each of my footsteps was a drop of sound in the stillness and over there by the wall the control console was ominously dark.

The whole place was just as the mining engineers had left it when they bugged out all of those decades ago. Racking, desks, chairs, ancient food containers, over-flowing rubbish bins and a thick layer of dust to confirm just how long ago that had been. All rather spooky, especially as there was just my head torch's single disc of light to pursue the odd unexplained noise into the surrounding dimness. As they say, it's not the dark that's scary, it's what's out there hiding in it.

And then I saw something.

Over at the far end of the cavern was where the power feed came down from the PV/wind farms on the surface. One of my more worried glances stopped at an explosive flash mark up the wall that surrounded a gap in the cable. The cable was composite-covered solid copper and something had bitten right through it, even if whatever-had-done-so's blackened and crispy remains now decorated the surrounding wall and floor.

At least it looked like a simple fix so I got straight onto it. One new section of cable later and several red lights popped up on the console. A collective momentary groan from the fan assemblies, but nothing more. No movement, no lights, no nothing.

And then I saw something else.

Stretched across the nearest motor assembly was what looked like dust-coloured netting. There was a dark bulge in the centre, with thin skeins extending out and one particularly hefty strand restraining a fan blade. OK, another easy fix, but as I took a step forward that bulge started moving.

I stopped. So did the bulge. Looking more closely, I could now see that there was a dark shadow at its centre. Every single hair on my head stood on end.

The miners and their planet-wrecking activities had left CS1 pretty much bereft of native animal life, but let's just say I'd heard the stories. Anything could be, and probably was, lurking down here but my IFF had taken this opportunity to decide it couldn't see a thing. My somewhat justified WTF-type response did eventually get it to concede that there were similar patches of netting on the other two motor assemblies, but it still couldn't see anything to worry about. Which was just great.

Icy little feet were marching up my spine as I flicked a quick glance around. Those fans weren't working. I could see what was stopping them, but a dark something moving around inside that patch of netting? Those icy feet changed to dribbling lines of cold sweat, but c'mon, surely I could deal with it. I mean it wasn't even that big.

Close by was a table that had a convenient length of metal pipe leaning against it. Perfect for the more hands-on approach. An exploratory swing, it swished through the air and the resulting clang left satisfactory dents in both the table and metal pipe. Just the job.

Gripping my low-tech approach to whatever might be in there, I slowly made my way towards the netting. The dark bulge started moving, and as soon as I was close enough I reached out and gave it a poke with my pipe. Two pincers popped straight out and clamped around the end.

I leapt back in shock, the pipe also jerking away, but with it came more of those pincers, a head and an even larger scaly body. I scrambled backwards, frantically trying to flick away the now very animated creature which dropped to the ground and ran towards me, pincers agape. What few of my wits still functioned lifted the pipe and smacked it down as hard as I could. A very satisfying crunch but an absolutely indescribable smell socked me in the nose, only increasing as I gave the rest of the animal the same treatment.

I changed hands on the pipe and took a deep breath. My "Shiiit, what the hell was that?" echoed around the machine hall, but the only answer I got back was the IFF's "Juvenile, Sand Crab generic. No longer a threat."

Marvellous. Thanks for that.

A few more breaths and the unmoving pile of mess was still there, still unmoving, still revolting, and as for that smell? Well, essence of everything unpleasant was where it started and I didn't want to go anywhere near where it ended. Still, leaving aside the fact that something longer than my arm, with massive pointy pincers, had suddenly appeared and gone straight for me, I'd sorted it out pretty quickly. Another look around just in case anything else was lurking in the dimness and I was off to the next patch of netting, forewarned as well as forearmed.

Much the same thing happened with the second net's resident and the third was no different. However, that smell was now so all-pervasive that every nose hair was curling up into my head just to get away from it. A screwdriver cleared the remaining netting from all three fan assemblies and I cannot begin to describe my relief as each fan slowly groaned into life.

I stuck the screwdriver back in my belt and was just making a firm and very swift way towards the exit when echoing down the air tunnel from the surface came a sound. A sound like a worried creature makes when she's coming down to see what has just happened to her babies which, of course, I'd just squashed all over the floor.

Those little nightmares were bad enough, but Mummy? Or even Daddy? Believe me, the best place to view wildlife is not in a deserted, dark section of tunnel whilst on your own. I scarpered straight out and didn't look back.

Annoyed Mummy noises plus that dreadful smell pursued my panicked scamperings back along the tunnel, with our now-working ventilation system helping to spread the indescribable olfactory memorial. I ran into the market under the quizzical gazes of nearby marketeers, whose general amusement changed to choking disgust as the vile smell socked them in whatever passed for their noses. My own panting breaths turned to choking coughs as I staggered away from air so thick you could cut chunks out of it.

Wobbling step after wobbling step kept me just in front of the advancing miasma, but the second part of my deal with the Smuts was starting to make its presence felt. Cold beer, and as much of it as I could drink. It was the only thing that could possibly cure my nose of that smell.

El Shitto was its usual welcoming self and even Dougie's greasy smile didn't stop my first glassful start to sloosh away images of grappling snappers and general skittering. Also, I was in luck. A good friend and irregular regular walked up to join me at the bar, with his absolutely perfect timing saving me from Dougie's unwanted scrounging.

An interesting guy is my mate Dane. He and his partner Ruth lived in tunnels right out in the middle of the equatorial desert where they'd built a strongly fortified hab for their ever-growing family. Dane and I are both standard Terran, but his partner Ruth is hybrid Terran/Duje. I met her once. A lovely lady no doubt, but not really my cup of tea. Her eyes are too large, in the wrong place and all of those sensory tentacles down the front are just too much of a distraction, even if her purple skin is pretty cool.

Local jokes go that Dane wasn't aware that Dujes had children in litters and when they started arriving, man, they REALLY started arriving. He was left walking around with the wide-eyed expression of someone who'd unsuccessfully tried to stop an overwhelming torrent by hammering a very small plug into a very large hole.

Ruth's Duje side made her ideally suited to the darkness out there in the sticks, but like me, Dane needed light, and more importantly, the occasional beer. Even better, he had zero patience with Dougie's scrounging.

I got the beers in as Dane's nod and a wave to Silent Bob received their usual answering thousand klick stare. I couldn't understand why he even bothered, but the chink of glasses, a refreshing slurp and it was time for a very welcome and long overdue catch up.

Dane always had some of the best stories and just the thought of him driving around in those deserted, pitch-black tunnels made my skin crawl. As for what he drove? Well, a homemade pile of wheeled junk built to fall apart was my best description and how it ever got anywhere was beyond me. I started to tell him about my brush with the snappers in the ventilation machine hall, but he just laughed, countering with the observation that I should see what was further out in the tunnels.

His view was that there was plenty of space for everything to do what they wanted, well away from us, and good for them. Fair enough, but as doing what they wanted probably involved eating anything that couldn't run fast enough, I'll just refer you back to his crappy old vehicle and my day today. He didn't stop laughing.

More beers arrived and Dane was into his first story. Several months ago, he'd come to the market using a new and hopefully quicker route. Bit of a struggle, roof cave-ins, lots of animal tracks, same old, same old, apparently. He'd been careful to lay out a trail of GPS pingers just in case he got lost, but when he tried to go back, they'd all disappeared.

Now we both had to agree that this was pretty strange as the unwritten rule was that you didn't touch. Anything out there could be life or death to someone, and where would you be if someone walked off with something you'd left out there for later?

He did eventually make it home, but Dane had obviously led a very misspent youth. The next time he came in, every one of his pingers was updated to comply with the rather worrying design principle that no problem's too big or too small that can't be solved with just the right amount of high explosive. As he said with a grin, he didn't much care who'd taken the pingers and actually, as far as he was concerned it could even be those almost mythical Aquatics who were supposed to live deep in the planet's crust. He'd just wait and see who was walking around minus a limb or two before asking any questions.

By this time we were sufficiently lit up to find the whole thing hilarious, raising our glasses to the only truly civilised Terrans on CS1, before falling off our stools in paroxysms of laughter. This definitely needed more beer, and it would have been rude not to have had at least one more, with another to keep that one down and maybe a final slurp to ensure adequate hydration on the way home. We did, after all, live on a desert planet.

Eventually, Dane's usual "What's mine is yours and your family is mine if you die" seriously weird military salutation rounded off the proceedings and we staggered out. Dane rolled off to goodness knows where and I started making my rather wobbly way back. The journey did seem to be a lot longer than usual although being well-hydrated was a definite worry off my mind.

OK, so this morning I'd left everything shut up tight, security ID with the Flivvers, nice and safe.

My hab door was open. A large pile of my stuff sat alongside it. A female Flivver was standing in the doorway, one hand under her chin/beak/whatever, watching as I walked up.

I knew that loan of my security ID was going to be a bad idea.

5
Flivvers, flivvers everywhere

Those two unblinking black eyes never left mine as I came to a halt in front of her. I knew who she was of course, that senior council member from the hive down the tunnel who'd been so good to me, but what the hell was going on? She was standing there like she owned the place. I was about to say something, but she waved me in through the door before I could say a word.

Gleaming clean and tidy was an understatement. My perfectly positioned piles of stuff had been cleared away and I could see nearly all of the floor. Everything was so clean and tidy that the cleaning drones were probably off sulking somewhere. Rather ominously, a heap of bags now intruded into this newly freed up space and several Flivver hammocks swung gently in my large back room.

"Franky, your hive was a disgrace," said Chitichca, my translator's best attempt at her Flivver name which, quite frankly, was unpronounceable by any Terran set of vocal cords. "It was not even fit for a Terran to live in," and she'd nearly said "dirty Terran." Flivvers are fixated about how clean and tidy they are and how dirty and unpleasant everyone else is. I had to concede that in my hab's case they probably did have a point.

"We have spent nearly half a rotation cleaning everything so it is fit for you to live in," she continued, with a very strong emphasis on the 'you'.

Anything else she might have been implying flew straight over my head, as I was still trying to understand what the hell was happening.

"Since you arrived on this planet, we have always done our best to help, and now we need you to do something for us."

My heart sank. Her face looked exactly like my Mum's used to when I was really gonna hate what came next.

"We have been looking after someone who was left on this planet with no family and no friends, just like you," she said. "Living in our hive is making her very unhappy so she needs somewhere else to live." She paused to look around the hab. "She also needs to learn about her Terran heritage. We know this will be a surprise, but everyone thinks it is acceptable payment for all of the help we have given you since you arrived here."

OK, so I could see where this was going but as I opened my mouth to object, she continued: "Soffee, can you come out here please."

My mouth was still gaping as another Flivver appeared at the back-room door, but this was no Flivver. Terran/Flivver feathered head, blue feathered arms ending in hands with clawed fingers, Flivver wings sprouting out of her back and shoulders, no tail, Terran legs bending the right way and claws instead of nails peeping out of her trouser bottoms.

Yep, that particular mixture had head-butted me in the stomach yesterday evening, but it was back to the same question I'd had then. What the hell was she doing here? Hybrids were made by bad people to do bad things. Making them was totally illegal and cost a fortune. From the look of it someone had tried to make a Terran who could fly, but why then dump her out here in the middle of nowhere?

Soffee opened her mouth and a strangled Flivver-like noise came out. My translator said nothing for a second, popped up <Flivver

dialect - translating>, paused, popped up another <Translating> but that was it.

"She cannot speak our language very well," said Chitichca, "so I will translate. She says your hive was very dirty but she will live here now that it has been cleaned."

I stammered back that she couldn't live here, I didn't want her here, I knew nothing about kids, I couldn't possibly look after anyone and anyway why should I, but my bleating tailed off as Chitichca threw me another of those mother-knows-best looks.

"We have helped you many times and never asked for anything in return," she said. "All we need is the loan of a room where she can live."

Chitichca then looked at me with what may have been a kindly expression. "Ever since I handed you that payment from your crewmates, we have seen that you are a good person. I know that you have no family and few friends, but you are the only Terran we trust. Part of the hive will move in to help look after Soffee and you will not have to do anything."

She then definitely smiled. "I have your 147 credits, given with heartfelt thanks by" <Untranslatable – Flivver family name/hive> "for rescuing their children." She extended her clawed hand in which was balanced a shiny metal pile.

Every single coin plus those Karma just-desserts stared straight back at me and you know what? She'd got me. What could I do? These Flivvers had indeed been very helpful, even if it was now pretty obvious they'd been setting me up since I'd got here. I truly was in hock up to my eyebrows, but I didn't appreciate this well-planned ambush. I also didn't know anything about kids and actually, now I could see more of her, I didn't know anything about stroppy feathered adolescents who didn't speak Terran. Also, what was a hybrid like that doing here and what had she been made to do?

My keen-eyed interrogator stood there looking at me, obviously expecting a reply.

"Looook...," I tried, "she can't live here and your hive can't live here either. It's my hab, there's not enough room and anyway, I like living on my own and also-"

But these feeble bleats were swept away as she interrupted: "We have moved people into your hab to look after Soffee. They will be part of our hive, just living inside your hab. You have six whole rooms, which is far more space than any one person needs. You can keep on living your life as you have been and you will not even notice we are here."

Her black eyes seared into mine as she turned and wrapped the child in a hug, her head doing the full 180-degree Flivver-neck thing.

"She is very precious and must be taken care of," and with that, both of them disappeared into the back room.

I stood there dumbfounded, surrounded by cleanliness, the sudden absence of people and a feeling like I'd been cracked over the head with a mallet. Where the hell had that come from? I'd had a great evening with Dane then walked straight into a Flivver hive being transplanted into my hab without so much as by your leave. I was still trying to make sense of it all, which admittedly wasn't helped by those glasses of El Shitto's finest, when Chitichca came out again.

"Now remember," she said, closing the door firmly behind her, "there is nothing you need to do. Your hab can provide everything we need and Soffee will ask her protectors if she needs anything. I will be back tomorrow to make sure everything is alright and I am always available if you need my help." With that final jaw-dropping statement she walked out of my hab and I was left alone with my new lodgers.

I caught the dazed reflection in my food unit. Several choice phrases were mouthed before I looked around my pristine hab once more. Shit, I needed a shower and, whatever El Shitto might be doing to the old brain cells, a substantial medicinal drink.

The long hot shower helped, but as I punched in for some food plus an extra-large nerve-stiffener, it still felt like I was in the middle of a bad dream. A ping from the food unit and I slumped back into my chair to contemplate the rather dubious plateful smiling back at me. The back-room door cracked open and a single, yellow-rimmed pitch-black eye appeared.

"You might as well come out," I said. "Looks like it's all yours anyway," repeating myself after ensuring my translator was working.

The door slammed shut, so I left her to it and applied myself to din-dins. Once that hit bottom, I sloped into the control cabin to look at the usual nothing that was happening out there. After a couple of minutes watching, well, nothing at all, I sloped back and flopped onto the couch, staring at the ceiling.

That wasn't working, so I called up one of my favourite Old-Earth films. As usual my eyes were drooping in the first five minutes, but I caught the blue streak racing across to grab a bag before racing back.

"Oh well, what the hell…bloody CS1…" was my final thought as I dropped off to sleep.

A loud chittering screech jerked me from sprawled out on the couch fast asleep to wide awake in a single gasp. Not the best way to start the day, and nor was Soffee's face, up close, nose-to-nose. My involuntary flinch and matching "What the fff…" got another screech and a finger pointed at my translator.

I fumbled it out, checked it, stuck it back in again and waited to see if anything happened. Another screech had the same result, so with a venomous look she flounced off into the bathroom, her face glaring at me to follow.

When I got there, OK, so she obviously didn't understand how the plumbing worked. I placed my hand on the 'Flush and clean' and her expression was a picture. As soon as the cycle finished, she tried it herself. Her hand went up for a second go, but we couldn't stand here all morning playing with the khazi. I needed to get myself ready and I shooed her out, hoping that today was going to be a lot less exciting than yesterday.

I was just getting some breakfast down my neck and wondering what else could possibly go wrong when it did. The hab IFF proximity alarm sounded and the front door delivered a stun discharge. Oh shit, we've zapped somebody. Despite the excited shouts from the

IFF telling me we were under attack I told it to stand down, and ran outside.

Chitichca was lying sprawled flat on her back, surrounded by three very worried, loudly chittering females. They must have walked straight up to the front door, ignored the IFF's warning and tried to get in. And then everything got just that little bit more exciting as Soffee's anguished screech raced past to join in the fun.

This was only going to end one way, and that was badly for me. The three Flivvers came hustling past bearing a barely conscious Chitichca, with Soffee following and leaving a particularly poisonous look in her wake.

I needed to stay out of this and in fact, Chitichca had said that I wouldn't have to do anything at all. Maybe I should go straight off to work? I leapt back inside, grabbed my stuff and was just sauntering out when I was confronted by an irate Soffee who made it very clear that I was wanted inside, now, and actually, even quicker than now.

Chitichca was lying on the couch being comforted by several of the Flivvers and they were really giving me the evil eye. I did feel rather embarrassed, so I tried giving her my best grovelling apology even though this wasn't my fault, surely?

She held out her hand. "Franky, thank you for looking after Soffee so carefully. Your hab has protected her, but you must tell it who are friends and who are enemies."

An indignant screech that was obviously the Flivver equivalent of a "Humph!" preceded Soffee as she barged past to lie down next to Chitichca, chirruping and stroking her feathers. I apologised once more and this time seemed to be let off, grudgingly, even if Soffee never stopped looking daggers. A final apology and I backed away, Chitichca's airy wave pursuing me down the tunnel and only adding to my dread about what I would find when I got back.

Hundred-year-old mechanicals built to last fifty years can eventually be made to work if you apply enough effort, or at least they can if it's me applying the effort. The Smuts' clients, a bunch of Dujes, were already there waiting for me, clustered around the burrower and making the right sort of noises. They got in. They fiddled about. They drove it around. They had another fiddle then pronounced themselves happy bunnies or whatever the small fluffy Duje equivalent was.

All of my fingers and toes remained crossed as they drove off down the tunnel and the Smuts declared themselves happy, their friendly insults bouncing off my remaining mental worries that were of course, an open book to all of them. I even got a bonus on top of my standard rate, but you know what? After last night's drinkies and the unexpected Flivver invasion, I needed to get back to my hab. Who knows what was waiting for me.

And what was waiting was a swirling flock of Flivvers, tails out, wings open, arms waving, all chittering loudly and the air full of that strong part animal/part perfume Flivver smell. They immediately retreated into the back room away from the Terran bad smell that had just walked in. Chaos to silence in no time at all and there I was, all alone, even if the closed door and scattering of blue feathers rather gave the game away. They stayed there all evening and actually, it was a lot less kerfuffle than I'd been expecting.

The next morning was just me and silence, so before anything changed I got straight off to work. That evening I came back to the same momentary cloud of noise and feathers which yet again disappeared, leaving me to another quiet evening.

The next day was the same, as was the next, and almost by accident we seemed to have established a way of living together. When I was out, they did whatever they did, and what I now knew were female hive protectors did their best to keep the lid on. Every night I'd arrive back to Soffee flouncing about the place in whatever state of chaos that currently reigned. Everyone would then disappear into the back room, preceded by an extra portion of Soffee-flounce and succeeded by the customarily slammed door. I would get out of my work clothes, have a shower and see what the food unit could produce for dinner.

I was rather proud of that food unit. It loudly proclaimed itself to be a 'Megameal 1200 - Feed your hive!' or at least that was what it said-ish in Flivver and was certainly the most advanced I'd found anywhere. A lot of the options were decidedly toxic to those of a non-Flivver persuasion, but totally bang on for my new and eagerly flocking guests.

Every Flivver was charmed that my food unit was made by Flivvers, for Flivvers and produced, as they put it, real Flivver food just for them. I never got around to explaining how everything going through the hab's plumbing eventually got back to the Megameal via a digester and compactor. There's a time and a place to go through that whole circle of life thing and I never found either the time or the place.

With the Flivvers being fed and doing their best to keep a low profile, I sort of had my hab back, even if Soffee's ever-present disruption seasoned with exaggerated flouncing never went away. Also, after the first couple of weeks I noticed stealthy sorties out of their room, followed by an irresistible wave of Flivver feathers, bits and pieces, food remains and anything else they obviously thought needed a home.

I didn't really mind, but had to put my foot down when one day I came back to find two of them set up in my bedroom. I mean, Flivver hives are totally cheek by jowl, but c'mon, really?

It was the one thing we never managed to resolve. To them, six rooms for one person was unbounded luxury and all of it should be shared. The fact that I was no longer living on my own, which Chitichca asserted had been "...very unhealthy and worrying for all of us," seemed to be adequate justification for pretty much everything they did, even if I was never going to have them living in my bedroom.

In the odd reflective moment, what Chitichca had said about Soffee being unhappy did raise its head for inspection. My own life had been a succession of feeling like a grudgingly tolerated spare part. There'd been Old-Earth in that mega-hab we barely existed in, then Servcon and all of those ships, but that was the life of a reltimer. I didn't know anything about how Flivver hives worked, but maybe I could do something to help make Soffee's life a bit happier.

Applying my mighty brain to the problem didn't exactly magic up a solution, but ancient whispers from my lovely Mother did. She'd always said that having plants around the place solved any problem and here I was on CS1, life full of problems and no solutions. What better than to try out my Mum's suggestion from five hundred years ntime ago?

Of course, getting hold of a Terran plant on CS1 was an interesting problem, but the next time I went through the market I had a word in the ear of a gene-tweaker Ontos gal. Several favours later plus an astronomical number of credits and there in front of me was a nice little plant in a pot, everything genuine Terran of course.

This came home, to be greeted by the usual flounce, flounce, flounce that went flouncing past. However, the flouncing paused as Soffee noticed what I'd put on the table. She stood there looking at it, a glance at me, then another flounce back to her room with the door slammed shut.

The next morning, the plant had gone.

A couple of days later, I dropped by another stall. This time a custom-made enamelled badge shaped like a blue-winged Terran/Flivver came home and was left out for inspection. In flounced Soffee, but she stopped next to the pin. I studiously concentrated on shovelling down my tasty plateful as she flicked another quick glance, reached out, picked up the pin and had a good look. She then flounced back to her room, but this time the flounce was less pronounced and the door wasn't slammed quite so hard.

I figured we must be making some sort of progress, so a couple of days later I swapped another favour for a badge of a generic Terran. That evening, when I walked into the hab, the door to the back room was open and there were Soffee and Chitichca looking at my plant, which now seemed to be producing a flower.

Soffee turned and I could see the blue-winged Terran/Flivver badge pinned to a dungaree strap. "Hello Franky," she said in an oddly accented Terran, before turning back to Chitichca.

Well, you could have knocked me down with a feather, even one of theirs. I put the new pin on the table and started getting out of my work clothes. There was a gentle touch on my arm and it was Chitichca. She said nothing, just stroked the edge of her wing down my arm before going back into Soffee's room. So, what was that all about? My IFF didn't register a threat so I figured, well, I just figured.

After that, things kept getting less fraught, even if we were still occasionally home to Ms. Shouting, Ms. Screaming and Ms. GetOutOfMyWay (...door slam!). Soffee was also starting to use the hab's AI, and several times I had a quick look at the stuff she had up on the consoles. Judging by the way she immediately hid them with her wings and hustled me away (...door slam), she was teaching herself Terran but didn't want me to see. Maybe she was just getting used to having some of her own space. Good for her.

Week followed week, month followed month and even though my hab was now a lot fuller of people, wings and feathers than it had been, life was pretty good. Also, Soffee was now trying out her Terran on me, which was nice. I'd got rather tired of hearing the world exclusively through my translator implant.

One day I walked in and there was Soffee and one of her minders sitting in front of the main console. She came across and dragged me over.

"I've bin learn 'bout science and what you do," she said rather proudly as she pointed to the large schematic of a mining mechanical. She then flicked across to another screen which had some sort of biped-oriented combat vid on pause.

"I find this when I look," she said equally proudly.

"Okaaay..." I said. "So why d'you want to look at that?"

"Mother, the one you call Chitichca, say I should look at what hab AI have. It help me learn Terran and I learn other things she think good. I find this," and she started the vid.

"AI show me to protect myself," she said over the noises of people hitting each other. "Is no worry to keep me safe and I stop those" <85% xlate confidence – Description? Defamatory? Insult?> "hurting me. Is what protectors do," she finished, as if that was all the explanation needed.

Ummm. Well, that obviously meant more to her than it did to me, so I took the standard interested-but-whatever approach.

"Well just you be careful," I said. "Don't hurt anyone."

For some reason Soffee kept returning to that growing collection of unarmed combat vids, and if only to stop her constant pestering, a particularly unguarded moment saw me agreeing to help. That evening we tried the first on the list, entitled 'Selected defence arts from Flivver history' or at least that was the best translation I could get.

Well, defence it may have been, but it looked more like twenty ways of clobbering someone before they clobbered you.

Our first attempts at trying to do it were quite amusing. Her wings blew up clouds of blinding dust, flapped everywhere and got in the way. However, she adapted very quickly. That hybrid physiology gave her both Terran strength and Flivver lightness which meant that as soon as she got the hang of the moves, she was lightning fast and packed one heck of a punch.

Those wings were now weapons in their own right, confusing her opponent, me, and clouting them around the head and body. The next person who tried giving her a hard time was going to get a very nasty surprise was my idle thought as I rubbed the numbness out of a dead arm.

I did keep warning her that she must be careful not to hurt anyone. After all, she was now giving me a succession of lumps and bumps and I was an adult Terran, not a small, bird-like Flivver. I'm not sure she took any notice.

6
Hab, hab on the range

It's funny how you can slip from one version of reality to another without realising it. Before the Flivs took over my hab, I'd been trundling along on my own, keeping out of trouble, minding my own business, earning a crust and moping about how crap my life was.

The new reality which had snuck up on me was so very different. There were Flivvers and feathers everywhere, there was that Flivver scent - half perfume, half body scent, half something else - overlaying my, ahem, more manly version, with that non-stop chittering an ever-present background. I'd even turned off the IFF. I mean, with the whole place full of Flivver protectors, who would even think about trying anything?

On the odd occasion I came back during the day, Flivvers seemed to be oozing out of the walls, with Chitichca always there in the background keeping an eye on both them and me. They might have thought my hab was large but I'd never seen so many sentients packed into such a small space. However, they always made sure I had somewhere to sit, eat, and do Franky-stuff during Franky-time, so it worked out pretty nicely. In any case, I was out of here as soon as any FTL ship arrived, so they might as well get used to the place.

One really good thing was that Soffee had finally found some friends, three Flivver females collectively known as 'The Girls' or at least that was my translator's best attempt. There was a particularly poisonous group of kids who were always teasing her, and on occasion I'd see a desolate, almost abandoned look steal across her face. Having three new bosom buddies was definitely what she needed, although another problem then immediately presented itself.

All three were identical. So, to help this ignorant Terran tell which was which, they started wearing different coloured clothes. Of course, they immediately started swapping these variously coloured clothes between themselves, with equally immediate fits of helpless laughter when I got their names wrong, again.

The whole native Flivver communication thing was always my biggest trial. It's a complex combo of speech, facial expressions, body posture, specific placing of limbs, involuntarily produced scents, all wrapped up in layer upon layer of context relating to status and hive seniority.

To anyone but another Flivver this was largely invisible and even just the basic chitters, clicks and screeches gave my translator a hard time. So, in a post-everyone-falling-about-laughing moment I decided I'd give the girls Terran names, so at least I'd be able to get my mouth around them. Circe, Scylla and Charybdis - which quickly became Chary, as Charybdis just caused blank stares – seemed to me like a great fit.

Unfortunately, the girls were outraged. Apart from the fact that Flivver names are a combination of family, status and other Flivvery things, what was the leader of another hive, and a dirty Terran at that, doing giving them names? Definitely a combined Oh Shit/WTF-moment, and my offer that they could give me a matching Flivver name just made matters worse.

My feeble intellect finally managed to drag itself out of the hole it was digging by telling them that Circe, Scylla and Charybdis, sorry Chary, had been fearsome Terran females who'd dealt with their enemies in various dreadful ways. This seemed to work from a Flivver point of view and I was eventually let of, if very grudgingly. As far as Soffee was concerned, she just looked at me and mouthed: "Songs of distant Earth?"

Now, relativistic space travel was great fun, but with every FTL jump came that substantial jump forward in normal spacetime. You'd leave everything you knew decades behind, but still carry forward your old way of speaking, social attitudes and highly devalued currency, none of which was any kind of joke. I mean, look at me. I'm twenty-eight years old reltime but I've lived across the best part of five hundred and fifty years ntime. The Old-Earth I'd left behind was over-polluted, over-populated and generally over-everything. As for five and a half hundred years later? Well who knew, but I could guess.

Every FTL-travelling species had their own version of the songs, and those Old-Earth names for the girls were just another verse from my particular song book. As for how they affected the clothes-swapping game? Well, the wrong name for someone in the wrong clothes reduced everyone to total hysterics. Any social faux pas I'd committed were obviously not a big deal, and especially not when taking the piss out of some dirty Terran.

I never really appreciated that to the Flivvers, giving the girls Terran names said that I had a hive and the girls were welcome to join it any time they liked. Now I certainly didn't know that I had a hive and I also didn't know that everyone was constantly reading far more into what I said than was ever intended. My general impression was that they found me baffling, rude and completely alien, even if their natural tolerance and good manners meant that I constantly got away with far more than I ever realised.

For this and, I'm sure many other reasons, the rest of them generally left me pretty much alone. Soffee and an occasional girl did start coming along to see what I did for a living, and during that first visit, Soffee tried getting into the guts of a mechanical.

I'll tell you what. Never again. The girls had to spend the next day cleaning oil, grease and other mess off her feathers and no one wanted a repeat performance of that. Flivver miners had turned this planet into a wasteland, but after Soffee's little escapade I couldn't see how a feathered species could possibly have done that and not ended up permanently covered in gunge. Maybe they had a special engineering caste who did the dirty jobs? Who knew, but feathers and mess certainly didn't mix.

Even after that little excitement Soffee still occasionally came along, even if probably more from boredom than anything else. One afternoon, a particularly uncooperative piece of machinery was causing me problems, and she very quickly left me to frenzied hammering and floods of swearing. I was just finishing off when a person-to-person comm from Chitichca popped up on my HUD.

"Franky, Soffee has been involved an accident. Can you come and help?"

My only thoughts were of the unprintable variety, but I dropped everything and ran. And of course, guess what? There in front of the hive was a completely untouched Soffee doing her best to look totally innocent. Unfortunately, the youngsters lying on the ground looked anything but, and the animated crowd surrounding them looked pretty unimpressed. Everyone was making a lot of noise and before I could even draw breath, Soffee started.

"You know those who nasty and horrible to me? Well, I walk past hive, do nothing, and they come out say horrid things. They push me and hit me and I very worried because they so many. I use what we practise, but only so I not hurt."

It all came out in a single breath and with such contrived innocence that I started to smile, just catching myself in front of the collective tension now aimed in my direction. I raised an eyebrow before turning back to the growing group of agitated adults and, oh joy. There was Chitichca come along to join in the fun. Her furious expression told me everything that I needed to know about what she thought about Soffee, me and anything else I might be thinking about.

"Why did Soffee hurt these children, and why did you teach her how to do this?" she said. "She is not your hive's head protector," and there followed a machine-gun exchange of chitters between her and Soffee, all far too fast for my translator to get anything but the first bit.

"Hold on a minute," I tried butting into their full and no doubt frank interchange. "She's always being bullied by these kids, so what did you expect?"

"But she hurt them," said Chitichca, turning back to me. "She must be punished."

The guileless, innocent Soffee flipped straight into the irate version, hopping from foot to foot with infuriated chirps and flaps of her wings. I sighed as the wave of anguish crashed over me from both sides, but you know what? Soffee looked like she'd done OK and good for her even if Chitichca was probably right about the inadvisability of those combat vids. Still, I hated bullies and it was about time those kids got a smack.

I told Soffee I'd deal with it and she should get back to the hab. She stood there glaring, before slowly sloping. Her furious departing glances and whispered chitters only made things worse.

"You knew what these kids were like," I said to the even more enraged Flivvers, "but you didn't stop them. Well, she can defend herself now and good for her."

"But she is not your hive's head protector," said Chitichca, her voice so annoyed that I almost did a double take. "She cannot do this," and her fury flew right past me, straight up the tunnel and into Soffee's retreating back.

I looked into Chitichca's face and realised, yet again, I was out of my depth. All of my time on CS1 she'd been there in the background, watching, guiding, tweaking, and now she and all of these irate Flivvers obviously thought it was all my fault. Well, I wasn't a Flivver and their trying to absorb me into the Flivver way of doing things was a right pain in the arse.

"Look, I don't care," I said to the raised voices and outraged expressions. "These kids have been pots of poison forever and you did nothing. Soffee can now protect herself so they'd better watch out."

I was about to continue with what, in my opinion, they could go and do with themselves, but managed to keep my mouth shut. There was no point in arguing, especially just me against the whole hive. I mean, I hadn't even done anything. I was sure it would all calm down once they couldn't see this dirty Terran taking Soffee's side, and with that thought I turned and strode up the tunnel.

Their outraged noise died behind me as the hab came into view. Soffee raced up with a great big grin plastered all over her face.

"Enough," I said, waving my finger in front of her nose. "You did some pretty serious damage back there."

"But they know what protectors do," she proclaimed proudly. "Mother say I now head protector so I have hive to protect," and with that mystifying statement she turned to walk beside me looking like the proudest person on the entire planet.

The hab was deserted and Soffee disappeared straight into her room, leaving me standing there in solitary splendour. All around was wall-to-wall Flivver hive, and that well-remembered Franky's hab? Long gone, matey boy. As for what I'd just been dragged into? Well, obviously more than just a dust up between Soffee and those kids, but really? I sighed and my body sagged. I needed a break from this nonsense and I needed it right now.

You'll no doubt remember me mentioning the unbearable heat on the surface which made troglodytes of us all. Well, it's not actually the heat that's the problem, it's the timing.

The daytime sun will flay the skin off your back, but that's just it. The daytime sun. When the sun goes down, the heat goes straight up into that cloudless sky and everything gets a lot more civilised. Sure, it's then dark, and there's things out there hiding, and no doubt waiting, but as long as you keep your eyes open you're pretty safe. And guess what? Just a quick stroll up the tunnel was an old environmental door.

A quick walk up the left-hand tunnel into the dimness, a bit of a heave ho and there we were. Silent desolation spread away into the darkening distance, junk piles merging into sand dunes and just a hint of sunset cracking the horizon. No Flivvers. Perfect.

The flinty-dry breath of breeze tickled my hair and I spread my arms, a heartfelt "Aaaah" greeting the ocean of stars staring right back. Alluring, mocking, and as always, supremely indifferent.

"Franky, what you do?" dropped into the silence.

"Shiiit!" was all I could manage, and there was Soffee standing silhouetted in the doorway. "What the hell are you doing here?"

"I follow," she said, having a good look around. "Why you come here? Is just sand and rubbish."

"Yeah, maybe," I said once I'd got my breath back, "but sometimes you've just gotta get out and breathe some air. I mean, look at it all. Isn't it marvellous?"

"But I know is here and you know is here," she said, looking around again. "Is always here. Why you come?"

"Oh come on," I said, "surely. It's the wide-open spaces, that sea of stars. On Old-Earth I'd spend hours just looking up and sure, the sky was pollution soup, but all of those worlds and peoples? I mean, what's not to like?"

I couldn't stop myself smiling.

"Well, I s'pose," said Soffee, obviously still not impressed, "but hive is here. Why you want go to other worlds where no hive?"

"OK then," I said. "If you don't like the stars, isn't it nice to just come out and get some fresh air?"

"But air is fresh in tunnels," she said. "I know you keep fresh. Out here is too open and sky bit frightening." Her gaze strayed upwards. "Where Old-Earth?"

I pointed. "Over there. See the top star in that line of three? Crazy really. That light's been on its way here for what, five hundred years before I was born."

A brief flashback, blasting into space, leaving the 'Blue planet' which hadn't been blue for an awfully long time. I wouldn't go back there if you paid me, but I'd swapped that craphole for this craphole and ironic didn't begin to describe it.

Soffee was still gazing at the thousand ntime year-old dot of distant Sol, silent, thinking. She stuck out a hand, looking at the wisps of ancient light that were striking it.

"Is very strange," she said, "this light coming 500 hundred years before you alive. I see why is Old-Earth, but where is New-Earth?"

"Well yeah," I said, "that's just it. Us reltimers' view of things is pretty outside of normal spacetime and any place we've been's already way old. That light's just limping along playing catchup. Tell you what. Where'd you come from? I can point..." but a hand on my arm stopped me.

"I not from Flivver home planet," she said. "I think I not from any planet."

Idiot!

Idiot!

Shit, shit, shit!

"But surely everyone's from somewhere," came out before I could stop myself.

"Someone bring me here," she said, "but no one know where from. Maybe I not from any place."

"Heh look...," I tried, "I didn't mean... but you know...," then shut up before anything worse came out. I knew all about that whole hybrid multi-species artificial cell line quagmire and probably so did she. You just didn't want to go there.

The remains of the breeze cooled my foolish sweat as gentle night whispers only served to emphasise the size of my big mouth. Soffee glanced back at the dim speck of Sol and her shoulders sagged.

"I know you like here," she said, "but I think we go back. Is dangerous."

I just managed to catch myself before any additional stupidity popped out. Soffee's reaction to Chitichca's frustrated "you're not a hive-protector" utterances were obviously a big thing for her. Get in the way of that at your peril.

"OK boss," I said with a smile. "I'll try and remember."

Soffee was sniffing the air. What could she smell?

"I think we go," she said. "Funny smell is getting stronger and I think is dangerous."

My IFF wasn't showing anything, but then it hadn't seen those little horrors in the ventilation machine room. Soffee carefully shut out the dark behind the environmental door and her best watching and worrying stayed full on all of the way back to the hab.

The next day everything seemed pretty much as it had been before, although there was still a whisp of something between her and the Flivvers. That being said, her much-exaggerated hardass reputation spreading through the market didn't do her any harm at all, as well as providing freshly minted gold dust for the marketeer's feeble attempts at humour.

Chitichca kept on with her unobtrusive presence, dipping in occasionally to make sure Soffee was OK and actually, now I came to think about it, doing much the same for me. Our shouting match seemed to have been completely forgotten.

Several weeks later she pulled me aside for a quick word. Always a bit worrying those 'quick words', and just like when my Mum used to have the same words about something I'd done, or not done, or even worse.

Anyway, this particular chat was about tech implants, or rather, Soffee's lack of. Now, that was indeed an interesting consideration. I lived on my tech implants - HUD, IFF, translator, remote sensing, tox screen, medical nanos - but I'd never come across any neural implant packs on CS1.

A bog-standard organic/tech implant might be possible, but on a hybrid? I mean, who knew what sort of central nervous system she'd been given, and believe me, there's nothing worse than a tech implant going wrong because it doesn't match the implantee's organics.

Soffee looked like an accident waiting to happen, but Chitichca's customary Mother-knows-best expression wasn't having any of it. Still, I'd been here before with those Mother-knows-best arm twists. The only thing that worked against Flivvers was a multi-pronged delaying approach, more battle of attrition than reasoned discussion.

So, first off, I had the hab AI do a quick scan to make sure that the implant insertion process wasn't going to fry her nervous system. A rather worryingly confident affirmation came straight back saying all was well.

Next, I tried the excuse that I'd never done an implant on someone like Soffee before, ever. That was greeted by the Flivver equivalent of scoffing disbelief.

So, the final weapon in my armoury. A quick dig around in my odds and sods box, but blast! There, looking straight back at me was the tech/organic interface stuff I'd been keeping as my own spares. I was out of excuses.

With a pleasing trust in my expected abilities, the girls had already removed an area of blue down from behind one of Soffee's ears. That pinky-blue patch of skin now joined the expectant faces looking back at me, and there was nothing for it. I picked up the brain/tech interface auto-inserter, positioned it over the patch of skin, pressed down firmly and stood back with fingers, toes and both buttocks crossed.

Worried chittering from those watching didn't exactly help my anxiety levels, and the drilling, cutting and other noises from the auto-inserter just added to the tension. Soffee gave the usual succession of involuntary twitches as a hole was made in her skull and micro filaments synched into the various parts of her brain stem. As each stage completed, succeeding tell-tales lit up on the auto-inserter and finally there we were, a full line of greens. The auto-inserter dropped off, and there we had a standard brain/tech interface multi-socket protruding from just behind her ear.

I wriggled in a translator plus standard HUD implants and her initial starts and surprised expressions from the initiating direct injection feeds were a picture. The next hour or so was the usual game of her getting used to the sprays of info now being displayed across her left eye, together with the constant chattering of the translator. She had to make several uses of the handy bucket, but any tech implant newbie will tell you about the initial mental loop the loops and their inevitable consequences.

Over the next few days, the full benefits of what I'd installed quickly became apparent. My suggestion that she power her new implants by adding piezo-generators to whatever she was wearing merely earned me another in the long line of you-stupid-man looks. Credits were burning holes. New clothes beckoned. Time to change the wardrobe.

Of course, the new translator also opened up the sorts of conversations that teenage girls have with more adult members of the various species involved, all of whom should know a whole lot better. Still, great fun for everyone and I even managed to bask in whatever expert engineer-type reflected glory came my way.

The funny thing was, my life kept getting better and better and it was all down to those Flivvers. Work was great, I had plenty of money to spend and every evening I got back to a hab where at least Soffee asked me, in Terran, how my day had been. Occasional visits to the surface gave my mental rats an airing, and even Dougie had become less of a pain.

I still had the problem of how I was going to get off this planet, but as the only thing to do was wait and see, I might as well have a good time while I waited and saw.

7
Off-planet, in a bad way

You know how they say you shouldn't wish for something too much, as it might actually happen? Well, this particular wish made its presence felt after a very successful day at work. In fact, it had been so successful that liquid refreshment was definitely in order.

Also, Soffee was getting rather arsy about why she, the head hive-protector, couldn't go with me to El Shitto and make sure I stayed safe. So, it seemed like an ideal time to kill two birds with one stone as well as show her the error of her wish.

We walked up to El Shitto with all three of the doorman's eyes giving both me and this brand-new customer their fullest attention. The usual look, the usual hesitation then he waved us in, Soffee's eyes growing wider and wider as we walked up to the bar.

Dougie sidled up, slimy, ingratiating, shit-eating smile, holding onto Soffee's hand for far too long and tonight he actually seemed to have had a bath. Extraordinary.

It was busy, but Dougie found us a place, carefully smarming Soffee into a seat that he'd specially found to fit her wings. He then raised a hand, and blow me down, the first round was on him. The Barkeep was already pouring mine, and Dougie managed to find something suitably Flivveresque for Soffee. I had to smile at her grimace and holding it up to the light to see just what the hell this actually was.

Still, I'd had a good day. We raised our glasses to continued success, and once Soffee saw that people chinking glasses together was not actually threatening, she started to relax. A second round of drinks arrived, again courtesy of Dougie, which made the "Oi, you Terran arsehole! I want a word," bellowed into my ear so much more annoying, especially as it was accompanied by a jab in the back.

I turned around with my choicest riposte armed and ready, but nothing came out. There were three military-spec suits, 3m high, fully armoured, with each user's head staring out of the opened-up helmet and weapons clutched in massive hands pointing straight at me. Totally state of the kick-ass art and equally totally overkill, but maybe that was just my perspective.

The biggest and ugliest guy leant in, nose-to-nose, eye-to-eye.

"I said, craphead, we want a word."

"Oh Shit!" was my only thought as I recoiled away from the bad breath and detailed close-up of his face. But hold on a minute. No one's got suits like these. Who are these guys?

Personal hygiene certainly wasn't this one's best friend, but alongside the earth-moving dog's breath was a flicker of ozone. Hell, they've just come down from orbit, and then the really important thought struck home. Shiiit. If they're down here, then they've left an FTL ship up there!

These and other thoughts fluttered across my twitching wits as the other two goons circled around, weapons out and obviously dying to use them. Soffee had ghosted off to one side, Dougie was at the other end of the bar and I was locked into this doughnut of empty space. Mr Dog's breath's gaze flicked across to Dougie with an almost imperceptible nod. So that was where those oh-so-generous drinks had come from. The bastard! I'll bloody kill him!

"OK MISTER Franks, you're coming with us," thundered into my face, interrupting the Dougie-you-bastard thoughts with more bad breath and a spray of saliva. His armoured hand grabbed hold of my shoulder but came up short. Soffee blocked our way, fighting crouch, wings held open, knife in one hand.

"Come on girly," said my suited friend, "out of the way."

"I head hive-protector and you not take Franky," ground out as the other suits circled back, red targeting dots bouncing all over her head, wings and body.

"Soffee, don't," I managed. "There's nothing you can do. Go and get Chitichca," but she was not impressed with that at all.

Mr Suit-man lifted his weapon and its red targeting dot flicked onto her face.

"Yeah," he said, "Soffee," smiling as he said it, "listen to the man. We've got no quarrel with you," and he turned to me. "What's a Fliv doing backing you up? You some sorta weirdo or something?"

"Please Soffee," I said. "These guys aren't kidding. Go and get Chitichca," but she just kept standing there, eyes flicking between all of us.

Ohhh nooo, she's going to do something, but her wings slowly folded back as she straightened up.

"I go, but I come back," she said, her gaze flicking around the room to pause on Dougie, before she ran out.

Matey-boy nodded to his companions and I was frog-marched straight out after Soffee.

I just about managed "What the...hell do...you...want?" as I staggered past the door guy, now completely immobilised with binder-web. However, my captor was far too busy looking around to answer, and so were his mates.

"Look...you must...have the wrong...person. Why d'ya want me?" came pumping out as we trotted across the market, travelling through a tunnel of stunned silence as everyone stopped to watch the extraordinary sight going by.

We whipped into the tunnel leading up to my hab and my spirits started to lift as we approached the Flivver hive, but they were immediately dashed. It was silent, deserted, no sentinel, no Soffee and no anyone.

Straight past and then up past my hab. It was now only a couple of environmental doors before we hit the wider tunnel system. I really hoped we weren't going up there, but I'd be fried in the sun if we went outside. Damned if we did, damned if we didn't, but I probably had more important things to worry about.

My favourite environmental door appeared out of the gloom and everyone fanned out, weapons drawn, alert as hell. They really seemed to be expecting trouble, but who from? Not Soffee, surely? Their three helmets snapped shut as my captor fumbled his gun back into its holster and thumped the door release.

A burp of superheated air smacked me in the face, my eyes screwing up tight as blinding sunlight came streaming in. Sitting outside was a knackered old mining crawler with another gun-toting minion standing alongside and looking very eager. An idle thought wondered how the hell they'd managed to find something, anything, that worked, but this was trumped straight away by the mental whinge that my day was looking bad enough without them dropping onto that.

Matey boy renewed his grip and dragged me across to the crawler, the sun searing my face and scorching wind cooking everything else. A door flicked open and in we bundled, the door snapping shut behind.

Everyone started to relax, armoured helmets popping back to reveal what was inside. Pretty basic Terran spec, although there'd been a lot more inter-species shenanigans than was good for them or anyone else. Large, hairy and angry. Best examples of anyone's gangster henchman poster boys.

There were several jerks from the superannuated drive train and we started moving. Up in front were two more guys wearing suits and one of them was looking straight at me.

"So this is the famed engineer we've come all this way to find," he said. "You certainly look the part, but can you fix a ring-ship?"

"Well you didn't have to kidnap me," I said. "I'd have probably come along if you'd just asked."

My questioner smirked. "Yeah well, we stopped asking long ago 'cos people kept saying no. Our ship needs fixing and you're the lucky guy."

Great. Weeks if not months off-planet on some wreck of a ship. Still, work was work and these idiots had no idea what an engineer cost. Could be a better day than I'd thought.

"OK, fair enough," I said, "but my time costs. Gotta pay the bills you know."

The temperature plunged twenty degrees as each goon's hand dropped to their sidearm. The main man was, however, still wearing a smirk.

"Look smartarse," he said, "I'll put it another way. You come along, fix what you can and we'll take a flight. If everything works then maybe I'll bring you back again, or maybe I won't. Whaddya reckon?" That smile said he wasn't asking.

I was about to answer with something typically stupid, but something more sensible raised its mental hand for attention.

"Tell you what,' I said. "If I fix your ship then you can give me a lift out of here. I don't mind where and if anything breaks on the way I can fix it. C'mon, that's gotta be a good deal."

Judging by their expressions, preferred remuneration was probably along the lines of an impromptu space walk without a suit. However, they needed someone to fix their ship and I seemed to be the guy.

"Ummm," he said, staring at me. "Maybe I'm feeling generous. You fix our ship and we choose the destination. Could work, but no promises."

The sheer delight on my face was probably not a great negotiating technique, but this was my golden ticket. I turned to the nearest gorilla guy with the beginnings of a high five, but his expression said better not. Looking back at matey boy, his face had changed, and I felt my smile stiffen. What wasn't he telling me?

"Yeah," he said after a moment's pause, "there's something else we need you to do," and my neck hairs started to prickle. "We need you to find something."

The hairs on my neck were now on tippytoes.

"What do you mean, find something?" I said. "Surely you can find something on your own ship?"

"Yeah well," he said. "We sort of permanently borrowed it and there's stuff we need that we can't find. You know how it is."

"But why don't you ask who you got the ship from?" I said.

"That'll be difficult," he said to muffled titters. "They're a thousand lights back and breathing space."

An icy chill shot down my spine. Only the sound of us moving. Everyone was looking at me, waiting.

"Okaaay," I said through a suddenly dry mouth, "what have you lost?"

"Bit difficult to explain, but we'll see about that once you've got the ship working."

Thank goodness the guy alongside him chose this moment to break in, calling out that we'd arrived. With no choice about being here, I wasn't sure I wanted to hear anything more. Everyone's look had now switched to what was outside and yup, it was a standard orbital pod, shining out there in the sunlight with fuel vapour streaming away in the wind.

A bit of a shiver from that time five years ago and actually, I was amazed they'd managed to land it here at all. This landing grid was wrecked, and they'd either had Lady Luck on their side or the pod AI was really good. Knowing CS1? Definitely a lot of both.

The guy nearest the door knocked it open and the searing wind blew in as he leapt out and ran to the pod. Repeated hammering at a switch finally gave a set of steps flipping out down the nearest landing leg, and up he went as everyone baled out after him. The heat and sun were awful and going up those steps was even worse, but eventually I tipped in through the entrance hatch. The outer pressure door swung shut and the inner door swung open to let in a blast of blessed cool air.

Pretty standard pod really. "Make me a pod," says Daddy, and his little girl uses the bits box plus ten rolls of packing tape to make what we were now standing in. This one looked like she'd then kept her animals in it, which I guess wasn't so far from the truth. The seats?

Well, not exactly hygienically clean, so I took pot luck and started strapping myself in.

The automated blast-off timer started counting down. We got to eleven seconds and it stopped with lots of warnings and flashing red lights. One of the goons got out of his seat, went over to the offending console and started hammering away at a keypad. One by one the red lights flicked off and the alarms stopped shouting. A final key stroke and the countdown restarted.

Zero arrived with nothing else complaining and that oh so familiar rumble filled the cabin. We were off, the ground disappearing faster and faster as we powered up into the sky. It had been far too long, and you never forgot what taking off from a planet's surface is like. That thing from childhood, you know, slipping the surly bonds of Earth, dancing the sky on laughter-silvered wings or some such nonsense. Anyway, this take off was like I was climbing back up to where I truly belonged, and the max G take off elephant sitting all over me was just further validation that I'd finally made it.

The launch boost cut off and we curved round into orbit, those five dead years disappearing behind me. Below us, CS1's yellow planetary disc slid by and there, further out, was a ring-ship, growing out of the blackness and dwarfing our pod. I really had been stuck on this crappy planet for far too long.

8
Ring-ship

The pod manoeuvred up behind the gently spinning ship, making sure it gave plenty of room to those three enormous rings suspended out from the main body. I'd not seen many ring-ships this big, and strewth, that main body was at least half a klick long. Where had they got this thing?

Control transferred to the ship's main AI and we slid in towards the docking bay, our pod now dwarfed by the vast mottled expanse across which we were crawling. Closer and closer, reassuring bleeps, pings, a bump and then sprays of green lights to say that we'd docked. A final check from the pod AI and indeed, there we were, safely docked.

Everyone eased out of their seats, and with the usual comments about what climb-out Gs did to the nether regions, we floated out into the pod bay. The first thing I noticed was that every control panel was showing more red lights than I'd ever seen before, anywhere. I glanced back to where we'd just left and icy fingers clutched at my heart. Our own pod's control panel was the same shouting sea of red and there it was, another of those records you hoped you'd never break. A pod that shouldn't have been able to fly had just got us up through the planet's gravity well, docked safely at a dock that didn't work properly, and no one had died. A tribute to the designers no doubt, but what were these guys doing in such a complete crock of crap? Or, more worryingly, what had they done to make it such a complete crock?

The entry lock to the main body swung open and aaaah, that unforgettable ring-ship smell. Oily mechanics, sewage plant, sweaty locker room and everything overlaid by that essence of pine which Terran environmental engineers think makes everything OK. You just didn't want to know what the Shonat equivalent smelt like. Waiting for us was another guy, as large and grubby as the rest of them and wearing a very worried expression.

"Faizal's gone," he said in a sort of whispered squeak. "He went to his room but never came back. He's gone, no sign of him, nothing. I don't know..." but was brought up short by the Boss-man's raised hand.

"Woah there," he said flicking a quick glance at me. "Let's not frighten the kiddies. We're back now and we've got our bloody engineer. Let's get it together and make sure he doesn't disappear before he's fixed the ship," and there was a snicker of amusement all around. "C'mon you," grabbing me as he moved off in front of us.

All eyes except mine were on the Boss-man, but I was transfixed by the sight of that brightly lit comms space stretching away down the main body. It was a scabby white, scuffed and scraped from decades of reltime travel with machinery, pipes, handholds and openings dotted everywhere. Aaaah. Daddy's home!

We were floating about in this weightless centre of the rotating ship, but out in the rings there'd be whatever approximated to these guys' 1G. We just had to get there. The walls of the central comms space were littered with handholds, but I'd been standing on the surface of CS1 for far too long and knew exactly what I wanted to do. Everyone's minds with but a single thought on that one and we leapt into the wide-open space towards an elevator labelled with a great big 1. A bit of an untidy landing, but pseudo-gravity was now grasping at us with its tenacious claws.

"Right," said the boss-man, "I've given you access to the ship. Your job is to fix it so we don't die. Our job is to get up to Ring 1 for a shower, a shit and something to eat."

I opened my mouth to say that was all very well, but was forestalled by the barrel of his sidearm being stuck up my left nostril.

"Now would be better than later, OK?" he said with a nod and a raised eyebrow. My matching nod had him and his mates disappearing into the elevator, leaving me in what my HUD was now telling me was as dangerous a place as the pod we'd just come up in. It had started pulsing an above-normal radiation warning and I could smell ozone, hot stressed metal and melting plastic. Never a good sign.

I hop-skimmed down the main body towards the large armoured door with a red light flashing above it. As it cracked open, my radiation alarm went up a notch and the stronger smells of over-stressed engineering made me cough. There was a red glow coming from the doorway to the control room and as I went in, there was the source.

Every single console and indicator board was lit up. There were reds everywhere. Even worse, there was a rash of non-standard equipment and everything seemed to be fudged together with wires and tape. Even the auto-repair systems were knackered. No wonder the Boss-man had been a trifle terse.

I was still trying to get my head around all of this when I was engulfed by a wave of electronic shouting. Unfortunately my HUD had told the ship's systems' AIs that I was an engineer and every one of them was now complaining about how deep in the doodoo we were, how I had to do something about it right now, and me first please.

I hopped over to the main console and asked the ship's main AI - you know, brain the size of a major asteroid, follows the rules, no personality, boring as hell - for a summary. And there it was. The ship belonged, or more accurately had belonged, to a group of Terran traders who'd been very naughty on the repairs front. No shit Sherlock there, but more interestingly they'd been accelerating away from Servcon when the ship had slowed to pick up a pod, after which they'd resumed their acceleration and jumped.

This jump had been somewhat random due to the confusion over who was in charge, and I'd already met those responsible for that. From what I could see, my new friends had then flown all over the galaxy sowing death and destruction wherever they went. This flying visit to CS1 was just that, a flying visit to pick me up.

So, thanks a lot guys, but at least the main AI had some good news. We had plenty of spares and anything we didn't have we could make using the nano-fabricator on board. So, at least with a little bit of luck we weren't going to die, although it was probably a race against time and all of those red lights.

Difficult to know where to start, but having air to breathe and a fusion reactor that wasn't about to blow up was a good start. So, I went, pursued by all of the AIs that couldn't understand why I wasn't doing something for them first.

Several hours later and I'd managed to sort out some of the most urgent reds, and several hours after that I'd managed to sort out the auto-repair systems. So, we were no longer about to die, or at least not immediately. Trouble was, I'd now been up for the best part of two days and was showing some serious reds across a lot of my own critical systems.

The nearest rest room was the manky mess you might expect, especially as there'd obviously been a mix of species living here over the years. Still, you've gotta go when you've gotta go, but as soon as I walked in I could feel my hackles rise.

Something was wrong. It was nothing obvious, nothing you could put a finger on. My IFF and HUD weren't saying anything, but there was something here that just wasn't right.

I looked around the mess, but my eye was drawn to the multi-species food unit up against the wall. Ah, hot beverage here we come, but hold on a minute. Where were the lights? Where was its welcoming electronic smile?

It was only then that I saw what had rung those mental alarm bells. A finger-sized hole had been drilled, or rather burned, through the front of the food unit. Below it was someone's half-hearted attempt to mop up a whole lot of sticky something that had oozed all over the floor.

9
More ring-ship

Putting my eye to the hole I could see right through the food unit and the wall behind. To my left was another hole, together with a similarly failed attempt at clearing up some sloppy mess underneath. Now you didn't have to be a genius to work out what had happened, but one or maybe two someones shot and killed wasn't something you saw very often, and definitely not on a ship.

You've got to remember that the whole point about travelling around in space is the staying alive bit while you travelled. Space is permanently waiting to kill you, so doing anything to help is pure lunacy. Sure, all kinds of things happen on the ground, but in space you do not blow holes through your enemy. That ultra cool state of the art hardware you're packing will make a nice neat hole in them, but also the ship's wall behind and anything else on the way out to open space to let in the vacuum. These psychos who'd picked me up must have been the luckiest people alive, to well, still be alive.

A worrying thought, but I had much more worrying reds back in Engineering control to worry about. So, grabbing something from one of the less well-ventilated food units, I went back to the ever-changing console light show.

That food and drink, whatever it was, really hit the spot, but you know what food and drink does to droopy eyes. I could hardly stay awake, and the sirens' song of the rest room's grubby hammocks was becoming more and more difficult to resist. I did remember to send a quick message back to my hab to say I was OK, but no one was listening. They were probably already celebrating my disappearance and their unexpected ownership.

I slipped into the nearest unsavoury but very welcoming net hammock and dropped straight off to sleep...to be rudely awakened by a sharp prod in the ribs. My eyes jerked open and there was Mr Boss-man's face, nose-to-nose, up far too close and personal with every one of his various skin problems all too evident.

"Wake up you idle bastard," was his shouted opening gambit through a spray of saliva. "There's still plenty of work to do so get yer lazy arse out of that pit."

He was even scabbier than I remembered and the flecks of spittle strongly seasoned with a lifetime's worth of no personal hygiene was a very rude awakening. I tried turning over, but my reward was the muzzle of his sidearm rammed into my ear.

"I said get up!" he continued. "This isn't a holiday."

"Look," I said as my head was levered back upright, "I've been on the go for two days solid and I'm knackered. I've fixed the priority 1s and I'll fix everything else you've broken after I've had some sleep."

He stood there staring at me, before disappearing out of the room. He came back with a strange smile cracking his face.

"Well you know what you're doing," he said, "but I want this ship ready as soon as bloody possible. I'll be watching."

He flicked two fingers at his eyes and back to me as he walked out. I flopped back into my noisome hammock and quickly re-joined those rudely interrupted dreams.

A number of refreshing hours later I swam awake, even if being greeted by that manky old rest room was almost as bad as matey-boy. Grabbing a drink, I staggered out to see what had been happening, and what had been happening was the main systems continuing to get themselves back online. So, thank goodness for that. Definitely time to leave Engineering's rather robust atmosphere and get along to the much more civilised main control cabin.

I suppose it was that old grunt versus owner thing. The real work got done in Engineering, so Engineering was hot, grimy and a real mess. The main control cabin was where the captain watched, airily waved a hand, and then the proles or main AI got the job done. OK, so I'm somewhat prejudiced, but I had to say that this ship's main control cabin was everything I'd always imagined. Bright white, lots of curves, lovely seats, fully integrated wall-to-wall consoles and clean, or at least it would be as soon as the bots had cleaned up the current owners' mess.

It was what those consoles were showing me that made my jaw drop. I'd already seen the mechanical guts but everything else was, well, something else. The ship was ancient, built four ntime centuries ago as a cattle-class transport for air breathers. Successive owners had then updated, added and changed so much that the original builders wouldn't even have recognised it. I almost couldn't believe my eyes.

We now had those three rings which provided comfortable interstellar accommodation for three hundred souls. Which was all very nice, but it was the stores where everything flew straight out of the window. My scrambling for parts had been a taster, and the full inventory was amazing. There were things I'd never seen before. There were things I'd never heard of. There were pods. There were suits. There were piles of stuff which had no practical use but price tags to make your eyes water. Of course, how it had all got here was not a nice a thought and a slap on the back and the exhortation to stop pissing about was merely further emphasis of that.

"I've never seen anything like what you've got here," I couldn't stop myself saying.

"Yeah," said the Boss-man, "always liked the good things in life. Always wanted to see the galaxy as well, but you know how it is. Those other species bastards with their noses in the air thinking they're so bloody special? Well, I never had your skills but no one's calling me

Terran trash no more, no sir. They can all burn," a cheery punch to my arm. "And d'you know what? That's exactly what they did."

His smile was as chilling as those mad, bad eyes. "You know something," he continued. "It's nice you're here. I needed someone to talk to. Those guys?" and he waved his arm at the door. "Animals, the lot of 'em."

There was an awful silence. I could feel myself wanting to say something, anything to break the stare of those godawful eyes, but luckily he started talking again before I beat him to it.

"Anyway, remember me saying I needed you to find something? Well, here's the thing. This ship's been around forever but I can only find the flight logs since we got on. There's nothing before that and I need you to find it."

"That should be easy," I said, wearing my best watch-the-expert-at-work expression as I told the main AI to put up the full set of flight logs. The expected flood of data came straight back and I turned to the boss-man with my best ta-dah expression.

"Yeah, genius," he said, decidedly unimpressed. "That's what I got. Have a look where it starts."

You know what? He was right. For a ship this old the entire log only started four reltime years ago, the best part of a hundred years ntime.

"Ship," I asked again. "Give me access to every log from commissioning to date." The ship came straight back with what it had just had given me, but that made no sense at all. I turned to the Boss-man and his sardonic expression had changed to a more menacing snarl.

"So there's yer problem, and your ticket out of here," he said. "Find those missing logs and we're good to go. Don't find them and you're breathing space. You get me?"

My desire to ask why those old logs were so important was interrupted by an alarm flashing, which was probably a good thing. By the time I'd sorted out that problem he was long gone, and I was left to my repairs, the re-furbs, his mysterious task and even deeper contemplation. His top priority may have been getting everything working, but I was starting to see that my top priority had to be self-preservation.

That last reminder of space being deep, endless and entirely air-free merely added to the urgency. I had to find myself a suit.

Terran suits come in all shapes and sizes, generally bipedal and ranging from strap on exoskeletons to AI-controlled 3m high armoured leviathans. In the larger ones, the user sits totally enclosed in a sealed environment, with full mobility and as much weaponry as you could strap on. Trouble was, the bad guys on this ship had been making full use of theirs, and the after effects of them living in their suits for days or weeks at a time didn't bear thinking about. I didn't want to go anywhere near that, but this ship had plenty of others. Even if they didn't work.

I'd already come across a room marked suit spares. Just the job you might say, but on further inspection? Wow - nice! Definitely spares, but very much on the destructive end of the scale. They had enough weapons and ammo to start a small war and all very plug and play.

I started by secreting some of the more repairable armoured suits around the main body, with added selections of choice goodies to keep auto-repair busy. Of course, getting suits ready to go was one thing. Getting to one before any trouble hit was probably another. I'd just have to see what happened.

The days kept marching on, and the list of things needing repair was finally starting to get shorter. Any work in the accommodation rings required either the Boss-man or one of his loping simians to be in close attendance, but for some reason no one was interested in following me into the cavernous main body. No one wanted to talk about Faizal either.

Now I know that micro-gravity wasn't everyone's cup of tea, but they really weren't keen on that main body space. Most of it was storage, massive rack upon massive rack holding all of the stuff they'd pinched, and even I had to admit it could be pretty spooky down there on your own. In fact, several times I'd have sworn blind there was someone in there with me, but I couldn't see anything and neither could my IFF. Maybe it was just a flashback to that machine room on

CS1, as there couldn't possibly be anything dangerous lurking on a ship? Surely?

Whatever was going on, or not, the next time I saw Mr. Boss-man he was wearing a fully activated suit. Following behind were the rest of the menagerie, also fully equipped. I did momentarily wonder whether they'd suddenly become worried about me, but I was just part of the plumbing as far as they were concerned. I told them about the noises I'd heard, or when I couldn't put my hand on something that I'd just put down, but all I got was that look from the boss-man as he stomped past. Maybe it was their planet-sized guilty consciences making them twitch? Who could say?

And talking of twitches, I'd left repairing the main armaments until very, very last. So you may well ask why, if everyone in space was such a goody two shoes, you'd need main armaments. Well, I'd never come across a ship with them before, but I guess it's better to have something you don't need, than need something you don't have. From what I could see on the usage logs, these guys had both needed and used the main armament many, many times, and it didn't take a genius to guess what for.

My quick look past all of the warning lights didn't make things any better. A massive bank of super-capacitors feeding enough power into the emitter to punch holes in anything I could think of, and all sitting on the edge of a nervous breakdown. Get it wrong and we'd be an expanding cloud of debris visible from the surface of CS1. So, I'd replace anything that might even just be thinking about having a problem and then we'd test, test and test again.

I got there eventually, but still held my breath as I told the IFF to fire a quick shot into the nearest patch of empty space. A flash on the weapons indicator and some dim and distant civilisation was going to have an interesting version of first contact if they happened to be in the wrong place at the wrong time. Still, greens all round and the IFF asked me whether I wanted to take another shot.

A big NO to that one and I slumped back into my chair. I was now surrounded by a sea of green and for the first time in almost forever, everything worked. In fact, the ship was totally unrecognizable from the junkyard I'd been dragged into and hell, even the cleaning bots were on the cusp of making the place habitable. OK, so I hadn't forgotten about that first golden rule of space engineering, but with the Boss-man's comments about suit-less space walks I'd had other things to worry about. FTL beckoned and the sooner we were off, the sooner I was out of here.

I'd only ever known his varied collection of evil grins and snarls, but on hearing this good news his face did finally crack into a jagged smile with an added friendly punch to seal the deal. The sniggers from his assembled minions were rather worrying, but I didn't care. We were finally off and if I never saw CS1 again it would be far too soon.

10
Every jump is a leap of faith

All of this time I'd been up in the ship fixing things, CS1's baleful yellow glare hadn't stopped reminding me about everyone still down on, or even below, the surface. In a gap between the Boss-man shouting, stomping off, coming back and shouting some more, I sent a final message to the hab saying I was off, but got no response. Flivvers were always going to be the hive and the hive was always going to be the Flivvers, but I was rather sad that they'd dropped me that quickly. I'd miss them. Life in the hab really had been something else.

I then reminded the ship's Navcom to get a move on before the Boss-man came back shouting at me to get a move on, and like now you idle bastard. The IFF was already fully active, on the ball and ready to shoot anything that even thought about being a threat, but really? Gimme strength. There was nothing for tens of lights. Still, if that's what the Boss-man wanted then that's what the Boss-man got. I wasn't going to argue. In any case, I had far more important things to worry about, like making sure the jump worked.

Our test jump track popped up on the Navcom and there we were, CS1 to the nearest system. We'd have thirty days' acceleration to get to our one tenth light-speed jump threshold and then we'd jump into betweenspace before coming back out again ten light-years later. The ship's elapsed time for the jump would be about a day reltime while normal spacetime would have been sadly missing us for around four years. Everything looked good. The Boss-man looked happy. Assuming all went well, this jump would be my ticket back to civilisation and I could hardly wait.

We orbited round to our correct launch trajectory, the main engines fired and we pulled away along our jump track. The Boss-man was still happy, but I stayed glued to the consoles. FTL travel involves far too much complexity and danger to be left on its own and even if the ship was showing all systems go, I didn't believe a word of it.

We were at our max comfortable long-term acceleration, 1.25G, which was going to be pretty unpleasant if you weren't in deep-sleep or wearing a suit. To my request, the Boss-man and his goons were having none of it. They were happily ensconced in their suits and I'd just have to lump it. Of course, they knew nothing about the various working suits I now had secreted around the ship, but I was keeping those aces up my sleeve for when any unplanned spacewalks might get suggested.

The days stretched into weeks and everything was still looking good, which was why the urgent and unexpected comm popping up was a bit of a surprise.

"Oi you," was the Boss-man's charming opener, "I can't get any comms from Green."

He was Red suit and the rest of his cohorts were going by other colours of the rainbow, obviously some ex-military garbage. I checked the console and you know what? He was right. Red, Blue, Orange, Yellow and Purple were still shining bright, but I couldn't see Green. In fact, Green wasn't anywhere. I reported this back and in fairly short order Red plus the other colours of the rainbow appeared, fully tooled up and very obviously ready for action.

"Strewth!" I said, "What's happening?"

There was too much gesturing and shouting to make any real sense, but I did catch "...and I bloody told you we should have done something. First Faizal and now Benji. What the hell are we gonna do now?"

That didn't sound great, especially as whatever they hadn't done now involved the disappearance of someone wearing a military spec suit. Any further thoughts were interrupted by a red light on the main console announcing the emergency opening of one of the airlocks. An IFF advisory popped up showing Green's ID attached to something that was now spinning away from the ship. Almost certainly Green suit then.

A momentary silence then the Boss-man growled out: "Anyone got Orange? My IFF's just dropped him."

Glances flicked around, but no one said a word. What the hell was going on?

"Right," ground out the Boss-man, "we end this now. There's only one of them and I want it breathing space. Got it?"

Everyone else didn't seem so confident, but he turned to me with a terse: "Stay here and keep watch," before heading off towards the storage area, followed by the rest.

I called out "Don't you want to go and get Green..." but he obviously had more important things on his mind.

My gaze flicked between the IFF console and the suits' receding backs. What the hell was going on? One, or maybe two, suits had just been taken out, but by who? These military spec suits were pretty much indestructible. I probably needed to keep my head down and actually, staying here suited me just fine. It was the safest place I could think of and with the Boss-man and his minions spoiling for a fight, I was very happy staying away from that.

Locking the cabin door made me feel a bit more secure and I went back to looking for Orange suit. Despite my best efforts I couldn't see it anywhere, but hold on. We'd just done an unscheduled garbage dump and there in the rapidly dispersing cloud of debris was what looked like the remains of Orange suit. A more detailed scan said mechanical plus organic remains and there we were. Two suits plus occupants dumped out of the ship and no sign of who'd done it, even if the bad guys certainly seemed to know.

I was still staring at the consoles when there was a half-heard, half-felt thump and a sea of alarms lit up. An external camera flashed up a spray of debris flying into space, mainly hull plating, atmosphere and the remains of Yellow suit. Auto damage control was straight onto it and the main AI informed me in an almost self-satisfied manner that it could see no tell-tales from Yellow suit.

I'd never seen an AI take sides before, but it was reporting the ejection into space of yet one more of the pirates who'd taken the ship from its previous owners. I wonder what the ship thought of me?

"Red," I called out, "We've now got Green, Orange and Yellow out in space. Also, why the hell are you using explosives?" I muttered an additional "...you bloody idiots," under my breath.

"Wasn't us," the Boss-man replied. "Yellow was on point when that explosion knocked a hole in the hull and sucked him out. We'd have followed if our suits hadn't held on."

"I'm not getting any comms or tell-tales," I said. "It'll take us days to go back."

"Nah, leave 'em," came the reply. "They're toast. You stay there and keep your eyes peeled. We're going in to get the bastard, so hold on tight."

Shiiit! So there was now a definitely identified "bastard" who was knocking off the bad guys. I probably needed to try and let him/her/it know that I was one of the good guys before I was next on the list. But how?

The remaining suits were now spreading out into the main storage area, but apart from auto repair bots beavering away at the hole in our hull there was no other movement. I could see the standard statuses from all across the ship, temperatures, air pressures, greens, ambers, reds, etc, but then I saw something that was not so much odd as strange.

A small section in one part of the storage area was showing exactly the same set of status values. They were static, unchanging and approx. 3 meters square, which never, ever happened, especially with a whole lot of suits tromping around. And then this block of status wrongness started moving. I got the ship to check it, but there were no errors indicated, just this block of static values tracking away from the bad guys. It kept on moving, heading towards the main door, where it dissolved into the usual random variations.

Some sort of anomaly? Telemetry playing up maybe? At least some of the sensors would have thrown a wobbler after that explosion, but a block of static readings migrating about the place? I'd never seen anything like that before, ever.

The click of a hatch behind me and I turned, a bright flash of light before someone turned them out.

11
Alarums and excursions

My head slowly spun up from the dim and dingy depths and what passed for consciousness did its best to stop breakfast re-appearing. The nail which someone had knocked through my eye also didn't help, although the sea of nausea when I gingerly opened the other was even worse.

I was staring out of a suit visor.

I was in a suit.

Shit - I've been tossed into space, but that thought was no sooner there than gone. In front of me was internal hull plating. I was still inside the ship, and my HUD intruded to tell me I was in one of the refurbed suits I'd hidden in the storage area. Life support was on, but everything else was off. How, why and who all popped up, but a moment's consideration said that I was still in the ship, so don't worry, or at least not yet. I'd already thought of this sort of thing and had a cunning plan. There's more than one way to activate a suit and during the refurbs I'd made sure they'd respond direct to me.

My HUD made the connection and passed the activation key. Everything started coming up, and as soon as I had control, I turned to face the room.

I was looking down the barrel of a hand-held energy weapon. At the far end was an odd-looking hand, with an arm attached that led to the shoulder of an alien species I'd never ever seen before, which was both interesting and worrying at the same time.

The weapon tapped my visor and I raised my hands. A mouth opened and some very odd noises emerged. After a momentary pause, my translator managed to translate: "Don't move," followed by "I shoot hole." <55% xlate confidence – Terran base>.

Not as useful as it might have been, but "Don't move" was fairly self-explanatory, as was "shoot hole."

I had a better look and this guy/gal was definitely a new one on me. Around my height, three eyes, three legs and three arms/tentacles, one of which held the weapon pressed against my visor. One beady eye kept looking at me while the other two scanned back and forth, constantly flicking to a screen embedded in one of its arms.

"I think we're on the same side," I said.

No response.

I tried again. "I was kidnapped to fix their ship but I'm not one of them."

Still nothing, although with those revolving eyes, who could tell?

We were in one of the rooms right at the back of the storage area, and obviously where this guy thought was a good place to stash someone. A massive mental leap wasn't required to see that this was the mysterious "bastard" who'd been removing the bad guys and I could only give thanks that it hadn't chucked me out after Green, Yellow and Orange, and let's not forget that guy Faizal. Still, this guy obviously hadn't even started, and as if to echo that thought I got an IFF alert saying the bad guys were starting to quarter back towards us.

The Alien's mouth gave a squirt of sounds which translated as "Stay quiet, here," <75% xlate confidence – Terran base> before it disappeared into the room's ventilation duct.

And that was a bit of an "Oh Shit!" moment. Those psychos wouldn't need any excuse to follow up on their long walk out of short airlock promise, and they'd be even happier now that they had the chance of a two for one with me and this Alien. The Boss-man's IFF tag was getting closer and closer and I'll tell you what, I was starting to panic.

But hold on a minute. Get a grip, you idiot. They were over there and I was here. I was wearing a nice new suit. The Alien was four up and wanted more. I'm sure I'd read somewhere that the enemy of my enemy was my friend, so maybe things weren't actually that bad. Maybe I could even help my new buddy somehow and then it would definitely not chuck me out. Maybe. Possibly.

My addled brain slowly emerged from its growing funk and a quick call to the IFF came right back with a solution. The main AI could re-configure the storage area so that the bad guys were funnelled into one place. The Alien would then have a ready-made shooting gallery and I'd be well away from the mayhem. Definitely a plan.

Of course, getting it to work was going to be a bit more of a challenge, but I knew the ship and the bad guys didn't. A stealthy call to the main AI explained what I wanted and it leapt into action, setting things up for the required move and flicking up a helpful diagram to show me exactly what was going to happen.

And then of course, you know how it is. Do something quickly and there's always something you forget. The main AI's rejig started, being faithfully replayed on its cunning little diagram, and guess what. The bad guys were being channelled straight at me. I hadn't told the main AI to direct them elsewhere, it was being as helpful as it could, and by the time I saw what was happening it was too late.

The final clunk of the new config merely confirmed this, but I was bumped off the wall by an answering thump. The first of the bad guys had got to the other end of my set of rooms and marked the occasion by throwing in a grenade. There was a second thump as the rest of them joined in, so I suppose my plan to get them all together had worked. But where was the Alien?

Another thump marked their continued progress and what the hell was I going to do? Get out of the room and I'd be shot to pieces. Stay in the room and I'd be blown to pieces. Not great options either way and my mind was spinning as another thump counted down to my doom. Those psycho bastards were now just two rooms away, and it was only then that I remembered all of those tasty little additions I'd made to the suit refurbs. A frantic shout to the suit and everything started mounting up, but it was too late. Or it would have been if something hadn't exploded right outside my door.

I was thrown back and a spray of projectiles followed, punching holes through the wall in front of me. One of the bad guy's suits came banging in through the door and thumped against my leg, a large smoking hole where its chest used to be. I was still frantically trying to make sense of the confused tactical display, but torrents of fire were hosing everywhere as the bad guys opened up.

Readiness greens popped up on my after-sales add-ons, but it wasn't immediately clear what I could do. The Alien kept flicking in and out on my IFF, loosing shots, disappearing, re-appearing, more shots, and all the time being pursued by the bad guys' fireworks. The comms were flooded by shouts and screams, but it was all just swearing, panic, more swearing, and they never stopped shooting.

I poked a finger around the door frame to see if the mini-camera could give me a clue and got an immediate targeting solution. I fired, adding my own streams of destruction to the crazed cascades outside. The bad guy I'd shot at fired straight back, shredding even more of the walls and floor.

The Alien materialised out of the ventilation duct and dropped to the floor. In contrast to its former pristine self it now had holes oozing blue/green gunk, with more streams of projectiles greeting its appearance. My suit was thumped back as a chunk of its frontal armour disappeared and these guys were going to keep on going until the only life signs were theirs. It was like being in a fully immersive shoot-em up game, except that the other players really were trying to kill me and there was no pause or reset button.

I grabbed the closest Alien appendage and heaved its body behind me. One eye flickered open and an arm/tentacle lifted a small control unit. I reached across and it tried to say something, but that wasn't going to work in the vacuum left by the bad guys' shooting holes in the ship. It fiddled with its arm control and this time my translator picked up a person-to-person comm: "When close, shut door press main button," <90% xlate confidence – Terran base>.

I looked at what it was holding, a small screened unit with buttons, but which one to press? The bad guys were almost on top of us so I kicked the remains of the door closed and pressed them all.

There was an almighty explosion. Everything snowed out. Flickering back came alarms saying something really bad had happened, while all around me chunks of the storage area spun off into space. And then, if you can believe it, a priority jump alarm blared out.

I'd completely forgotten that we hadn't stopped accelerating towards our planned jump. No one had told the Navcom to stop. Standard maxima and minima hadn't been exceeded. It was doing exactly what it had been told to do and now was the time. And that was what it did.

Wham! Out of normal spacetime we jumped.

12
Jump back

Alarms shouting, red lights flashing, but actually all indications showed that we'd made a pretty good jump and were in the pipe five by five. My IFF was showing just two organic life signs, so we'd obviously left the rest of the bad guys decorating normal spacetime when we jumped, and thank bloody goodness for that.

Something bumped against my suit and as if to mirror the alarms, there was my poor Alien buddy, even more knocked about and still breathing vacuum. I grabbed him up and pushed into the cloud of swirling debris which was all that remained of this part of the ship. The main door to the rest of the ship showed a big red light, but just over the way was an internal lock and that, thankfully, still showed a green.

I headed straight for it, trying my hardest not to look at the flickering expanse of betweenspace showing through the gaps in the hull. Urban legend said that anyone looking directly into betweenspace lost their mind as well as control of their bowels, and now wasn't the time or the place to find that out. The internal lock saw us coming and the door swung open, snapping shut behind as air came flooding in to banish the vacuum.

However, the outer door was one thing but the inner door was entirely another. The main AI wasn't sure whether it wanted us in the ship after what had just happened and, I suppose, you could hardly blame it. So, while it thought about that, I called up the Medlab. One rather frank exchange of views later and finally, both it and the main AI were happy to crack open the inner door. I duly deposited the Alien onto the waiting Medbot and then made my way towards the main control cabin to see what sort of state we'd been left in.

That homely red glow was not exactly unexpected, and you'll no doubt remember what I said about no one but a complete moron firing a weapon inside a ship? Well, large bites out of the hull plus extensive peppering of holes said all you needed to know about that. My first plaintive question asked where the hell to even start, but the auto-repair AI was already spraying bots all over the place and I just grabbed hold of anything it hadn't already sprayed.

At least none of ship-critical systems were showing any problems. These were still sitting pretty behind their built-in armour and the ship was still nicely lodged in betweenspace. And then a couple of rather worrying reds popped up. It was all a bit like being back on ship when I'd first got here.

The next half day was a continuing litany of damage, damage, and more damage, but as the main priority 1s started to disappear, I noticed that the background noise was changing. The auto-repair and I were making good progress repairing the ship, but it would seem that this was not being matched by the Medlab's attempts to repair the Alien.

I suppose its slathering at the mouth type response to our new and oh so very different patient should have tipped me off, but you know how it is. I'd walked into the main control cabin. The ship was coming apart. Or it had stopped working. Or both. In the scheme of things, one sick Alien wasn't really at the top of my priority list.

It was only when the screaming reds started to abate that the Medlab's reports had a chance to bubble up high enough to get my attention, and there we were. This Alien really was alien. In fact, our entire civilisation had never seen one before. The Medlab could pretty much fix anything it knew about, but it knew absolutely nothing about this guy/gal. So, where to even start when 'normal' was completely uninformed guesswork?

I was pulled away to deal with more continuing nasties, and once I'd done that I was dragged along to see what state the storage area was in. So, back into my suit and wow! Wide open to deep space was where everything started and my alien mate's hiding place was spectacular more by its absence than its presence. Auto-repair bots were scurrying around all over the place, but what really smacked me between the eyes was the green bloodstains.

Now, you must've been in a situation where everything kicks off and you've just got to get on and deal with it. It's only some time afterwards when the shakes start, and seeing that green blood all over the place was my moment. I'd pretty much accepted that the bad guys had got their just deserts, especially as they'd been threatening me with a long walk out of a short airlock ever since I got here. It was those smears, the sprays all up the walls, and I was jerked right back to the gunfire, the explosions and the complete panic.

It looked like a child had been painting, there was so much green everywhere. I was stunned, horrified, and my skin crawled. I mean, if it hadn't been for my alien mate then those bloodstains would be red, not green. And what had I done to help? Sit in my suit and panic was about the size of it.

Another of the Medlab's reports popped up but I didn't bother checking it. I knew what was there and actually now I came to think about it, I'd been ignoring them as I didn't really want to know what they said. The Medlab's guesses weren't working. It had run out of things to do and I probably needed to get up there and see what was happening before it was all just a bit too late.

So, I left the damage, the green smears, the shouting alarms. I took off my suit and made my way to the Medlab. Every step told me how much I owed the guy and how little I'd done to help, and somehow that just made it all worse.

I walked in and there the Alien was. Still as stone, limbs spread out, dressings everywhere, tubes and wires, scurrying microbots, and every monitor's red lines diving downwards. My civilisation's state of the medical art and it couldn't do anything to help. Sure, it was trying as hard as it could, but the guy was dying quicker than it could find things that worked. What a mess.

I stood there looking at the still and silent saviour who'd stepped in to save me and I felt quite sick. What if it had been me lying there in some Alien Medlab came my whispered thought, but the immediately answering mental sigh gave the answer straight back. I wouldn't have been there. I'd have been running for the hills, and yet this guy had jumped straight in, no hesitation, and I'd done pretty much nothing.

The monitors chirped and clicked as a background to these shameful thoughts and the more I thought about it, the worse I felt. OK, so I'm not some hairy chested man of action, but surely I could have done something, anything, but what? People trying to kill me? Someone stepping in, killing them and in the process saving me? A day ago, I'd been floating through space minding my own business and now we had seven dead crewmates, a wrecked ship and this very sick totally alien Alien. It was almost impossible to believe really.

New alarms were screaming on my HUD and I really needed to get back. A hand rested on the Medunit with a whispered "Thank you" was the best farewell I could think of, but that was pretty feeble I know. Maybe the Medlab could still pull something out of its medicinal hat, but what? I had no idea. Just like the Medlab.

Unspoken reproach pursued me back to the main control cabin and I just couldn't seem to think straight. Those ship repairs had been a convenient distraction from the fighting, the nearly being killed and the witless fright, but I couldn't escape what I'd just seen up in the Medlab.

I sighed and tried to find something, anything, to take my mind off it, but it wouldn't go away. And actually, it was all rather strange. I'd always been on my own, looking after myself, and I'd certainly never had anyone do anything for me like this Alien. It was all very strange and I wasn't sure that I liked how I was feeling.

And then, a ping from the Medlab. Nothing more to say. It couldn't detect any life signs. The Alien was dead.

"However," continued the Medlab in its usual cheery fashion, "I now have better physiological specs which will be useful if we come across any more of its species."

I wasn't really listening, my feelings of guilt overlaying everything. Despite myself, I couldn't stop my eyes being drawn to the flickering of the ever-changing consoles, but hold on a minute. What was that?

My eyes jerked back to one of the consoles and there it was. A single readout that smacked me right between the eyes. The main AI was reporting that there was just a single living organic on the whole ship.

Me.

Just me.

No one else.

No one else with any claim to the ship.

Except me...

...and that must mean that I owned the ship, or at least it was mine because no one else did.

Just in case I'd missed anything critical I started right at the beginning and thought it through to the very end.

Nope, I hadn't missed anything.

I really did own this ring-ship!

Myriad possibilities burst across my imagination, dispelling the dark thoughts and blossoming into showers of galactic exploration and untold excitements, but other more sensible thoughts quietly raised their hands for attention. Those let's go out and tear the galaxy apart thoughts slowed, stopped spinning around and grudgingly sat down as my previous ponderings came back to whisper in my ear.

So, it really did look I owned this ship, and as its last official and unofficial owners were floating in space there was no one to argue about that. And actually, it all felt rather odd. If I'd been on any of those ships the pirates had boarded, they'd have found me. I wasn't, so they'd come and found me on CS1. And then, a totally alien Alien had appeared from nowhere to get rid of the bad guys and keep me from breathing space. Fate and karma had been smiling, the both of them, and that was more than a bit worrying.

Anyway, here I was on this lovely ship, but I was on my own. I'd always wanted to have a ship, but now that I'd actually got one, how good was that actually, really?

Let's face it, I was twenty-eight reltime years old and had been travelling through ntime for over five centuries. Most of that time I'd been stuck in the bowels of ships and when you thought about it, the travel bit of reltime travel might have been OK, but the rest? I mean, money? Hah! Home? Hah! Friends? Hah, yet again! I'd made more friends on CS1 than I'd ever made anywhere, and I really missed them.

I now had a ship, but the more I thought about it, the more I realised that aimlessly wandering through ntime/reltime really wasn't that great, especially when you were on your own. I'd had the best time ever with those Flivvers on CS1 and now, I could go back and see them. Sure, we were still flying through betweenspace and we'd have to complete the jump before we jumped back, but that wasn't a problem. I could do just what I wanted.

The more I thought about it, the more it just got better and better. OK, so my life was still lit by red indicators saying "We're all gonna die" but I could fix that. It's what I did.

We made the jump back into normal spacetime without any problems and I was straight onto putting back all of the external bits that the bad guys had removed. OK, so some of the patching wasn't exactly official spec, but as it kept space out and the air in, what more could you possibly want?

A couple of weeks later and the Navcom almost yawned when I asked for its quickest flight plan back to CS1, and I had to laugh. For the past five years, all I'd ever wanted was to get away from CS1 and yet here I was, heading straight back as quickly as possible.

A final check with the main AI and it was greens across the board. Deep-sleep beckoned, but I couldn't quite resist just one more look around. After all, this was my ship, flying in a system that our collective civilisations had never visited, and it was my ship. I just couldn't stop telling myself that.

My tour eventually led to the waiting sleep unit, where I was duly prepped and engulfed. My last thought as I drifted off was that I was finally living the dream, even if CS1 wouldn't have stopped being the nightmare it had always been. I'd just have to get there and see whether it was as bad as I remembered it to be.

13
CS1 redux

The ship jumped back into normal spacetime well inside the CS1 system's heliopause and Mr. Navcom got straight on with doing the necessaries. The main AI kept me asleep throughout the main deceleration phase and actually, there was nothing a mere organic could have done anyway. System manoeuvring was far too complex for anything but the Navcom so I slept the Gs away until it was time to be dragged out of the interstellar deep and dreamless and dropped into the waking-up pit of hell.

Deep-sleep is basically one step away from being dead. Your brain and body have been shut down to almost nothing and as for those maintenance nanos inserted where the sun don't shine? Best not think about them, especially as being brought back up that great white corridor is more unpleasant than you can ever imagine.

The Dujes were the first to come up with deep-sleep, and we just copied what they did. Wherever it came from, my welcome back to CS1 was the usual slow warm up and then blam – wake up ya bastard! Definitely something that you never, ever, wanted to do again and yet here I was, doing it again, just one more time.

By the time my stomach had stopped deciding it would rather be outside than in, we'd slipped into a nice parking orbit. CS1 was still glaring out at the Universe as balefully as it had been when I'd left and the Navcom popped up confirmation that while I'd aged only three reltime months, CS1 hadn't seen me for the best part of nine years. Hopefully the Flivvers would have looked after my hab, but then it struck me. Maybe they weren't even there. Shit, I hadn't thought about that.

Other more worrying thoughts flitted across my death-warmed-up state of consciousness and the Navcom's reminder of our upcoming drop window was a welcome distraction. I told the main AI to get a pod ready and started kicking my dormant thought processes into getting the ship nice and secure from unwanted intrusion. Having got hold of it quite by accident, I didn't want anyone returning the favour while I was away.

A readiness ping from the pod AI and thankfully the Medlab's wake-up shots were finally doing what they were supposed to do. I made my way along to the freshly repaired pod bay and there was my best armoured suit being swung out to meet me. A thumbs-up from its AI and I floated across, the suit wrapping itself around my still rather fragile self. Up came the fully-integrated view, full sync was established, and I made myself comfortable in the nicely integrated 360 info-bubble as our drop window approached.

The pod pushed out into a good descent and down we dropped towards the same landing area I'd left three months ago for me, and nine years ago for everyone else. Our retros blasted away the dunescape now obscuring the landing grid and I must admit that absence did not make the heart grow fonder. CS1 was still the same shithole I'd left, even if who cared about searing temperatures and blasting hot winds when you're comfortably sat inside a suit?

The one I was in had a full military spec, heavily armoured, equally biped/quadruped and totally state-of-the-kick-ass art. The cleaning bots had even fully cleaned it, which was a nice change from the lived-in feel these things usually had. I'd loaded a shoot-first-ask-questions-afterwards tactical AI persona and we had full loads of the most lethal weaponry ever devised. It and I were seamlessly integrated and it was more like having a whole new body than a mechanical exoskeleton. So, just the thing for landing on CS1 after nine years away, and anything that might be waiting had just better watch out.

The pod finished its landing checks while I had a good look around and it was actually worse than I remembered. Piles of rubbish, wrecked buildings and everything disappearing under boiling hot windblown sand. Every single entrance tunnel was sealed up tight, but readiness greens across the board said it was time to go. One more look around and out I baled.

The suit sunk knee deep into the windblown sand and dropped forward, its hands sinking elbow deep. A bit of struggle to get out and we stayed on all fours as we moved towards the nearest entrance tunnel through a fifty kph sand storm.

The door panel was scoured opaque, so I tried the backup operating handle. Another good heave but it was jammed solid. In fact, the door looked like it had taken some pretty serious damage before being hammered shut. Still, a suit trumps such problems and by applying more brute force, it shuddered open.

The entry bay had sand sloping up to the top of the inner door, packed down hard and clearly not going anywhere. Still, no problem as there were plenty of others to try. Back outside and the suit scrambled its way across more drifts of sand to the next door. The IFF told me that it couldn't see any drones or mechanicals and there was a complete absence of radio chatter. It was firing up its targeting array just in case. The long-range sensors deployed and after a detailed scan, the tactical displays showed, well, pretty much nothing.

All around me was the same unending sand I remembered, but there was also a lot more rubbish. Wrecked mechanicals, sand-blasted broken concrete and everything engulfed by long slicks of sand running away downwind. The place was a total junkyard.

At the next entry door the suit had to dig its way in. Same opaque touch panel but at least the door was properly sealed. The suit applied the requisite brute force and the door juddered open to reveal a clear entry bay. In we went and the suit carefully re-sealed the door behind us. If I hadn't known any better I'd have said that it seemed a little worried.

Once the outer door was shut it was pretty dark, but the inner door opened into a blackness that was almost tangible. The suit's image intensification flicked on and all around me was green darkness, green stillness and green silence. I knew exactly where I was, but where had this darkness come from? Even long-range scans from the IFF showed nothing. We needed to get along to the market and see just what had been happening whilst I'd been away.

The suit strode off down the tunnel, launching drones into the darkness. They sped off as we crunched our way through a scattering of rubbish, their feeds showing more rubbish, the occasional dim ceiling light, but nothing else. Something really bad had happened here, but it had happened long ago. And then we walked into the market.

I stopped, almost not believing what I was seeing. The suit's lights played across piles of rubbish sitting there in the silent darkness. No stalls, no people, just the remains of lives scattered about where there should have been that busy market I remembered so well. The suit reported that the air was breathable if very stale, so the forced ventilation system was obviously not working. A brief mental smile at that.

On my request it gave me a small squirt of the outside air to try. Dry decay and more like the inside of a tomb than a living place. This whole place had been trashed, but where was everybody, those hundreds, those thousands of Flivvers, Minos, Smuts and everyone else?

We started weaving our way through the stacks of rubbish, heading for the tunnel leading to my hab. As we got closer, the suit started excitedly reporting marks of scattered gunfire, but they were old, old news. The tunnel was just as I remembered it, and then finally some evidence of life. A scattering of lights ran up the tunnel although they weren't in the ceiling. Knackered old fittings lay scattered across the ground, joined by odd lengths of wire and lines of scuffed footmarks.

Pinpoint reflections scattered away down the walls and the suit IFF flashed up a warning of multiple organics. It then called back the drones, as we didn't want to worry anyone now did we?

Up ahead was a silhouetted corner and I had a quick peak around it. Yep, just as I'd hoped, the Flivver hive with a wide-open pool of light at its entrance. A happy throng of children played in the tunnel, with small groups of adults chatting away as they kept an eye on things. I was so pleased to see somebody, anybody, that without a second thought I walked straight up with a happy cry of "Hi, I'm back!"

Not my greatest move. How would you feel if a 3m high, heavily armoured mechanical biped you'd never seen before suddenly appeared out of the gloom? Screeching alarm calls, petrified youngsters making a dash for the hive entrance and a rank of protectors forming a protective line was their version.

I just stood there like an idiot as everything kicked off. And then a spray of gunfire flew past, missing me but carving up the tunnel walls and adding to the general mayhem. I backed away as quickly as I could, telling the suit to put away its weapons. We dissolved back into the tunnel's dimness as the last of the Flivvers ran into their hive and somebody turned out the lights.

Well, that wasn't the best thing I'd ever done. In fact, I was a complete idiot and it was lucky no one had got hurt. The suit helpfully told me that the tunnel was now clear, but I was still cursing myself. CS1 was not the CS1 I'd left and I needed to start taking a lot more care.

I waited while the suit did a more detailed scan but the green image-intensified tunnel was still empty. So, a quick hop, skip and a jump and I was past the hive and walking up towards my hab. I'd come back and talk to the Flivvers once I'd seen what they'd done to my home.

That lovely hab appeared out of the murk and the suit stopped sulking, eagerly announcing a new potential target of interest. Indeed, there was a light in one of the windows so someone was definitely home. Trouble was, after my complete cockup at the hive, how was I going to play this?

The IFF's initial tactical assessment showed that the whole place had been heavily fortified. I was just thinking about how I could get closer without spooking the occupants, when the light in the window went out.

OK, so they knew I was here. The suit gleefully reported that it could see a couple of anti-personnel mines that might be a problem, but in such a way that it was really saying: "...and now, PLEASE, can I do something about it?"

We were well out of the mines' range so I told it to pipe down. If there's a problem with suits, and especially one with the sort of shoot first and don't worry afterwards-type of persona I had in this one, any operation was generally a success but the patient invariably died. A collection of debris where my hab had been wasn't how I wanted to say hello, so softly, softly was the best policy while I at least tried to keep everything in one piece.

"Hey you in the hab," I called out. "This is Franky. I'd like to talk."

A window cracked open and the barrel of a long gun pointed out. An IFF targeting alarm went off as the gun fired and a large projectile hit the suit's chest. The suit brought up both hand-held blasters but I told it to put them away and get out of sight down the tunnel. They obviously weren't keen on talking, but from what I'd seen so far, maybe that wasn't entirely unreasonable?

The suit muttered away to itself as it changed the bullet-spalled panel, but I told it to pipe down and stop whinging.

"Hey," I called out again, "I really do just want to talk. Look, I'll get out of my suit if it makes you any happier." The only reply was silence.

The suit had now added one or more organics to its threat assessment and quickly followed up with a matching set of tactical options. The least lethal was a gas grenade with multi-species barf/crap/general insensibility capabilities, but I wouldn't make friends and influence people using that. I tried calling out again, this time in multiple languages. More silence. I tried calling out some more, but while they may have been listening, they certainly weren't answering. I then tried inching up the tunnel to see if I could see anything, but a loud bang and another spalled suit panel told me that probably wasn't going to work either.

I just wanted to see inside the hab, but whoever was in there obviously didn't want me anywhere near it. Maybe a gas grenade was a good option, but wouldn't that just piss them off some more? No idea really, but if I could get myself in, maybe they'd at least have to talk? The suit was pretty relaxed either way but I couldn't stay there forever. Without thinking, I stuck my head out to have another look and just missed catching another projectile.

Pretty annoying really, but having come all of this way I didn't want to leave without seeing my hab. Also, I wasn't too sure what the Flivvers would do if I went past their hive a second time. So, maybe a gas grenade was the least bad of the available options and there was only one way I was going to find out. I'd just have to deal with any of the fallout when it worked. When it worked? Hah! More like if it worked, but before I could talk myself out of it, I told the suit to do the necessary

The grenade flew straight in through the hab's open window. A thud, then gentle tendrils of gas started leaking out of the window. Nothing more, except that someone closed the window. That knockout gas was supposed to work pretty quickly but the only effect I could see was that I'd probably pissed them off even more. The suit eagerly suggested a selection of more lethal options, but you know what? Maybe I just needed to put myself out there and see what happened.

"Heh, whoever's in the hab," I called out again. "I know it's been nine years but this really is Franky. Look, if you let me near to the hab I'll open up my suit and you can take a look."

Silence in the dimness.

Silence and then more silence in the dimness.

I gave it another minute and repeated what I'd said.

Finally, a voice echoed back, short, sharp and to the point.

"You do it!" and a duplicate appeared in my HUD, the significance of which I totally missed.

OK, so let's see what happens. I walked up the tunnel and positioned myself right under the single working light. Then, despite the suit's frantic imploring, I told it to pop the helmet. A pause, the suit's equivalent of a sigh, and the helmet slid open. I took a lungful of the dead air and sat there waiting, an imaginary target painted on my face and a knot growing in my stomach.

More silence...

...and then, a rattling from the hab door. The front end of that long gun poked out and pointed straight at me as the door swung open. The suit's and my IFFs were going wild and the growing knot in my stomach was joined by every sphincter in my body slowly tightening.

Behind the long gun was a large and robustly built adult Flivver, full coverage sand suit, boots and helmet, blue wings arching up nearly as high as my head. Quite a sight. It slowly came down the steps before even more cautiously walking towards me, the rifle never leaving my face.

14
Nine years on

Neither of us said a word and I didn't move a muscle, especially with that weapon aimed at my head. The Flivver came to a halt and each of those cramped sphincters managed to tighten up just a little bit more. An arm went up. Ohhh shiiitt...but it was just to slide the helmet back.

"You come back," said a voice with that oh so familiar Terran/Flivver twang.

A pause.

"Soffee?" I said, but the Soffee I knew was young Miss Strop-a-lot from three months ago. Ntime/reltime eh? But actually, this was the first time I'd ever come back to someone who was time-slipped from the last time I'd seen them. Very odd indeed.

She was still staring at me. "Where hell you been? You go forever and now you come back. Is so much time," and she paused. "You not even say goodbye."

"But you're still here. That's great. What the hell's happening? The whole place is wrecked," I gabbled out.

She said nothing, then: "Yes, is changed. I think we go in hab. Is dangerous out here."

My suit opened up like a flower and her whole body posture softened. Everything I'd seen so far had been pretty bad, and she obviously hadn't been sure I wasn't something worse.

I told the suit to keep watch and followed her into the hab. Extensive defences had been added and I could see a couple of projectile-strikes across the front. She obviously hadn't been joking about the danger. We walked through the heavily armoured main door which closed behind us with a hefty thunk.

It was just as I remembered it, even if the only thing saying Franky was a snap pinned up on the wall. It was of me, sitting at one of those food stalls in the market and laughing at the snapper. I half-lifted my arm to point.

"Good times, eh?" and was about to continue but Soffee's expression said probably better not.

She put down her helmet and rifle. "I flush out gas," her face expressionless. "So, you welcome home."

She sat on one of the command chairs and I rather gingerly sank into the depths of my very old and saggy couch.

"My Terran not good," she said. "I speak Flivver," and a burst of strangled chittering flew across at me. But you know what? I'd come all this way and wanted to hear her speak Terran.

"Your Terran's great," I said. "I've come ten lights just to see you and I want to hear your voice," and very deliberately turned off my translator.

She threw me another burst of Flivver, but I just wiggled a finger at my ear and shrugged. She tried again, but I just gave another finger wiggle.

"OK," she said after a pause, "I use Terran, but I not speak for many years so is bad. I sorry," but I did get the beginnings of a smile.

Looking around, the whole place was even more chocka than I remembered. Flivver stuff festooned the place, with the usual dusting of feathers. Three months for me, but she'd been living here for nine years. That was a very long time indeed.

"So where you go?" she said. "When men take you I go get girls, but we too late. I very sorry we not save you," and I was amazed to see tears in her eyes.

"Hey," I said, "don't worry. You wouldn't have been able to do anything with those suits anyway."

"But I head hive-protector," she said. "Protector not lose anyone from hive or she not good protector." She paused. "Today, hab AI tell me ship come. Is nine years. Where you been?"

"Yeah, sorry 'bout that," I said, "but that's reltime. I did send you a couple of messages, but no one answered. Did you get them?"

Her disbelieving expression was my only answer to that, even when the hab duly played back my messages from nine years ago. OK, so they were pretty blah, blah, blah, but let's face it, I'd never expected to come back here at all.

The final message finished and we sat there in silence looking at each other. I tried something else.

"So where is everybody? It used to be wall to wall in here."

"Scylla and Circe go to hive and Chary go to entrance tunnel," she said. "Your suit make big panic." I started to smile and she continued: "You lucky they not stop your suit." I stopped smiling.

"So they're still using my names then?" I said, but all I got was a slightly annoyed, slightly baffled look.

"But of course," this with the clearly unspoken "You stupid man" addition. "They hive names so of course they use."

The silence after she spoke dripped unspoken meaning. The pause lengthened and I felt a shiver run down my spine. The whole atmos was really odd, almost like I'd done something awful but only she knew what it was. I could feel my mouth opening to break the silence, but she beat me to it.

"OK," she said with a sigh, "I tell you what happen. You leave with Terrans in suits. I stay living with girls and Flivver protectors. There plenty food and water and I also know your safe places for things we need."

At my expression she threw up her hands. "You not want me have nice things?"

I had to smile, but the whole situation was becoming more and more surreal, sitting here in front of this previously awkward, stroppy young Terran/Flivver who was now anything but. Of course I knew about the whole "knew them as a child and now they're an adult" ntime/reltime thing, but this was so very different and I didn't know why.

I glanced around the hab, the worn metal, the collapsing furniture, the Flivver stuff everywhere, and for the first time it struck me how totally crap it was for those waiting in ntime for reltimers to return. I'd been away just a couple of months but she'd been here nearly half of her life.

"All go well for couple of annuals," she continued as these thoughts flickered across my mind. "Flivvers think it cool I look after your hive and when I give them credits," again that shrug, "they think we both totally cool. They think you sort of hive head, even if strange hive with you Terran and you leave without me and girls."

Ummm. That was a very odd thing to say.

"It all go wrong when Aquatics living under planet appear," she continued. "They say they need tech. Minos and Grunts say they not take shit from scum-sucking aquatic sub-species, but scum-sucking aquatic sub-species come along anyway."

"But those Aquatics are a myth," I said. "Surely they don't exist?"

"Oh they real," she said. "They left here by miners like rest of us and they come in mechanicals and take things they want. Minos and Grunts fight, but Aquatics take and leave big mess. We work to make Market OK again, but then ship appear in orbit and send down pods. They offer people flight off-planet if you pay price. We know it not you so hives stay, but this offer very bad. Everyone start stealing to buy seat. It all go mad and not safe anywhere."

"But hold on a minute," I butted in. "No one down here had much of anything. What were they stealing?"

"Well," she said, "you know. People say they poor but everyone have emergency fund. There lot of fights for emergency funds. Hives have things but we also have weapons. Other people not have many weapons so we keep safe and I not lose anyone."

She gently stroked the long gun by her side, which I now recognised as mine, last seen locked away from her and, indeed, anyone else.

"But how?" I said. "You didn't know anything when I left." To her sour expression, I added: "C'mon, you know you didn't, even if you look like you've got it all under control now."

"But is friend of yours from sand desert," she said. "Dane, he help. He say you and he swear oath to help families if you get killed. He think me and girls Franky family so he come and help. I also think this."

"But why would he think you were my family?" and, neatly inserting even more of my big foot into the even bigger mouth. "I never thought he was serious. It was just messing about over some beers."

A long, hard and very direct look from her, before she took another breath.

"So... stealing start and everything big mess. One day Dane appear and tell me oath you make. He teach me and girls how to shoot your guns and defend hives, which you not do, or show me." Another accusing look.

I just shrugged. I mean, any three-for-two deal's too good to miss even if I'd never let kids get their hands on guns. In fact, I'd never used them myself, even if I wasn't going to tell Soffee that.

"So where's he now?" I asked.

"He help then go before bad chaos," she said. "He really save us, as everyone stealing for seat price and it all total piece of shit cake."

I snorted with laughter, but tried to get my face straight as she stared back at me. "You always use words like total piece of shit cake," she said.

"You're right," I said, "I do, and they're exactly the right words."

She gave me what I think used to be called an old-fashioned look.

"Girls and I shoot first raiding party. Our two hives good friends and we too powerful for people to rob. Some try but we fight them off."

"But what's all this hives stuff?" I asked. "I know about Chitichca's hive, but weren't you all members of that? Where's the other one?"

Another pregnant pause, before another sigh.

"I head hive-protector and I protect our hive while I wait for you to come back."

She looked straight at me, her face expressionless yet again. It was like she was trying to explain something really simple, to someone really stupid, even if I didn't have a clue what she was on about.

"More and more people leave planet," she continued. "Whole place is now big rubbish dump like you see and soon is no more people can pay. Ship leave. We know Aquatics stay, as ship only for air-breathers. Other people go to tunnels. Dane live somewhere under sand sea but we not know where."

"So how long ago did the ship leave?" I asked.

"Six years."

"You mean you Flivvers have been on your own for six years?" I said, to her briefest of nods. "Wow. I don't know what to say, but I did come back. I'm just sorry it took so long. Anyway, what's happening now?"

"Humph!" she said. "What happening? I tell you what happening. Wind and PV farms break and we lose follow-sun grid. Aquatics take air fans so air not good. We have water but food very bad as bug farms not work. But hab is secure," she finished proudly. "Your hive wait for you and you come back, although I only one think you will."

I sat there, rather stunned. I'd come back expecting a quick "Hi, it's me," and everything would be back to normal. As for CS1 being totally wrecked and this totally transformed Soffee sitting in front of me balanced on her own pile of unstated assumptions? And this new hive? I'd just never thought through what might have happened while I'd been away.

Still, I now owned a ring-ship and was about to cast this gleaming pearl for inspection when my suit popped up an alert, matched by a red light on the hab console. Soffee leapt to the window but I wasn't too worried. The suit could deal with anything out there and actually, I'd better check before it did just that.

Out of the darkness materialised two rather elderly Flivvers and a sentinel, with the suit eagerly informing me it had weapons locked on and I only had to say the word. I told it to stand down and the Flivvers continued their walk unmolested. It must have been a very frustrating day for that poor suit AI.

Soffee and I walked out to face our visitors, the first of which performed an extravagant bow.

"Franky," he said, "you are very welcome back to CS1. Your time away has been long in the memory, but head hive-protector Soffee has looked after your hive through all of those years."

"It's good to be back," I replied, "but I can see there have been many changes while I've been away."

"You are right," he replied, "but our hive and yours are allied and we look forward to continuing prosperity, especially now that you have returned. As a welcome, we invite you and head hive-protector Soffee to a meeting of our hive council," and he bowed again, this time sweeping his arms and wings to point down the tunnel.

Now, no one outside of a hive, and especially not a Terran, ever gets invited to a hive council meeting. The sweeping arms and wings plus collective floating question mark said that this invitation was for right now and I caught Soffee's smirk as she watched the dim light of understanding dawn. She was obviously something senior in this Flivver world order and for some reason my confusion seemed to be excellent entertainment value.

"That is very kind of you," I said, trying to ignore her mocking look. "I have travelled far and missed civilised conversation while I've been away," but this was so weird. Here I was, in a dark tunnel, on a deserted planet, about to meet a full Flivver hive council and the only person I'd got on my side, or maybe not even that, was Miss Snigger-a-lot standing right next to me.

Miss Snigger-a-lot, who flicked back to head hive-protector Soffee of this new hive I'd been hearing so much about, turned to close the hab door. She was obviously ready for what came next, but me? I was floundering. She gave me a quick glance and started off after our three guides, leaving me to trot along behind.

"What are we doing?" I whispered.

"I am head protector in hive," she said, straight face, not a hint of a smile. "Head hive-protector is also honourable term for someone who is closest to hive head. We go to meeting with other hive," and she opened her stride to catch up with the three in front.

I followed along with much the same feelings I'd had when Soffee plus hive protectors had been parachuted into my hab. I'd been back on CS1 for just an hour, those Flivvers were back in control, and I was back in the dark. Bloody marvellous!

15
The last hive

Down the tunnel we walked, the Flivvers leading in line ahead. The hive's pool of light grew out of the murk and there was the main doorway flung wide open, a large Flivver standing on either side. That door was almost never opened, so maybe this wasn't a dream after all? Maybe this whole hive/hive head/head protector/hive council meeting thing was real? You had to laugh really. Scruffy, hairy-arsed Terran engineer to Flivver royalty in nine years and one step. How the hell had that happened?

Soffee was engulfed by a swarm of females who swept her away down a side corridor. She was at least a double head-height taller than everyone else and her wings were correspondingly large and even more magnificent than I'd first thought.

They disappeared around a corner and my guide directed me down a large corridor towards a rattle of Flivver chittering and chattering. The corridor was perforated by other corridors and everywhere was that well-remembered smell that made Flivvers exactly what they were, Flivvers.

The chittering died away as I came out into a large, brightly decorated spherical chamber, only the sound of my footsteps breaking the circle of silent attention. It was Flivvers, Flivvers everywhere, with a circle of elders seated in the centre. A Terran chair had been placed in a very obvious gap and several steps behind it were three large adult females, dressed similarly to Soffee and wearing the colours I recognised as the girls' favourites. OK genius, these are the girls, only nine years older. All three of them stood there looking terribly formal, their eyes staring straight ahead across the sea of Flivvers.

The collective stare of myriad eyes bore down on me and I still couldn't quite believe what was happening. Here I was, a Terran sitting with a Flivver council, as head of another hive. Flippin' crazy or what?

Soffee appeared in a space high in the ceiling and that sea of faces looked up. A momentary pause, before she fell forward, dropping down until at the last moment her wings opened, several mighty flaps killing her speed and the blasts of air knocking everyone back a step as she landed right in front of me.

She'd changed out of her full coverage sand suit into a slim fitting blue and yellow all-in-one. Two ornate scabbards poked up between her wings, each one topped by a matching handle. The two pins I'd given her all that time ago were pinned tightly together on one breast.

Her wings opened wide as she brought out my old-style Personal Defence Weapon – another three-for-two bargain there – and presented it to me with a bow. Just imagine a vast bird of prey suddenly taking a very close and personal interest in you and that's what it felt like. The solemn, if not too solemn, expression on her face told me that there was a lot in play here, especially as the Soffee I remembered would never have given me this much, or indeed any, respect.

"Do what I do," she murmured as she retrieved the PDW, slung it over one shoulder and stepped behind me. The Flivver council seemed entirely happy with this play-acting, but "Do what I do"? What the hell did that mean?

The council head stood up, smiled and d'you know what? It was my old friend Chitichca. Talk about circles being squared.

"Franky, friend of my hive, it is good to see you back after your long journey. All honour and good wishes to your hive and we extend the hand of friendship and alliance."

At that, Soffee gave a couple of strong wing beats, screeching out a deafening, "Ayee, Ayee, Ayee," right behind me. I jumped clean out of my skin but luckily fell straight back into it as the surrounding Flivvers repeated her cry, its echo disappearing down the corridors. This was something I vaguely remembered from a twenty-things-you-need-to-know-about-Flivvers visual, an all-hail-our-leader-type call from the hive's head protector. Just another piece of weird wackiness after my day so far.

"As you can see," Chitichca continued, "we have used your gifts wisely. We are secure, have all of the water we need and this is all due to our hives' alliance, your kind gifts and head hive-protector Soffee's skills." She bowed her head. And waited.

Shit, it was my turn.

"You are very welcome," I said, frantically trying to think of something even vaguely sensible to say. I mean, it was more of this Flivver social stuff and yet again I was the only person who didn't have a clue what was going on. "We have been friends for many years and it is always a pleasure to help my friends. However, you must tell me what has happened. I see that there have been many changes while I have been away."

The mood changed. There was an echoing silence into which Chitichca dropped: "We are the last two hives left on this planet. Most other entities except those in the planet's depths have left."

She then continued with much the same story as Soffee had told me, but it petered out into another gaping silence, almost as if she wanted me to provide a final full stop. I glanced at Soffee who was standing there looking as big and powerful as possible, but she just flicked her eyes back and forth between me and Chitichca. So, thanks for that then.

"OK," I tried, "it looks like much has changed while I've been away," but my head was spinning. I'd dropped from my new reality where I'd got a ring-ship, to this even newer reality where CS1 had been trashed and everyone was now expecting me to say or do something, but I didn't know what.

I needed to get out of here before I dropped myself into it, but flicking a glance at Soffee didn't help. An outline of a smirk and lights dancing in her eyes said that she thought this was all great fun, but what was she expecting me to do?

"I am honoured to be invited to your meeting and you are always welcome in my ha... hive," I continued. "I now need to discuss all of this with Sof... head hive-protector Soffee and rest after my long journey. I thank you for your welcome and let us plan to meet again soon."

As I stood up, Soffee moved around to stand in some sort of formal protective pose. My attempt at a comradely bow to the Flivvers was a comedic two step around those wings, before I turned and walked towards the main corridor, pursued by a rising sound of excited chittering.

All of the way out Soffee walked in front of me projecting her best protector pose, wings partially open and nearly brushing the ceiling. However, as we walked into the tunnel, her wings folded away and her shoulders started to shake with silent sniggers, turning to quiet laughter as we walked along.

I wasn't sure what she was laughing about, but she didn't say a word. We got back to the hab, the IFF popped open the main door and in we walked. By now Soffee had stopped laughing and was looking at me with a happy smile.

"So, what was all that about, and why were you laughing at me?" I said.

"I not laugh at you," she said. "I laugh at how hive look at Terran who hive head. They half-shocked, half-not-sure and is very funny."

"Well that's great, but next time please give me some sort of heads up before you hang me out to dry."

"No one hang you out to dry. Why you say that?" she replied, her smile fading. "I just very happy you come back and it funny that hive want to treat you like hive head but can't bear it."

OK, so more Flivver social stuff then but Soffee obviously knew what was going on so she could deal with it. I glanced around the hab and there was the Terran plant I'd given her, sitting on a little shelf all by itself. It looked old and tired but still had a few leaves and the remains of a flower. Not bad for a simple gene tweak and my eyes moistened, thinking of the good times now long past.

Soffee dropped her head to one side. "Franky," she said, "you really not understand what happening?"

I must have been wearing my best blank expression so she paused. "OK, so I try make easy for you," and she sat down in her chair while I sunk back into that couch. "I child in your hab. You live there and Flivvers look after me."

"Yeah, great," I interrupted, "but I didn't have a choice. You lot just moved in."

Soffee lifted her eyes ceiling-ward. "You not wonder why step-mother, person you call Chitichca, get Flivver protectors to live here? They want me out of hive but they worry. Other Terrans they know not nice people, so protectors live in hab and make sure I safe."

She smiled. "But they see you good person and they trust you. They even think you make good head of new hive."

"OK…" I said, "but this was just payback for all of the help they'd given me, surely? I mean, a Terran in a Flivver hive? It just doesn't happen, ever."

"But you know how Flivver hive works," she said. "OK, you don't know so I make simple. You Terran and I half Terran. I need place to live and Flivvers think you need hive, so is good idea. Also, you very lucky. I have sister, and she crazy. They keep her in main hive as she not safe out on own. But she leave on ship which sell seats, so you safe."

I sat there with my mouth open, again. More WTF-type info indeed and it made me wonder what other little gems Chitichca might have secreted in her Soffee-plan that she hadn't told me yet.

"So when were you going to tell me that I'd grown a hive, or even ask if I wanted one?" I said. "I mean, don't get me wrong, I like Flivvers, but a hive? Really?"

"Mmmm," she said, considering, "I see how is maybe not fair, but I need safe place to live. Also, I tell you now, and with me as head hive-protector I protect both hives and we all safe."

"Yeah, maybe," I retorted to her happy grin, "but what did Chitichca mean when she thanked us for the gifts?"

Soffee's eyes flicked across to where my strong box used to be and before she could say it's all gone matey boy, I stepped over to the secret panel. Several years' worth of the hard-earned should have been smiling back at me but indeed, matey boy, it was all gone.

"You didn't give 'em the whole lot?" I asked, but what a stupid question that was.

"You leave me with only girls as friends," she said. "I not know if you come back and they only ones who help. Longer time you away, more time they think you not come back." She paused, before her hand came over to rest gently on mine, claws brushing my wrist, feathers tickling my skin,.

"How you get back?" she said. "Where your ship?"

That hand was a bit of a surprise, especially when she slowly tightened her grip.

"Look, you mustn't tell anyone," I said, "but I've got a ring-ship in orbit. You remember those guys who took me? Well, it's theirs, or rather it's now mine."

"We saved," she said, her whole face relaxing, eyes glued to mine. "I wait and I wait and people make fun when you not come back, but I know you come back." Her voice broke, tears welling up and trickling down her cheeks. "And you have ship. I can't believe. Is miracle."

And it struck me yet again what a tough cookie this striking lady was. She'd been stuck here through seven shades of hell, she'd managed to keep the two hives safe, and all the while she hadn't stopped thinking I'd come back.

"I so glad you come back. I think you leave for ever," and she burst into tears.

Ohhh shit, was my only thought as I did the first sensible thing I'd done since coming down here, absolutely nothing.

She leaned forward and buried her face in my neck, a warm, damp patch spreading across my shoulder. My reflex action of giving her a comforting hug stopped at those huge wings. I mean, what were the touch/don't touch, go/no goes here anyway? I had no idea. I was still trying to make up my mind when a red IFF alert flipped up, the main door popped open and my suit's helmet stuck itself in through the door.

"Hostile activity inbound. Contact at the Flivver hive in less than ten minutes."

16
First contact

Perfect bloody timing, but if the suit was worried then so was I. I disentangled myself from Soffee's tears and ran outside, calling back that the suit and I had this covered. The suit engulfed me, ready for anything and eager as hell.

"Sorry to interrupt you," it said, with what I'd swear was a verbal smirk, "but there are two unidentified mechanicals coming up the tunnel, with others following."

It flicked up a tactical assessment and sure enough there they were, but who were they? Everyone kept saying we were the only people still here, but of course we weren't. Those fabled bloody Aquatics, and I could guess what they were after.

We raced down through the Flivver hive's ball of light and were engulfed by the eerie green image-intensifier darkness on the other side. A sand-covered auto-digger shell appeared and we stopped, taking cover behind its remains. The suit popped off a couple of drones and their whines disappeared down the tunnel, the feeds slaloming from side to side as they raced off towards what I could now hear was the distant sound of tracked vehicles. The suit popped up an estimated range, quickly followed by a manual or auto-targeting request. Better safe than sorry, eh?

"Manual to me unless I can no longer respond," was my response.

Its "Affirmative" came back with a definite air of disappointment and I was straight back to that surreal game on the ship, although this time I had the advantage. Full loads of solids, mini-rockets, RPGs, grenades and blasters should be enough to sort out anything I could think of. I just hoped I didn't have to use them.

A mechanical edged around a distant corner and moved up towards me.

"Hey you," I broadcast on wideband. "Stop right there and identify yourself."

It kept on rolling and a second one appeared, both bog-standard tracked crawlers, although these had armoured windows plus some unusual hardware scattered across the top.

"Assessment?" I asked the suit.

"I can take both with 100% probability to breach first strike, on your command," was its reply as two targeting points came up.

"No," I said, "what are they?"

"Two heavily armed tracked vehicles with supporting bipedal mechanicals following," was the equally unhelpful statement of the bleeding obvious.

"I say again, stop and identify yourself," I broadcast. "I will shoot if you come any closer." At that, both vehicles ground to a halt.

A wideband transmission came back: "We are looking for whoever owns the ship in orbit. We wish to use it as well as the landing ships it carries. Once we have access, we will leave this tunnel."

The translation carried a clear implication that the speaker was not in the least worried about its ability to get what it wanted. A bit arrogant I thought, but they were probably assuming I was as much of a pushover as the last group of CS1 inhabitants had been.

"You can't have the ship or the pods, so I suggest you go back to where you came from," was my reply.

Rumour had it that these Aquatics were pretty wild, but it was worth at least one polite refusal before we bopped them on the nose. Unfortunately, my answer was both mechanicals starting to move, heading straight for me.

"OK," I told the suit. "Knock 'em out, but watch the back-blast."

Two missiles flew out of the suit's backpack. Turrets on both mechanicals flicked around and shot the missiles out of the air, but they were far too late for the suit's RPG. A massive explosion punched out the front of the nearest mechanical and gouts of water, bits of the machine and undoubtedly its occupants flew everywhere.

The suit leapt back up the tunnel as a missile from the second mechanical obliterated the auto-digger.

"OK," I gasped, as let's face it, moving quickly in a suit was pretty uncomfortable. "How do we get the second bastard?"

At that moment, Soffee's voice came across person-to-person. Stone me, her embedded tech still worked.

"Franky, what happening?" she said. "Flivver hive locked down and me and girls come to help."

"No!" I shouted. "Stay away. There's far too much crap flying about for anyone not in a suit and we've got this," although judging by the IFF's latest update, I wasn't so sure.

"I not leave you like last ti-" but the suit's "Confirm auto control?" interrupted our exchange.

"Confirmed," was all I could manage before we were up and running towards the remains of the auto-digger. The suit squirted a full sitrep up to the ring-ship, requesting a new orbit over the top of us and a couple of fully provisioned pods down here. It then squirted a quick comm to my own pod, telling it to destroy any unwanted visitors.

A full auto-control tactical display flipped up in front of me and the suit fired everything it had at the second mechanical. One moment it was there and the next, a cloud of debris and multiple shockwaves jolted past. The suit bounced out into the clear air beyond, but came to a skidding halt. A large group of bipedal mechanicals had appeared around the corner and were looking very eager to see what had just happened to their tracked mates.

I was shaken like a stone in a can as the suit fired another salvo. Each weapon was individually targeted and the nearest six bipeds blew apart. Their mates, however, weren't hanging about and the suit was knocked backwards, sliding around on hands and feet as several projectiles spanged off the outside. The HUD was shrieking critical damage, energy losses and other bad things but the suit never stopped firing as it hopped about, dodging the streams of projectiles coming our way. Those bipeds were also doing the same as our shots chased their leaping forms with explosions and gaping craters across the tunnel walls.

Standing, running, jumping, my suit just kept on firing. Biped after biped was going down, but we were also taking hits. The suit's right arm blew away and then we lost the lower part of our left leg, and still the bipeds kept coming.

I now had a sea of reds to match the shrieking alarms, and it was a good job the suit was in control 'cos I could hardly think. The continual leaping about and over-energetic drumbeat of incoming projectiles was shaking me past the middle of next week, and then another red popped up showing criticals on the suit's internal impact protection.

An explosion in the tunnel wall and a hail of rock fragments blew off the suit's remaining leg. We bounced across the floor but the suit's remaining arm still kept firing. The HUD popped up, asking whether to keep on firing or direct remaining power to life support as we couldn't have both. Some choice, especially as those bipeds weren't going to stop coming until we were in pieces all over the floor.

Another massive thump and we spun into the wall as an immediate bale-out flash ate the display. Clouds of stars and I could just about see a large piece of suit lying next to me. Internal systems were out and I couldn't move. We really were screwed. One more hit and I'd be red fruit jelly all over the floor.

And that would have been that really, except that Soffee dropped into my nightmare. A vision of sand suit, helmet and wings appeared, her rifle thudding down across my visor. She fired, her face a picture of anger and despair, hitting first one biped and then another as they dodged about. I tried calling to her but the noise was deafening, and then she ejected her last cartridge case.

The rifle bolt worked back and forth but she really was out. She glanced down at me, then back along the tunnel, before slowly standing up and dropping the rifle. Her helmet fell to the floor as both wings arched up behind into a massive blue hemisphere, her head in the centre with its feathers opening up into a matching blue halo.

"What are you doing?" I screamed, but no one could hear. She was a sitting duck, but the bipeds paused. They hadn't seen anything like this before, and what was it doing?

She sucked in a massive breath, then the most incredible sound ripped through the tunnel. A cross between a screech and thousands of nails scraping down thousands of blackboards, at a volume making it the loudest sound in the known universe. My suit shut down into close protection mode and Soffee just kept on shrieking.

With each blast of sound, the targeted biped ran into an invisible brick wall and dropped to the ground. Of course, those still moving weren't standing about doing nothing and several projectiles punched holes through Soffee's great feathery disc as she turned from one biped to another, each one getting its own dreadful shriek. A final sonic blast and the last biped slumped to the floor, leaving just an aching silence behind.

Two eyes, black holes in her blue death's head, stared down the tunnel. Her gaze flicked back to me and the surrounding feathery halo started to collapse as her wings crumpled. Both eyes turned upwards and she sagged, momentarily holding herself before collapsing to the ground in a big blue feathery heap.

17
Good guys - 1, Bad guys - 0

What readouts I was still getting said no threats indicated, and from what I could see they weren't kidding. I punched out of my suit and there it lay, a limbless torso plus helmet, scored over with impact marks. All around me was mechanical debris, appearing and disappearing through the swirls of choking smoke that caught in my throat and tickled Soffee's feathers.

I bent down to see if she was OK and out of nowhere three Flivver females appeared. Each was wearing those old colours and yep, they were the girls alright and it was straight back to Soffee plus girls equals everything going pear-shaped. They looked to be pretty tooled up and yes, durr-brain, they really had always been hive protectors. That was why they'd made friends with Soffee. These thoughts chuntered through my wool-gathering wits as they shouldered me aside and picked up Soffee's still-unconscious form.

"Are you coming," was tossed over Circe's shoulder and they were off.

I was about to do the same when another group of Flivvers appeared out of the murk, halting and bowing towards the girls who were now hurrying away up the tunnel with Soffee.

"We owe you and head hive-protector Soffee our thanks," said one, gazing at the smoking carnage. "We know these machines. They are used by the aquatic beings who previously terrorized the inhabitants of the tunnels."

His gaze flicked back to me. "Your weapons are much more powerful than ours but your suit has been destroyed. What will happen when they return?"

I was still staring at the mess down the tunnel and seemed to be the only person wondering what the hell had just happened. The Flivvers didn't seem in the least surprised, but then I suppose they'd lived through the previous years' chaos and this was just more of the same.

I walked up to the nearest biped, which was some sort of armoured suit with the viewport now looking like someone had smacked it with a lump hammer before smearing lumpy soup around the inside. Undoubtedly the remains of its unfortunate occupant and we had enough cans of that particular foodstuff for a sizeable picnic. Trouble was, and those Flivvers had just said it, they'd be back. We had things to do, and the first of those was to get out of here and see how Soffee was.

Straight back up the tunnel and the main hive was shut up tight. Up to my hab and this now seemed to be bursting with people. As I walked in, a cramped path opened in front of me, feathered arms pointing to the equally chock-full front cabin. I pushed my way through and they started fluttering their wings, quietly chittering away with something that my translator couldn't even begin to translate.

Soffee was lying in a sort of cradle, with several females sponging her down with a straw-coloured fluid. That stroppy teenager I remembered was long gone, and I probably needed to get outside and leave them to it.

A council member was waiting as I came back out to stand in the small remaining area of empty space.

"Do not worry," he said. "They are looking after your head hive-protector Soffee and paying you a great compli..." but he was interrupted by a group of Flivvers struggling up and dumping the remains of my suit by the hab door. Kind of them, I suppose, but it was clearly just bits.

"We should wait out here until she is well enough to see you," continued my new friend. "Also, I am not sure how many times I can bear hearing how brave you were and how lucky your hive is to have head hive-protector Soffee."

My translator was picking up all sorts of nuances, like he was implying far more than he was actually saying. It was probably just more of that Flivver comms thing and the aches and pains from my suit's impact protection were starting to intrude. I needed to sit down.

"We have not seen a hive-protector scream" <90% xlate confidence> "for many generations," he said. "Protectors have always been able to hurt their enemies with the power of their voice, but legend says that the protector dies. Your head hive-protector Soffee's..." and here he hesitated, "...Terran heritage, obviously makes her strong enough to make the call many times. She is truly a mighty protector."

"Well, it was a new one on me," I replied. "Almost like it was controlling her rather than she was controlling it."

"Oh, the action is quite involuntary," he said. "It is triggered by the hive, or those that the protector holds dear, being in great danger, and continues until there is no more threat," and he paused, before, "or the protector is dead. We have always wondered why she and her sister were hidden here. Maybe someone was worried about people finding out what they could do?"

He was staring at me, his silence again implying volumes, but what? Soffee was probably the only person who could tell me, but she was out of it and here I was, on my own, yet again.

A long waiting pause, before: "In the past, these Aquatics have always got what they wanted and they will be back." He looked at my suit's remains. "It is a mystery what they think we have, but they obviously want it very much."

I mentally groaned. OK, here we go.

"They saw my pod coming down," I said, "and they want my ship."

The old guy gave the Flivver equivalent of a sharp intake of breath and wide-eyed surprise.

"Aaah," he said. "So you have a ship. What sort is it?"

"It's a ring-ship with three rings, maybe 300 plus passenger capacity," came out before I could stop myself.

His look flicked back, quizzical, calculating but, it has to be said, quite open in that way Flivvers have of not trying to hide what they are thinking.

"Anyway," I continued, "we need to start making some plans 'cos they won't stop now."

He opened his mouth to reply, but at that moment Soffee came storming into the cabin. She looked pretty worn out, but apart from the obvious holes punched through her wing feathers, remarkably well.

"Hey, you're OK," I said rather lamely. "I was really worried."

She marched straight up. "Why you not say bloody suit lose arms and legs but you not hurt?" she shouted at me. "I see IFF and I think you die and now you have joke with," and she pointed an accusatory finger at the old guy, chittering out something so rude that my translator couldn't even begin to translate it. She followed up by shaking her finger in my face.

"I wait so long for you and you make me so worried and I...you...aargh!" before turning and marching straight out again.

Everyone around me was smiling. I think I preferred the flouncing to the marching.

"She must be feeling better," said my companion. "Protecting the hive is core to a protector's being and she also knows that you are not as indestructible as everybody thinks."

"Well, she's right about that, but it's nice to see she's feeling better. I was really worried."

He shrugged. "Our protectors are armed with Terran weapons provided by head hive-protector Soffee and they were ready to help. However, we knew you would protect us and if that did not work, head hive-protector Soffee would destroy them. And that is what she did."

"Well, that's one hell of an assumption...," I started, but stopped as I realised that anything I might know was nine years out of date. I was still dying to know how she'd found that she could melt her enemies by screaming at them, but that was probably a question for when she wasn't shouting at me.

"We are not fighters," the Flivver continued, "and we are happy to ally with your hive. We know you Terrans love fighting and your hive has destroyed our enemies," and he smiled, opening his arms in that universal I-told-you-so gesture.

While I was still thinking about that, Chitichca appeared. She stepped up and took my hand, which Flivvers never did, but then this was Chitichca. Always there and always doing what was necessary to make things work.

"Franky my friend," she said. "You and your head hive-protector Soffee have our deepest thanks, but we must talk about how you will get us off the planet before the Aquatic beings re-appear."

Great. So good news obviously travelled fast. At least the old style behind-the-back-manoeuvring had changed to a more direct face-to-face style. Franky was back so let's use his ship and hoo-bloody-rah to that. But you know what? Flivvers are fixated with everyone, regardless of their species, having a hive. I had no family and few friends, so Chitichca and her minions had given me a hive, ready populated. Everything had then been shared, Soffee had protected them, and now the whole Flivver world and his wife were planning on hitching a ride off-planet. Made perfect sense to them and that was the way it was going to be.

I looked at Chitichca and I'd place a large bet she knew exactly what I was thinking. It was more than a little odd to have found a new mother, from a different species, half a millennium after the first, but there's worse things that could happen I suppose. Admittedly, the start of a ground war hadn't been top of my list, but we were where we were I guess. As if to emphasise this, an IFF projection popped up with some worrying timescales attached. The best said we needed to get our arses in gear. The worst? Well, you just didn't wanna know.

A much happier looking Soffee was now standing alongside Chitichca and both of their expressions said that they were well ahead of me. Chitichca's best Mother-knows-best expression was also present, so I guess that in this case Mother did indeed know best.

"OK," I said, raising my hands in mock exasperation, "let's assume we're gonna try and get everyone up to the ship. What are we talking about?"

"There are two hives," said Chitichca in a chiding tone. "We have 141 adults, 145 children and the crèche. You have 5 adults. We will bring food and drink, but everyone can use your sleep units for the journey."

Now that last bit was more of a question than a solution, and a jolly good question it was. I'd already used one of the sleep units getting here, but that was the only one I'd looked at. The rest were showing as working, but there's showing as working and 'showing as working.' Get into the wrong one and you were going to wake up dead. Still, we'd only need sleep units if we had people needing them, so I'd worry about sleep units when everyone was off-planet.

"OK, sounds good," I said to the waiting Soffee and Chitichca, "but I guess we need to get moving. I'll start by talking to the ship and you two look after the hives. We'll touch base again when we know what's what."

They turned, chittering to each other, then calling people in, firing off instructions and very obviously far more on the ball than I was. I'd better start getting my act together.

18
We are leaving

The swell of Flivvers was already starting to move with a purpose but that was all very well for them. They had two forces of nature barking at their heels. As for poor old me? Without those two pairs of skewering eyes it felt like my brain was liquifying prior to dribbling out of my ears.

I stretched back into the couch. The clicks and creaks from my aching back added to the muffled imprecations from passing Flivvers as they had to hop over my outstretched legs, but I was still trying to get my head together.

Several more deep breaths and come on, shape up, stop messing about. A tentative wiggle of the mental gear stick and I tried opening a comm to the ship's main AI.

You know what? I shouldn't have worried. The various AIs down here had been keeping the main AI up there fully in the loop, and in almost no time at all we had some potential what-ifs to look at. I had a look through the more likely ones, checked the numbers, checked the feasibilities and found that we couldn't even begin to do what we needed to do in the times the IFF was giving us.

The main AI went away with a promise to come back soonest with something that might actually work, and I was left with the lingering thought that it had all been going so well. Still, a refreshing drink always made things better and there was the good ole Megameal flashing its enticing options. Buttons pressed, a five second wait, but cough, gag, yeuck! Soffee hadn't been joking about running on dregs. If this was all we had then getting off CS1 had just gained a whole new priority.

My cringing taste buds were interrupted by the main AI's new and improved timescales, but they still didn't look great. Flivvers aren't really possessions people and they pretty much do what the hive needs, no questions asked. Trouble was, there were three hundred and they would have to leave their home carrying the barest essentials, and all in half an hour please. Also, let's not forget the hive creche. Just the thought of moving every single one of those precious eggs, without them breaking, filled me with horror.

Unbidden, that old joke about how Flivvers laid eggs that large - lots of shouting, screaming and tears spurting out of their eyes - flashed across my mind, but come on now, concentrate. The Aquatics were still out there and we needed some protection.

A quick comm to my pod and it started powering up all of the suits and semis it had onboard. I needed them over here, but they mustn't shoot anything until they'd checked their targets and checked them again. Every single one of them had the same tactical persona as my over-eager suit, and we didn't want any over-eager AIs being, well, over-eager.

Confirmations flicked up across the board and I focused back on the room, but I was sitting in an oasis of calm. Everything had transferred outside where waves of people ebbed and flowed across the tunnel and some of the younger ones were even flying above people's heads. Quite a sight.

"Franky, sorry mate, can I have a word?" dropped into this maelstrom, Silent Bob's face poking around the door.

"Shiiit!" I managed. "You still here? Come on in."

"So you came back," he said, wandering over and perching on a couch arm. "Dane always said you were a complete moron not knowing what you'd got here, but that's the both of us, right?"

I stared back. I don't think I remember him ever saying a word and yet here he was, all words and no thousand klick stare. "But there's nothing here," I said. "Everyone's been trying to get away for ever."

"Yeah maybe, but I like it." He smiled as his eyes flicked across the door and the noise beyond. "Me and Dane had some pretty wild times before this place and CS1's OK, even if it has now all gone to shit."

"But surely you want to get away?" I said.

"Nah! You mad?" he said, slowly rubbing his hands together. "No one on your case, no previous? I love it here."

"But I've got a ship," I said. "I could take you away with us if you want."

"Yeah, you and that bloody ship. One fool to another? Take care of your own 'cos one day they're here and the next day they're gone. Believe me, there's a lot worse out there than there is down here," and he kicked the small bag he'd brought with him. "That's my whole life, but it's all I need."

We both glanced at the door as several distant thumps interrupted. Those blasted suits are shooting Flivvers! Shit, shit, shit, but an advisory popped up to quell that thought.

"3 hostiles destroyed," came the terse report. "Long range scanning indicates multiple hostiles coming in from all directions."

"Ok, get everything deployed," I shouted back rather superfluously. They were already well ahead of me.

"I've got some suits coming in from the pod," I said to Soffee as she raced in, doing a double, then a triple take at Bob. "They've just stopped 3 of those things we destroyed earlier but they're coming in from everywhere."

She opened her mouth to say something, but ran out again with just a passing glance at Bob. He watched her go, a smile creasing his lips.

"Dane asked me to keep an eye on your family, sorry 'hive'," cocking an eye at the door as his smile opened into a laugh. "Yeah I know, you didn't know you had one but those Flivvers eh? Hive, family, blah, blah, blah." He shrugged. "Your Soffee's pretty serious shit and for some reason they also think you're great. You've got it made," but was interrupted by more distant explosions.

"Well she's not my Soffee," I said. "I mean c'mon, she's just a kid, and anyway, how'd he know I was gonna come back?"

"Oh come one," he said with a big grin. "You're a big soft dollop, Franky Franks. You were always coming back, and ntime/reltime'll do what it always does," but a chorus of not-so-distant explosions interrupted him again. "Look, whatever. I'll try and help but good luck. You're gonna need it." He smiled, flicked a finger to his forehead salute, picked up his bag and walked out. I blinked. Yet more oddness in this whole mad day.

Two suits came racing out of the gloom, closely followed by a couple of wheeled semi-autos. They weaved up to the hab and skidded to a halt in a cloud of sand, all very obviously tooled up and ready for action.

Everyone gave them plenty of room, as well as looking on with some alarm. The more heavily armoured suit walked up and opened, ready for immediate boarding.

"Good to see you," I said. "What's happening?"

"We used the same entrance you did," it replied. "We came across 3 hostiles, which we dealt with, but there are now 4 streams of mechanicals converging on this location, and others heading for the landing grid. The ship has launched two of the larger pods which will be down in 30 minutes, best estimate. Main armament is cleared to fire as soon as the ship is in range."

"Sounds great," I said. "Trouble is, we'll need two trips for each pod and the refuelling turnaround'll kill us. You're gonna have to make us some more time."

Soffee and Chitichca were standing off to one side. I flicked them a glance as I continued: "None of the enemy can get anywhere near here or the grid. We may have to leave you behind. I'm sorry."

"We are looking forward to destroying as many of your enemies as we can," came the surprisingly gung-ho reply, backed up by a summary popup of what had already bitten the dust. No wonder those Aquatics were so pissed off.

"You see," piped up Chitichca into this exchange. "Terran engineer already has protectors. With Soffee and her friends you have even better protectors."

Easy for her to say, especially as my IFF view of the world was showing something a lot worse.

The two semis plus other suit moved off down the tunnel, leaving just the opened-up suit behind. Stomach-clenching doubts were adding to my worries, and the more details the IFF gave me the more everything clenched. We really were stuck between a rock and a very hard place. This had to work first time or, well, just or.

"OK," I said to Soffee and Chitichca, "we've got three pods and they'll each take about fifty people. It's a real squeeze, so no more than one bag each. I need the first fifty of yours ready in five and the next two right behind."

They just stood there looking at me.

"What about others?" said Soffee.

"Oh yeah, sorry" I said. "The pods'll go up to low orbit, drop their passengers off, come straight back down again, and yes, I know," to their questioning faces, "we don't have enough time. We'll just to have make some."

Soffee's worried face also had a question: "How people get to landing grid? Only working exit is environmental door, and is too far to walk." She paused. "Also, you wear," and she held out a sand suit.

"What's this?" I said. "I'm fine with what I've got."

She stood there holding out the sand suit. "Is important," she said. "Please."

"Look, we don't have ti..." but I ground to a halt under that piercing gaze.

I sighed. More Flivver malarkey no doubt, but everyone had stopped doing what they were doing to watch. Another look at Soffee then I grabbed the sand suit and ducked into the hab, shrugging off my outer clothes and slipping on the sand suit. It fitted OK, but why all the fuss? And then I saw it. Those winged Terran/Flivver and Terran emblems had been added to the chest pocket.

I went out again and the crowd's body language said that my wearing this was really important. Totally baffling. I smiled at Soffee.

"Happy?" I said.

"Very happy," she said. "Thank you."

"Right," I said waving at the hab, "this vehicle plugs a hole to the outside, so we're going to have to move it. It's the shortest walk to the landing grid so let's hope it works OK?" addressing the now rather sceptical expressions on both Soffee's and Chitichca's faces.

They looked at each other, shrugged, then moved back towards the ever-growing mass of waiting hive members. More distant thumps and matching shockwaves, and an automated advisory popped up. Four more hostiles were down but the suit was obviously having so much fun it couldn't be bothered to tell me in person.

I jogged back into the hab with every mental finger crossed. This thing had an emergency righting capability and my plan depended on that still working after all of those decades stuck in the tunnel wall.

I told the hab AI what I wanted. It came straight back with a list of reasons why this was a really bad idea. I repeated what I wanted, and with the equivalent of an AI sigh, it started setting up the hydraulic rams.

Tracking info from the two pods coming down from orbit showed them on final approach. We'd need people out there as soon as possible, and while I could see Soffee trying her hardest to marshal up our first group of fifty, their lack of enthusiasm was palpable.

"Soffee, how are we doing?" I called out.

"First group ready," she called back.

"What about the other two? They'll need to go straight out after."

"Nearly ready and rest coming. Last group has slow people, crèche and hive records. They very slow."

"Well we can't wait," I said. "They'd better get a move on."

I was interrupted by a suit with more bad news.

"We are still in control but they have brought up heavier weapons. Best estimate is they'll be with you in less than an hour."

And all we had to stop them was a handful of suits and semis.

19
First away

The chorus of distant thumps with attendant shockwaves had become an underlying rhythm to our preparations and the collective nervousness was almost palpable. An IFF popup showed our two pods landed safely and deploying suits to give us a safe passage to the landing grid. I suppose we'd soon see about that then, wouldn't we?

"Right, you lot," I called out through the door. "As soon as we've got a hole I want the first group out and then the next two. We're really short on time so no messing about."

There on the main screen in the hab's control cabin was a helpful red button saying 'Automatic righting - Push to initiate.' I leant over and did exactly that.

Several massive thumps creased the floor and we lurched to one side, clouds of dust coughing into the tunnel. More mechanical grindings, then there was a screech of tortured metal as the hab tore itself away from the wall. A blinding bar of sunlight skewered into the tunnel with a scorching cough of wind right behind.

A rather superfluous "Manoeuvre completed" advisory popped up on the console and I raced back into the tunnel. A sea of blue faces punctuated by wide-open eyes greeted me. I turned. Wow! There was debris all over the place and my hab looked like some giant child had tried to bend their toy in half. Over everything was a deathly silence, broken only by the sibilant swish of wind blowing past outside.

"C'mon then, snap out of it!" I shouted. "Let's get moving. Now!"

The stationary tableau broke as Soffee raced past, a wave of Flivvers following close behind.

"You're in charge and I need those pods in the air like yesterday," I called after her. "They'll come straight back down again after they drop you off, but you've got to get moving."

Soffee just ignored me as she chivvied the first of the Flivvers up to that blindingly bright hole, and no one looked even vaguely keen. And who could blame them? I was being baked alive just standing here and where they were standing must have been blistering. Soffee's shouting and shoving finally got the laggards moving and the girls' coming in to help really started to get things moving.

Finally, the first group was out and the second followed right behind. A particularly toasty gust blew past, and my skin tightened as I stepped out of its way. Looking past the moving file of Flivvers, I could see a growing group of the old, the ill and the very young, some being supported and some on self-propelled stretchers. Everyone was sagging in the heat and I couldn't even begin to think how we were going to get that lot across to the landing grid.

And then, to make my day complete, out of the dimness staggered several litters holding swaddled-up egg shapes, the flippin' crèche for goodness' sake. Close behind were four Smuts and even a Grunt, which nodded a greeting alongside the Smuts' chorus of welcomes and thanks for the lift. Silent Bob limited himself to a smirk and a wave as the Smuts' sent their parting jest about my novel approach to hab engineering.

Flickers of activity were now coming in from the landing grid as the first over-heated Flivvers got there. Soffee and the girls were everywhere, rushing around in that hideous sunlight and chivvying the less enthusiastic passengers. Even with their insulating feathers they must have been frying alive.

I opened a comm: "Soffee, you needed to be off five minutes ago. Anyone messing around gets left behind."

No reply.

I started saying it again but was rewarded by an immediate: "Franky, we know. Everyone loading and we leave as soon as possible."

"That's great," I replied, "but you've gotta go now."

"Franky, we know. Stop calling."

I left her to it, but couldn't stop looking at our assorted slow-coaches plus that bloody creche. At best we'd have barbecue plus scrambled eggs. At worst? Just didn't bear thinking about.

"Shit, shit, shit!" was my only conclusion but I was distracted by yet another cluster of distant thumps courtesy of the suits and semis. That bright red circle on my IFF tactical display just wouldn't stop contracting around us.

Then, finally, a launch prep notification from one of the pods, followed by another and then the third. Soffee's was last and it looked like they might actually take off some time soon, which thankfully rang a bell. We didn't want any ship and pod-related IFF incidents, now did we?

"Ship," I called up. "Special directive, effective immediately. Terran/Flivver hybrid identified as Soffee has standard priorities and command privileges. All commands from her should be obeyed with no reference to me."

The main AI's confirmation overlayed the continually changing dispositions of our suits and semi-autos. They'd started off with full ordnance loads, but everything was being used up at such a frantic rate that I was having trouble following the lightning-fast cuts and thrusts. Six hostile mechanicals had now broken out onto the surface and were heading for the landing grid, but they were just a small part of the constricting sea of IFF indications that seemed to be everywhere.

'Six hostiles destroyed' came from the landing grid, but was immediately replaced by more red dots. An interrogative popped up from my suit, still standing there almost quivering with anticipation. I told it to wait, and the AI sounded very disappointed. Its mates were out there having fun so why weren't we out there with them?

"OK Franky, we leave now," Soffee popped up through the madness. "I send girls back to help."

A final wink as she stuck out her tongue to accompany the roar of the first pod's boosters. The girls came racing in through our brightly lit entranceway and man, they were roasted. Each picked up a water container and poured it all over herself before grabbing another and trying to drain it. I ran over to my waiting suit.

"Hey!" I called out to the girls as I mounted up. "Are you OK?"

They winced and covered their ears, so I tried again with less of the speaking across the planet level of volume and more of the commanding presence to give people confidence level. Circe chittered to a group of elders who were sitting alongside the hab and they chittered back before gesturing that there were still more people to come.

"We can't wait," I said. "If they aren't here soon, they stay here."

The suit IFF's best guess was that we had less than thirty minutes before the first Aquatic walked up and knocked on the door. Another report from the landing grid showed hostile mechanicals everywhere. And the ring-ship's armament was still ten minutes away. It was so close that everything was starting to squeak.

An earth-shaking detonation and a massive wall of sand flew past. I was OK in my suit but everyone else was knocked flat.

"What's happening?" I called out, but there was nothing.

I was about to try again when "The hostiles deployed a mine," said a semi. "Suits 2 and 4 and semi-autos 1 thru 5 have been buried and the landing grid has been damaged. I would advise that you evacuate your current location immediately."

I opened up a channel to Soffee. "How are you doing? We could really do with you back down here."

There was a momentary pause before her laboured response under blast-off Gs came back. "Pod say 30 minutes. Will let you know."

From what I was seeing thirty minutes might as well be thirty hours.

"Look, we may not have 30 minutes. I'll give you a final go/no go and if we can't get away then you get the hell out of here."

My suit shook from another shockwave and I could see that Soffee was getting the same feeds.

"We not leave you," she said. "We not leave anyone."

An IFF report popped up saying that the landing grid had repulsed another attack but they'd lost a suit and there was even more damage. I checked my feeds and checked them again, but there it was. The landing grid was now just bent metal.

How the hell were we going to land our pods?

20
It all goes a bit semi

It's amazing how you wrack your brains, and then you wrack your brains some more, and it's the power of unbidden lateral thinking that has the final throw of the dice. A great big seven came sliding in, and you know what? I'd been looking at this the wrong way. It wasn't the landing grid that was the problem. The real problem was finding somewhere where the Aquatics weren't, and close enough so that our passengers didn't get roasted alive getting there.

And you know how it is. First one thing, then another. Just up the tunnel was a collection of semi-autonomous transport bodies, or trucks, left by the miners long ago. Wheeled, designed to go over that blazing hot sand and each would hold at least fifty Flivvers. A suit could pull one, so I guess we had some transport. And then, the final piece of the jigsaw. Five klicks from here was a mess of salt flats, and they were as flat as their name suggested. Perfect to land a pod on. Problem solved.

I checked with the suits and got cautious agreement that they could probably pull a truck for five klicks, probably, maybe. Soffee came in on the conference and told us she could plot new descents. A final check and yep, we still had three fully working suits. I told them to disengage and get up to trucks like smartish.

There was an intense flash outside and a gust of air blew in, preceded by a scattering of people and even hotter than usual. Soffee had a gleeful smile plastered all over her face.

"This cool," she said. "You not tell me I can get ship to use weapons. I call up ship AI to see how can help and it ask what to shoot. I say melt anything not friendly and it just do it."

"Yeah, sorry" I said. "Forgot to tell you. You've now got full access to the ship in case anything goes wrong down here."

Silence.

"You give me your ship," softly whispered, face expressionless, bottomless black eyes floating in a sea of blue.

"Oh come on," I retorted, "I wasn't going to leave you here. If I don't make it then you'll certainly need a ride out."

She was looking at me just like she had in the hab.

"So you really come back for me." Another whisper. "I knew," cutting the connection as a tear welled up.

So, what was that all about, but I had other things to worry about. A much closer explosion blew its cloud of debris up the tunnel. Running out of this came three suits. They weaved their way through the throng of people and disappeared up the tunnel towards the trucks.

"Right," I called out to the waiting masses, "we've got a new plan. Everyone needs to get along to the trucks up the tunnel and they'll take you to where the pods are gonna land. Girls, you're in charge."

The girls looked back at me, their wtf-expressions slowly changing to concern.

"Yeah, I know," I said. "The landing grid's damaged so we need somewhere else. We've got three suits and each can pull a truck. You'll have to make sure we get everyone in."

Still no one moved and the expressions being tossed about were largely of the what is he talking about variety. There was no Soffee around to help, so I thought I'd better try on this hive chief thing for size and get things moving.

I struck my chest with a clenched fist and raised my arm over my head. "Success to you all and may your gods go with you." OK, pretty corny and lifted straight from one of my favourite films but hell, I was making this up as I went along.

More surprise flicked across the girls' faces but they straightened, mimicked my salute and started moving people up the tunnel. Chitichca was standing to one side, a smile creasing her lips. Her gaze was on me, but it flicked to the girls and then back again before she started ushering her Flivver council members after the milling crowds.

The IFF had been trying to get my attention and when I had a look, I almost wished I hadn't. Pulling out those suits had left us with just a partially mobile suit and a semi between us and the Aquatics in the tunnels. There were still two suits at the landing grid, but the Aquatics were starting to circle around behind them and us. We did have those three suits up the tunnel, but they were pulling trucks, not fighting bad guys.

There was another massive flash from outside, followed by another, but that was it for the ten minutes re-charge time, and probably for this orbit as well. My eyes focused back to the tunnel, and wow! From milling crowds to just me, the only movement being dustings of sand swirling in from outside. I'd had some good times here, but it was time to go.

Those trucks were further up the tunnel than I remembered, but sure enough, up past the environmental door and a line of sand covered shapes appeared out of the gloom. I could see all three girls trying to get the Flivvers loaded up and then, a massive explosion. A suit had placed an explosive charge against the tunnel wall and a bulwark of light flashed in through the hurricane of sand and dust that blew past.

People started picking themselves up from that little surprise, and the suits got straight on with clearing a way out for the trucks. That didn't take long and back they ran to stand there waiting as the girls chivvied in the last few passengers. Tailgates were slammed shut and with a succession of mighty heaves, each truck lurched out of its burial place and slowly rolled out through the brightly illuminated exit. And there I was again, all alone, even if my final looks were fleeting as I ran straight out after those clouds of dust now headed for the salt pans.

It was full afternoon sun, air temperature eighty C and well over a hundred on the ground. I was OK in my suit but we really couldn't hang about. The trucks' passengers would be heating up in their rolling ovens and those Aquatics would have seen us leave.

A fountain of sand, and the suit shuddered as it returned fire, bringing me back to the job in hand with a bump.

"Target destroyed," popped up and I handed over full fire control so it could do its thing while I tried to do mine.

A quick peep from Soffee said that she could see us, and was syncing the suggested landing area with my suits. At the same time, our remaining suit and semi in the tunnels flashed up that they had run out of ammo and were attacking the hostiles hand to hand, which must have been a sight to behold.

Two 'no carrier' advisories popped up and then nothing. The remaining suits at the landing grid were now coming after the Aquatics and providing a great diversion as they turned yet more machines into scrap metal. The trucks were making good time and we only had a couple of klicks to go. Three landing countdown timers popped up and there were our pods, dropping down nicely on final approach.

'Hoo-bloody-rah!' was my enthusiastic response, but we weren't there yet and the ship's main armament was still behind the horizon. We'd get our passengers to the pods no problem, but as for loading everyone up while the never-ending supply of weaponised mechanicals kept shooting at us? We were so out of time that the bad guys were in the process of walking up to say "Boo!"

A triumphant shout from Soffee as her pod dropped into its billowing clouds of rocket exhaust. The nearest truck stopped and the passengers started baling out. The second pod touched down just as the next truck arrived but we had a serious problem with the third. It was half a klick behind and not moving.

I could see the massive flash burn down one side as I raced across. The truck was still in one piece but everything on the flashed side was fused. Hopefully no one was hurt but we were nowhere near the pods and that needed to change as soon as possible.

I ran up and applied brute force to the problem. The addition of my suit's heaving caused the truck to lurch forward but the suit which had dragged it there was nearly out of power. I told it to keep on going until it had minimum power to operate and then drop off to keep the bad guys' heads down.

It must have been completely knackered as almost immediately I was the only suit moving the truck. Several minutes more extreme heaving and a sequence of red warnings had started to fandango across my HUD, but we were finally getting close to the waiting pod and no one had shot at us yet. Scylla flashed up that she couldn't open the melted doors, so after a final heave my suit started tearing its way through the back of the truck.

Our partner suit was doing a great job making the bad guys' lives difficult. Also, we'd somehow managed to find ourselves behind a small dune which was good shelter from whatever was headed our way. I tried calling up the other suits for a bit of help, but no chance. They were far too busy sorting out their own passengers.

Increasing HUD alerts and Soffee's squeaks of alarm told me that we really needed to get a move on, and as if to emphasise that very point, my suit started loosing off at the distant specks in my IFF that were growing ever closer.

The first of our truck's passengers stumbled out into the fierce heat and staggered towards the pod. There was a furious banging on my suit's leg and there was Bob, wrapped up in a sand suit with a pretty serious piece of hardware over one shoulder.

"Get going, I'll keep their heads down." He knelt, and with an avalanche of sound, loosed off something at an approaching speck.

"We can't leave you," I shouted back. "You'll be killed for sure."

Another rocket propelled something flew out of his launcher and he leapt for cover.

"Nah, I'm staying. Stop pissing about and get the hell out of here," and this time he loosed off a salvo.

I was in a cauldron of total insanity and then, would you believe it, a pallet holding part of the hive crèche edged out of the back of the truck. Everyone was using far more care and attention than we had the time for, so I raced across, grabbed it out of protesting Flivvers' hands and carried it across to the pod. Straight back again to grab both remaining pallets, and another quick hustle left the three pallets stacked in the pod's shade ready for loading.

The fronts of two mechanicals poked over the top of our sheltering dune and my suit fired at both. They blew apart and right behind them two more noses poked into view. The suit sorted those out, but the straggly line of people wobbling their way towards the pod seemed to be taking all of the time in the world.

There was nothing for it and I scooped up the nearest slowpokes and ran. Definitely one of those never before in my life-type experiences for each armful as we raced through the super-heated air firing away at the bad guys. Their shocked expressions will stay with me for the rest of my life.

Low ammo and energy warnings were coming up all over my HUD, but we finally seemed to be getting somewhere. One more sweep for a final straggler and then suddenly, out of nowhere a large unfriendly giant drop-kicked my suit into the air. Sun, sand, sun, sand, then a monumental crash as I hit the dirt and my passenger flew through the air to wrap herself around a pod's leg.

My eyes slowly un-crossed to a cracked visor covered in red popups and my HUD's shrieking alarms. I was alive, but I was alive, sealed inside an armoured can and nothing worked. I'd been hit by an energy beam together with some sort of RPG, which the suit had just about managed to absorb but was now dead remains, severely knocked about and welded up tight. I was in full sunlight, on red hot sand and starting to cook.

Chary and a Smut appeared. Over Chary's shoulder I could see several more mechanicals appearing over the top of the dune but you know what? After all of that banging about, I was in that happy place where there was no hurry, what will be will be, and if it's going to happen, it's going to happen.

However, what did happen was truly extraordinary. A crater opened up under those mechanicals and up from the sand came two massive toothy jaws, closing with a snap and dragging the mechanicals down into the sand. I blinked, looked again, but sure enough there was just a final metal corner disappearing under the surface. Saved by a flippin' Sand Crab, which should have been extinct but wasn't. Extinct or otherwise I'm guessing it wouldn't like what it had grabbed for lunch, but that was its problem not mine. I had other things to worry about.

Chary and the Smut were trying to lever open my suit and what was left of its systems finally managed to pop up a distorted 'Emergency exit?' tell-tale on the cracked visor in front of me.

"Yes!" I shouted.

Of course, voice recognition was down and nothing happened. I tried the lower-tech approach of prodding the indicated green button with my nose. Various emergency exit processes worked as designed and the suit blew apart, vomiting me out onto blisteringly hot sand in the blazing sunlight. Flat on my face to up on my feet with no apparent muscular effort. Shit, that sand was melting. How anyone hadn't caught fire was a mystery.

Luckily none of the suit's jettisoned remains hit Chary or the Smut and we staggered across to the waiting pod, my exposed skin scorching as the rest of me broiled. Three steps to go and Chary disappeared into a thunderous explosion, the wall of sand knocking me off my feet.

Frantically scrabbling out of that fiery blanket, I leapt to my feet once again, swaying in the wind as I brushed myself off. In front of me was a sandy pile with feathers poking out. I dug in my hands and snatched them right back again – 'flippin' ouch! Wrapping my hands in my sleeves, I tried digging in again and this time grabbed out a very tousled Chary, still alive, but only just. It took a couple of attempts to heave her over one shoulder and we staggered off towards the pod's steps.

Every step on the pod was red-hot agony but with help from the Smut's hands heaving against my backside we eventually fell into the airlock, my able assistant falling in on top of me. The outer door slammed shut and the inner door swung open to let in a wave of cold, soothing air.

I heaved Chary out into a mess of Flivvers who were chittering about and showing no sense of urgency, although our sudden appearance abruptly stopped the chatter. A sea of eyes watched me smear blood everywhere as I dropped Chary into a seat. She needed serious medical attention but we had to get out of here. I slapped on a Medi-hood and ran across to the command seat, screaming at the Navcom to get us off.

"Ready to launch on your command, although passengers are not ready," responded the pod AI.

"Launch immediately," I shouted as I started strapping in.

The Navcom hesitated, but its "five, four, three, two, one" counted down and the engines fired. Clouds of rocket exhaust blanked out the sun as the all-encompassing thunder of perfectly firing main engines gave me all of the confirmation I needed that we'd finally made it off this hellish sea of sand.

Even so, my stomach remained knotted as the take-off Gs squashed the rest of me down into the seat. Those bastards on the ground weren't going to let up that easily, but Bob's voice cut through my worries.

"Born to burn you lucky bastard! Anyway, I'm off. Have a goo..." and a succession of blinding flashes cut him off as the ring-ship's last laugh scorched the ground below us.

Those shots must have fried everything, as we continued powering up towards the welcoming arms of unending space unmolested. Higher and higher we rose, the planet's horizon doing exactly the same as it shut those bloody Aquatics away from us behind a continent of sand.

Safe at last.

21
All away

Launch acceleration had pretty much finished when Soffee's face popped up on the comm screen.

"Why your face all red and covered in blo…" Her voice faltered. "What happen?"

"Yeah," I said, "bit tight at the end. Chary got blown up but I think she's OK. We also lost Bob."

"Who Bob?" and her face changed. "Oh, Terran in hab. Him Bob?"

"Yeah, he was helping keep the Aquatics off. The ship's main armament got him as we took off," and then Circe interrupted to say that it wasn't Chary who'd got hurt but Scylla who'd borrowed Chary's sand suit, and they all started worrying about Scylla. Soffee told Circe and Chary what I'd said and they all piled in with questions, questions and more questions, which I did try to answer, but eventually they got bored with my monosyllabic grunts and left me alone. A Medbot appeared and sprayed something cooling over the burns that were really starting to make their presence felt, but it all felt a bit weird. Mentally I was still out there on the sand with Bob, who the ship had killed, by accident.

The ring-ship's Navcom had started marshalling our pods into line for docking, but I was floating high above it all, looking down across the pods and the planet yet seeing nothing. I mean shit, I'd hardly known the guy. His whole life in one small bag. He'd looked after Soffee, helped us get away, and now he's gone. Just amazing really.

"Franky," intruded into my thoughts, Soffee's eyes pitch black, gazing at me. "You OK?" Her eyes flicked to the Medbot. "You very quiet. You sure you OK?" An affirmative grunt from me, but she didn't look convinced. An update flicking up from the main AI gave me a convenient excuse to look away.

Everything looked to be under control, but those Aquatic bastards hadn't finished, I was sure of it. They were planning something, and of course, as soon as I thought about it, I got a red flash from the IFF. Something had just been launched from the planet's surface and with it, for added emphasis, came a wideband transmission.

"This is a message for the sentients who have just taken off. We wish to use your ship. We will destroy it if you do not comply with our request. You have one standard minute to reply."

We now indeed had a great big dot coming straight up towards the predicted orbital track of the ship. The briefest of chats between Soffee and me and I was put in charge, so thanks a lot for that. The IFF then added that even if we could shoot whatever this thing was, we'd still be hit by the debris. Its only solution would be to give the missile a pretty vigorous nudge to move it off course, but we'd run out of suits and all of our pods were full of people. Oh yes, and the ship had tried moving, but so had the missile, and the main armament seemed to have no effect on it.

Then, finally, some good news. It appeared that actually, we did have a pod with a suit still onboard. It hadn't been able to join the fun on the surface as its legs didn't work. Big maintenance oops on that, but a quick diagnostic check said that while it couldn't walk, everything else was working just fine.

Multiple IFFs with but a single thought and the most pyscho AI was promptly loaded before the suit was dropped out. Off it powered, looking to loop out then come in from the side and knock the missile of course. If, that is, the plan worked, and if, that is, it wasn't hit by any counter-measures, and if, that is, it even managed to hit the missile at all.

The ship's IFF popped up a nice green vs. red plot showing the suit's track. The missile was now coming up at more than twenty-five thousand klicks per hour and the suit was coming nicely in to kick it in the whatsits. A collision window of nanoseconds. No trouble at all, or at least according to the IFF.

The missile saw what was happening, but it couldn't move very much as it still wanted to hit the ship. The suit powered in, all guns blazing, and the IFF's green vs. red lines disappeared into nothingness. The promised cloud of fragments flew past and that seemed to be it. A clear plot, not a peep from the bad guys and I guess they'd finally shot their bolt.

I sagged back and a xylophone of agony started playing across every single one of my bruised and badly mistreated body parts. There on the console was the pod universal clock and I had to laugh, catching myself in mid-gurgle as everything complained even more. I'd arrived on CS1 less than five hours ago as the guy who was just visiting. I'd left as the guy who'd saved a whole Flivver hive or no sorry, two Flivver hives, got them up here and was now about to fly them off somewhere. One hell of a day, and it wasn't even half done yet.

Murmurs of astonishment interrupted my jumbled thoughts as our pod came up behind the ship. Everyone on the pod was a grounder, and what with CS1 below, the black expanse of space above, and now the ring-ship's travel-beaten face expanding in front of us, end-to-end astonishment didn't even come close. The main AI pinged me to say that Soffee was already making friends, and if she wanted to help get those Flivvers onto the ship then she was very welcome. The Flivvers would probably expect it anyway, so why make life difficult for myself?

We docked without incident, to be greeted by Soffee's, Circe's and Chary's happy smiles as the air lock door opened. To Soffee's very obvious amusement the two girls gave me that ill-advised salute before they all whisked Scylla away to the Medlab.

My passengers were enjoying floating about in the zero gravity as they filtered out, even if they were all totally oblivious to how close they'd been to floating about in zero gravity, but in little feathered pieces. I caught my reflection in the viewport and it wasn't great - haggard, red blood all over my face, khaki blood smeared everywhere else and a liberal seasoning of CS1 sand. Passing Flivvers were giving me a wide berth and I couldn't blame them. I looked just like the dirty Terran they'd always called me and I didn't smell that great either.

A sea of Flivvers was floating about in the pod bay and those pics, vids and "Look where we are – where are you?"-flashes were going to go on for ever. Trouble was, a new operating equation had started to intrude. Flying person + zero gravity = accident waiting to happen. People were finding that moving around in zero gravity was one thing, but stopping before you hit anything was entirely another. A growing number of injured had already followed Scylla to the Medlab and that wasn't going to stop anytime soon.

I pushed through the throng, all the time keeping a very close eye out for any incoming feathered, guided missiles. What a relief it was to get to the main control cabin, and my whole body sagged as the door clunked shut behind me. Finally, some peace and quiet. Away from all of that nonsense. Of course, the main AI was straight in, hassling me about the whole what, where, when, how, who, but you know what? After the last five hours I just told it to get us out of here as soon as possible.

Of course, an immediate whinge from the Navcom saying that it couldn't just head off anywhere, so I told it to take us to Servcon. I didn't care how, just get us out of visual or indeed any kind of range of the bad guys as soon as possible.

Its best attempt popped straight up in front of me, but I didn't even look. I mean, Servcon, the centre of the known Universe. How difficult could it be? A quick nod and the ship started setting us up to leave orbit, the Navcom adding that we weren't going anywhere near visual range of our friends on the surface even if it didn't exactly use the word 'friends'.

I stretched out my poor aching body in that comfortable chair and enjoyed the silence, even if reflecting that with three hundred Flivvers clogging up the accommodation rings there was no chance of me getting anywhere near a hot bath. However, I knew exactly where there was a hot shower and a clean set of clothes, just for me.

That Engineering rest room was still a complete craphole, but it was my complete craphole, as well as being a totally Flivver-free zone. I was going to stand in that lovely, hot, micro-G shower and let everything go very, very wrinkly, and then I might just stay in there some more.

22
Every journey begins with a single step

After the usual manoeuvring and positioning, the ship was soon curving away from CS1 at standard max bearable acceleration. We had thirty days to minimum jump speed and then it was twenty years ntime to Servcon and who cared about the reltime? There hadn't been a peep from the Aquatics and we'd soon be travelling fast enough that they couldn't do anything anyway.

Our passengers, on the other hand, had plenty to do, spreading themselves all over the ship and playing their brand-new game 'Let's set up our new hive in the accommodation rings.' Soffee was chief caller and the girls were lending their able assistance. Rings 1 and 2 had been allocated as the new hive residence, or hive space, but you've got to remember that Flivver hives are tightly-knit colonies, more flock of birds than hive of bees. Their hive space had to be arranged just so, and trying to move three hundred people into two large metal doughnuts was causing all sorts of problems.

They'd already divided up the previously plain white-walled rings using drapes of cloth, after which they'd attacked the paint stores.

The ship was now alive with happy chitterings, and the smell of drying paint had overlayed the almost over-powering Flivver body scent. Trouble was, you can tell people, you can tell people and you can tell people, but sooner or later they have to find out for themselves. There was only standing room in the Medlab.

As for more general problems? Well, three hundred feathered beings leave an awful lot of mess. The main AI had been pretty relaxed when they'd first come on board, but it was all of those shed feathers. They floated everywhere. They clogged the aircon. They got into everything else. It was just one more thing after another for the auto-repair systems.

Still, auto-repair was there to fix things, so what was it complaining about? What was really starting to get up my nose was the constant flivvering about, 24/7. It never stopped. In the hab they'd always made sure I had my own Franky-space and time, but here on the ship they were everywhere. They'd already made it very clear that both Rings 1 and 2 were now their own space, not mine, and they would have probably taken Ring 3 as well except that Ring 3 was in an even worse state than the Engineering rest room.

So, here I was stuck down in the main body, with just the aforementioned Engineering rest room for sleep and the usual necessaries. Which was not great, especially as this was my ship.

There was also a peculiar dynamic playing out around me, and when I say around me, it was actually between Soffee and the girls. It seemed that everything had been trickling along quite nicely when I'd been far, far away and probably not coming back. However, now that I was back, and both hives were living together on the ship, Soffee and the girls seemed to be testing out how this new arrangement was going to work between me, them and everyone else on board.

Of the three girls, Scylla was definitely the most disruptive, especially with the kudos of having been injured in her protector role. As soon as she was out of the Medlab I was given that ill-advised salute together with a gentle caress from one wing. With Chitichca this had just been friendly, so when Scylla did it I reacted in much the same way. You know, quick smile and nothing more.

Well, it would appear that Chitichca was one thing but Scylla was an entirely different ball of wax, or at least judging by Soffee's reaction. She told the girls in no uncertain terms to stop doing the salute and stay away from Franky. Stay away was the strict translation, but my translator added a whole lot of untranslatable Flivver additionals to her irate chitters. She then followed up with a right mouthful directed at me, and my surprised and spluttered protestations of innocence just raised her eye crests even higher.

She looked me in the eye, paused, then told me in no uncertain terms that Chitichca was one thing, as she was "third sex with no sex" <75% xlate confidence>, but the girls were entirely another.

"Now hold on a minute," I replied, "Flivvers aren't really my bag and we couldn't do anything anyway 'cos we're not even the same species," although this jocular attempt to lessen the tension went down like a lead balloon.

There was a long silence. "You like Flivvers," she muttered eventually. "I sure dirty, moulting, egg-less" <80% xlate confidence> "Scylla try anything once," and stood there for a moment before walking out, leaving me in a sea of confusion.

To be fair, I think that both of us were having an equally hard time getting our heads around what was happening. My three months reltime absence had taken Soffee from a stroppy kid to this equally stroppy, if very capable, adult. Of course, any reltimer is well aware of the whole ntime/reltime changing ages thing, but this was the first time I'd actually known a child, who'd now become an adult, and here she was right in front of me. In Soffee's case, I'd disappeared, she'd fought her way through everything that had happened on CS1 and then, out of the blue, I'd turned back up again. So, difficult for me, but for her? I couldn't even begin to imagine.

Also, I was starting to find that every time she flitted past, almost before she'd left I was looking forward to her next flit. And she was one hell of a flit-er. Keeping a low profile in the main body made my life reasonably trouble free, but she never stopped racing around helping the other hive get fitted into the ship. It was exhausting just watching her.

Anyway, after our little Scylla-contretemps things were a bit awkward, but it soon settled down. Soffee started using the wing stroke down my arm as part of her greeting, but only when other people were watching. She was also working hard on her Terran, and the fact that we were the only people who could speak it without using a translator seemed to make her very happy. The girls settled up in the rings and that also made a difference, although whether they were just getting on with their jobs, or avoiding me, remained to be seen.

I tried mentioning what was happening to Chitichca, but even my best attempt at explanation was met with the sort of look you'd give a small child asking a very simple question.

"Soffee and her friends are just trying to find a way of living with you in your hive," was her only comment.

I must have looked confused, as Chitichca tilted her head to one side before continuing: "I know Terrans do not understand the subtleties of our culture, but I know that you try. Terran communication is so one-dimensional, but I know you have a good heart," which left me even more baffled than before.

OK, so I'm no innocent and could guess what was going on, but with Flivvers? I generally had a big enough problem getting to know Terran females, let alone other species, and with Soffee being the one that was filling my thoughts, well, I could feel my head starting to spin. I mean, three months ago she'd been a child, but now she was an adult. And I know that's just ntime/reltime sticking the boot in, but it still felt wrong, even if it wasn't. If you see what I mean.

I think the real problem underlying all of this was that I'd expected to be on my new ship, with my friends, having a good time, but that wasn't happening and I had no control of what was happening. OK, so both the fight with the bad guys and then the battle to get away from CS1 hadn't exactly been business as usual, but they'd happened and we were here. I'd just assumed that I'd get back to CS1, say hi, some folks would want to come along for a trip and there we'd be.

Instead, three hundred Flivvers had come onboard and taken over the place. They didn't want me anywhere near them, they were doing what they wanted, and it felt like there was a big party going on that I hadn't been invited to. And I was stuck down here in the main body on my own.

At least Soffee's regular flying visits were a ray of sunshine. Every time she appeared I tried to get her to stay longer, but no, she was too busy. I tried calling her up for a chat wherever she happened to be in the ship, but no, she was too busy to talk. I tried suggesting that we organise some time for a drink and a chat but yep, you've guessed it, she was too busy. The best I could get was a quick here and there every time she went past, even if it seemed like she was enjoying the break from those pursuing Flivvers more than talking to me. I did try looking up what the ship had on the whys and wherefores of Flivver social interactions, but that just gave me a headache.

Another morning, another solitary breakfast, another bowl of food unit goop. Halfway through, a random advisory popped up showing Soffee racing from Ring 1 to Ring 2.

"Hi," I called out. "What are you up to? Everyone's ignoring me and I'm bored."

"I go help with creche on Ring 2," she replied.

"Would be nice to see you some time." I said. "If you can find the time."

"Maybe I get down this afternoon. Everyone think I run ship, so I think you have to be extra nice to me," said with a grin that I tried to respond to, but actually, it kicked off all of that annoyance which had been building up.

"Good for you," I said, "but I feel like a guest on my own ship. They don't want me anywhere and I'm stuck down here in that crappy old Engineering rest room."

Her faced changed. "But we allied hives and allied hives share. They very happy to be away from CS1, but Flivver hive not work like

Terrans. They leave their hive space and all very worried about living in your hive space. Also," and she paused, "whole hive still very upset you throw their crèche around. You being Terran just make worse."

"Oh come on," I said, "I didn't throw it around. I got it to the pod before any of the eggs got damaged. I mean, what did they expect me to do? Leave it out there for those Aquatics to find? They should be grateful we got away and stop with the whinging."

She looked at me. "I know is not fair, but no one outside hive can touch crèche. They very shocked Terran touch eggs. They glad you help but very shocked."

"So that's just great then isn't it?" I said. "They took over my hab and now they've taken over my ship and I'm stuck down here. Also, no one gives a shit about what happened to Bob or the suits and semis we left behind. It's just take, take, take and they never stop complaining."

I could feel the steam coming out of my ears. "I mean strewth, they should have stayed down on CS1 if everything here's so crap," and I came to a shuddering stop, my angry face glaring back at her.

"I sorry you not happy," she said after a long pause, "but they leave everything and must have new hive space. I promise I make our hive space as soon as I can. Is OK?"

"D'you know what?" I said. "You do what you want. I'm sick of the lot of them."

She looked back, opened her mouth as if to reply, but closed the comm instead. I sat there furious, but actually now that the anger was seeping away, I knew I'd been a bit of a prat, as well as scuppering any chances I might have had. I couldn't fight how another species worked. Flivver society was Flivver society and they weren't going to change, however much I wished they'd sometimes have a bit more consideration for Franky society.

I sat there twirling my spoon in the remains of breakfast, to be surprised by a double brain tickle as a couple of Smuts appeared. They gave me their thanks for picking them up and, rather surprisingly, made a point of saying that they were glad to see me again.

"Hey, no trouble at all," I thought back. "It's good to have some friends on board."

"We can help you run the ship…anything…just ask. Also, we can talk to the Flivvers for you," even if that made little sense. Look at where talking to the Flivvers had got me so far. Still, at least the first bit was useful. I was way over my radiation limit and someone else taking their share of the rads would ensure I wasn't the only fool here who glowed in the dark.

We had a quick conflab and off they went to have a look around, leaving me to sit there stewing in my own annoyances. And then a thought popped up. This was my ship. The Flivvers couldn't tell me what to do. I could go anywhere I liked, and you know what? I was going to go and do that right now.

I leapt to the nearest elevator and short seconds later walked out into a cloud of Flivvers all busy flivvering around. Their shocked reactions were a picture, but their good manners assured me that I was very welcome even if they obviously wished that I wasn't there. Well, it was my ship and I hadn't come up here just to go straight back down again so I wandered off in a random direction, leaving much perplexed confusion in my wake.

A couple of minutes into my impromptu tour and I was starting to feel that perhaps this hadn't been such a good idea. My presence was creating a storm of tumult, and the politeness with which they greeted me, this uninvited intruder into their hive space, made it all so much worse. I'd just come to the conclusion that maybe I needed to get out of here as soon as possible, when a floor to ceiling drape was yanked aside.

A hive council member was standing there and what could I do but come to a stumbling halt. She opened her arms and bowed before inviting me to a council meeting, with the clear implication that this must be the very reason I was here. Which, as you can imagine, was a complete surprise, but I returned the bow with as good a grace as I could manage and said that I would be delighted to attend. As the words left my mouth, they were closely followed by the thought that I had no idea what was going on, but I'd just have to wing it, as usual.

I followed her into the forest of cloth and was just wondering whether they knew how much it all cost when we brushed through another ruched hanging and out into a large cleared area. The full council was sitting in its customary circle and I was ushered towards a Terran chair that had been placed right beside Chitichca.

Everyone stood up and bowed.

"Franky," said Chitichca, "we sometimes forget how little you understand about us, and for that we apologise." She looked around the rest of the council. "We are forever in your debt and offer our deepest thanks to you and head hive-protector Soffee for getting us away from the planet. We are very sorry that your friend was killed and that you had to leave so many of your mechanical protectors behind. We honour them all," and they must have been feeling particularly guilty, as the thanks just kept on coming.

Eventually I was able to butt in and thank them for their thanks, say that my hive and their hive would forever be joined in friendship, blah, blah, blah, and it all became a bit of an I love you, you love me, fest. We had just started with a second round of nicely traded expressions of mutual admiration when Soffee appeared, taking up her hive protector stance with a particularly expressionless face and a gust of intriguing Flivver scent that I hadn't smelled before.

The mutual expressions of friendship and gratitude continued, but eventually we got down to the real business of the day. It turned out that they were worried about the journey to Servcon, as there wasn't enough Flivver food on the ship. The ship could, of course, generate almost unlimited quantities of microbial/fungal-based multi-species concentrates but the fastidious Flivvers and their discerning palates regarded these as, well, only fit for Terrans and probably dirty ones at that. It was almost funny that while they'd been fine with these on CS1, now that they were on a ship they rather seemed to think that they deserved better.

Beggars can't be choosers was the observation on the tip of my tongue, but I managed to keep that to myself. I now knew we had enough sleep units to put the whole hive to sleep, and that was the obvious solution to their food problem. However, the consternation when I raised this for consideration was extraordinary.

I couldn't understand why they were throwing themselves about over something so simple, but I suddenly realised that some of the council members thought I was suggesting they got into coffins. I was about to add some clarification when Soffee stepped in with a withering glance in my direction. The noise level quickly dropped as she explained what a sleep unit was and that I hadn't been suggesting that we permanently cut the numbers of their hive to fit the available quantities of Flivver food.

Oops!

I was just ducking another of her best you-stupid-man glares when out of nowhere, a bright red IFF alert popped up.

23
Step two

My eyes unfocused as I scanned the details glowing there in front of my left eye. You couldn't make it up if you tried.

"My deepest apologies, but there's something I need to check," I said, nodding a "You've got this," to Soffee before bowing out and racing through the fabric forest down to the main control cabin.

Sure enough, there on the main IFF console was a single red trace, coming straight at us and undoubtedly some new delight courtesy of our oh-so generous Aquatic friends.

"OK," I sighed, "so what's going on this time?"

The IFF stated that something very big, very fast and very nasty had been fired at us from CS1's surface, and in fact much bigger, much faster and much nastier than what we'd used the suit to get rid of. Its light had only just caught up with us and there was another demand to stop or they'd destroy us.

So, same old, same old really, but what I couldn't understand was what they thought they were doing. We were only days away from jump speed, their missile couldn't catch us, so why even bother?

"Have you tried the main armament?" I asked the IFF.

"I fired a full spread but this had no effect. The missile has now separated into two separate projectiles and is manoeuvring to defeat our targeting."

"OK," I said, "so what's our best projection for hitting jump speed against when they'll hit us?"

The IFF's best guess was rather worrying, as these things were a lot closer than I'd first thought. Four days and closing against our five days to jump speed.

"So why didn't we see it?" I asked.

The IFF was almost apologetic when it said that the missile had obviously been stealthed, although where they'd found anything like that on CS1 was a whole new question.

"OK," I tried, "so what if we increase our acceleration to 1.5G?"

Both the IFF and Navcom came straight back that 1.5G would give us a good margin, although they advised that everyone would need to be in sleep units. So, a solution pretty much in line with what I'd already told the Flivvers. No problem, right?

I told the Navcom to start upping our acceleration and then passed the good news to Soffee. She could deal with any Flivver complaints and I'd be staying awake anyway just in case. So, first things first, get into one of our last remaining suits before that extra G kicked in.

Everything was just folding itself around me when Soffee popped up a comm to say that the Flivvers were starting to make their way to the sleep units, even if the chorus of complaint was deafening. I mean, really? We'd pretty much decided they were going to use them anyway so what was the issue? You've just gotta love them Flivvers haven't you.

The first deep-sleep indicators started coming up and it was at this point that a Smut decided to add its own perspective to what was happening. I almost wished it hadn't.

"We recognise those projectiles. They were a project we did for the entities you have been fighting," but the finisher was the best bit. "Each is jump-capable with homing capabilities in both normal and betweenspace."

So, that was just bloody marvellous. They could get us before we jumped, in betweenspace, or out the other side in case they missed the first two opportunities. I didn't even know such things were possible, so many thanks to the Smuts for their unexpected addition to modern weapons technology, which was now aimed right at us.

"But hold on," I said. "If you had FTL capability, why the hell didn't you leave CS1 long ago?"

"We acquired a basic FTL ship that was no longer capable of supporting organics," came straight back. "Our customer provided detailed specifications and the price was excellent. We were not able to fully test it and we certainly never planned on being that test, but we will be very interested in seeing how the projectiles perform."

I sat there digesting this rather breath-taking reply, which if nothing else gave you interesting lessons on how yer average Smut's mind works. In any case, there was nothing we could do but run for the jump, and we'd worry about that whole chasing us through betweenspace and out the other side bit once we'd got there.

A rather odd-looking suit coming into the cabin distracted me from my mental cursing of the Smuts and their ingenuity.

"I come and see what you do," said Soffee, for it was indeed she. "Also," this time directing a thought at the Smuts, "you must go to sleep units now."

They grudgingly agreed, pitching back a final request that I send them all of the data we were collecting on the missiles. Assuming we were still there of course.

"I suppose I'm not going to get you into a sleep unit," I asked. "Whatever have you done to that suit?"

"You having fun in here," she said. "I want to see fun and I never see jump before."

"Yeah well, it isn't a game," I replied. "Those bloody Smuts have built missiles that can chase us in and out of betweenspace and that's a serious problem."

"But Franky," she said. "This is all game for me and girls. Is not fun game, but game we play to keep hives safe. Part of game is suits. Me and girls not like wear them, but we make changes so they fit us and we also not want wires and tubes automatically going in without us say OK. That really disgusting you know."

"Well I didn't make 'em," I replied to her accusing expression, although she was right. Fully integrated suit mount-up inserted things into every bodily orifice where things came out of, in case, well, you know, things had to come out. It wasn't a whole lot of fun and just the thought, let alone the actuality, was bad enough. I only used full integration when I absolutely had to, and for a female it was probably even worse.

Her customised suit had an interesting shape. She'd chosen one of our largest and most heavily armoured suits, which gave plenty of room down each leg for the wings, as well as aligning with the whole hive protector thing. I only hoped she was wearing it fully integrated, as getting out for a bathroom break under 1.5G would be a right pain in the arse, if not everywhere else. She'd now mirrored the face plate and it was a bit worrying not knowing how much trouble I was still in.

Our suits were now transferring themselves to the cabin wall in preparation for the start of standard high G user protection. A sequence of continual forward, backward and sideways rolls would share those 1.5Gs across all orientations of our various body parts as well as ensuring that body fluids stayed where they should. The motion sickness was just an added bonus, even if my visor had now gone opaque to try and help.

The main AI reported that we were now bang on 1.5G acceleration, everyone was in deep-sleep and all was well. There was nothing else to do except wait for the jump point, "or the missiles" was my mental addition.

It has to be said that being stuck in suits didn't exactly help with the atmosphere between Soffee and I, but actually, her attitude wasn't what I'd been expecting. Our conversations started off polite if rather strained, but they gradually loosened up and it was almost like she was the one that was worried, not me. So, maybe I'd got away with being a complete prat? Maybe the shared adversity of being stuck in these suits had sort of flushed out everything we'd said, and that odd meeting with the other hive council as well? Who could tell, but at least both of us being stuck in suits would give me the chance to talk without her continually racing off.

Time passed, the main AI remained confident and the pursuing missiles stayed outside the collision envelope. We both took regular clumps around the ship for a change of scenery, but ultimately all there was to do was lie against the wall, check the ship, check out the onboard entertainment, talk or sleep. There was sometimes just the hint of an odd atmosphere, but it was nice having the time to talk.

Soffee just kept skating around the whole issue of the Flivvers being on board, but I didn't press it. I mean, if she wanted to talk about them she would. If she didn't, she wouldn't. Also, her Flivver view of the world turned out to be quite helpful with some of the things I'd been worrying about. Those sacrifices made by the Alien and Bob for example. They just wouldn't leave me alone, but Soffee's view was both Flivvery and straightforward. There must have been some sort of hive protector thing going on with both of them. They'd done exactly what you'd expect a protector to do, they were heroes and we should honour them.

I was a little surprised when she first said it, but it obviously made perfect sense from her perspective. Maybe it should for mine? I had my ship and we'd got away from CS1 because of what they'd done to help, so maybe this protector thing did make sense? After all, my world was becoming more and more Flivver-like. Them as hive protectors perfectly fitted this mould, and even if I couldn't stop thinking about what they'd done, it did make a lot of sense.

The appearance of the jump countdown timer was a welcome relief from our days in the suits. Apart from anything else, it definitely showed that we'd make the jump before the missiles hit us. Also, I have to admit that all of the various hygiene problems intrinsic with extended suit wear were starting to make their presence felt, and I can only imagine how Soffee must be feeling.

Our time to jump counted down. Hours, then minutes, then seconds and I was just starting to relax when a cacophony of alarms exploded. Fifteen seconds to go.

"Stay here, I've got this," and I raced off the wall and down to Engineering. Through the radiation lock and sure enough, there was the jump field console lit up like a beer ad. Shit, shit, shit! The Navcom and IFF were now adding their noise to the general shrieking, and then Soffee joined in, just to make things less stressful I'm sure.

A quick diagnostics' check and puffs of smoke also helped identify the problem. Out with the old, in with the new, base reset and everything back on line. Greens across the board and the jump field started charging. Only then did the Navcom bother to pipe up that we'd lost only nine minutes, although it didn't say how close those bloody missiles were.

I raced out of Engineering as the stationary fifteen showing on the countdown counter flicked to fourteen and kept on going down. The decreasing seconds pursued me back along to the main control cabin and wham! We jumped.

24
Step three

It's impossible to describe what an actual jump feels like. When you're in, you're in and when you're not, you're not. Some say it's like being turned inside and out again and again, while others say they experience something like a state of bliss. Me? Everything momentarily stands still, a bad hangover appears, disappears and there we are.

My suit slid back into the command chair and everything in front of me said that the jump was good. We were nicely slotted into betweenspace, all apparent acceleration had ceased and everything was in the green.

"It very boring," said Soffee. "Does anything else happen?"

"'Fraid not," I said. "This is about as exciting as it gets."

She seemed disappointed, but pushed over to a suit mount point, dropping out of her suit with a flourish of wings, and floating back.

"Come on then," she said, "out of your suit. If nothing interesting, I show you our new hive space."

"OK by me," I said, my suit floating across to another mount point. "I just wanna make sure we know where those missiles are."

I ejected from the suit and floated back. The IFF was showing nothing, but added that it couldn't necessarily be sure there wasn't anything there until we'd jumped back into normal spacetime. I checked again but the answer came back the same, even if the IFF then added that if we couldn't see the missiles then they probably couldn't see us. Until we both jumped back into normal spacetime. So, even better.

I stared at what was in front of me, but there's only so much you can do. Also, I guess that being stuck in a suit for three days hadn't been as bad for Soffee as it had been for me. Her flowery cloud of Flivver scent was so overpowering that I could hardly concentrate.

A final check of the IFF, but there was still nothing showing so I guess it was wait and see.

"All right," I said, "Let's go."

We floated out of the main control cabin and into the nearest elevator up to Ring 1. Everywhere was still that wall-to-wall Flivver hive aesthetic, but it was rather eerie walking through endless successions of curtains and draperies with no one home. We came to a slightly plainer door, which Soffee opened and walked straight through. Her smiley cry of "Ta dah!" as she spun around with wings and arms spread wide open said it all.

I smiled at my own happily re-played phrase, but this was not the previous unsavoury captain's even more unsavoury mess. The whole place was spotlessly clean with the same Flivver aesthetic we'd been walking through now comprehensively transplanted everywhere. The only non-Flivver thing I could see was a normal table and chairs.

"We try to make hive space better than hab on CS1," she said. "I try to make like Terran space but I guess," and she paused. "I speak to Smuts and I know you not happy living with other hive, but I hope this nice here. Everyone feel better when they have own hive space."

"It's lovely," I said, "but we're right in the middle of the other hive. Won't they hate that?"

She looked disappointed. "But this our own hive space on our own ship. Can you see?"

I looked around but what was I supposed to be looking at? I raised both hands and shoulders in that big unspoken question mark.

"I know they think I'm a dirty Terran, and yes," I said to her sheepish expression, "I'm not stupid. But what am I supposed to be looking at? I just see you and this lovely room," but mentally kicked myself at her continued disappointment.

"Look, don't be sad," I said. "It's lovely, much better than anything I've had since Old-Earth." I looked around again. "Did any of my stuff get up from CS1?"

"Of course," she said, pointing proudly at a pile of bags and boxes. "I bring your stuff from secret store and I also bring mine. Your stuff not nice and need washing before you wear," smiling as she mimed holding her nose.

"What? You kept everything safe while I was away?"

Soffee's "Of course" expression looked like she couldn't understand why I was even asking the question.

"I specially save plant you give me," she said, pointing over to where it sat in a place of honour. "We also have bathroom just for us," pointing to a small door in one corner. "Just like hab."

"Blimey," I said half-jokingly, "I hope not."

She paused. "I know you find everyone being on ship difficult, but I also find it hard to know how Terrans work. You very different to Flivvers."

I sighed.

"Look, I like Flivvers, I really do, but I also find it hard. I mean, it drives me crazy. Why do they do things? What's good and what's bad? Do they like me? Are they only tolerating me 'cos they need a lift away from CS1."

She was looking at me as if she couldn't believe what I was saying, but her face slowly changed.

"But they thank you for saving them," she said. "Everyone thank you all time since they come up from planet."

"But how?" I said. "If it's that scent thing, I can only smell the general Flivver smell that gets everywhere."

She looked at me with a rather odd expression on her face.

"OK, I try explain. We not speak like Terrans. We use smells to say many things and we always know if truth as person cannot fake smells body make. Whole hive say many thanks and are very happy to be here. This is what you smell in ship. We use smell to say many things," and she paused, looking at me, waiting.

"But Terrans only speak using words," I said into the pregnant silence. "To me, they're just smells, even if you do smell lovely," and of course, the clogged up mental cogs finally started creaking round.

"So... is...that...you know...?" I started, but thought better of it before trying again. "So this smell in the ship is the hive saying thanks?"

"But of course," she said, rather exasperated. "That why I say you smell horrid in hab. We not understand what your smells mean and some very nasty."

"Yeah, sorry about that," I said with a smile. "Terrans do smell but it doesn't mean anything. Well, apart from maybe they need a shower," which got a smile back. "But you can see my problem? If I can't smell these smells then how do I know what's going on? Also, what's with that wing-stroking thing?"

"Oh, that very different," she said. "Is friendly, but can be more, depending on how person do it. Smell also involved. I know is difficult for you but is difficult for me. I try hard to understand how Terrans see each other, but I still guess."

"Oh, don't worry," I said, "we're very simple. If one Terran likes another, they give them a lot of attention and try to be as nice as possible to them. If the other person likes it then they do the same back. Quite simple, although probably not as reliable as the Flivver way of doing things."

She looked at me, before dropping an "Oh..." into the silence. "So...you...?"

"Yep," I said, "that's poor old me doing my clumsy best to say I like you. Obviously must try harder."

"I think you did," she said, a blush rising to her cheeks, or at least as far as you can say that when someone's face is covered in feathers.

"OK then, good" I stumbled on, my stomach clenching with embarrassment, "so that's OK then." She was looking at me, a smile creasing her lips as my cheeks reddened. "Look, you mentioned we've got a bathroom," I continued, grabbing at anything to fill that dreadful hair-prickling silence. "I need a shower, and I'm starving. Do you want anything to eat?"

"Is OK. You choose," and she knelt to start digging stuff out of her bags, almost but not quite ignoring me. I really wasn't very good at this Terran/Flivver boy/girl stuff was I?

I left her to it and went into the bathroom, leaning back on the closed door as I let out a sigh. She really was very lovely, and I was a complete idiot.

In front of me was a beautiful, sparkling-clean, full 360 shower, with hopefully all traces of its previous owner removed. I got undressed, stepped inside and the steamy deluge engulfed me. The simple pleasures are always the best and this shower was definitely the next best thing to that bath I'd been promising myself ever since we left CS1.

I disappeared into the endless, hot water luxury, but you know how it is. Eventually your fingertips, and probably other bits as well, start getting wrinkly. I turned off the water, flapped my way out of the clouds of steam and started getting into some clean clothes. Soffee was still deep-diving into a steadily growing pile of stuff, so I left her to it and went outside to find a food unit.

The nearest was only several dangling blankets away, and judging by its pristine condition our passengers' discerning palates had treated it with complete disdain. I asked for two Terran roast dinners plus a couple of Terran beers, then stood back to contemplate the acres of brightly covered fabric all around. A double ping announced the arrival of din-dins and I just about managed to grab it all with both hands, juggling my way back into Soffee's new hive. Judging by the splashing water and clouds of steam she was in the shower.

I took off the food covers and hoh yes indeedy, we had delicious portions of Terran roast dinner. Brown lumpy goo, orange lumpy goo, green lumpy goo and yes, you've guessed it, white lumpy goo. In fact, whatever the Flivvers might think, this ship's food units were pretty good, and the first slurp of beer always numbed the taste buds. The shower flicked off and to my surprise, out walked Soffee, drying herself with a towel. She stood by her lake of stuff, wings partly open and damp feathers clinging to her body. I didn't know whether she did this at home, but I couldn't take my eyes off her.

She had that odd mixture of Terran and Flivver features I've mentioned before. The wings plus massive musculature round her chest and shoulders were front and centre, but she was missing the Flivvers' pronounced frontal keel bone and their tail. Everything else flowed nicely down to her clawed toes, and all encased in a tantalisingly obscuring, but not too obscuring, layer of blue feathers that started light at the wings tips before darkening into her body. Also, now that she'd had time to attack the bathroom, I could see the obvious adult Flivver female feather crest and a line of darker feathers outlining each pointed ear lying flush along the side of her head. Topping it all off were those large, slightly slanted, deepest black oval eyes. In front of me was a mixture of the standard characteristics of a mature adult female Flivver and a mature adult female Terran, all put together in an absolutely entrancing combination.

She'd been in my thoughts ever since we'd got onto the ship, but now being here, with her, and that shower? The stroppy kid transplanted into my hab by the Flivvers was now anything but, and this whole situation was flying right outside of my experience. Here I was in the middle of a Terran boy/Terran-Flivver girl ntime/reltime thing, she didn't understand me and I didn't understand her. It wasn't so much scream if you want to go faster, but first wear this blindfold, then use a language you don't understand, and then scream if you want to go faster. And maybe she wouldn't understand anyway.

Still, I couldn't really complain as I sat there watching the most gorgeous woman I'd ever seen dry herself off and preen those feathers back into place. A quick glance in my direction and judging by the slight smirk that caressed her lips, she knew, that I knew, that she knew, that she'd seen me looking, and she didn't seem to mind. I mean c'mon, no one walks out of a bathroom with nothing on - OK, I know she's covered in feathers, but you know what I mean - unless they want to be seen and are fairly confident of the effect it's going to have.

I watched entranced as she slipped an odd-shaped shift over her head and it shimmied down over those feathered wings and arms. She came across to the table and closely inspected the food unit's best efforts, before picking up a spoon and trying a mouthful. A raised eye crest plus momentary pause said it all, but she took another spoonful, so it looked like I'd got away with it.

I raised my drink and she watched, before picking up hers. "Cheers," I said, "here's looking at you."

She took a sip but gagged and coughed. "What is this? Is disgusting."

"Oh yeah, I forgot, sorry. Food unit beer's a bit of an acquired taste."

"How you drink this?" she said. "Is really horrible, but thank you," placing it firmly back down on my side of the table.

We finished our meals pretty much in silence, and I was starting to feel a little bit nervous about what would happen next. I mean, she was leading, but I didn't want to do anything she might not like. A quick glance around didn't give me any help, so I made my way across to an inviting slew of cushions up against the wall. Soffee followed, and before I could say anything she flopped down and snuggled up, which was a nice surprise for me and quite a feat for her with those massive wings getting in the way.

"You know I really miss you when you go away," she said, her beautiful Flivver scent overwhelming me. "Everyone say you not come back, but I sure you come back, even if I have to wait nine years."

"But they all wished I wasn't there,' I said. "I'm surprised you even noticed I'd gone."

"Flivver hive doesn't count," she said. "They not want me in hive anyway. No one except mother nice to me and she not count either.

You first person on CS1 who nice to me, ever, and talking Terran make me feel like real person.

"I sorry I let Terrans in suits take you," she said after a pause. "I try protect you but they go too quick and I very sorry," and she snuggled up a bit closer. "Apart from girls, there no one I like in other hive and I miss you when you go. Now you come back and we same age, with new hive to live in."

"Yeah, and look at you,' I said, rather stunned by the pace of what was happening as well as being completely smothered by her continuing fragrant and feathery encroachment. "You've joined an elite group. Reltimers travel the galaxy and live for hundreds of years ntime. I mean, look at me. I've been around over five hundred years and I haven't really seen anything."

"But you had whole galaxy and you come back for me," she said snuggling even closer. "I know you would," and with that she lifted her head up and kissed me.

My heart leapt, my head exploded, and I could do nothing else but return that lovely kiss, wrapped in wings and feathers, engulfed in a world of just me and this lovely blue lady.

What went on for the next forty-five minutes is, as they say, history as well as being no business of yours, although I will say that those feathers get everywhere.

I was floating on my own little cloud under the dimmed cabin lights, stunned and enthralled by what had just happened. This wasn't the first time I'd met someone I really liked, and it also wasn't the first time they'd been from another species. Of course, most inter-species relationships are just that trying-it-on-for-a-laugh sort of thing and I'd certainly been hung out to dry once or twice. This just seemed so different and I couldn't believe how insanely happy I was.

Soffee stretched, her wings staying wrapped tightly around me. Two black, oval eyes opened, focused and I fell straight into their bottomless depths.

"Hello," she said. "Do we do it right?" giving me a peck on the lips before letting out a chuckle. "I have hive, I have hive chief and now I really have hive-chief," and she gave me a squeeze. "I think you lovely man even if you very strange," and she gave another chuckle. "Main AI say Terran male is called man and I looking forward to hive with my lovely man. But I not share you with anyone. Don't smile, is serious. Flivvers work different to Terrans and girls maybe want you as partner."

"But that's not fair," my protest a mere whisper into her ear. "I only have eyes for you, my lovely lady."

Soffee pulled back to give me a good look before snuggling back in again with a sub-vocal "Hmmph..."

After a while she said: "Now we have hive sorted, we must decide where we go in your ship. I know we go to Servcon, but hive cannot live there."

"But surely there's two hives," I said. "Not just one?"

She sighed and pulled away to look me in the eye.

"OK," she said, "I try explain again. You come back for me. Also, you rescue hive so they think you come for them too. This change you from dirty Terran into featherless, wingless, wrong-coloured person who maybe they trust. So, we have choices. We stay two hives is one choice. We link our hive with other hive is other choice. You not see but you sometimes act like Flivver hive head," and sniggering, she prodded me in the ribs. "I know is accident but they maybe accept you as head of both hives."

"Oh come on," I said, "there's no way that's gonna happen and anyway I don't want it. Not knowing I was head of one hive was bad enough."

She smiled: "Your hive have me and both hives scared of me. I control protectors and you have full seat at council. Mother being head of other hive help, but we still have to decide."

This was starting to sound more and more like an ongoing extension of the hab invasion. I certainly didn't want anything to get in the way of being so happy with Soffee.

"You know what I think?" I said, "This is all part of that conniving Chitichca's master plan. I'll bet you're in it right up to your neck."

Soffee opened her eyes wide and tried to look innocent. "That not fair," she said. "When I meet you, you very scruffy and I say dirty Terran engineer who shouldn't be on planet. How will anyone know you find a ship and come back to CS1? Everyone very happy you help and I also very happy you come back." A masterful swerve and totally avoided answering anything I'd just said.

"I must ask," she said, obviously trying to change the subject. "Why you call my step-mother Chitichca?"

"Oh that's very simple," I said. "When we first met, I asked what her name was but instead she told me her position in the hive. My translator translated this very badly as something sounding like 'Chitichca.' So, all of these years I've been calling her a very bad translation of 'Senior council member'."

Soffee laughed "Is what I thought. She very surprised when you call her that but she know how important sound names are to Terrans. She happy you give her name and she also flattered. Senior Flivver give person name when they invite this person to join hive. So, you accidentally give her big compliment. I think I tell her to call you scruffy, dirty Terran engineer and not Franky," adding another jab in the ribs.

I jabbed her back and this all turned into a very enjoyable wrestling match for the next couple of minutes.

'Look,' I said, after I'd been well and truly sat upon. "You two have your plans and I don't mind a bit, but you must tell me what's going on. You say they're my friends but everyone's always manoeuvring around me, and friends don't manoeuvre friends."

She stared into my eyes before laying her head back on my chest. "You are good, kind, man," she said. "I grow up like Flivver but I also think like Terran. I like you very much and I want permanent pair bond with nice man, and you are nice man," which was a very nice way of describing something and I liked it a lot.

"I promise I help make things better," she whispered into my chest. "Also, I try tell you before things happen, but try and do not always same thing," and she let out a squeak as I grabbed up a cushion to smother her giggles.

25
Step four

The fearsomely complex physics controlling how ships travel in, out and more generally shake it all about, in betweenspace was one of the many things I'd forgotten as soon as I'd learned it. In any case, the AIs had it under control and that left Soffee and I with nothing better to do than catch up with that nine years ntime we'd been out of each other's lives.

When we weren't wasting too much time on each other, Soffee kept cracking on with her Terran. Not being fluent really seemed to bug her, although I did find the way she'd drop in a Flivver word or phrase to substitute a missing Terran equivalent very endearing. She'd also turned into a lady on a mission to learn everything about me, but what could I say? I mean, I was Terran, sneaked my way off Old-Earth twelve reltime years ago, flown around the known bits of the galaxy as a space engineer, got dumped on CS1 five years ago and that was it. Pretty simple. No secrets worth keeping.

However, trying to get her to return the favour was a big mistake. She totally clammed up. Absolutely nothing. Complete silence. Didn't even want to look at me and then she walked out. Mental note to self to not do that again.

One thing that was less of an issue was me managing to lever her away from those verbs, tenses and vocab so she could go and see the Medlab. I'd gone there when I'd first come on board and the AI had been very surprised I was still alive. CS1 was a mincing machine for any organic entity and what it had done in those five years wasn't pretty. Soffee had lived there for most of her life. I was really crossing my fingers and toes.

The Medlab AI was initially surprised, and then very excited, about this new person who'd just laid down in front of it. A full set of scans, samples, and Soffee telling it to stop doing that, and that, but everything seemed to be working just as required.

"In fact, for someone who has been on CS1 for as long as she has, she is unnaturally well," was its comment, cooking up a special set of nanos and inserting them while Soffee wasn't looking. Apparently her full physiological spec showed a very odd mixture of highly conserved Flivver and Terran genetics but I immediately quashed any ideas about further investigations. She didn't need any more reminders about how different she was.

The next day started with an auto-repair AI doing the equivalent of shoulders raised, hands up and "I haven't the foggiest - whatcha reckon?" plus appropriate red lights on the console. Hours of faffing about later we finally got it sorted, and with my day pretty much done I thought I'd mosey back to the cabin, sorry hive. In I walked to be greeted by Soffee standing in front of a full-length mirror, looking at herself from all angles and obviously rather upset.

"When you look at me, what you see?" was the greeting as I walked in.

Without thinking too hard I replied: "I see the lovely lady I found on CS1 and who's the most important person in my life."

"But Franky, I not Terran and I not Flivver so what am I? Why I have these wings? I cannot fly and they get in way always."

"But you can fly," I said. "That thing you did in the CS1 hive was pretty damned impressive."

"But is not flying," she insisted. "I just fall then open wings as brakes. Is all show to make me big and powerful as possible."

Saying that seemed to cause her even more pain.

"Hey," I said, slipping my arms around her, "what's this all about? You're the loveliest person I've ever met and everyone's scared of you. Why would you want to be any different?"

"But I ask main AI," she said, shrugging me off. "Apart from sisters, I think I only person in whole galaxy who look like this."

She stood away, opening her arms and wings as she looked at herself in the mirror again.

Sisters plural eh? Very interesting, but probably not the best time to ask about that.

"But why would you want to look like anyone else?" I said. "It's a big galaxy, full of all sorts of people and they're all different."

"But Franky," she said even more insistently, "you standard Terran and you had family. All Flivvers have families. I was made in laboratory and where did cells come from? Maybe not even from person. I not Flivver, I not Terran, and I maybe not anything. Also, you not see people on CS1. After you leave, some Terrans get friendly with me. I like this until I hear one of them betting his friend he would be first to have sex with me. They laugh and slap hands together, holding money. They make bet because I so different and they think is funny. What does that make me?"

"But that's terrible," I said, completely shocked. "Who the hell was that?" but she was too upset to answer.

I tried again. "Look, scumbags are scumbags. I mean, whatcha gonna do about a scumbag? Yeah, nothing. And sure, I've got a family, but the last time I saw them was on Old-Earth five hundred ntime years ago. I'm centuries away from their timeline, and as for relatives? Who knows? At least you've got your sisters. All I've got is me."

"But you had family and you Terran from Old-Earth. My sisters and me just grown in laboratory. Where cells come from? Who make us? I think we just things and no one want us unless we do things for them."

"But I want you," I said, grabbing her hands. "Your hive wants you. I mean c'mon, you've made yourself a hive and you're a great and powerful hive protector. And you've got me," kissing the feathery tip of her nose, "who came all the way back just for you."

She eased into my arms but was stiff, all sharp points. Those people who made hybrids can't have any idea of the pain, grief and anguish they stack up in the entities they create, or maybe they just don't care? One hell of a legacy, but there we were. A quick hug and a kiss wasn't going to solve this one regardless of how much I wished it would, but what could I do?

Over the next couple of days, more worries appeared, and it was almost like the mirror episode had jemmied open long-locked mental doors to let all of the agonies confined within come cascading out. The more I listened, the more I realised how awful it had been for her on CS1, especially with the Flivvers. I mean, someone had dumped her there then disappeared. Chitichca had looked after her, but the hive had never wanted her. As soon as my hab came up, they'd moved her straight into there, and then the ultimate backhanded compliment. Please come and save us from the chaos. Just don't stick around after you've done it.

I'd never realised. Maybe I'm lucky because I've always known I'm pretty good, regardless of what any other self-important species may think. I mean, if they're so bloody advanced, why do they need me to fix their stuff? I've always been very happy just being me, but with Soffee it was oh so very different.

She'd only ever known CS1 and that was nowhere to find your place in the world. Being on this ship just made things worse. How would she cope under the bright lights of this new, wider, harsher world? Why was she here if no one wanted her? Was there any place anywhere she could call home? Truly adrift in a raging sea of uncertainty.

To try and cheer her up, in an idle moment I told her about Dougie's Treasure planet story, even if I did warn her that this was exactly what it was, a story, told by Dougie, after too many beers. She didn't even hear that last bit. The idea of a deserted planet seemed to strike a chord within her deepest being.

According to Flivver lore and legend there was a planet out there just like the one in Dougie's story. And guess what? It was ready and waiting for any Flivver hive that might need somewhere to live. Soffee had been longing for somewhere to call home her entire life, and here it was.

Now of course, every species had its own magical stories that answer the same basic needs and here was the Flivver version. Amazing really, but there you are, or rather, here we were.

I'd already done a fair amount of delving into the ship's innards, but what with one thing and another I'd had a lot of other things to worry about. I did warn Soffee that she wouldn't and couldn't find something that didn't exist, but that look of dogged determination said that I was wasting my time. I asked the ship for systems that matched Dougie's story and stretched back to wait for the expected nothing to be found.

A brief pause and my eyes nearly fell out of their sockets. I knew this ship was old but wow! What came back was its full four hundred years of ntime travel plus other stuff that went a lot wider. The main AI was very mysterious about why all of these details had been hidden away, but I could probably guess and I didn't care. This was a comprehensive log of our galactic civilisation's space travel and the ship had travelled, or knew about, everywhere. Well OK, not everywhere, but well outside anywhere I'd ever been.

More and more of these amazing details kept scrolling up in front of us, but Soffee was only interested in anything that looked like Dougie's Treasure planet. My eyes had only just popped back in again after the first lot of information, but sure enough, up came a system on the other side of the galaxy. High tech, sentients, Goldilocks zone tags, and out they fell yet again.

Soffee's triumphant face plus even bigger smile missed or ignored the advisory that this information was not backed up by any firm data. I did try asking her why, if this place was so good, no one had ever gone back to get some more details? She just repeated that Dougie's story matched the Flivver legend, and if the ship couldn't confirm the details then this just confirmed the planet's existence. If the details had been confirmed, the whole place would be colonised and so wouldn't be waiting for a Flivver hive. Circular argument well and truly proved.

She then pointed out that the most recent details were from a ship that had come back to Servcon with severe damage to its power grid, and that's where more of Dougie's story kicked in. Servcon also noted that two beings had left the ship, one a Terran and one some other species, which was an additional detail that Dougie certainly hadn't mentioned. So, the Terran was probably Dougie, but if this second person was a stowaway then maybe the planet wasn't so deserted after all.

Soffee just shooshed this all away. It was obvious that having found a potential treasure planet, the whole idea went right to the ache in the depths of her soul. I'd travelled enough to not really care either way, but if she was happy then so was I.

In any case, it was about time I did some of the heavy lifting and how better to do that than find her this new home. We still had the slight problem that these details might yet dissolve into the morning mist, but I'd get the main AI to try and confirm them when we got to Servcon. After all, if Servcon didn't know, then nobody did.

26
Servcon – my kinda place

Our month's journey through betweenspace really flew by, especially as it was just Soffee and me and plenty of time to enjoy that. The discovery of Dougie's Treasure planet had really seemed to ease Soffee's fears and the thought of having somewhere to live was now her sole guiding star. I only hoped that Servcon could provide us with some real, concrete, info, otherwise we'd be making that 50k light jump pretty much on a nod, a wink and a funny handshake.

Into all of this, the Navcom's warning that we were about to jump back into normal spacetime was a bit of a nasty surprise. Those weeks had been the most relaxation I'd ever had, but it was time to start getting ourselves ready for normal spacetime and whatever might be waiting for us when we got there.

Down went the jump counter and out we popped. The IFF kept its closest eyes out but despite the usual string of warnings and worries, it couldn't see anything and neither could I. We'd come out into the same old deep, dark, blackness of space and there was nothing to see for millions of klicks.

A standard day's-worth of worrying later and it was obvious that if those missiles had been following us, they weren't doing so now.

As to why that might be? Well, who knew. The Smuts had said they hadn't been able to test those marvellous new capabilities they'd designed, and anyway, betweenspace was betweenspace. Anything could have happened and probably still could. It was probably just easier to assume that those Smuts hadn't been as good as they thought they were, and we'd see what happened if anything did. Or not.

Up to this point, Soffee and I had been enduring the post-jump deceleration in our suits, as she'd wanted to see what happened when we came out of the jump. More fool her I might have been brave enough to say, but we did leave the waking up of the girls, the Smuts and a selection of the Flivver contingent until we'd slowed down to approach speed. Servcon was growing out of the star-spangled blackness and I tipped the ship's main AI the wink. It was wakey, wakey time and the best of luck to them all.

The Central Servicing and Control centre, otherwise known as Servcon or its alien equivalents, started off as a Duje mega-satellite/relay station when they were the only sentient species flying FTL. Early explorations led to first contact with several non-FTL sentient species and being as how the Duje were caring, sharing sorts of guys and gals, they gave away their FTL interstellar tech to anyone who asked.

Thereafter, and almost by accident, Servcon found itself in the loose centre of a growing intergalactic collective, floating in deep space halfway out from the galactic core. It was pretty much the city of gold for any wannabe space farer and, with Old-Earth going to hell in a hand basket, exactly where I'd wanted to be. How I managed to get there is a long story for a longer evening and an even better bottle, but I won't bore you with that. Let's just say that once I got there it was my base for the next five hundred years ntime, culminating in my, ahem, slight embarrassment when those bloody Shonats left me on CS1.

The original Duje relay station was now absorbed into an ever-growing artificial rocky planetoid that was honeycombed with living spaces for all of the sentient species that made Servcon, well, Servcon. A complex inter-species management and security structure purported to run the place, although as you might expect, the real power lay with ever-changing groups of a decidedly criminal persuasion. Still, commerce is commerce and as long as you didn't interrupt the flow of money you could pretty much do what you wanted, as long as you made sure that the right people continued to get their percentage.

CS1 had pretty much cleaned us out of a whole lot of essentials and I also needed a skilled pair of eyes to check some things on the ship that didn't look quite right. In addition, five decades away from civilisation had made some proper R&R pretty much top of my list. Servcon specialised in providing anything any sentient species could possibly want and I'd already found out that my lovely new ship had a seriously large credits balance, all nicely up to date and inflation-proof as per galactic ntime/reltime standards. This was going to be my best trip ever.

We were greeted by the landing grid AI requesting full ID, why we were here, any special requirements we might have and after a polite pause, informing us of the landing and processing fees. I passed over our details and, as the ship's new owner, was immediately upgraded to an enhanced level of service, which I equally immediately declined as it more than doubled the price.

Eventually, after a lot more to-ing and fro-ing the Navcom was passed a track to our allocated docking bay. We weaved our way in through the patchwork of ships from every epoch and species, and I could see that we'd already been flagged up as the new guy in town. A large figurative target was pasted all over us and people were starting to circle, ears pricked and licking their collective lips. We'd need to keep our wits about us and no mistake.

Most of our newly wakened passengers had now managed to get themselves down to the main control cabin, standing reasonably bright-eyed and bushy-tailed with every faculty giving our approach their fullest attention. The Smuts were pretty much "Whatever, it's Servcon," but most of the Flivvers had only ever seen CS1 and their reactions were a collection of stunned surprise. My to-do list was primed and waiting, but before I let anyone out they needed full instructions on the Servcon shark-tank and how to survive it. Servcon was, after all, Servcon.

"OK," I said to the circle of eager faces, "I need you to listen up because this is really important. We're now at Servcon, which is an artificial planetoid filled with every known sentient species. Think of it as a larger and more dangerous CS1 market and you won't go far wrong. Everyone'll be out to get you, so don't look like a tourist and don't flash the cash. Always make sure you know how to get back here and if you don't know what's going on, call me."

I could see trepidation replacing the initially unrestrained excitement but that was a good thing. Servcon was, after all, Servcon.

I thought for a moment. "Oh yeah, and don't take any weapons. You'll get immobilised, and the ship'll be fined. Anyway, have a good time and be careful."

Excited conversations started as I turned back to the console. Jobs, jobs, jobs to be done before I had any fun and games. People started to wander off and I did wonder what cunning plans were being hatched behind my back. Well, best of luck to them as it was time for me to dive into the murky depths of Servcon commerce. A deep breath and I started right at the top of my list.

Servcon commercial negotiations are a full contact sport and in I went, every transaction a comprehensive shouting match. They couldn't possibly provide what I wanted at that price. Where had I been, expecting such low prices and immediate delivery. This was civilisation not some primitive planet, etc, etc, etc. Of course, as soon as we'd agreed the deal, immediate expressions of deepest appreciation, please don't hesitate to come back, they would deliver everything immediately. Just as soon as I'd paid in full.

It was a long and weary journey across the slippery slopes of Servcon retail to the paid and delivered high ground on the other side. Hours later I just about made it, slumping back in my chair absolutely exhausted. Gimme strength, it didn't get any easier. Still, everything would be delivered in the next couple of hours and finally, it was time to go out and have some fun.

I turned from the console to find Soffee waiting there at my elbow. She'd changed into a rather fetching pair of dungarees in blue and yellow, with matching lightweight combat boots and her two pins securely attached to a dungaree strap. I don't think I'd ever seen her wear anything other than variations on your basic dungarees, but wide shoulders and large wings meant that little else fitted. Finishing off the whole ensemble was what I think used to be called an Alice band, highly polished metal, very retro. She didn't have a bag but then what did I know about the dressing habits of a well-dressed female Terran/Flivver?

She stepped forward. "While you keep us safe, I also busy," she said. "Long time ago you give me two hive pins and I make you this."

She opened her delicately feathered, clawed hand to reveal a silver ring, decorated with the intertwined motifs of her two pins in blue and yellow.

"Is made with silver I bring from CS1. Silver is mine and now I give to you."

Wow - no one had ever given me such a nice present. In fact, no one had ever given me a present, full stop. Soffee was standing there almost holding her breath, rather tense for some reason. A bit odd, but I was still somewhat lost for words. I tried the ring on and Soffee breathed out, a massive grin splitting her face. After trying a few more fingers we found that it fitted perfectly on the third finger of my left hand. It looked pretty good. Nice and chunky, a perfect match for her pins.

"It's really nice," I said. "No one's ever given me anything like this before," and as she was looking particularly lovely I gave her a hug and a kiss. Good old Mr Perceptive could tell there was something else going on, but what did I know about anything? A perfect end to a hard morning's work.

We needed to explore that kiss a little further, but eventually I surfaced. "So what do you wanna do?" I said. "I've got to talk to an engineer about something on the ship but apart from that, Servcon's your oyster."

I'm not sure she understood the world is your oyster-reference, but she was getting used to my collection of arcane expressions.

"You know anyone here? I want to meet someone who look in my eye and smile when they tell me I make big, bad mistake with you."

"Oooh, harsh," I said. "There may be a few of my old reltimer friends, but any ntimers'll be long gone. In fact, this whole place has changed so much it'll be a bit of a voyage of discovery for me."

"OK," she said, "in that case I think I just see what make Servcon, Servcon."

I gathered her into my arms and, as she was looking particularly sweet, gave her a quick peck on the end of her nose.

"Your wish is my command lovely lady," I said. "Just give me two minutes and I'm all yours."

I returned as quickly as I could, noticing Soffee's glance to make sure I was still wearing her ring. We got into a pod and flicked across to the nearest air-breathing airlock complex, the 'Secure' ticker popping up to confirm that the ship was secured against any sort of intrusion. I didn't trust Servcon any further than I could throw it and everyone better have their IDs with them or they'd be waiting in line until I got back.

Out of the pod and down a wide tunnel, that expanded into the boisterous bustle of the main air-breather Servcon habitat. It was an enormous space, brightly lit and far larger than I remembered, crammed with buildings, walkways, stalls and people. Shops, clubs, bars and anywhere else that might provide you with fun and games detected two new customers and flooded us with ads, recommendations and money-offs, our HUDs frantically turning down the volume to stop us drowning in drack. Multitudes of different air-breathing species milled about and the air was alive with chatter, noise and general hubbub.

Soffee's eyes were wide-open black discs and her hand clenched tightly around mine. Of course, I was doing my best to look like the cool dude who'd seen it all before, but I couldn't help smiling. Servcon really was my kinda town. Every being walking past seemed to have been surgically improved to within an inch of its credit balance and as for the clothes? They were obviously the height of fashion, but to my untutored eyes, everything bordered on the utterly bizarre.

Trouble was, we both rather stood out in this sea of tweaked perfection. Me, I was just my usual rather scruffy, lived-in, self, but Soffee? There wasn't a single person who looked anything like her and even amongst the oddities walking past, she was almost floodlit. Surreptitious pics, vids and live feeds were being posted, broadcast and tagged by everyone going past and the whole of Servcon would soon know that someone very different had arrived.

We kept on with our casual wandering, just taking in the sights and doing our best to ignore the constant attention when there was a tap on my shoulder. This turned into an over-friendly pawing down one arm and I turned, to be greeted by that all too well remembered shit-eating smile.

Yep, you've guessed it. That complete tool Dougie. Last seen thirty-five ntime years ago in El Shitto but now very much here and looking sharp as a razor in a brand-new black suit. The change from greasy barfly to this new persona was as amazing as it was really bad to see, but then he always came up smelling of roses.

"Franky, as I live and breathe" he said, still clasping my hand, "and Soffee," who was wearing a shocked and almost horrified expression. "So you both made it off CS1. Isn't that great? Best friends reunited."

"How in hell you get here?" said Soffee straight back, annoyance replacing her initial shock. "Last time I see you, Minos chasing you for money they want back. How you get here instead of broken bits all over rocks?"

Dougie took a step back, raising his arms in mock horror as that smile spread even wider.

"Woah, hold on," he said, "let's let bygones be bygones, surely. I could ask you how you got here and where you found that lovely big ring-ship everyone's talking about. You, my good friends are a marked man and woman, but come on," raising an index finger to tap the side of his nose in that oh so well remembered gesture. "I won't tell if you won't."

Soffee took a step forward. "I not trust you and Franky not trust you," she said. "Go away before I tell him what I promise I do next time I see you."

Dougie blenched and swallowed, his smile crumbling. "Woah there," he said. "No harm done. I was just saying hello but you're obviously busy. I'll leave you in peace," and with that he slithered off into the crowds, disappearing like a puff of smoke in the wind.

27
Servcon – maybe not my kinda place

I blinked, looked at Soffee then back to where Dougie had just disappeared into the throng. Talk about bad dreams coming back to haunt you.

"What the hell was that?" I asked.

"Him complete bastard who bet on me," she said. "He try rob us during chaos and I nearly shoot him. Only very bad people hire person like that. Still," she continued with a growing grin, "he have at least 30 years extra on us, so he go boil his head in bucket of sand-crab sick."

"Wherever did you learn such an awful expression?" her answering smirk saying exactly where. "Anyway, maybe we should give him a break. You do meet the most interesting people on Servcon." Soffee's expression said exactly what she thought about that.

I felt for her hand and we started walking again, but Dougie appearing right in front of our faces had been more of a shock than I'd realised. Still, that was Servcon, part cornucopia, part Pandora's box, and I had really missed it. I was about to say something similar to Soffee, but her worried expression brought me to a stop.

"What's wrong? You look like you've seen a ghost."

"Is not right," she said. "Everyone staring and three people following," and of course, what do you do when someone says that? Yep, you look around. Anyone even remotely suspicious immediately becomes part of the scenery and indeed, all I could see were milling crowds. I turned back to Soffee and her worried expression had been replaced by an exasperated sigh with eyes raised skywards.

"Yeah OK, sorry," I said. "I'm an idiot."

"Can we just find some place where people not staring?" she said.

"You're imagining it," I replied. "It's just Servcon being Servcon."

"Don't be silly. I only person who look like me and my wings big blue flags." She gave them a shake which was answered by a metallic rattle behind her back.

"Yeah, I s'pose," I said after another look around. "Look, I was gonna get you a welcome to Servcon present. Anything you like. Just for you. We'd also be out of sight in the shop, if that works."

"OK...." But her eyes never stopped their unceasing movement. "I think I look big mess. Maybe some nice clothes like people wearing?"

"But you look great," I replied, that immediate response which equally immediately earns a well-deserved withering look straight back, with bells on.

And of course, as soon as every bottomless credit-pit in the area had parsed out "...present" and 'Anything...' the hosepipe of drack changed to ads guaranteeing anything a female of any species might desire. Bit of a lottery really, so Soffee picked the nearest high-end clothes store and off we went, following the directions towards an ominously very plain and unassuming shop frontage.

"I wouldn't want to go anywhere they'd let me in" was the phrase that crossed my mind, and the full remote body scans we received only emphasised that. Waiting for us was a heavily armoured, if immaculately coutured, Grunt doorman and the whole Old-Earth Rhinoceros the size of a brick shithouse-thing told you everything you needed to know about the spending power of their clientele. Or at least it told you what the owners wanted you to think.

Without a word he swung the door open and followed us into the wall-to-wall marbled haute couture shark tank, standing guard as the door closed with a solid clunk. Out of nowhere an equally immaculate Duje assistant appeared, wide smile, deep bow and welcoming arms spread wide.

"Welcome dear gentlefolks, to the premiere clothing experience on Servcon. I can see from your reltime industrial aesthetic that you have been away for decades. Are you both looking or do we just have Madam?"

"My friend is...." I tried but Soffee had it covered.

"I look for something smart but casual, easy to move," she said. "I also need carry things but no one see them."

Our Duje helper spread her arms even wider. "But Madam," she said, "we entirely understand the Flivver Protector aesthetic. May I also say that Madam's Terran is very good. Please come this way."

Turning to me she continued: "We will be busy for some time sir. Please follow my colleague who will provide you with refreshment," her polite manner actually saying: "OK matey-boy, bug out. She's all mine."

Soffee and the assistant swept across to the other side of the room, a cascade of semi-opaque curtains falling from ceiling to floor behind them. Another immaculately dressed Grunt appeared at my elbow and waved me across to the side of the room where a well-stocked mini bar had miraculously appeared. I sat down and a chilled cocktail glass equally miraculously popped up, no doubt filled with something very tasty and even more expensive. The Grunt stood back to watch.

I looked at the glass and a nano-tracker alert flashed up on my IFF. Cheeky beggars, they'd spiked my drink! However, a quick pulse through my fingers and everything became just more proteins adding to the flavour. I shook my hand to get rid of the tingling and risked a sip, as fragments of Soffee and the assistant's conversation drifted back to me through the dividing curtains.

"Backless, Madam, backless is what Madam needs to play to her strengths, especially when wearing cultural jewellery...Ah yes, I do see...well we always recommend non-absorbent, unless Madam is prepared to throw garments away after one encounter...all fabrics are flame-proof but unfortunately not stab-proof...in that case I would recommend stab-proof and energy beam resistant lingerie, all completely invisible, of course..." with other intriguing snippets floating across to add to my interest.

Servcon was, after all, Servcon and as far as I was concerned Soffee could have whatever she wanted, as if I had any say in the matter anyway. I must admit it hadn't occurred to me that the protector aspect might make things difficult, although the assistant was obviously trying her very hardest to please. And then both of them disappeared.

I blinked and looked around, but with some relief saw them on my HUD in another room. I looked at the Grunt, who was looking down at me.

"Don't worry," he said, "we're fully screened and no one's coming in without my say so. She'll look great. They always do," and he started attending to a titanium reinforced fingernail that sat alongside the lethal end of an integrated beam weapon extending down one massive arm, or at least what passed for an arm in a Grunt.

Tweaking finished, he looked back at me. "There's a whole lot of people interested in you. I saw the flags when we scanned, but that's cool. You're totally safe in here," and he paused. "I wouldn't think you'd need any security with her around."

Those lots-of-interest and needing-security comments were rather worrying. However, Soffee was obviously having a good time and the shop would protect us, or at least until we'd paid the bill it would. So, relax!

"Let me get you another drink," said my minder. "It'll take 'em at least another half hour and I can add kill-alch if that's your bag. Just let me know."

I was still worried about Servcon's not so sudden interest, which in my experience was never a good sign. Still, it was too late now and leaving out the kill-alch would undoubtedly dull the pain of the bill that Soffee was busily running up. A new drink appeared, and once firmly slurped I sat back and tried to relax in front of the brainless drack oozing out of the multi-screen attached to the arm of my chair.

"Franky, what you think?" butted into my idle appreciation of something entirely forgettable.

Soffee stood there wearing a slimmest fitting all-in-one, its dark blue material subtly offsetting her lighter blue feathers. Flecks of yellow traced her figure from neck to toe, where an immaculately dainty pair of boots peeped out. As she turned to look at the reflections in myriad mirror panels that blinked in and out to follow her gaze, the whole garment flowed around her. The trousers were slim and figure-hugging with the integrated top following her curves all of the way up to the shoulder, backless as they'd been discussing. She looked absolutely stunning.

"Madam should try opening her wings to feel the fit," said the ever-attendant assistant.

Soffee slowly un-furled her wings, extending them out and out until they filled the room. She gave a gentle flap.

A tornado blasted past, picking up my glass and smashing it against the wall. Both the Grunt and the Duje took a step back, shock plastered all over their faces.

"Good fit," said Soffee. "I flap my wings and everything stay just right."

"We do of course offer a full flying guarantee with all of our garments," said the assistant, watching rather warily as Soffee folded her wings back in again, "although we have never seen anyone with wings quite as large or as powerful as Madam's."

"You look absolutely gorgeous," was all I could say to Soffee's even wider grin. "Backless definitely suits you. Trouble is, I look like a complete scruff."

"Is no worry," she said. "We think about that. Go with guard and try on clothes we make," and there was the Grunt, gesturing to a door in the wall.

I walked through and a friendly voice called out: "Welcome, dear customer. Please remove all of your clothes and step into the cubicle."

Well, that was all a bit too much of a WTF for my liking, but I could hardly walk straight out again. I got undressed, walked into the cubicle and was greeted by an avalanche of spraying, washing, shaving, grooming and general fiddling about that most men have never had, ever. Slightly stunned, I stepped back out again, squeaky clean, rigorously shaved, generally tweaked and twiddled and ready for the brand-new pair of fresh, clean shreddies sitting there waiting for me. A male Duje assistant had also appeared, laden with new and very comprehensively Soffee'd clothing, which he helped me into before I was marched out for inspection.

What I'd been slid into was a male, non-avian version of what Soffee was wearing, cut just as snugly and unbelievably comfortable. The fabric was soft as a butterfly's wing and the nap showed our intertwined Terran and Terran/Flivver pin motifs. Everything had been made from scratch but then with Soffee's unique requirements, that was probably pretty much of a given anyway. I had to admit that I'd never, ever, looked so sharp and as for Soffee? Well, she looked good enough to eat.

After the obligatory twirling, mutual self-congratulation plus hyperbolic admiration from everyone in the room, "Happy?" I asked.

"I very happy," she said, "and this lady help with other nice things."

That sounded ominous, but with Soffee so very happy I couldn't be anything but even happier.

"I wear mine and you wear yours," she said. "For first time on Servcon we look like we own ring-ship."

I nearly retorted that looking so good was also a pretty good disguise as no one would ever recognise me, but I limited myself to a smile and raised eyebrow. The hovering assistant came straight in, ready as ever.

"We will have everything transported to your ship so there is nothing to carry," raising an eyebrow in that universal expression saying "OK pal, time to pay up."

Soffee went off to get herself ready while I direct-synched with the shop and settled the eye-wateringly large number she'd managed to run up. Whilst the flood of credits gushed from me to them, I discretely asked whether the shop had an alternative exit.

The Duje smiled. "But of course sir. As soon as Madam is ready, my colleague will escort you to our high carbon dioxide habitat entrance."

Soffee waltzed up preceded by a big smile. With general expressions of interest, thanks and please come again as soon as you likes from everyone around us, we followed the Grunt through a discrete side door. As we walked along, I whispered: "So what does that 'full flying guarantee' mean?" but Soffee's withering glance and hand squeeze with just the tips of her claws poking into my skin told me to shut up and stop asking silly questions.

"Standard air breathers, right?" our attendant grunted.

"Yep,' I said, "20% Oxygen, less than 0.04% Carbon Dioxide and we should be just fine." The Grunt ran his hand along a shelf and pulled down two emergency breather units.

"This room opens into one of the high CO_2 habs," he said. "Very handy for dropping a tail and these breathers will get you back to an airlock. You've got about ten minutes."

I fitted the patch across Soffee's face and as soon as I got a green, fitted mine. The Grunt waved us through a pressure door and slammed it behind us. The outer door swung open and my HUD flashed up a high Carbon Dioxide alarm as we walked out into the new habitat.

"Don't worry," I said to Soffee who was now clutching my hand rather tightly. "We'll lose anyone who's following us and the main hab's just through that lock over there."

We were definitely the odd ones out and some serious staring followed us all of the way over to the big blue airlock light. Maybe my attempt at ducking out of sight wasn't going to be as effective as I'd hoped. A rather bored guy in a suit scanned us in, the door clanked shut, a flow of air, another door popped open and there we were back in the main air-breather habitat we'd just left.

"Well that was unexpected," said Soffee, dropping her breather into the bin as we walked back into familiar surroundings.

"Yeah sorry," I said, "but I wanted to make sure we'd lose anyone who might be on the lookout," but three steps on, she tensed.

"Same three people follow us and don't look," she said squeezing my hand. 'How they know we here?" But of course. You couldn't escape Servcon's 24/7 360-degree view of everything.

Soffee's happy expression had disappeared. "Franky," she said, "I really worried. Buying clothes was fun but assistant keep asking questions. Everywhere we go, people stare and follow us. Can we find person you need then go straight back to ship?"

"Whatever makes you happy," was my only response and we moved off through the crowds towards a tunnel I vaguely remembered. The garishly decorated entrance led us down past lines of shops and stalls and all the while Soffee stayed glued to my side. Our desire to blend in wasn't exactly helped by the fact that in her new clothes she was even more striking than she had been. In fact, we both stood out like big blue flags.

I was just starting to worry that I'd chosen the wrong tunnel when sticking out of the wall was the sign I'd been looking for. Wazzap??? - scene of many previous festivities that probably needed to stay previous. The alcoholic fug of its predominantly Terran/bipedal lookey-likey clientele washed over us as we slipped in through the door and the sniggers and those aren't regulars-type looks pursued our attempted secretive walk to the bar. They still had their well-remembered and rather marvellous selection of beers, and I got Soffee a real orange juice. Her "What IS this?" expression was a picture.

"Relax," I said once we'd found a quiet corner to hide ourselves away in, but her eyes hadn't stopped flicking around. "If we don't find anyone here there are other places we can try."

Various highly amusing comments were still bouncing around the place: "Who brought the birdie," "Squawk, Squawk," "Pretty Polly" with matching smirks and thumps on the shoulder to reward each of the comedians. Still, all part of the game in a place like this and everyone would soon get bored of sharpening their razor-sharp wits on the newcomers. I hoped. Unfortunately, small groups were forming, splitting, re-forming, eyes directed our way and whispers passing around that there was something new to see. Definitely not what I'd wanted.

Sitting as we were, I could now see what had made that metallic clanking noise behind Soffee's back. Backless was definitely what Madam needed to play to her strengths and the pair of short swords she had down there were pretty serious items of cultural jewellery.

And then, Ohhh Shiiit. A Terran, clad all in black and in fact looking just like Dougie, appeared out of the crowd. I knew these guys and really wished I didn't. His eyes were locked on Soffee as he slowly walked towards us.

"Welcome," he said, talking to me but his gaze never shifting from Soffee. "I heard from a friend of yours that your good self and a, I'm sorry but I'm not entirely sure what sort of entity your companion is, had arrived on Servcon and I wanted a word." His eyes flicked to mine as Soffee slowly moved around in front of me, arms crossed, staring straight at him.

"Verrry interesting, and very expensively dressed. Looks like a Terran/Flivver hybrid. Plenty of Flivver. Excellent. Tell me, is this Harpy yours, or is she a friend?"

"She's a very good friend," I said quietly. "What's it to you?"

"Well..." he said, considering. "I heard that one of the older colony ring-ships had arrived, new owners, lots of credits. You got off it and here you are. You won't know me but I represent a group that, err," and here he smiled, "sort of helps administer this part of the station. We're very interested in your ship and your lovely companion."

As he said it, he was looking Soffee up and down like she was a piece of merchandise. I prodded her in the back but all she did was unfold her arms, her eyes staying glued to the Terran who had now been joined by three others, all dressed like him and actually, exactly like him.

Great. So he's brought along some clones and all undoubtedly combat trained to hell and back. Still, at least they didn't look armed.

"Do you know any fusion reactor engineers?' I said over Soffee's shoulder. "We need someone to check out our mass-converter and then we'll be gone."

He looked at me and then looked back at Soffee.

"Tell you what," he said. "We'll find you an engineer and you can lend us your Harpy," and with that, two of his companions made a grab.

Soffee took a step back as her hand reached up to the Alice band on her head. She snatched it off and with an elegant backhand flick threw it straight at one of her attackers. It flew between them, snapping straight before burying itself in his right eye. Even before the agonized shriek and matching spurt of blood she'd drawn both swords up over her shoulders. These came singing down, chopping into both of the next guy's arms before being yanked out as her immaculately cobbled boot kicked him in the stomach. Down went his head and she helped its path to the floor by chopping it off, neat as you like.

The original guy and his remaining companion were now scrabbling backwards over the tables and chairs in complete disarray. Soffee leapt forward and decapitated both of them, the sword strokes continuing round to cross over her head as she finished with a loud shriek.

That ear-splitting crescendo was greeted by a stunned silence, the thumps of her final victims' headless corpses hitting the floor and adding additional punctuation to the widening pools of blood spreading across the floor. Soffee stood, wings slightly open, spattered by her attackers' blood, slowly swaying as she chittered at the room. My first thought was that it was a good job the Duje assistant had recommended non-absorbent, but non-absorbent? Really?

Soffee stepped forward and wiped both swords down the back of the nearest body. The whole place was an unmoving tableau, shocked expressions following her every move. She yanked her lethal projectile out of the first guy's face then dipped it into a convenient jug of water. The water clouded as she gave it a quick shake and the drips were removed on the back of his jacket. A twist, an answering click and it was an Alice band again. She slipped it back over her head then demurely checked herself in the mirrored bar panel.

"I think we go," she said, starting off towards the door. A wedge of rapidly opening space preceded her and I followed close behind. We got to the entrance, her swords went back down between her wings and she started walking briskly up the tunnel as if nothing had happened.

"Pretty to watch and all that, but what the hell just happened?" I gasped.

"I do what Protectors do. I protect. No one take you like on CS1 and no one take me. Cultural jewellery useful as well as pretty." Her smile was chilling. "You see others?"

"What others? I saw the ones you sliced into bits but the whole place was full of people."

"They not Terrans," she said. "They follow us into bar and by time Terrans try and grab me I see seven. I wish Dougie there as well," she finished almost wistfully.

"But seven of what?" I said, still rather behind in all of this. "I didn't see anything. Also, why did he call you a Harpy?"

"I obviously what they think is Harpy," she said, "but seven people now chasing us."

A quick check behind and sure enough there were indeed a number of very single-minded entities all dressed in black, knocking people out of the way in their haste to catch us up. We exited into the main cavern and struck out through meandering groups of onlookers who looked on with a great deal of interest as this blood-spattered version of the Soffee-entertainment rushed past. Soffee was so busy with her HUD getting out an all points 'Back to the ship' bulletin that she didn't notice.

Now, the thing about Servcon is that there's no police or indeed any formal law enforcement. The various criminal groups are left to get on with it as long as they keep a reasonable amount of order. I seriously doubted whether Soffee's recent escapade came even close to a reasonable amount of order and those people chasing us were only a small part of the station's unofficial management team who were now undoubtedly very interested in what had just happened.

We dashed into the main lock entrance tunnel and it looked deserted. My IFF was giving me all sorts of red alerts and then a line of black-clad figures slid out next to the lock doors, standing like people do when they're holding powerful weapons and really, really want to use them. We got closer and closer before coming to a halt in front of this black roadblock. The gal in front slowly, loudly and very ostentatiously cocked her weapon.

"Drop your weapons and lie flat on the floor," she bellowed. "You have 5 seconds to comply," and then a smirk. "C'mon then birdy, if ye think yer 'ard enough."

I glanced at Soffee, before switching my gaze back to cocked-weapon gal as she counted out "...4...5" then fired. A sea of pain erupted, and I just had the briefest moment to think "Non-lethal..." as everything slid sideways into a deep, dark hole.

28
Outstaying our welcome

A warm, gritty surface pressed into my face as a pair of clawed feet swam through the slowly dispersing fog. I just about heard: "He awake," before feathered hands grabbed my arms and levered me off the ground, everything swaying and wobbling as my head did its best to stay attached.

"Franky, you OK?" echoed in my ears and Soffee's face joined Circe's. A little shake. "Franky, can you hear me?" then both faces looked away down what looked very much like a tunnel.

Everything slowly oozed back into focus and I just about managed to dribble out: "What...hell happen...?" as Scylla and Chary appeared. They stood there clutching their own versions of cultural jewellery and the same sorts of remains that Soffee had left in Wazzap??? were now decorating the floor all around us. I could only guess that Soffee and the girls had shown that gal exactly how 'ard they were.

"We must get back to ship," said Soffee. "Lot of people come up tunnel," but I was still trying to stay upright while not looking at the large red puddle I'd just stepped in.

Those knockout shots are awful, just like a whole-body dead leg. A deep breath and I tried to get something, anything, to work, but no chance. I tried again and this time my legs sort of answered the call, even if a drunken stagger was about the best I could manage. No matter, as I was swept along in a moving thicket of feathered arms and wings. The girls were trying to help, but Soffee swatted them away as her greater strength and height started making the right sort of difference as we wobbled up towards the pod.

The acceleration then deceleration as we zoomed over to the ship didn't exactly help matters, but the pod bay's zero gravity was so much better. My hand over hand float to the main control cabin was just what the doctor ordered and the way I felt, gravity was severely over-rated.

"You're going to have to stop saving me," I said to Soffee who was already busy, prepping for departure. "What am I gonna do when you're not around?"

Without taking her eyes off the consoles she smiled and unfurled a wing to stroke down my arm, much to the girls' annoyance as they tried to navigate around this new movement hazard.

My HUD was now flooded with alerts and alarms. Various mates of the chopped up bad guys seemed to be wanting to have some pretty serious words and even official Servcon management had woken up. Under Soffee's prompting the Navcom started to un-dock the ship, but a general advisory popped up that the landing grid had locked us in. Servcon management was also telling us in the strongest possible terms that we needed to open up and let in a security detail.

Not entirely unexpected I suppose, and I told the main AI to tell the landing grid that we were detaching anyway. It had ten seconds to decide and then we'd be off, whatever it decided. Luckily, the landing grid was no fool. It thought about the potential damage, the repair costs and our readiness to do exactly what I'd said. It complained about the potential damage, how much this was going to add to the docking fees and then paused, before grudgingly opening the docking clamps. All the while, I was busy activating the ship's main armament and launching suits to go off and hide amongst the other ships.

We slipped away from the docking area, all the while being pursued by streams of irate and threatening communications. Still, our main armament was tracking and they could go forth and multiply as far as I was concerned.

And then, a comm pinged up as another of those all-in-black Terrans appeared.

"Captain," she said. "I'm very sorry about the recent misunderstandings. We need to have a talk about how I can be of assistance in resolving them," which sounded ominous. Whenever someone really important is being really polite, you just know that something really bad is about to happen.

"We don't need any help," I replied. "We're moving towards our jump track and we'll be out of your hair as soon as poss."

"But Captain," she said, "of course you are, although we do need to discuss how your Harpy and my group can get better acquainted. Also," and she paused before giving an exaggerated sigh, "some of my people are very anxious to answer the challenge she issued after that unfortunate incident in the bar."

"Challenge?" I said to Soffee, who was watching with some interest.

"I said I meet anyone who threaten my hive and I kill them all. No one want to meet me, so they cowards."

So that was great. We're in the middle of something really serious and Soffee's having a pissing contest with the bad guys. Still, whatever. We needed to get out of here.

"Look, we're leaving, and now," I said back to the console, but the view at that end was panning back to show a couple of black-clad guards manhandling three Flivvers, one of whom looked just like Chitichca. In fact, as the woman who'd been talking pulled this Flivver in front of the camera, that's exactly who it was.

Shit! We'd missed doing a full crew check before we left.

"You're probably not aware that you accidentally left some of your crew behind," our black-suited friend replied. "Surely you're not going to leave them here?" and she gave Chitichca a shake. "Tell your captain."

Chitichca flicked her a glance of pure poison before turning to me.

"Franky, friend of my hive," she said. "Unless you turn around they will destroy your ship. Soffee, you have always been special to me and I do not want you come to harm. Do you remember the stories I used to tell you?" and with that she started chittering away, waving her arms and wings in some sort of mime show before two guards wrestled her back out of view.

"If you want your crew members back then you'll turn around, no choice and no argument," said the re-appearing Ms Black-suit. "I'll swap them for that Harpy and maybe we'll give you free passage out of here. Still thinking about that one though. You've got a minute to decide," and the feed clicked off.

I looked at Soffee, expecting, well I don't know what I was expecting, but what I saw was a look of wonder.

"Mother acting out my favourite story," she said. "Protector rescue head of hive by making hole in wall of prison. I think Mother say we make hole in Launch Control so they escape."

"But that won't work," I said, "Any holes'll let in space and they'll suffocate."

"But you send suits," replied Soffee. "They go get Mother and other two. Also, if Launch Control destroyed, she not target us and we escape before they make repairs."

Well, didn't sound like a great plan to me, but the Flivvers standing around the cabin looked pretty relaxed.

"These people are from your hive," I said. "Are you happy with what your hive head is suggesting?"

The most senior looked at me as if he couldn't understand why I was even asking the question.

"But that is what our leader and head hive-protector Soffee have said, so that is what will happen," he said.

A glance back at Soffee and her look said what are you waiting for? Well, I could think of many things, but they had a plan and I didn't so I placed a nice fat targeting cross on Servcon launch control and told the IFF to fire on my command. I then told the hiding suits to get over to Launch Control and retrieve three Flivvers who were about to be ejected into space.

That given minute was all too short and Ms Black-suit duly re-appeared. "Well, then," she said, "what's your answer? Captain?"

"I want to see my crew and make sure they're OK," I replied.

The view panned across to show our three Flivvers in the hands of black-clad goons. I winked at Chitichca and pointed my finger upward. She smiled back as I said: "Fire!"

The weapons-fired indicator popped up and the feed from Servcon Launch Control got rather confused. The ceiling disappeared, being replaced by the black of space as everyone was sucked off the floor. The comm fuzzed out as our three Flivvers opened their wings and flapped into a sea of static.

The IFF informed me that the main armament was ready to fire again, so I told it to shoot anything that looked like it needed it. It fired again, and judging by the targeting information another person's day was going rapidly downhill.

The suits had now come alongside the damaged Launch Control and were engulfing our Flivver friends. I shuddered to think what an un-modded suit would do to wings and feathers, but it was a whole lot better than breathing vacuum. They powered straight back, keeping as low a profile as possible they ducked in and out of the docked ships. The IFF fired once more before informing me in a rather smug tone that all immediate threats had been eliminated, and I could see what it meant. Each target area was now a shallow crater framed by expanding clouds of debris.

Of course, we'd been lucky that Servcon wasn't armed with anything but anti-debris defences, but who'd ever have thought of attacking Servcon? Still, the inhabitants would be OK as we'd been very careful not to shoot anything vital and damage control was already on the case. Even so, no one was ever going to forgive or forget this little escapade and we needed to get out of here like now.

Our three retrieved space walkers came back on board and were whipped straight up to the Medlab. The Medlab AI stuck them into

Medunits and expressed itself supremely confident that all would be well. Let's face it, with all of those Flivver injuries it'd been dealing with since we left CS1, it knew everything it needed to know about Flivvers.

"I hope you can see what I meant about the whole Servcon experience," I said to the expressions of bewilderment surrounding me. "Anyway, that's all sorted and I s'pose we'd better get a destination keyed in," smiling as Soffee's face broke into the happiest of grins.

"We go to Dougie's Treasure planet," said Soffee to the Flivvers. "Franky heard about it on CS1 and Servcon give us details. It totally matches End of Rainbow Nirvana," <65% xlate confidence-context uncertain> "for hive. I know, is Dougie, but we try. If no good, we try somewhere else."

Everyone looked pretty relaxed with Soffee's explanation which, I suppose, made perfect sense from a Flivver, as well as her, point of view. Also, strictly between you, me and anyone else, Dougie's planet was probably the only sensible option we had. Planets with breathable air and no inhabitants didn't grow on trees, and I certainly didn't know of anywhere else even vaguely sensible. Also, we had to go somewhere and we had to go now.

I started telling the Navcom about the course, but a HUD advisory flashed up for immediate attention. "Shit, what now?" was my only thought, but it wasn't actually bad news, just odd.

The main AI had been looking for Harpy references and a spray of information started pouring across my left eye as it regurgitated everything it had from Old-Earth mythology. So, just more Songs of distant Earth from my friends in black, but what came next was very interesting.

There was a report from an organisation called The Science Federation of Earth and the Exoplanets, or SFEE, describing some research they'd done on Terran/Flivver hybridisation. Viable hybrids had been created, but these had been taken away by one of the Flivver scientists into some unknown reltime. A side note said that the hybrids had been healthy, with much augmented Terran and Flivver capabilities.

Very intriguing, but just as I was about to ask for more info, I paused. This was one hell of a Pandora's box to open and it was Soffee's, not mine. That awful curiosity everyone has that demands to know about things that we really shouldn't was nagging away at me, but this wasn't the time, the place or even my decision to make. And then, thank goodness, the Navcom stopped me from doing something really stupid by distracting me with our shiny new jump track.

It had gathered enough information from Servcon to get us plus or minus several lights for a final destination but actually, that probably wasn't so important. Everyone would be in deep sleep anyway, so the Navcom could hop us about as required and we wouldn't even know the difference. It was just the size of the jump that made me pause. I mean, my biggest jump had been about two thousand lights, and this was twenty-five times that. Still, at least with a jump that size we'd be well away from our current problems when we got there.

Before I could talk myself out of it, I told the Navcom to get started. You do something and you're damned, you don't and you're still damned so what the hell, eh? I looked over at Soffee, but she was slumped in a chair and not looking so good. Her hand was pressed against a patch of khaki growing across her stomach, and a matching peep from the nearest Medlab agent confirmed a dangerous wound. Recommendations for urgent medical attention arrived right alongside a second Medunit.

"She caught me and I very stupid," she said with a wry smile. "I not wear stab proof underwear like shop-lady say. I also get my nice clothes dirty," but she didn't object to the Medunits grabbing ahold and whipping her off to the Medlab, pursued by my concerns that she hadn't gone up there sooner.

Several minutes later and the Medlab came back with its usual confident prognosis, leaving me to finish watching the Navcom get us moving. A second Medlab summary interrupted, this one being even-handedly positive and medically cryptic. It had now fully analysed this new organism that I hadn't let it look at for long enough last time, and it would be ready for the next one I put in front of it.

The report finished by offering me its congratulations, but why and for what wasn't immediately obvious. More dubious Medlab humour no doubt.

Still, we were now on our jump track that didn't go anywhere near Servcon – good – but the ship was still travelling in entirely the wrong direction – bad. So, there'd be several weeks of pretty extreme manoeuvring before we started our acceleration to jump speed – even worse. Deep-sleep was strongly recommended and that sounded great to me. My last couple of hours had definitely been ones to forget and I'll bet Soffee wouldn't object to some restful deep-sleep under the watchful eye of the Medlab.

Telling everyone they needed to get into sleep units generated the expected chorus of complaints, but if you fly in space, you gotta deep-sleep. I mean, what did they think they were gonna do? Stay awake for all of those reltime months/years flight time? Gimme strength...

I followed the Medbot bearing a very sleepy Soffee across to her sleep unit, those bottomless black eyes never leaving mine. A net of manipulators flopped her in, and a smile tickled the corners of her mouth as she slipped away. She was going to wake up in exactly the place she'd always wanted to be and just couldn't wait.

Everything quietened down as even our most vociferous complainers got themselves loaded into sleep units. It would have been nice to spend more time on Servcon, but I guess short and hectic was always going to be the name of the game with Soffee and the girls around. In any case, we were safely away and the ship was in charge. It would take us right across the galaxy to Dougie's Treasure planet, and I was going to sleep all of the way there.

29
The other side of the galaxy

Franky

The Medlab sandman kept us sleeping safely all of the way across the galaxy and the Navcom did exactly the same on the flying front. Fifty thousand-ish light-years later and out we popped. The Navcom had a quick look around, made another jump and there we were, a tiny fragment of our civilisation in the vastness of other species' space and stars.

Of course, we may have arrived safely, but Dougie's tales were still just that, tales. This was a new system, very far away from anything we knew and I had every confidence that we'd find things here we couldn't possibly expect. So, safety first, and the Navcom jumped in well outside the system's heliopause.

Run silent, run deep for the first couple of days, but apart from some automated wide area traffic-type scanning, there was nothing. The IFF was at max code red, every tactical and strategic system was ready and if even a speck of dust had hiccoughed we'd have heard about it. But there was nothing. Not a peep. Maybe Dougie and his story hadn't been so crazy after all. The Navcom obviously thought so, and after a couple of weeks look/see we started our deceleration in towards the single planet orbiting around in the Goldilocks zone.

I'd told the main AI to wait until the ship was nicely decelerated before waking up Soffee and I. Let's face it, coming back from the edge of existence was bad enough without being squashed into the nearest hard object while you did.

This wake-up seemed even worse than usual, except that Soffee bounced right up, bright eyed, bushy tailed and racing down to the main control cabin before I'd even approached the death warmed up stage. The Medlab's helpful comments about Flivvers recovering faster than Terrans, hybrid vigour, blah, blah, blah, didn't help one little bit.

When I could walk without falling over, I followed her down and there we were, nicely positioned on the other side of the sun to the planet we'd come all of this way to see. As for the planet? Well, it had air-breather Goldilocks-zone characteristics and no one was shooting at us. The IFF wouldn't stop bleating about that automated scanning we'd seen coming in, but most civilised systems had wide area traffic management and this looked pretty much the same. So, all looking good and I definitely needed a nice, hot drink to soothe my aching particles.

"You very suspicious," said Soffee as I sat clutching my drink.

"Yeah, and that's why I'm still alive," I said. "All we know is Dougie's story just before he fell off his bar stool and I still don't believe a word of it. Even the ship's best info says just what he said and I don't believe a word of that either. Hope for the best but expect the worst, eh? Also, however do you look so good when I feel so bad?"

"Maybe is because I only think good thoughts," she said. "Also, is hive-protectors' job to go to new planet before anyone else, so I make plans before girls wake up."

I choked on my drink. "Oh come on," I said, "be sensible. Just you and the girls?"

"Protectors always go first to new planet," she said, "so me and girls go first. I ask main AI to wake them. Also, Medlab say I well so nothing to worry about."

That feeling of me, the hopefully immovable object, being nudged by the definitely irresistible force standing there looking at me wasn't something I was going to win anytime soon, especially feeling as bad as I was.

"OK then, you and the girls," I said, but spoiled it by grinning and getting a well-deserved prod in the chest for my trouble. "But you've got to take some backup. A couple of the Smuts, you know, safety first and all that?"

The expected huffing and puffing started but, "Come on," I said, "it's a brand-new planet and anything could be down there. I mean, look at CS1. The Smuts'll just make sure you've got all your bases covered."

She opened her mouth, but I continued: "Look, this is standard stuff for any new planet, and this one's Dougie's. You really have got to take care."

My mention of Dougie did give her pause for thought, although I could see she was still rather upset about losing her protectors-only getaway. Before she could change her mind I told the main AI to wake up the Smuts, the Grunt, the other-hive council plus a couple of their protectors. Severely raised eyebrows at that, but we needed more people awake otherwise I'd be the only person left on the ship.

She did make me promise that no one would follow her down until she said it was OK. Of course, she knew and I knew that she was going to do whatever she wanted anyway, so anything could happen. I'd just have to hope that the Smuts would make the right kind of difference.

The next couple of hours involved Soffee racing around at high speed, followed by newly awakened girl after newly awakened girl wobbling after. The equally wobbly Smuts finally made it, although I could tell they were suffering just as much as I had.

They greeted my plan for two of them to go along with Soffee and the girls with more of a "You reckon?" than the confident assurance I'd been hoping for. Still, we all knew exactly what they were letting themselves in for, so I wasn't exactly surprised.

Soffee and the girls suddenly disappeared, and while I had another look at the IFF's security assessment I grabbed myself a quick snack. This sudden peace and quiet was really quite relaxing after all of that rushing around.

A readiness popup from the pod AI interrupted my contemplations, and then wow! Look what just walked in. Soffee and the girls, fitted out by that shop on Servcon as four seriously fashionable but terminally badass-looking protectors. And, they weren't even packing any hardware yet. Or were they? Who could tell, but they were going to knock anyone they met down there stone dead, even if that was figuratively rather than literally, I hoped.

They were messing about, laughing and joking, but obviously keyed up and dying to go. Soffee gave me a final talking to about being careful while they were away, and I couldn't stop smiling. They were off to the surface of an alien planet and I'd be back here safe and sound. That Flivver protector perspective, I suppose. Anyway, the girls dragged her off to the pod and it was only the more leisurely pair of Smuts that needed to get along before they were off.

A comm from the pod flicked up and there they were, all four of them looking back at me through a cloud of riotous excitement. The Smuts squeezed in behind and I got a final "We'll try and look after them" squirt from one, followed by both pairs of eyes mentally rising to the ceiling.

"Have a good time and look after yourselves," I said. "I'll be very upset if you don't come back safe and sound."

They just grinned at me.

"Do not worry, my lovely man," said Soffee. "We now have good protector plan which is much better than any Franky plan. Everything is good and we try very hard not to break anything," although the excitement in faces and twinkles in eyes told a very different story.

The pod's readiness alert popped up and I raised my hand in a goodbye wave. I looked at them, they waved at me and we all shouted: "Launch!"

30
Planetfall

Soffee

My gaze flicked to the viewport as the silent acceleration pressed us back into our seats. Those motionless stars were a backdrop against which the only thing moving seemed to be the rapidly retreating ring-ship, but that just showed how fast we were going. I could hardly believe that we were finally off, but the growing bubble of excitement in my chest told me that yes, this really was happening.

Scylla, Circe and Chary sat there entranced, but I couldn't take my eyes of our receding ship. Franky loved every bit of it, but all I could see were the dents, damage and centuries-worth of repairs. Ring-ships were very much the quantity not quality end of interstellar travel. From the outside, this one looked like a barely functioning collection of the spare parts that had been added throughout its long life.

The lumps and bumps smoothed away as the ship receded, eventually becoming a perfect snapshot of three rings spaced around the central main body. It was still the same centuries-old collection of repairs, but at this distance you could hardly tell. I lifted my hand and the end of one finger obscured everything but the tips of the main rocket exhausts that peeped out from behind a claw. The snapshot got smaller and smaller until it smoothed away into just one more bright dot shining in the dark continuum. Space was suddenly very large and frightening out here, however safe Franky said it was.

Regardless of that, the girls were having the time of their lives. Excited chitters filled the cabin and it really was lovely being away with my dearest friends. We'd only survived CS1 by working closely together and here was a whole new planet to explore. The suggestions about what they wanted to do became ever more ridiculous, and the peals of laughter greeting each new idea slowly lulled me off into a gentle sleep.

I was jerked awake by the pod AI flicking up our first view of the third planet, a tantalising smear hiding behind the sun's fiery edge. It slowly solidified, the sun's wavering curtain of super-heated atmosphere drawing back to reveal a clean planetary disc, brightest blue as it hung there in the black almost like it was waiting for us.

At this distance we could see a dense layer of objects surrounding it, but there were no indications of what these might be. The closer we got, the thicker this swarm became, but it soon became clear that we were seeing nothing more than a fat torus of mechanical debris orbiting the planet. These unknown remains of equally unknown alien craft were constantly colliding with each other, adding more and more debris to the halo of high-tech wreckage that started exercising our short-range defence systems as we came into orbit. Only advanced civilisations had the time and energy to loft that amount of technology into space, but why was it all in pieces and why couldn't we detect anything alive, anywhere?

We now had a superb view of the planet's surface, and it truly was a revelation. At least half was liquid sea and the landmasses were a patchwork of artificial construction, each surrounded by open country dotted with smaller developed areas. The planet's equator had unbroken construction across every landmass, but nothing to indicate that there was anyone alive down there. Dougie's tale of an advanced but deserted world was coming true right in front of our eyes.

After several orbits, and with everyone still exclaiming over new points of interest which immediately replaced the previous orbit's points of interest, we got the first flickers of RF. Sketchy traces, here one moment, gone the next, and the pod AI edged us over to see if it could find a better orbit. On the new track we got more of these same radio transmissions, definitely artificial, but they were gone almost as soon as they appeared.

The girls looked at me and I looked at them. The transmissions were coming up from a vast city spreading along the edge of one of the planet's seas and we were in full agreement. A city, all of that water, evidence of life and it was right below us. I told the pod to start making preparations to land.

Over the girls' continual chittering, the pod AI first dropped out a comms relay and then started giving us regular reminders to strap in before we started our descent, Franky's distant helping hand no doubt. We came back around the planet, up came our descent window, the pod made final adjustments and we dropped out of orbit.

The ride down was flawless, but as we came out of communications blackout the pod reported that it could not re-establish connection with either our comms relay or the ship. This was immediately followed by an assurance that atmospherics or hull ionisation could be the cause. So, nothing to worry about.

The city below was now horizon-wide as we dropped down across its expanse of urban gridwork. A final re-direction from the IFF, the rocket engines fired and we were crushed into our seats as everything outside disappeared behind churning clouds of rocket exhaust. A final thump and there we were, landed safely on our new planet after a journey of fifty thousand light-years.

Gentle sun, blue skies, and gently swaying native vegetation slowly appeared out of the whiteness. A sitrep from the pod said that we'd landed about a klick away from the city's edge and were in a secure location, whatever that meant. Franky's much stated worries about the dangers of new planets kept mentally repeating themselves, but the longer we waited for the pod to do its final checks, the more we couldn't wait to get outside.

The landing checks went on and on, but eventually the pod was forced to concede that we were free to disembark although it would, it said, keep its very closest eye on us.

"OK girls," I dropped into the unrestrained excitement swirling around the cabin, "before we do anything else, I want everyone in suits, fully integrated." This was answered by a chorus of complaints, but they knew the rules. New planet, no suit, no exit.

The suits swung open and in we stepped, the indignities of full integration starting straight away. At least these modified suits now asked first before applying anaesthetic and carrying out the most intimate procedures. Definitely an improvement on the first time I'd tried it, but not something you would ever choose to do, ever.

After the first involuntary gasps I called across to the Smuts, telling them to stay in the ship while we went outside, but I was wasting my time. They had been fully connected to the pod's systems ever since we'd left the ship and all I got back was an acknowledgement that they would keep watch.

As soon as my suit showed ready I ejected, closely followed by Scylla, Circe and Chary. We had landed at the bottom of a gentle valley, selected by the IFF so that no one in the city could see us. That was fair enough I suppose, but the first thing we needed to do was get up and out so we could see more of what we'd come all of this way to see.

My IFF synched up all four suits and we started jogging up the gentle valley slope facing the city. Each step gave a different picture of the native wildlife and it was difficult to believe that there could be so much life here, and then we crested the valley slope.

A flattish plain stretched away from us towards a distant line of hillocks. Behind was the valley we'd just come out of and beyond that the city extending out to the horizon. There was nothing moving and however hard they tried, the suits' IFFs could not detect anything that might even be pretending to be dangerous. We quickly decided that a plain with hillocks in the distance was a much safer bet than a large and deserted alien city, so left it very much for later as we started forward across the carpet of native vegetation.

My entire life had been lived in rock tunnels, with occasional visits to the sand desert up above. Being on the surface of any new planet would have been exciting enough, but here there was running water, plants, the sun was pleasantly warm and little fluffy clouds danced in a beautiful blue sky. Streams? Plants? Clouds? I had seen pictures of them of course, but having everything in front of me for real was absolutely breath-taking. I could have just stood looking at it all for hours, but a cry from Circe distracted me.

"Over there," she said, pointing. "Those lumps and bumps are like the piles of junk on CS1."

My suit IFF was now highlighting a number of lumps covered in native vegetation that were spread across the plain. I must admit that I'd missed them completely, even if the suits' rather terse response was that they'd told us about them as soon as we'd got out of the valley. Apparently, no one had been taking any notice.

More of these lumps and bumps were being flagged up, tall ones, short ones, some large, some small and all covered in weathered vegetation. The best the suits could agree on was that they were some sort of high-tech mechanical construction but devoid of any life signs. They could detect many living creatures all around, but nothing large and all seemed to be doing their very best to avoid us. The suit's IFF popped up several representations, but they were just small native creatures. Who could blame them if they were trying to avoid these four mechanical bipeds which had invaded their world?

We kept walking across the plain, passing more and more of these mysterious vegetation-festooned lumps. The ground was now starting to edge upwards as we approached those now not-so-distant hillocks. The air was breathable, it was a lovely day, the IFF could detect no danger and almost unprompted, a thought popped into my mind. I'd come halfway across the galaxy to be on this planet and it seemed like it had been created especially for us. I should be walking around in the air, not in a suit. I wanted to be out there and I wanted to be out there right now.

I almost didn't have to ask the girls, but my command to the suit to let me out was met with a blank refusal. The other three suits chipped in to say that it was far too dangerous. So, I asked my suit's IFF exactly what was the danger it was talking about. It thought for a moment and had to concede that none of them had been able to detect any dangers. Even so, I should stay in my suit on this new planet, as it might be dangerous.

Well, I certainly didn't need any over-cautious suit telling me what to do, so I gave it my very firmest command to let me out. There was a grudging pause before it slowly cracked open, giving me yet more warnings as it did so. I stepped straight out and became the first person to stand on our new world.

A light breeze ruffled my feathers, pleasantly warm with an intoxicating mixture of living smells. The sun was bright but had a coloured gentleness that did not sear the eyes. I bent down and took a pinch of the grainy soil. It was moist, organic, smelling alive. This was so different to CS1 that I could hardly speak, the lump in my throat turning to tears of happiness as I looked around.

Clicks, clanks and a chorus of chittering delight announced the unrestrained excitement of Scylla, Circe and Chary as they joined me in the open air. Typical Chary - she immediately ran to the top of a small rocky crest and leapt into the air. Flapping hard, she flew out, catching an updraft that filled her wings, lifting her into that glorious sky.

"We can fly!" she shouted, rising even faster as stronger lift bumped her outstretched wings. She turned in a circle, continuing to rise as the lift almost catapulted her away from us, higher and higher.

"This is amazing," she shouted down. "The plain goes on for tens of klicks around."

"Don't go too far," I called out, but my answer was a brilliant flash from the ground. Chary dropped with a screech, her wings pulling back as she dived straight back down again before swooping in for a very untidy landing.

"Something shot at me," she said indignantly. "I wasn't even doing anything."

Holding up her left wing we could all see the hole, neatly punched through her flight feathers and the charred edges tracing out a perfect circle.

"Lucky it only hit feathers," was Scylla's sniggered response. "You'd have been a large blue skid mark if they could shoot straight."

More sarcastic comments were interrupted by a Smut brain tickle, asking what had just happened. I replied that there was nothing to worry about as we had everything under control. It's "OK" reply carried strong hints of "Are you sure?" but I was already scanning the ground.

"Did anyone see where that came from?"

"One of the mechanical objects, as indicated, fired a high energy laser," was the eager response from my suit. "As soon as Chary took off she was being tracked. I can only conclude that the shot was fired when she became a threat. Shall I engage?"

"Yes, immediately," was on the tip of my tongue but I paused. OK, so Chary had been shot at, but we were uninvited visitors on someone else's planet. I looked at Scylla, but she just smiled, shrugged and looked at Circe. Circe looked at Chary and then back at me. I asked the suit for more information, but all it could tell me was that one of the mechanical lumps had woken up, tracked Chary, and then shot at her. And that was it.

The girls were looking at me, obviously eager to do something about it, but what? We hadn't asked for permission to be here and whoever had shot at us was just doing what we might have done to any unknown someone sniffing around our hive. We were clearly unwanted visitors and we needed to try and turn this around before first contact became a shooting match.

I raised an eye crest at the girls. "OK," I said. "They obviously think that we're a threat. We need to try and convince them that we aren't, although I do think we should get into our suits."

The three expressions that greeted that suggestion were universal in their disapproval. Scylla stated that she'd been happy to wear a suit when we got here, but now that the hive had been threatened the protectors must protect. We didn't need suits to do that and anyway, they could provide us with backup in case anything went wrong.

Circe and Chary piled straight in on top of what Scylla had said and it was clear that no one wanted to wear a suit. They seemed almost affronted by the suggestion and as Circe said, it was our job to prove it was safe and we couldn't do that while wearing suits.

I suppose that it was stretching it a bit to complain that someone had shot at us when we'd been the ones invading, but we were still the hive's protectors. We had come here to make things safe and we had our attacker in view. We just wanted to talk. What could possibly go wrong?

I had known the girls for far too long to keep any secrets from them and their affronted expressions disappeared into smiles as they saw what I was thinking. Everyone started laughing and joking about the sacrifices a protector had to make, but I was still worried. I didn't want anyone making sacrifices, especially when we didn't really know what we were doing.

Still, if we were just going to talk then our plan was simple. The locals had shown that they were happy to shoot, so we would use convenient rocks and other lumps as cover while we tried to get close enough to make contact. What might happen if they didn't want to talk, or if anything else decided to wake up and shoot at us, was a minor detail to the girls. They were happy to leave any problems like that to the suits.

"Understood. Passing tactical information," was the suits' only response when I told them of our plan and they seemed as confident as the girls. They also gave us four clearly marked paths to our target, all of which took us into danger whilst the suits stood well back and kept watch. The Smuts very clearly thought we were crazy, but did assure me they would do whatever they could to help.

The longer we waited the worse it would be, so we had a quick final talk and started off towards our suit-recommended safe paths. Scylla immediately caused a panic. Something scuttled away under her feet and she squeaked up into the air, drew her pistol and shot it to pieces. Everyone dived for cover, but stood up rather sheepishly as Scylla smoothed her dishevelled feathers back into place.

The air filled with jokes about how nice it was to have our own pest controller, and in fact, we were soon making so much noise that my suit had to warn us that anything for klicks around would know we were there. The girls didn't seem too worried, but this was a new world. Something had shot at Chary with a high energy laser. One shot on target and that would be it.

They did quieten down, but about a hundred metres from our target an IFF alert popped up. We had been scanned and something was powering up. The suits immediately sent an advisory showing their four missiles and eight energy weapons ready, targeted and waiting. They seemed confident. I wished I was.

We were now down on all fours and doing our very best to keep out of the mechanical lump's sightlines. Circe stuck her head out to have a look and was rewarded with a bright flash. A hole appeared in what she had been hiding behind and the matching spray of red-hot fragments pursued her back into cover. Judging by the rolling about and flapping of hands that must have hurt.

The suits fired straight back.

Four aerial flashes showed our adversary destroying each missile but it couldn't avoid the energy weapons. No more than a second and we were back to silence filled only by my suit telling me it could detect no signs of life.

After that, no one was in any hurry to do anything. We sat and waited, little comms flicking back and forth between us. A couple of minutes later the suit repeated its assessment and launched a drone to go and see what was happening.

Its whine whizzed overhead as it tracked in, the feed showing charred vegetation framing a neat collection of melted holes in the metal structure. There was indeed nothing moving. The suits' best guess was that this was some sort of landing ship but it had no more information. The drone circled around and we could now see several odd-shaped lumps scattered around the craft.

Tendrils of smoke curling up into the air was the only movement.

I had a quick peek and ducked back in again. Nothing happened. The suits were confident and so were the girls, although it has to be said that the girls' confidence was more along the lines of me going first and them following. My suit repeated its assurance and almost as an incentive, gave me a nice new track heading towards the structure.

Well, I was head protector and I had to go first. I slowly stood up, the sun shining down on me and the breeze rustling my feathers. Nothing happened. Scylla slowly got up, followed by Chary and Circe. Another burst of confidence from the suits and we all started walking towards the smoking box.

Up in front of me was one of those lumps that the drone had seen, a body-sized oblong encrusted with creepers. A handful of the bristly vegetation came away in my hands, dragging up a flap of clothing and exposing long tendrils stringing back inside. I dropped it back, dusting off my hands as I stood back up again. It wasn't for me to disturb the peace of whoever was lying there.

The suits now had some more information, but it was still scarce stuff. In essence, this was an alien ship surrounded by alien beings. They had been here for at least a hundred standard years, but even that was a guess. Scylla called over, saying that the metal box was indeed the remains of a landing ship, but like nothing her suit had ever seen.

A chorus of distant pops announced the suits launching a cloud of drones which whined off in all directions, their feeds pouring in as a map of everything around us started to build. That would certainly get a reaction from anyone out there, but who was out there? This alien ship was just mechanical remains left behind by its dead crew. We hadn't seen anything organic, sentient and alive.

We continued to dig around the alien ship while the drones flew out to their maximum range. All of the way there was country, city, roadways, buildings, wrecked mechanicals and even more alien craft, but that was it. No movement, no RF, no reaction and absolutely no sign of the creatures who had built this world.

I focused back from the drones' map to a horizon that was growing a broad band of orange up into the darkening sky. The girls were still messing about in the landing ship, but we needed to keep our eyes open. Just because we hadn't seen anyone, didn't mean that no one was here. Maybe they were watching, wondering who we were? Maybe they were nocturnal? With night coming we needed to get back to the pod before anything else happened.

I called across to the girls, but they were not in the least worried. This lovely planet was deserted. The suits had destroyed the landing ship which had fired at us. They, the hive's protectors, had protected our hive, could deal with anything else that might be out here so let them come. And it suddenly hit me. This planet wasn't different or alien. We were the Aliens. There were just the four of us and whatever the girls might think, we really did need to start taking a lot more care.

My worries were, however, laughingly dismissed by the over-enthusiastic girls. Sure, intelligent life had built those cities, but where were they now? We hadn't seen anything and everything would be fine. Nothing to worry about at all.

I wasn't anything like as sure about any of this as they were, but it was a very happy band of protectors that made its way back to our waiting suits under a darkening sky.

31
Second group away

Franky

Soffee's pod powered away and their track was good. They swooped by the sun before slowly curving around to meet up with that distant planet we'd come all of this way to see. A perfect run in, equally perfect orbital insertion, everything looking good and maybe I could finally relax. Except, of course, that anything looking this good just meant that whatever was going to happen hadn't happened yet. I wasn't going to take my eyes off them for a moment.

The other people I'd woken up were now starting to move around the ship, but they left me very much on my lonesome as I watched the whole of my hive having their new adventure. It was rather strange having Soffee so far away from me, but that was no doubt ntime/reltime paying me back for those nine years.

A never-ending stream of reports had filled in a lot of the blanks about this new world, but Soffee and the girls were taking their own sweet time having a look around. Still, I could hardly blame them.

We'd flown halfway across the galaxy to get here and they must be having the time of their lives.

The pod's reports kept coming in, everything kept looking good and finally the pod popped up a landing track. They launched a comms relay, a descent window appeared and down they dropped out of orbit.

Standard sitrep as they went into comms blackout and there was nothing for me to do but wait until they came out the other side.

Four minutes.

Nothing.

Five minutes.

Still nothing...

Six minutes.

...and just for a change, still more nothing.

A bit overdue, but here's the thing. Comms blackout is perfectly normal for any ship undergoing re-entry, although it's generally only three to four minutes max. This planet was nineteen light-minutes away, so what I was/wasn't seeing had already happened six minutes PLUS that nineteen minutes ago, my time. All of which didn't help. At all. They were still late.

I checked the IFF again, but no change. Nothing received. Not a peep. Nothing good, nothing bad, just nothing.

The Navcom upgraded its no signal received advisory to a more definite no signal received alert, but we should still be OK. If the pod's comms had failed, Soffee or the girls' HUDs would still be able to get a signal up to their comms relay. So, I may have heard nothing, but there was nothing to worry about, yet.

I tried asking a Smut to have a go but it just said they were too far away. Also, it couldn't – and here I got the telepathic equivalent of something untranslatable about shouting loudly in the dark – which obviously made sense to it but not to me. So, extremely frustrating, but what could I do? Nothing.

Ten minutes.

Then fifteen minutes.

OK, so they really should have re-appeared by now but I'd only ever seen one descent go wrong, and that was in my early days on a first gen ship. A knackered old lander in much the same state as the one those pirates had used had catastrophically failed. The very obvious trail of fiery particles had been its very visible epitaph, but we hadn't seen anything. Soffee's pod was our very best AI-controlled, fully automated, fail-safe and multi-redundant version. In fact, it was a lot cleverer than I was. It would never have started its descent unless it was absolutely certain that they were going to make it down safely.

"Ping their comms relay," I told the Navcom, but it had been doing that since they went into comms blackout. Still nothing.

My what-the-hell-is-going-on thoughts were now well ahead of the growing knot in my stomach, but were interrupted by the politely muffled sound of what, for a Flivver, passed as a cough. I turned from the console to see Chitichca standing there watching.

"I can see you are busy," she said, "but I wanted to know what is happening. Also, we all offer you and Soffee our deepest congratulations and best wishes," glancing at the ring sitting on my finger.

OK, so there it was, durr-brain. Chitichca was keeping an eye out as per usual and making doubly sure that I knew what was what. I'd already figured out that there was more going on than a just a lovely present, but as everything on Servcon had then kicked off I'd been a bit distracted. Still, if it worked for Soffee then it definitely worked for me and my smile at just the thought of that only increased the happiness all over Chitichca's face.

"Many thanks, old friend," I said, turning back to the console array that was still telling me nothing, "but we've got a problem. Soffee and her friends descended to the planet's surface, but we've not heard anything back from them."

She looked at the bank of screens, but they were still saying the absolutely nothing they'd been saying before she came in.

"You know," she said, "if there is anything you need, you only have to ask."

There was another no signal received popup, but that was it. I checked the Navcom yet again, but there was no signal, nothing we could see on the planet, so what was going on?

I felt her hand on my arm, which was not a Flivver gesture as those claws added a whole lot more to the gentle squeeze.

"I can see that you are busy," she said, "but I mean it. Anything we can do to help. We have protectors who are at your disposal, so please do not hesitate to ask."

The squeeze disappeared and she was gone, leaving me to, well, what?

It was that lack of, rather than presence of, anything that was so worrying. The pod and everyone in it seemed to have dropped off the face of the planet. We were too far away to see anything on the planet's surface, so all we had was radio comms.

It was just so frustrating, but you know what? I'm not the kinda guy who sits there with his thumb up his you-know-where and his brain in neutral. I was going to put a rescue team together and actually, I was going to do that right now. I know I'd promised Soffee I wouldn't go over there until she said it was OK, but I'd worry about that once I'd gone over there and found that everything was indeed OK.

My Dad used to say spare capacity and molto redundancy good, back of a fag packet bad, and that made as much sense here as it did for him on that over-heated, over-polluted, pretty much over-everything Old-Earth I'd left. So, over-provisioned and mob handed would be the order of the day and we'd see what happened, wouldn't we?

The easiest bit would be getting some pods prepared but almost immediately, the first big problem. Soffee and the girls were on the planet, so who would actually be available to go in mob-handed with me?

I shouldn't have worried. The remaining pair of Smuts had been following what was happening, and almost before I thought about asking they said they'd come. They also said that our Grunt passenger fancied a trip, so there we were, three people straight off. However, that was hardly mob-handed, so I thought I'd see what Chitichca's kind offer of protectors actually meant.

What it meant was two protectors ready and waiting to go, and guess what? These two highly recommended individuals with unpronounceable names were the kids I'd rescued from those Minos all of that time ago, now as adult as you like and both of them fully fledged protectors. We were, apparently, old friends and they were definitely looking forward to doing anything that they could to help.

It was almost a relief from all of my racing around and good to have a few words about times passed. Then, and I know, but I just couldn't help myself, I asked whether the Terran names Medea and Hecate worked for them now that they were joining our team. Where those two names appeared from I have no idea, but no sooner had they come to mind but straight out of my mouth. Even so, both ladies seemed happy with the idea. In fact, they almost seemed to expect the offer of new names together with the Flivver-implied invitation to join my hive. What Soffee was going to think about that I could only guess.

Anyway, we now had six people and that seemed like a good team. We'd take three pods plus a tanker and if that little flotilla couldn't sort out whatever trouble Soffee and the girls had got themselves into, it probably couldn't be sorted. And that's when the next problem came up.

I wanted to get over there as quickly as possible. Trouble was, no one was even vaguely happy about the hard acceleration that would involve. Several exchanges later and five people with their equivalents of arms crossed and no-flippin'-way expressions said that I was going to have to do it myself and they'd follow along behind at their own pace. We would no doubt see whether that would mean lucky me or lucky them.

A final chat, with the usual reminder about no one eating anything native when we got there. First contact was one thing, but us as diners and any local sentients as dinner was entirely another. I'd just heard too many stories.

I got myself straight off to the pod bay, but hold on a minute genius. I'd almost forgotten the most important bit. My ship, with only the CS1 hive on board plus no one in charge, equalled a recipe for disaster. Chitichca was the obvious choice, but as soon as I asked her, the tidal wave of joy that I would trust her with the ship, my hive space, everything in it, etc, etc engulfed me. She just wouldn't stop talking and all the while I could feel the time awasting and my feet atwitching. I eventually had to retreat down the corridor away from those protestations of never-ending gratitude and at the first corner I was off as fast as I could move.

I swooped through the pod bay to the waiting entrance hatch, and the pod AI was already swinging out a suit. It wrapped me up nice and tight, a quick synch with the onboard systems, and I handed over control to the Navcom.

Out we boosted at 4+G, the Smuts' final quip chasing me off as they wished my weak and feeble Terran insides all of the very best for the journey.

32
All down

Franky

Now, yer average Terran body has some pretty strict limits on the acceleration it can stand, and it's not as much as you think. Six hundred agonising seconds of said max acceleration later was in fact a lot more than I could think, and I just sat there gasping lungfuls of much needed air as the tanker slipped in to top up the pod's tanks. All too soon we were off again and I'd tell you how helpful the Navcom's countdown was, except that I didn't have enough breath to speak.

The next, the next and then the next, and even with the suit's best ministrations I was starting to feel like peanut butter being irrevocably squeezed into a suit-shaped bagel. Still, we were now really shifting and with a final pulse that nearly finished me off, there we were, peak speed and thank bloody goodness for that. A remote blue planetary dot was starting to ease out from behind the sun's flare and I just hoped that this whole crazy journey was going to be worth it.

The remote blue disk slowly solidified and our first long-range scan picked up the vaguest smudge of a perfectly landed pod. What a flippin' relief! Indications of suits moving about, whispers of RF from suit comms, but my pod rotating through one hundred and eighty degrees plus full deceleration kicking in removed any further contemplation of that good news.

The deceleration agony was, if anything, worse than the previous acceleration, and by the time we were close to the planet I was no longer peanut butter in a bagel. I was well chewed gum trodden into a crack in the floor by a herd of Minos. My suit was also going to need a pretty good clean.

We slid into a high orbit and, just as requested, I could see that the Navcom had put us several thousand klicks behind Soffee's comms relay. Definitely safety first. I reckoned that any planetary bad guys would shoot the first thing they saw going over, so being this far back would keep us nice and safe. The IFF kept its own council as to why they wouldn't just shoot anything that moved and be done with it.

The pod's close-range defence systems were now fully occupied with the cloud of debris around the planet, and our orbital track brought us nicely over Soffee's landing area. There was still nothing from her pod, but I could see lots of movement with four pods moving about the place. I tried pinging the pod, something between it and me was screwing with the comms. So, I'd leave that until later even if she'd still be absolutely furious I was here, especially after my promise. I'd just have to think of a really good excuse.

The next orbit brought me round again and the IFF excitedly reported a discharge from a weaponised laser. Whether that was good or bad I couldn't tell, and just as we slid out of view around the planet's edge, the IFF reported multiple weapon discharges from suits. So, she'd only been here a day and someone on the surface was already getting the benefit.

I couldn't wait to get down, but Soffee's night was approaching. Landing on a new planet, in the dark, was not a good idea and especially after all that shooting. Also, the Smut, Flivver and Grunt-laden pods were now making their appearance around the sun's edge and their best ETA was Soffee's sunrise. I guess I'd just have to wait until everyone else arrived.

A cloak of darkness spread across the surface of the planet, eclipsing Soffee and the girls. I could only hope they were getting their beauty sleep, but I wasn't, orbiting around, watching and worrying. However, the IFF couldn't see anything bad and eventually I did start to relax, even if only a little bit. Let's face it, this planet did seem to be following Dougie's story even if all of that shooting was definitely not in the script.

The new day's sun eased its way across Soffee's landing area and the slow-poke pods finally came sliding in behind me. Everyone was in pretty good shape so I guess idleness did have its own rewards. A quick conflab and the tanker AI wished us good hunting as our pods dropped out of orbit.

The descent was almost boringly normal. Halfway through the comms blackout, we fell through a layer of strongly charged particles and started picking up a lot of hull ionisation. Both would block most kinds of radio transmissions so we now knew why Soffee's pod hadn't called back. Another big relief.

The city below was an artificial half-pancake well over a hundred klicks wide, butting up against the sea and expanding into standard grid system urbanisation as we dropped. The sea was blue, the air was clean and it was rather like the pictures I'd seen of Old-Earth before everything was trashed. It was weird really, coming all of this way to a highly advanced planet whose inhabitants hadn't broken it like we had ours.

Dropping out of comms blackout, we disappeared straight into an indignant flood of radio traffic. Everyone was pleased to see us, but why hadn't I waited, you promised, you know you did, Soffee's black eyes almost raising blisters as she glared at me. Several flattened areas across the cityscape popped up as anomalies as we came down on final approach, but really? It was just another built-up area like all of the others I'd seen on my travels. No indications of movement or anything alive, so yet more confirmation of Dougie's crazy story.

Soffee's altercation with the natives had, however, left a big impression on the IFF. Its recommended approach was a landing some way off from where Soffee had come down, last-minute max-G pull-out and immediate armoured deployment straight after. Another example of our over enthusiastic AIs being over enthusiastic, but this time it was definitely Soffee's fault.

The last-minute max-G pull-out was as unpleasant as it sounds and we spent most of the time the pod AI needed for its landing checks peeling ourselves out of our seats and checking that our internal organs hadn't been squeezed out of where the sun didn't shine. I staggered across to the suit mount points and was unexpectedly joined by a Smut in their pod doing much the same thing. On the journey over it had amused itself by somehow squeezing into a standard Terran suit. Very handy, even if where everything fitted was rather mind-boggling.

The pod AI gave us a big green and out we both baled. A quick look around then we were straight off, racing across a large plain towards the distant dots of Soffee and the girls. The rest of our party disembarked in a much more leisurely fashion and with weather this nice, who could blame them?

The Smut and I pounded along, the suit's IFFs showing full tactical displays, alert as hell and ready for everything. Of course, the only thing that happened was us being greeted by slow sarcastic handclaps as we ran up to the waiting Soffee and the girls, the suits coming to a halt in their best tactical poses.

"Where you been?" Soffee called out, her grin matched by the grins on Scylla, Circe and Chary's faces. "We here for ages, all problems sorted and now you come in without asking. You look just like something from adventure story."

The Smut and I studiously ignored the muffled titters as we got out of our suits.

"Actually, you haven't been here for ages," I said, "but it feels like you've been away forever," and I folded her into my arms.

She squirmed out of my grasp, flapping my arms away, but not too fast.

"Welcome to my planet," she said, spreading out her wings and arms to encompass the vista. "What you think?"

"I think we've landed on someone else's planet but they're not here anymore. Maybe Dougie's story was true, even if you were sooo rude to him."

"Pah! Girl can be wrong can't she?" was her response as the walking part of my three-pod circus ambled up towards us.

"So, what you want to know?" she said, talking to me but keeping a worryingly close eye on the approaching Medea and Hecate. "Something shot at Chary, but we shot it back and there nothing left. We surrounded by alien ships and neither pod AI or suits have seen anything like before. I think we have everything under control."

I'd already synched with her pod AI and that just underlined her story. There wasn't a sign of any sentient organics and only the merest flickers of radio traffic. The city we'd landed next to showed a standard layout, with a large flat central area in the middle with what looked like an entrance going underground. In fact, scattered across the city were more of these entrances, but that was it. Just one enormous city with no one in it.

"Well, it does look like you've got it all under control," I said, coming back to Soffee and the girls' now even-wider smiling faces, "but I still can't believe we're the only people here."

Soffee raised her eyes skyward as she said they'd already scanned everything ages ago and the only reason they weren't out exploring was that they'd been waiting for us. I tried explaining that we'd been worried about not getting any comms, but her eyes raised skyward again said that she wasn't interested. Anyway, why were we so worried? I apologised again for spoiling her fun and I did think she rather liked the fact that I'd been so worried I'd come across at max acceleration. So, a good trade-off for that high-G agony, or at least just about.

The next hour, which stretched across a knocked together lunch courtesy of the suits and into the afternoon, consisted of all four of them telling us exactly what they'd done, with every story adding multiple repetitions and even more versions. It also included Soffee finding out exactly who were these two new Flivvers who'd come along so very unannounced.

Every answer to her whys, whats and wherefores got me another "I'll speak to you later" look and I was starting to think that maybe I hadn't got away with it after all. Still, Soffee and the girls seemed happy to welcome our two newbies into the fold, even if Soffee's mouthed "Medea?" "Hecate?" over their heads spoke of much future piss-taking to come.

And actually, this planet was so totally great it was very difficult not to be happy. Outside on CS1 during the day would have had the skin scorched off your back, and yet here we were walking around in the open air, the sun warming our skin and the wind tickling hair and feathers. Sprawling about, chatting, joshing and generally doing very little was a soothing balm that spread itself all over my own sleepless night worries, just as it seemed to be doing for everyone else.

"We could live here, couldn't we?" was Soffee's whisper that echoed through my mind, perfectly in tune with the swirls of wind soughing through the grass.

The afternoon was now developing into a bit of a party, especially after someone broke out the unofficial drinks. These lubricated the proceedings rather nicely, but in what seemed like no time at all the sun was creeping down towards the horizon and evening stars were speckling the sky. Unbidden, the suits had tidied up and were now breaking out a couple of prefabs. No one wanted to sleep in a pod, but sleeping out in the open was probably just a bit too much excitement for one day. The noises rattling about in the dusk from the local wildlife merely emphasised that.

Once the prefabs were up, the suits got on with dinner. There is nothing quite like your first hot meal on a new planet to really raise the spirits. More unofficial drinks helped but pretty soon my sleepless night was catching up with me and everyone else was also starting to droop. By now, the light had pretty much gone and a rose-coloured sunset gave the perfect backdrop for just one more round of stories before we finally called it a day.

Soffee, the girls and our two new protectors had already bagged the larger prefab so the expanded hive-thing seemed to be working just fine. The Grunt, the Smuts and I fitted ourselves rather snugly into the other prefab and there was plenty of good-natured banter as we got ready for bed. You know, body size, shape differences, body odours, what we'd done the last time we'd been in a prefab and with who, etc, but I was so tired I dropped off pretty quickly.

A couple of hours later saw me being dragged up from the sleepy depths by an IFF alert indicating movement somewhere off in the distance. Nothing identifiable and a drone had been despatched. By the time it got there, it was just vegetation, rocks and blackness and we all dropped straight back to sleep.

The first flush of dawn's early light tickled the prefab's walls as Morpheus' arms gently relaxed, leaving me to lie there dozing in the sort of air you get when four different people from three different species have been in a small enclosed space all night. I put my head back under the pillow and was just drifting off again when an otherworldly, keening ululation jolted me awake.

The IFF wasn't reporting anything but I fumbled my PDW out from under its impromptu wrapping of yesterday's clothes and stuck my head outside. In the fresh light of a new day everything was still as a picture. Circe was slowly circling fifty metres overhead, framed by the light morning sky. Her head went back and that same high-pitched keening cry splashed over us, jangling backwards and forwards between the vegetation-covered lumps. The others were standing in the door of their prefab, wings hanging open as they watched.

Chary ran forward and leapt into the air, flapping hard as she soared up to join her voice with Circe's keening song. Scylla, Medea and Hecate followed and soon all five of them were circling above us, their voices synchronising into an ever-growing swell of sound. I was entranced, but suddenly realised that I'd heard this before. It was Soffee's awful 'death screech' even if these cries were so much more melodious as they echoed across the plain. The cries abruptly ceased and our songbirds fluttered down to land in front of Soffee, being greeted by congratulations and a group hug.

"That was amazing," I called out as I wandered over. "I've never seen anything like that, ever."

"We very honoured," said Soffee. "Now full hive is here, we do ritual Flivvers do when they on new planet for first time. Is formal request to fly and live here, honouring hive and our new planet." Her eyes travelled around the girls. "I too heavy, even in lighter gravity," and her longing eyes told a story that tugged at my heart.

She slipped an arm around my waist and gave me a fierce squeeze. "I watch girls," she whispered in my ear, "and I watch new hive members you bring," locking her bottomless eyes on mine.

I didn't even bother answering. Doomed if I spoke, doomed if I didn't and anyway, next stop was breakfast. That first meal of the day should definitely be the best, and I was always promising myself that one day it would be. More max nutrient rations. Ummm...nice...

Everyone started digging into the suits' proffered selection of multi-species breakfast sticks and slicks, and plans started to be knocked about. What this actually meant was everyone saying what they wanted to do and not listening to anyone else. Discussions quickly became quite heated but, I didn't mind. I was just happy being here. I sat back to watch Soffee manage the various strongly-expressed opinions.

Eventually it was decided that Soffee, the girls, Medea, Hecate and the two Smuts who'd come over with Soffee, would follow a roadway into the city aiming for that interesting central square with the hole going underground. My two Smuts and I would fly off in a couple of pods to look at a city on the other side of the sea. The one person left, our pal the Grunt, would stay behind and look after the pods. His smile said that a day sitting in the sun was right up his alley.

By the time we'd agreed all of this, the morning was awasting and we needed to be away before lunchtime beckoned. We all wandered over to the pods and I got a fierce hug from Soffee. Her "AND make sure you come back safely as I not there to look after you," echoed in my ears as she let me go.

The Grunt settled back in the sun and waved us off with a smiling crude gesture. This was going to be a nice relaxing day for all of us. I was starting to like this place. I was really starting to like this place a lot.

33
Just when you thought it was safe

Chitichca

No one can understand what is happening. Soffee and her hive protectors have left the ship and now Franky is gone as well, leaving just me in charge. One hive passing control of their hive space to another is unheard of and people are very worried. Franky and Soffee would not do this unless they were planning something. And Franky is a dirty Terran.

A never-ending chorus of whispers and stories, but I think people are mainly worried that they will not be allowed to live on this new planet as their own. They have very short memories however. None of them would be here if Franky and Soffee had not got them away from CS1, and I know that Soffee has never stopped looking out for both hives. People and their prejudices have very short memories.

I have been very happy watching how Soffee has blossomed since Franky returned, and now he is wearing the hive-pair symbol she gave him. Terrans are such strange creatures, and I am not sure he appreciates what Soffee's gift actually means. However, he is a good person. He makes Soffee happy, and that is the best that any of us can hope for in life.

So here we are, half a galaxy away from CS1, floating in a ship that I have been left in charge of. His final entreaty: "Chitichca, please don't break anything!" was said, I think, as a joke, but why would he joke about something so important? I cannot begin to understand, but I will do my utmost to keep everything and everybody safe.

Since Franky left, I have been fulfilling my duty by staying in the main control cabin, watching the console screens and trying to make sense of it all. The rest of the hive council are, I think, rather put out by Franky only asking me to look after the ship, and they have left me very much on my own.

Yesterday, bright red messages together with a set of moving diagrams popped up on the IFF console. When I asked the ship what they meant, it said that missiles had been fired from the planet's surface. However, we were in no danger and after a while both the messages and red indicators disappeared.

Today there were even more messages. The main AI told me it had received a distress call from a ship in trouble. This overrode Franky's standard security directives and it was adjusting course to meet the ship. I, however, did not share its lack of worry about a ship that had appeared out of nowhere, fifty thousand light-years from anywhere we knew. I asked the main AI to wake up two protectors, just in case. You can never be too careful, especially after Servcon.

The two protectors eventually appeared, and were still very groggy from their high-speed awakening. Kichitit and Prichikit, two of my most experienced and trusted companions. I felt a lot more secure having protectors around me and I sent them down to the pod bay. The Medlab had already sent two Medunits and it looked like we were as ready as we could be for anything that might happen when the ship arrived.

The IFF had now recognised the ship as being Terran, which was odd. We were tens of thousands of light-years away from any of our galactic civilisation, so what was it doing here? The white spec approached us out of the blackness and despite the distress call saying it had hull and engine damage, it looked pristine. Again, very odd. The main AI took over local control and docking completed with no problems. The airlock opened and a black-clad Terran stepped out. She waved Kichitit and Prichikit over.

They disappeared into the ship and then, without warning, five black clad Terrans raced out. They spread into the ship, moving quickly and purposefully as two of them headed straight for me. An arm appeared around the doorway and a grenade was tossed in, instantly filling the cabin with clouds of smoke. Just one breath of that and everything went dark...

...until I slowly swam awake, still in my chair, but with the grinning face of a Terran right in front of me. Unfortunately, I recognised her all too well. She had been on Servcon when Franky shot the roof off launch control. Those awful Terran eyes with their black dot in the centre of so much white, the greasy yellow skin and even greasier black hair. Being that close to a skin covered face was not pleasant and she smelled even worse than I remembered.

"You Flivvers are so trusting," she said. "Still, we wouldn't have got in if you weren't, so good for you."

The rest of her team led in the hive council, obviously rounded up from across the ship. "Right," she said, "all we want is that Harpy. Hand her over and we'll be out of your hair, sorry feathers," with a smirk at her joke.

I was still struggling to understand what had just happened.

"But how can you be here on our timeline?" I said. "We should be nowhere near each other in either time or space."

"Well," she said, "here's the thing. We knew you were looking for this place so we followed you from Servcon. We had a little trouble synching our jumps, but you're here now so just give us the Harpy and we'll be off."

"But I don't understand why you came all of this way," I said. "She's just one person."

"Oh, you've no idea what you've got there," she said. "Look at what she did on Servcon. Everyone who's anyone wants their own organic sentient weapon."

"But any hive protector can do that," I said. "Also, if she's so valuable then why don't you make some more?"

"One of your protectors can't destroy things and stay alive can they?" she said. "Also, making them's the problem. It's not only illegal but very difficult. She's one of only three we know about and the other two've disappeared into reltime. What she did on Servcon means I can name my price."

She lent in towards me, the smell of her breath making me pull away. "So stop pissing about and hand her over. I might even let you keep your ship if you're a good little chicken."

"Well, you are too late," I said. "Soffee and Franky have gone to the third planet and you'll have to find her there."

She muttered a curse.

"So it has a name eh, Soffee is it? Look, you feathered piece of shit. I haven't come all of this way for nothing. Tell her to come back here or I'll start dumping your mates overboard. In any case, while you and I have been having our little chat, my tech has started taking control of your ship. Maybe we'll take the Harpy and the ship as well. What do you think about that?"

She called across to her team, telling them to get their bloody fingers out <95% xlate confidence>. However, one of them called straight back that five pods had been launched to the planet, with life signs showing that the Harpy was in one of them.

My black-clad questioner turned back to me, opened her mouth as if to ask another question then turned back. She called to her team and led two of them out down to their ship in the pod bay. There they threw out our two bound and unconscious protectors and launched straight off, accelerating hard into the blackness. Kichitit and Prichikit floated there in the micro-gravity of the pod bay, still and unmoving. Their life signs were low. What had the Terrans done to them?

"Hey you," interrupted my thoughts. One of the remaining black clad Terrans was looking at me. "My name's Dougie and I'm an old friend of Franky and Soffee. I am sure we can be friends about all of this but I need you to get over there where I can see you. My colleague gets very nervous when she can't see everyone and we don't want any nasty accidents, do we?"

"So you are the person Soffee told me about," I said to his smiling face. "I think she said the Terran scumbag she is going to kill the next time she sees you."

The skin on his face momentarily tightened, but almost immediately that false smile returned.

"I'm sure she was only joking," he said. 'We always had some good laughs on CS1. Now get your feathered arse moving and shut up."

He shoved me across the cabin and went back to the Terran female working at the console. The room fell silent as first one, and then another, green tell-tales appeared. From the accompanying chuckles and cracking noises she made with her hands it was obvious that she was pleased with what she was doing. I caught the eye of a council member, but he looked scared. I tried another, but it was obvious that anything we were going to do would have to be just me.

Time went by and alongside the multiplying green tell-tales, the IFF flicked up a series of alerts. There was a plot showing the flights of two missiles which had been launched from the third planet. They were aimed at the Terrans' ship and AI-driven intelligent targeting was indicated. This was then overlaid by a report saying that our ship's main armament was off-line.

The Terrans' ship was now travelling far too fast to get back to us and its passengers had obviously seen the missile launches. Their leader popped up on the console and shouted at Dougie. After a quick glance at the IFF console, Dougie shouted back that there was nothing he could do, and that just started more shouting.

I caught a brief flash of blue in the doorway. A face peeked around the door and then suddenly, Kichitit and Prichikit rushed in. The technician at the console pulled out a weapon. Kichitit saw the movement but the technician fired, a spike of light going through Kichitit's chest. Kichitit flopped and barged into Dougie.

Prichikit snatched out a flechette and threw it straight back at the technician who was now dropping behind her console. Its metallic flash flew across and stuck into the technician's neck, flicking open and nearly removing her head. Prichikit swooped through the spray of blood and grabbed Dougie, one hand gripping him by the throat and the other hand pressing a flechette against his eye.

The stunned silence was broken by her shouting for help. Council members leapt into action, flying across to pinion the now loudly shouting Dougie. Prichikit quickly checked the nearly headless Terran and shouted to the main AI for an emergency air flush. The cloud of blood started moving up towards the nearest vent as she turned to the still and lifeless Kichitit, who was jammed up against a console.

Her body was floppy as a child's toy, delicate tendrils of smoke trailing from a small hole burned right through her chest. I knew that they had been close friends but there was nothing I, or anyone else, could do. Prichikit tenderly picked up the body of her friend, burying her face in the limp wings as she whispered, clucking and rocking as a mother does when calming a child.

The baffled face of the black-clad Terran was still staring back at us from the comm screen and with a start, I realised we had our ship back. As if to emphasise this, the status of the main armament flicked back to fully operational with a targeting solution appearing against the Terrans' ship.

So, Soffee and Franky had indeed left a plan in place, but the keening from Prichikit told me that we had more important things to do. The Terrans and their ship could wait.

34
The second is never as good as the first

Franky

I got a final wave from Soffee and it all looked pretty good, you know, X marks the spot, optimal track, no anticipated threats, usual sort of thing. Everyone was now making themselves scarce and the Smuts' readiness advisory popped up alongside mine. It was about time we did some good old-fashioned recreational exploring and I was sure that the Smuts were also pretty excited, even if they'd never admit that to any bone-brained Terran.

Down went the countdown, up came the big fat zero and off we blasted, everything disappearing into the billowing white clouds. A good climb out, the boost shut off and over our intra-orbital parabola we went, curving down towards our targeted city.

Apart from my needless worries about the lack of comms and Soffee's disagreement with that alien landing ship, this planet had been pretty much as Dougie had described. So, when the IFF lit up with a shouting red missile alert, all I could do was administer myself a good mental kicking for not keeping my eyes open. Something was now tracking in out of the horizon, splitting in two and then in two again. Two of these projectiles were after me and two were after the Smuts. A brain tickle interrupted my mental cursing.

"Our IFF has given us a 50% chance of avoiding the projectiles and is requesting autonomous action. We have agreed and will see you on the surface."

Their pod started jumping around as my IFF asked exactly the same question, and almost before I'd started a "Ye.." we leapt upwards, my face banging into the console. Straight back down again and my world disintegrated into an impossible maelstrom of noise and wind. That couldn't be right, I could see the sky, and then a crash-hood snapped over me and everything flicked out like a light.

You'll no doubt know that "Where the hell am I?" feeling as you wake up in the morning, followed by a "What the hell did I get up to and with who?" follow-up? Well, as the greyness cleared I could smell burning, there was a worried voice shouting in my ear and my first proper thought was indeed what an amazing party that must have been. My second thought wondered why I was surrounded by flames and everything hurt.

Something grabbed my arm and started running through what, to my fevered mind at least, seemed like a flaming pit of hell. We'd only gone five agonising steps when there was an enormous explosion and up I flew into the air. Flames and the snapshot of a damaged suit spun before my eyes before my head was rammed through coarse vegetation and everything else tried to bend my neck past its elastic limit. A hearty thwack to the 'ole wedding veg brought me to an abrupt halt and that just added to the clouds of stars, watering eyes and breathless agony.

The agonising reality of spiky vegetation inserted where spiky vegetation shouldn't ever be inserted convinced me to sit back up again, and almost in my face was the remains of a suit which had absorbed an explosion by the simple means of disintegrating. Behind these remains were those of my pod. It was on fire, surrounded by parts of itself, also on fire, with other stuff scattered around a large crater that had been punched into the ground.

I tried getting to my feet, but every bone and muscle screamed that they didn't want to. Another attempt and I just about managed to inch myself up and actually, I probably needed to get away from all of that smoke and fire. The beginnings of a shuffle and I promptly fell over a piece of twisted wreckage. Even louder shouts from those sore body parts greeted my four letter attempts at describing the wreckage, but at least it was a distraction from the flames.

I managed to stagger away, but after the first few steps I came up short. I was in the middle of a woodland. OK, so it wasn't an Old-Earth woodland, but it was still a woodland. I looked back at the fiery destruction and back to the trees. Where the hell was I, and as that thought bounced around between my ears I was transported even further up the surreal creek by a Smut's brain tickle.

An involuntary glance around, but come on, get a grip. There weren't any Smuts here even if I was still getting that spray of telepathic information. They were both, apparently, OK. Their pod had been damaged by one of those missiles but they'd managed to land near the city we'd been aiming for. Unfortunately I was a long way away, or rather they were. My pod had spiralled off to crash about two hundred klicks from where they'd landed, and between them and me was a large expanse of mixed forest, scrub and rocky wastes.

And it hadn't finished yet. They might be able to fix their pod, and if they could, they'd come over and pick me up. They would also contact Soffee's group to let them know what had happened. The message ended with a rather worrying statement that I should keep a lookout for anything native, large and aggressive. And then my brain stopped itching.

Smuts can always tell when you're listening, even if I could hardly reply being two hundred klicks away. Still, they'd given me better news that I had any right to expect. I might be here, wherever that was on this bloody planet, but at least I was here and they were there. I just hoped that Soffee wouldn't immediately leap into a pod to come and get me, as whatever had just shot us down would undoubtedly try and do the same to her.

These thoughts flickered through my mind as the flames continued to consume the pod. Difficult to believe really - almost no time at all ago I'd been hugging Soffee and now I was here watching my pod go up in flames. You'd almost laugh if it wasn't so flippin' serious, especially as Soffee had wanted to get to this planet for most of her life. Be careful what you wish for, I always think.

Still, if there's one good thing about violent impacts, it's that everything tends to get thrown away from the point of impact. Of course, this throwing away doesn't exactly keep things working, but while the pod's internals burned themselves out I could at least start having a look at what had been projected about the place.

Almost immediately things started looking up. Embedded in a native bush type thing was my rather worse for wear emergency kit bag. I then found my PDW in its impact resistant gel case. Scattered about like edible confetti was an assortment of shrink wrapped, guaranteed to last for years, nutritionally balanced, packets of food. Tasted like, well not very much, but they'd keep you alive past the constipation capacity of your insides, or at least according to the small print. My HUD had also been busy, and by the time I'd finished getting my rather pathetic pile of goodies together we had a map and a much better idea of where I'd landed, sorry, planted.

As I'd guessed, I was stuck in a woodland. A brief flashback to other fun and games in other woodlands on other planets, but a woodland's a woodland right? Apparently this particular one stretched out past the horizon in all directions, with the odd bare hillock distributed here and there. The IFF then added that I should probably get to that higher ground, as the surrounding woodland provided a lot of cover for the local wildlife. And, of course, the way we got to higher ground was a walk through the woodland.

My eyes focused back from the HUDs best efforts and that was the second time someone or something had mentioned the local wildlife. Also, now I came to take a proper look at this woodland, what was it? The trees were more thickened vines than trees. The ground was covered in plant life, but it was odd shapes and with colours across the rainbow. In fact, some of it almost glowed. I'd also swear I kept catching movements out of the corner of my eye, but surely plants couldn't move?

I could feel my infallible neck hairs rising. Sure, we were on a new planet, but you know how it is. When everything around you is different, then that's fine. It's just different. Similarly, if everything around you is pretty familiar then that's also fine. It looks familiar. It's when everything around you is sort of familiar but sort of not that you start getting the shivers. And I was getting the shivers.

The flames had started to die down and it was pretty obvious that whatever might have been useful in the pod's remains was now charred beyond recognition. I'd collected together everything useful and if both the Smuts and the IFF thought that I needed to look out for wild animals, I probably needed to start doing that, and right now.

The track I'd been given through the woodland by my HUD's nice fat arrow was your typical path beaten down by things that walked. So, native earth, pretty flat and weaving off through the trees. Even with all of those oddities speckled around it was actually rather pleasant walking along in the mottled shade, and then I nearly trod on two large paw prints pressed into the ground.

I froze, and the whole woodland went silent. Well OK, not silent, but it still felt like something was watching. No alarms from the IFF. Nothing I could see. Just those icy fingers crawling up my spine. Whatever had made those prints was obviously not here at the moment, but it certainly had been. So, nice to have confirmation of the Smuts' and IFF's worries, but I really needed to get out of here.

I started walking again and this time a little faster. The trouble was I couldn't stop looking around, twisting and turning, not paying attention where I was walking, and that didn't help with those aches and pains from the crash. More and more were starting to complain, and the further I went, the louder the complaints were getting. I was just thinking that maybe a quick break might be in order, when the woodland in front of me opened out into grass and sky. Another couple of steps and I was out in the open, at the bottom of a grassy slope.

The HUD gave a triumphant "Ta dah!" but just where had it brought me? The flat plain of woodland still extended out to the horizon, dotted with the same speckling of hillocks that were no doubt just like the one I was on. The remaining trail of smoke from the pod's demise was the only thing above the greeny-brown expanse and was almost a punctuation mark for my arrival both there and here.

Turning back to the rising ground, I could see a line of rocky outcrops running left and right along the crest of the slope, but these weren't natural. Oh no, these weren't natural at all. Angles, flats, jagged edges, sprays of vegetation. It was a line of buildings.

All the HUD could tell me was that this was indeed a line of buildings, but surely that was good news? Buildings meant sentients, sentients meant tech and that meant help. Assuming, of course, that whoever lived here wasn't mates with whoever had just shot me down.

A formal roadway meandered out of the woodland edge and snaked up towards a creeper strewn gap in the buildings. I started following its cracked and broken surface and as the slope rounded off, the buildings had now extended up to three, maybe four storeys of cracked construction, with a matching line of more distant ruined buildings seen through the creeper draped gap in front of me.

Lines of doors and windows stretched away on either side, but they were just holes. No doors, no glass, just blank eyes staring back at me through lashes of encrusting vegetation. The damage? The vegetation? This was decades, maybe centuries, worth of decay.

I went through the vegetation festooned gap and there, in the centre of the ring of buildings, was a large dished area. A dishevelled mess of native grass, larger plants, sand and rock but nothing else really. Except, that is, for the extensive animal tracks all over the place and nothing small made tracks that big.

I wandered over to the building. The doorways had odd proportions, not very high and a lot wider than you might expect, but then they would do wouldn't they? Behind the first was an empty room and behind that was another even darker room.

The next doorway was the same, but I spun around as the merest breath of air tickled my neck. Those same ranks of empty doors and windows stared back. I couldn't see anything, I couldn't hear anything, but those neck hairs swore blind that someone was watching.

Now, the first rule of adventure is that you don't EVER go anywhere, and least of all a darkened room or building, without first knowing exactly what's in there. And of course, that's exactly what our intrepid hero/heroine does with the usual nasty consequences. Still, being a smarter sort of consumer, I got out the micro-drone I had secreted in my emergency backpack.

Up it bounced, its multi-prop whine triggering a cascade of echoes back from the ruined buildings, as its feed showed the walls, roofs, doors and windows plus that ever-present vegetation. The whole place was a ruin and actually, it was starting to give me the creeps. Ruins of your own civilisation was bad enough, but ruins of someone else's? Brrrh – made your blood run cold. Trouble was, if I didn't want to stay here I'd have to take another walk through the woods, and I didn't want to do that.

So, another randomly selected door and the drone showed me just more blank rooms, with the next door the same, and the next. Everywhere was empty, cleared out, the whole place gently rotting in the sunshine.

I left the drone to it as I kept a more general eye out and suddenly, fortune favoured the bravely random. The block I was now looking at was different to the one I'd started with and the drone had gone in through a door, then through another one further in, before finding a set of stairs running up the back wall.

It zipped straight up and found a long room running straight back out towards the front of the building. In one corner was a divided off space with the sort of plumbing that, regardless of species, was pretty self-explanatory. However, what was more interesting was the wire basket that had been placed alongside some bags and various other bits and pieces. The drone flagged up a quick evidence of sentient life flag then flew back to me out of the first-floor window.

Well, we already know the first rule of adventure, but there's also that essential first rule of survival, find shelter. So, a big tick for that then. I mean, if someone's stuff's already there, it must be a good place to stay. However, that's only the start survival-wise. The second rule of survival is to find water, and then there's the third rule, find something to eat, as well as the fourth, don't get eaten. With my day so far, maybe I'd just count myself lucky that I'd satisfied that first rule.

So, without too much thought I walked straight through the doorway, my head scuffing against the low ceiling as I headed in towards the back room. Sure enough, there was that flight of stairs. The treads were really odd, but then they probably would be wouldn't they? What was interesting, and worrying, however was the collection of odd-looking footprints in the dust.

I checked with the IFF. It couldn't see anything moving, I was already in here, so why not eh? The stair treads were so narrow that my foot slipped straight off on the first attempt. The second attempt was more successful, even if only having the front bit of my foot in contact was completely calf-cramping. Each succeeding step was even more agonising than the last and it was a real relief when my eyes slowly came up level with the floor above.

Walking away from me were a smudged path of those odd footprints and I just about managed to join them before my legs stopped working. A quick stagger across and there was the basket, a neat little collection of metal strappings twisted together and resting on a slab of concrete. Judging by the charred remains, whoever lived here used it to cook the dried vegetation lying alongside. However, it was that pile of bags that really rang my bell.

I bent to have a better look, but stopped. There'd been a noise, downstairs. I totally froze, listening so hard that my ears almost flapped. The IFF popped up a tentative organic indication, so thanks genius. Why only tell me now? Something, or in fact hopefully someone, had just made a noise and was now trying very hard not to make another, and I was an idiot.

My hands feverishly activated the drone and flicked it off down the room and out of the window. I dug into my bag for the PDW which, of course, was still locked in its carry bag. A loud crash as I dropped the magazine but it snapped back in, I pulled back the cocking handle and then slipped a multi-tool into my pocket. I mean, you never know, right?

The drone was inching its way in through the front doorway downstairs. The feed just showed an empty room, before the merest whisper of sound, something swung in from the right and everything white noised as the feed disappeared.

OK, so that went well.

Silence, followed by more silence only broken by subliminal sounds of something going on very quietly...

...and then more silence.

Whoever was down there knew I was up here and they'd been watching my every move. Now they had me exactly where they wanted and I could only hope that the longer things went on without anything bad happening, the better. I'd just better hope that whoever was downstairs thought the same.

There were a couple of gentle scrapes, just like something was coming up the stairs and trying very hard not to sound like it was coming up the stairs. The drone appeared, clutched in a slim tentacle. The tentacle placed the drone on the top step before whipping away, leaving the drone sitting there smiling at me.

More silence downstairs. I tried re-activating the drone, but Mr/Ms/Mx Tech-savvy downstairs was obviously way ahead of me and nothing happened. Shit, maybe I'd just better climb out of the window and run away but no, that wouldn't work. They'd be standing there watching my fat arse appear and that wouldn't be safe or even vaguely dignified. I'd just have to grab the drone and see what happened. They had, after all, given it back to me so were obviously expecting me to do something with it.

I inched my way across the floor, trying to make as little noise as possible. Not sure why really. It knew I was up here, it had placed the drone there, so who was I trying to kid? It just seemed like a good idea even if my progress would have been easy to track by the scuffles and heavy breathing. Also, that was pretty clever putting the drone right on the edge of the top step as they'd get plenty of warning when my hand grabbed it. Which is what I did before scuttling back, all attempts at stealth completely forgotten.

Downstairs was as silent as the tomb. I had a quick look at the drone. The main power pack had been disconnected and a metal box was stuck to the body with some tape. This box had several winking lights plus a lens. Great. They'd just seen the Alien they'd been watching for the past hour retrieve the drone, and then they'd had an even closer look. And I still had no idea who was down there. I reconnected the power pack and everything powered up with its usual cheery chirp.

What to do next, but my mind really was a blank. I'd got the drone back, but what next? Maybe they'd given it back as a peace offering? Maybe it was an invite to go down and have a chat?

Who could say, but in my experience, simple as possible is often the best approach. They wanted to see me and I wanted to see them. So, why not do just that? Before I could talk myself out of it I pointed the lens at my face and waved, before slowly walking to the top of the stairs.

Ensuring that the camera stayed pointing in my direction, I took a first step down, grabbing at the wall as my heel wobbled. Another step and then another, all the time trying as hard as I could to keep the camera pointed at me and my feet stuck to the steps. First contact was going to be bad enough without whoever was down there seeing this first example of a species they'd never seen before come tumbling down the stairs.

35
Exploration

Soffee

If there is one thing worse than seeing something too awful to watch, it is seeing something too awful to watch and not being able to do anything about it. My stomach churned as red traces chased across our emotionless HUDs, both pods twisting and turning away from the missiles tracking in towards them. They were doing their best, but first one and then another red line changed to 100%-hit probabilities and they weren't going to get away from that.

The first missile smeared past the frantically evading Smuts' pod but the second punched straight through Franky's. A wave of damage reports flooded back. The Smuts' pod was still under control but Franky's plunged down towards the planet in an uncontrolled arc, down, down, down before disappearing into ground clutter.

I couldn't seem to breathe. What were we going to do? What was I going to do? He'd come back. We'd flown halfway across the galaxy and now he was gone. Bottomless black despair dissolved into five sets of wings wrapping around me, and we were here, the Smuts were there and Franky wasn't.

I couldn't even think straight but suddenly, a telepathic shout from hundreds of klicks away. The Smuts were alive. They had made contact with Franky and he was alive.

Tears of relief and deepest ragged breaths as I swayed in my friends' embrace. That Franky! He may be alive but I'm going to kill him the next time I see him, the Smut's words chasing away my jagged thoughts as I stared unseeing at the still smoking patches where the pods had just taken off from. Another shuddering breath and I couldn't stop crying. Why does he do this to me? Why am I so angry when he does? I'd waited nine years and now look what just happened. But he's safe. He's well. Get yourself together. Now.

The group hug opened and I slumped to my knees. Everyone was smiling and gently stroking my wings, but it was still almost like I was on the outside looking in. I really didn't seem to be here. A deep breath and then another, but the shock wouldn't go away. This planet was dangerous. We had all better start taking a lot more care.

The far distant Smut had already told us what it knew before disappearing back into nothing, and that was another thing. Those wretched Smuts. Hadn't they ever heard of a conversation? But Franky was OK. I hadn't been able to save him on CS1 and I almost hadn't been able to save him here. I was going to go over there right away and get him, but a Smut standing nearby butted into my chaotic thoughts.

"It is likely that whoever fired those missiles will do so again. We do not know why they didn't shoot at us on the way down, but as soon as we launched our pods they destroyed them. You must stay here. Our friends are in a much better position to find Franky."

My gabbled response was a rather curt assessment of why I disagreed with those last statements, but the girls chipped in with their agreement. A suit also came in, agreeing with the Smuts.

I started to hand out another piece of my mind, but my anger petered out. They were right. We were here, two of our pods had been destroyed and the Smuts and Franky were now over the ocean. Going over there now would not achieve anything except losing another pod and probably those in it. We were protectors. The best way to protect our hive was to find whoever had fired those missiles and stop them.

Another tickle in my brain answered that thought.

"We know Flivver ways and this must be difficult for you. You should consider all of us protectors and leave retrieving Franky to those over the sea. You can then concentrate on finding out who is directing these defences and do something about it."

I looked around at the Smuts, the girls, Hecate and Medea, and the Grunt. They could all see the good sense in what the Smut had said. Two Smuts were over there and would find Franky. We all had protector work to do and the sooner we started, the better it would be for all of us.

"Alright then," I said, "let's start getting ready for our part of this job."

That raised a smile. People turned away to start getting ready, but I could see that the girls were still rather shocked by what had happened. After several raised voices over the simplest of things, the Smuts and the Grunt stepped in, waving us to go and sit down. They then got straight on with getting things ready and, I have to admit, I was happy to watch. To my voiced thanks, a Smut responded with something sympathetic if totally untranslatable.

By the time the suits were fully prepared and marshalled into line, the usual laughing and joking was bouncing around between us again. I called everyone together for a group hug, which was respectfully declined by the Smuts and the Grunt, and it really looked like we were ready to go.

The girls and I got into our suits. A cloud of drones leapt into the air and everything came up in full tactical mode. I was confidently informed that everything was under control and there was nothing at all to worry about. Which was easy for my suit to say. We would no doubt soon see how true that was, but whatever happened we were protectors. Only their gods would be able to help anyone or anything that got in our way.

A mental nod to the Smuts and we started walking along the meandering roadway that led towards the city. The Grunt waved us off before turning back to its guard duty, a large weapon clasped in equally large and capable hands.

Cracked and uneven concrete marked our path across the gently undulating and trouble-free plain. The suit IFFs were on such high alert that it was almost an anticlimax when we crested the final slope and there was the city spreading away from us right out to the horizon. Our cracked pathway changed to a clean, well maintained road surface and before we knew it we were straight into the still and silent cityscape.

Lines of identical single storey buildings extended off down the road, walls painted the same colour as the gravel surrounding them, and each fenced off from its neighbours. They were immaculate, seemingly freshly painted, the gravel brushed perfectly flat. The IFFs could see nothing, not a movement, not a sound, not a soul. It was almost like the residents had gone like they normally did each morning, leaving their pristine houses to bake in the sun and await their return.

Every hundred metres or so identical roads went off left and right, each lined with more identical buildings and extending out to distant vanishing points. Circe wandered over to have a look at one of the houses and I was about to tell her to be careful, but what was the point? There was no one here, and nothing moving.

Her suit dwarfed the firmly closed front door, so she went around to one of the windows. There, her video feed showed a large room full of what was obviously the local's best version of interior design. It certainly looked very tidy, but covered in dust. No one had lived here for a very long time. In fact, as far as we could see, all around us was just too clean, too tidy and almost sterile, like we were in a full-sized model city before the people had been added.

We kept on walking and coming up to the next junction, spread out on one side was a scene of total devastation. Several blocks had been flattened, with only scattered jumbles of rubble to mark the demise of whatever used to be there. What was strange was that the damage started and ended exactly along the roadways bounding each block, almost as if the destruction had been carefully limited to fit exactly into each precisely defined rectangle.

My suit indicated that a large bomb or projectile could have caused the damage, but it had no idea why the destroyed areas were so neatly defined. Also, whatever had happened had happened a long time ago, leaving just these odd rectangles of rubble as blots amongst the unbroken matrix of buildings stretching away in all directions.

"Can anyone see anything at all?" I called out, but no one could see anything that wasn't exactly like what was in front of me.

A red IFF trace popped up, then two more. These three red dots were moving in a tightly packed group several klicks away and the suits came together into a protective ring around our suit-less companions. The drone which had sent us the notifications was already speeding off to investigate.

Its view whipped across the cityscape, concentrating on a faintest shading of dust that was rising into the air. Our view rose with it into a hover and there we were. Three mechanicals were driving down adjacent roads, each of them sweeping dust into a long line that was gobbled up by other mechanicals following close behind. As we watched, one of the sweepers stopped and turned in towards a building. It reached out, extracted a broken window which it threw to its sweeping companion. A new window was inserted and the pair of mechanicals resumed their sweeping path down the road.

"So that's why everything's so neat and tidy," I murmured, being answered by amused comments about how we could do with something like that to clean up after Franky. Everyone was obviously in good spirits, especially as we now had firm evidence of an existing co-ordinating intelligence, but what was it? Where was it?

The suits were picking up the same faint, bursty transmissions we'd seen from orbit, but so widely distributed that there was nothing that could be traced. The drone kept on watching, but it really did look like the mechanicals were just sweeping along the roads and making repairs as they went.

We had a quick discussion and everyone was still eager to go on. In fact, Chary pointed out that the buildings were changing from what we'd seen so far. Maybe we were getting closer to whatever intelligence still lived on this world?

She was right. The buildings had indeed grown both upwards and outwards, and some had ornate frontages which were covered in colours and symbols. Maybe we were moving into a shopping or business district? Wherever we were, the only movement was those mechanicals and these now seemed to be scattered right across the city. The IFFs were doing their best to track every one, but whatever they were doing, they were doing it while staying well away from us.

The buildings continued to grow in size as we continued down the road, their ramparts rising ever higher. We seemed to be entering into what was almost a canyon, with our footsteps and the whining of drones echoing between the buildings.

A weather flash from the pod Navcom broke into our contemplation, showing bad weather coming in from the sea. After the lovely weather we had been having, that was difficult to believe, but a glance upwards saw that the previously bright blue sky was disappearing behind filmy clouds which seemed to thicken as we looked. Whorls of dust had started to curl around the buildings and an updated weather advisory popped up with the urgent recommendation to seek shelter. Strong winds and torrential rain would likely hit us within half an hour.

Torrential rain? Who would have thought it? I would love to see any rain, let alone rain that hard, but the weather warning underlined the Navcom's recommendation, especially if all of that water was going to drop out of the sky on top of us.

"We're only about 5 minutes away from that square, so let's get a move on," I called out, glancing down at our pedestrians. Flicking them a quick apology, I picked up the two Smuts and deposited one on each shoulder. Circe picked up Medea and Hecate and we sped off down the road.

The lines of buildings converging in front of us slowly widened as a distant line of buildings revealed itself. The road opened and we ran out onto a vast, featureless plaza. In all of the emptiness there was just a single feature, a small round building right in the centre, sitting there like a pill on a table top. The whole place wore a neat, silent emptiness, across which the rising wind scuffed eddies of sand. The suits were expressing worries about being stuck out here with no cover, but that was just their IFFs worrying.

I sent Scylla off to have a look at the nearest buildings while everyone else headed towards the pill-like structure in the centre. This was where there had been some indications of an entrance going underground and we all wanted to see that.

As we approached, our suits spread out to provide full defensive coverage and before I could say anything, one of the Smuts dropped down from my suit. It walked towards a hole in side of the building, sidled up to one edge and peered cautiously inside.

"It's just a tunnel running through to the centre of the building," it said, before disappearing into the hole without another word.

My "What are you doing?" got no response, so I re-directed a drone, its feed flying in over the Smut's head and down the tunnel towards a bright flare of light at the end. We couldn't leave the Smut on its own, so I moved across and followed straight after. My question asking whether it didn't think that this was rather dangerous, got the response that it could not detect any sentient life so it did not consider what it was doing in any way dangerous. To my further question asking who, in that case, had shot missiles at the pods, it did not bother to answer.

We walked out into a circular space, bounded by smooth inner walls several stories high. In the centre was a large fenced-off hole with a ramp dropping down out of sight around the edge. From the drone hovering above we could see it circling down into darkness.

The weather had now really changed. Scatters of rain had started to fall out of a bruised purple sky and gusts of wind were coming from all directions. Both of the Smuts had declined suits before we left and it now looked like they were sorely regretting their decision. They and our protector sisters had a firm grip on the nearest suit leg and were imploring us to get out of the weather as soon as possible. The Navcom's weather warning repeated itself, with the strongest recommendation to immediately seek shelter. Wind speeds were increasing and heavy rain would hit very soon.

A drone dropped down the ramp hole. It went as far as it could before radio contact was lost and then came back to its signal-loss failsafe position. The ramp surface looked easily walkable and there was dim artificial lighting set into the walls. The other drones dropped down after it.

"We need to get under cover," I called out. "What about the ramp? Anyone got any ideas?"

"These buildings have doors but they are much too small," said Scylla, who was still outside investigating. "Also, I can't see what's inside."

"OK," I replied. "Can you have a look and let me know?"

There was a quickly chittered affirmative and I turned back to our assembled and even more miserable-looking party.

"What do you think?" I said. "Down the ramp or wait and see if the buildings are any good?" but Scylla broke straight back in.

"I've made some holes but these buildings are full of tech and other rubbish. There's no space for anyone, so I say go down your ramp. Also," this with an amused tone in her voice, "straight after I broke in, one of those cleaning mechanicals turned up and it's now patching up the holes. So, even if we did go in, we'd have to break our way out again."

A particularly strong gust of wind blew past and my suit swayed, shifting its feet to maintain balance. The Smut holding onto one leg gave me an indignant "Get on with it!" which was echoed by everyone else not in a suit and holding on for dear life.

OK, I thought, decision made.

"We're going down the ramp," I called out. "Scylla, get back here and follow us down."

I picked up both of the Smuts, Circe picked up Medea and Hecate and we ran for it. Even for a suit this was now quite hazardous as gusts were showing in excess of a hundred kph, and just to make matters worse, all of the water in the sky suddenly dropped on top of us. Pursued by the wind-blown deluge, we raced down the ramp away from all of that weather.

Dim artificial light and the suits' image intensification lit the way, with our drone cloud dropping down the centre of the ramp in front of us. After several more circuits, an IFF warning popped up. We all came to a halt and Circe's and my very uncomfortable passengers jumped off. The drone cloud had also now stopped at the very bottom of the ramp and their feeds showed a vast dimly lit space extending away from them.

A proximity alert blared out. Scylla's and my suits spun around, mounting blasters as two of the cleaning mechanicals we had seen earlier came thundering down towards us. Everyone scattered to the sides of the tunnel and I shouted out not to shoot. The mechanicals stopped, turned around, then sat there unmoving.

"They must be sheltering from the weather," said Scylla and indeed, water was streaming off them.

"Is everyone OK?" I called out.

"We're fine," Scylla called back, "although those two mechanicals nearly got melted."

No one seemed too worried apart from our poor pedestrians, all of whom were calling out variations of being cold, wet and having a dreadful time.

The two bedraggled Smuts left the equally bedraggled Medea and Hecate and walked slowly up the ramp towards the mechanicals. Each mechanical was just like the ones we'd seen earlier, except that these had some sort of a cockpit at one end.

I called out a warning but the Smuts took no notice. One of them started fiddling with one of the mechanical's cockpit edges, and with a hiss and a creak a large panel swung upwards. From the Smuts' selected telepathic blowback, the cockpit was configured for a 4 or 6-limbed entity. From their rude comments it was obviously an odd shape.

Before I could say anything, one of them leapt in. The cockpit lights came on and the panel swung back down again, locking shut. The mechanical jerked forward then stopped, with corresponding squawks of alarm from our suits' IFFs. It lurched forward again and started moving up the ramp.

The same panel on the other mechanical swung open and the second Smut jumped in. After a brief pause, the lights came on, the cockpit closed and the mechanical started moving up the ramp after the first. All we got from the drivers was a brief telepathic statement saying that they were taking the mechanicals for a test drive and would keep us updated.

Smuts! What a species they are to be near.

36
Another of those aliens

Franky

I'd been concentrating so hard on not stumbling down the stairs that the first chance I got to see what was waiting was after I'd stepped onto that lovely flat floor. Standing there watching was a three-legged figure, with all three of its arms clasping bags and all three of its eyes having a very good look at me.

Well I've seen you before! Or, correction, I've certainly seen one of your mates. This guy, gal, whatever, was the spitting image of my friend on the ring-ship and even though I'd now seen two of them, still a totally new species. Hey, maybe I'd finally made contact with one of the mystery natives. These and other thoughts chased around between my ears as we stood there looking at each other. Each of us undoubtedly looked equally strange to the other but then that's the whole thing about being alien isn't it?

I tried a friendly "Hi, what's happening?" but unlike its mate back on the ship it obviously didn't understand a word.

I repeated what I'd said, and this time my translator also had a go. Still no reaction. OK, so maybe a lower-tech approach would work better. I bent down and scratched out an approximation of my pod, the planet and an arrow showing me crashing onto it. There was a definite reaction this time, together with a blurt of sounds and waving of arms that my translator immediately and helpfully professed to know nothing about at all.

Still, pretty pictures were obviously working so it bent down and drew the same kind of diagram I had, this time adding a star shape to show where it had come from. So a good start. It could understand a picture and so could I, but this crucial moment was interrupted by what I can only describe as a long, blue, multi-jointed, hairy arm/tentacle flying in through the door and jerking my companion outside.

A split-second's mental paralysis, but I activated the drone and flung it out to see what was going on. I then grabbed my PDW and slid along the wall to the outer doorway, keeping as flat as possible to avoid any other unexpected tentacular intrusions.

The drone was up and away, stopping several storeys up where its feed showed a large blue creature having a really good look at the Alien. A blue arm/tentacle was wrapped around my new friend while another administered a good prodding. Judging by both creatures' body language, they were clearly not the best of friends.

What I could do was not immediately obvious, especially as the big blue guy was several times bigger than me. However, I'm pleased to say that I didn't follow my head's advice to stay out of the way while the big blue animal dealt with the Alien. Instead, I followed my gut. I stepped out of the doorway, lifted the PDW, and as that blue head turned to have a look at this new creature who'd so suddenly appeared, let auto-targeting put half a mag into it. That was only going to end one way and its body slumped to the ground, flicking my tripedal friend out along the ground like a bowling ball. I had a quick look around before stepping smartly back into the doorway, watching and waiting in case anything else turned up.

The drone zipped over the slumped and oozing blue job, gave it a firm thumbs down, zipped over the Alien, gave it a firm thumbs up, reminded me to check my magazine and started circling back upwards. Its feed pulled back to show our ring of buildings sitting inside a large circular grassy area edged by that never-ending woodland. An overlay of three red indicator dots popped up, converging fast, coming right at us and no more than half a klick away.

Firing the PDW is nothing if not very, very loud and as well as me being slightly deafened, any living creature within a couple of klicks was going to know exactly where I was. Luckily, the drone was well ahead of me and indicated that one of the towers on the opposite side of the amphitheatre appeared to have a way to the top and, more importantly, all of the entrances were small. The IFF confirmed that me and my new mate could get in and nothing the size of our attacker could get in after us, probably, or at least hopefully.

I ran over to the Alien who was lying flat out on what looked like its back. Grabbing an arm, I pointed to the base of the indicated tower and started helping it up. It was still pretty groggy and having something like me grabbing hold of its arm didn't do much for its grip on reality, especially after that blue job. However, three legs were obviously better than two and it sped away towards the doorway in the base of the tower.

In we ran, both of us doing our best to avoid the low ceiling and assorted debris. We raced for the back staircase and it was those same thin steps all over again. Up we went, then straight up the next set, and then the next, higher and higher and hopefully further and further away from our pursuers. I was completely out of breath, but having large blue creatures chasing after you was one hell of a motivator.

We finally got to a room that didn't have any more stairs going up and both of us dropped to the floor, gasping for breath. My drone feed showed the first of our pursuers bursting out of the forest, with two more close behind. Four-ish metres long, high as me, six legs, multi-jointed arm/tentacle at each shoulder and a large head with well-equipped mouth. Exactly like what had just grabbed hold of my alien mate.

Each was clearly on the lookout as they ran in through that gap in the buildings, sniffing the air and keeping a close eye on their fallen comrade. One cautiously walked up, had a good look and then a very good sniff before calling out to the others. My translator had no idea what it was saying, but I could probably guess. Something like "Where are they?" or "How are we going to catch them and eat them?"

One lifted its nose for several vigorous sniffs before padding across to the base of our building. It tried to get in but was far too large. It then tried shoving an arm/tentacle in through the doorway, but that didn't work either. Its two mates came lolloping up and after much conferring, three heads lifted up to stare straight at me looking down at them.

I glanced back at my alien friend but it obviously had far more interesting things to do. Pieces of tech were spread across the floor and it gestured for me to pass the drone control. I handed it over then went back to watch the blue guys. Several minutes later I felt a tap on my arm and it was the Alien, waving at my bag with a "Can I have a look?" type gesture. I replied with what I hoped sounded like a friendly affirmative, before looking back outside.

Two of our pursuers had now decided that they were going to try climbing up the outside of the building. At the same time, the drone's low power alert went off, which was not helpful. We'd soon be blind to anything I couldn't see out of the window. I just hoped nothing was coming up the stairs.

There was another tap on my arm. I turned to see that my friend had picked up a power pack and was jiggering a connection to one of its own pieces of equipment. Gesturing at my earpiece, an arm/tentacle came straight up and plucked it out of my ear, to be connected into the growing collection of bits. It was obviously trying to get our two techs to talk to each other, but doing so using all three arm/tentacles at once, with a separate eye assigned to each arm/tentacle. Impressive, if more than a bit weird to watch. Still, I'd be interested in seeing how that all went.

It was well on the way to connecting up every bit of tech we had, but interestingly, everything was plugged into my main power pack. It must have been completely out of power. I was amazed. When did anyone ever run out of power? I was still watching when the drone flew in through the window and landed. My friend reached across and started connecting it up to its tech stew.

I was brought straight back to what was happening outside by scrabbling, slipping and what was undoubtedly those blue jobs' version of bad language. I'd been badly distracted and looking out of the window, the closest was no more than a couple of metres down and using all eight of its limbs to hold onto the vertical wall.

I swung the PDW into my shoulder and let rip, which at that range chewed a large gooey hole in what was looking at me. It flopped, falling onto the second creature which was clinging on just below. Piercing screams followed both bodies as they bounced down to the bottom of the building, hitting the ground with a soggy thump. The remaining creature walked up to the unmoving bodies and spent a long time checking them over. It then sat back on its haunches and stared up at me.

I must admit that as well as being deafened, again, by the PDW, I was rather sickened by what I'd done. OK, so these guys were after eating me and my alien pal, but while I'd talked the talk, I'd never actually walked the walk. That was only the second time I'd ever fired the PDW and the amount of death and destruction it dealt out was truly shocking.

I had another look out of the window but the remaining blue creature was still sitting there staring. There was a noise behind me and I jumped, but it was only the Alien who now had a small piece of equipment attached to its head whilst it made noises and watched a little screen. Looked like it was having fun so I went off for a quick recce down the stairs.

As I staggered my way down, it struck me that I'd never, ever seen anything like this place. It seemed to have been built and never finished, or maybe finished but everything had then been ripped out. Also, the Alien couldn't be a native, as any native wouldn't be camping out here in the wasteland. The whole planet had obviously been built by an advanced civilisation, but where was the tech, the people, or even the rubbish? Even if they'd decided to go off somewhere else, no one cleans up before they leave. It was just very strange and I couldn't make head or tail of it.

Back up to the top room and the Alien was still deep in its game of making tech stew. As I wandered over, an arm/tentacle offered me my earpiece back with a gesture to stick it in my ear. Hey, it was even wiped clean. Nice.

The Alien grunted. There was a momentary pause before the translator said: "Can you understand?" <55% xlate confidence>

I smiled back. What a flippin' genius.

"I understand," I replied. "Can you understand me?"

Judging by its blank expression I knew the answer to that one. It fiddled some more and then looked back at me. I repeated myself.

The answering expression said that it had definitely got something this time and we immediately celebrated by shouting at each other and not listening to anything the other person said. Several seconds of enthusiastic chaos later we paused, both of us rather embarrassed. The Alien had another fiddle and then we started on a more measured test.

It turned out that just like me, my new friend had been shot down while attempting to land. She, or at least that was the translator's best opinion, belonged to a species local to this part of the galaxy, although a long way away. They'd detected signs of high-tech life on this planet a long time ago, although with the RF time delay being many hundreds of years, what they were getting was centuries out of date. They had sent an FTL ship to investigate but it hadn't returned. She had then been sent out in another ship, but as we'd both found, landing on this planet could be hazardous. Her being attacked by large flying creatures after she'd landed was merely one example of this.

Anyway, she'd been here for at least a standard year, surviving in the various deserted buildings that were dotted about. She was sure that there was working tech somewhere, but her translation tech failed just as she was explaining why she'd been avoiding the cities.

After more fiddling about, she continued with comments about the native animals, including the blue jobs, and was sure that she'd never come across any of the sentients that had built the world. As far as food went, she'd found enough to keep her going by eating very small amounts of things she'd found, and then only eating larger amounts of what hadn't made her sick. She'd done a fair bit of exploring but that was limited by time spent avoiding the larger carnivores, all of which seemed pretty keen on eating her.

That took a bit of time to get through, and then it was my turn. She was fascinated by the fact that my party consisted of four different sentient species, one of which was telepathic and one of which had wings and could fly. The idea that I was one species and Soffee was at least half of another was something she found both hilarious and rather shocking. I could tell that she was wrestling with whether to ask the more obvious boy/girl questions, but maybe she was just too polite.

I mentioned that I'd seen another of her species and immediately disappeared under a slew of questions, most of which I couldn't answer. She seemed to think that this individual was the pilot of the ship they'd lost, but if that was the case then how had he found himself on my timeline, on a ship half way across the galaxy? Obviously a key question, even if a complete mystery, and I could tell she wasn't going to leave that one alone.

Now, everything I've just recounted is a much-summarised version of the long and confusing conversation we had between the two of us. The differences between our languages, understandings, social confusions and the dodgy quality of the Alien's home-brewed translator meant that it took several hours of mutual incomprehension and misunderstanding to get just this far.

We did eventually arrive at the following conclusions. Here I was, on the surface of this planet, with minimal food, water and tech, limited ways of protecting myself and no way of communicating with the rest of my party. Here she was, on the surface of this planet with only native food and water, limited tech via my borrowed power pack, even fewer ways of protecting herself and no way of communicating with her ship.

I said that we'd seen no ships in orbit on the way in and while that was obviously a bit of a blow, I don't think that she was surprised. I did offer to take her back to her home planet, but got the distinct impression that while grateful, she reserved the right to refuse a flight in such a primitive ship. Tech prejudice from a stranded Alien. Marvellous eh!

All of this took a lot longer than a couple of hours and by the time we'd got as far as we had, the light was going. A quick look out of the window confirmed this and my IFF also added that it couldn't see the remaining blue creature, even if there were now other types of native creatures scavenging around the remains of the blue guys. It was only then that my alien friend said that she wanted to go and retrieve the bags she'd left in her room.

Okaaay...so she wanted to leave our nice little haven and go outside. Where the blue guys were. Not sure that was such a good idea, but she was really keen. And, of course, I couldn't let her go out there on her own, now could I?

Her quizzical stare said it all, and I suppose that my resigned acceptance meant the same in any language. I had another quick check of my IFF, but she was already off down the stairs. I raced after her, or at least as fast as I could with those hellish treads, and by the time I got to the bottom she was out of the door. My IFF was saying rather worrying things about all of the animals that were about, but she was OK about it so out I went.

I gave the vigorously snacking natives a wide berth, and took up guard by her doorway. She didn't hang about and I was handed a couple of bags as she brushed past on her way out. The scavenging creatures were now taking a lot more notice of us than they had done, but their feast was obviously still a lot more interesting.

There was the expected game going back up those flippin' stairs, but the Alien was very happy when she had all of her retrieved stuff spread out in front of her. Me, I could still feel those chills down my spine. Everything here seemed to want to eat us and I'll bet those smaller animals below wouldn't have any trouble getting up the stairs. I had another quick check, but the IFF seemed pretty relaxed even if I wasn't.

Turning back to my alien friend, she'd obviously decided it was dinner time. A parcel of toxic-looking native vegetation was being unwrapped, and she offered me a piece. Nice of her I s'pose, but I've never been a veggies kind of guy, and especially not the toxic native variety.

Still, what I had in my pack wasn't much better, and a quick delve around demonstrated that. NutriTech - all of your multi-species nutritional needs in one bar, perfect digestive transit guaranteed. Another ntime/reltime special and this one was nearly ninety-six ntime years old. I could only hope that the equivalent reltime years were somewhat shorter, but it was, what it was, what it was would at least keep me alive.

My first bite showed that these things really do not go off, flavour notwithstanding, and it was actually quite companionable sitting there with my new friend. Unfortunately, my nutribar only lasted a couple more mouthfuls and that eat by date suddenly reminded me of how far I was away from everyone. How the hell was I going to get back, especially with all of those blue jobs sniffing around? If the Smuts couldn't fix their ship then I could be sitting here for a very long time.

The only light left was a deep purple from the close of the day and it was nearly dark in here. The Alien was tidying away her stuff, and with limited power supplies I guess we were back to bed at dusk, up at dawn.

My IFF had a final look around and declared itself satisfied, assuring me that it would remain on guard. I wasn't really ready for sleep, so I offered to take the first watch. The Alien's reply seemed heartfelt and I guess that after a year down here on her own, she was pretty happy to have someone looking out for her while she slept. I'd only been down here a day or two and I knew exactly how she felt.

It was going to be a long night.

37
Ring-ship and Flivvers

Chitichca

The responsibility of a hive chief is to look after their hive. Anyone who dies must be ushered on to the next plane of existence in a manner that is both just and fitting. It is the worse possible karma for a hive member not to be able to move on correctly, and the whole hive is left incomplete until they do.

We had already left a hive member unburied on the surface of CS1 and now there was a protector who had given her life helping throw the Terrans off our ship. The person on CS1 would have to remain there, hopefully to find peace in its sandy wastes, but I would make sure that Kichitit was laid to rest in the proper manner. We could only hope that both of them would forgive us and not blight our journey.

The Medlab had already given me every assurance that it would take the greatest care of Kichitit, but there was still a certain unresolved something floating around the ship. It was an uneasiness, a gap in the circle, almost like the sacrifice had been in vain. The hive was incomplete and we could only wait for planetfall to make things right.

Also, two of the council had sought me out. Their stridently expressed opinions started with what we should be doing for Kichitit, and then they moved onto how we should pursue the Terrans' ship and destroy it. It was the only way to make up for our loss and would make sure that we would be safe. Indeed, it was a tempting thought, but the Terrans were no longer a clear and immediate threat. Custom dictated that only clear and immediate threats could be directly pursued and custom was what kept our hive safe.

The discussions just went round and around but I could not stop thinking about our two lost souls. It was an IFF alert that finally interrupted. Missiles had been launched from the planet. They had divided into intelligent clouds of independently controlled projectiles and these were targeting the Terrans' ship. The Terrans had diverted towards the fourth planet and maybe these missiles would do for us what my two colleagues wanted?

I had already been reprimanded for my lack of attention to their sage advice, their words not mine, and they stormed out to go and find any other council members who might agree with what they were saying. I was left on my own, mulling my own thoughts, when out of nowhere the face of the black-clad leader appeared on the main console.

"I know you're watching us," she said, "and I need you to start shooting those missiles with your ship's main armament. As an incentive, I've put everything about you and that Harpy on an FTL probe and believe me, my friends on Servcon are nothing like as reasonable as I am. You'd better start getting those missiles off our tail or I'll be launching that probe." Her comm dropped.

A tell-tale on the console showed that she was about nine light-minutes away. I leant back for a think and as I did so, those two council members returned, bringing the rest of the council with them.

"Wait," was my answer to their strident calls for attention. "Wait. You must hear this." Over the continuing clamour I told the main AI to replay the Terran's message. It did so, after which there was nothing but silence. "Regardless of what we do, I am sure they will launch that probe and we will never be safe. Destroying their ship will not help."

The oldest member of the council cleared his throat for attention, then had to clear it again for the noise to die down.

"I remember when Soffee and her sister first arrived on CS1," he said. "I also remember when several of you described them both as rubbish that not even the Terrans wanted. We only gave them a chance because our hive head," and he nodded to me, "took them in."

To the mutters coming back from several council members, he continued: "Look at where we are now. She protected us through the chaos. Then Franky came back and she convinced him to take us off CS1. The planet is already trying to destroy those Terrans and what with their threat to launch that probe, I really think we have other things to worry about."

Vigorous discussions broke out and he leant in towards me.

"Most are on our side," he whispered, "but ever since her fight with those two," pointing at the two noisiest council members, "they hate her very existence. If people start agreeing with the..." but he was interrupted by another IFF update.

There were now six separately co-ordinated clusters of missiles, all converging on the Terrans' ship. The planet was also scanning our ship, with indications being that any missiles left after the Terrans' ship had been destroyed would switch towards us.

The IFF then added an advisory suggesting why the Terrans' ship was being targeted. Their initial track had looped outwards before starting back in towards planet 3. To an observer, this could have looked like they were leaving the system. The cross-system passive scanning had changed to a much tighter targeting solution and missiles had then been launched. The IFF concluded that there must be an intelligence on the planet that did not want any ships to leave, although it could offer no explanation why.

The conversations around me continued as I digested this information. An advisory popped up saying that the Terrans had destroyed the closest inbound projectile cluster. Then, another advisory came up saying that they had destroyed another one. Their ship was close to slipping behind the fourth planet, but this came with an approximation flag as everything we were seeing was already nine minutes old.

Unexpectedly, the Terran leader's face re-appeared on the console. Even for such an unattractive species she really was quite dreadful to look at, especially with those awful white eyes staring back at me from her pallid face.

"You'll have seen we're having some success, but this is your last chance. Start shooting or that probe'll be going back to Servcon whatever."

I flicked off the comm, but at least the appearance of that hideous face had stopped all of the arguing.

"She is nine minutes away so she may not even be alive, and she could have already launched that probe. However, I have an idea."

Our two noisy council members muttered something about this being all very well, but they couldn't make decisions without hearing what my idea was, and anyway they had a plan which was much better than anything I had, and so on and so on. However, time was passing and they were in a minority. I would risk it.

I opened a comm. "We now have full control of our ship," I said, "and whoever is controlling those missiles is doing exactly what we want. You think we are stupid, but it is you who has forgotten that the round-trip time for travel to Servcon and back is at least fifty ntime years.

"If anyone does come here, they will find a planet covered in hives that are ready and waiting. I say do what you want as we do not care about your threats," and I closed the comm. "They will receive that in nine minutes."

There was silence as the significance of what I had just said sunk into my listening and now more appreciative audience. Small bubbles of whispered conversation started.

"I have always said it was a masterstroke making you head of the hive," murmured the oldest council member. Raising his voice, he continued: "I suggest that we agree with what our hive chief has said and start making plans in case those missiles start targeting us."

"You lot have no idea how valuable that Harpy is," dropped in the voice of Dougie. "They'll come for her and you'll get what's coming to you, don't you worry."

I turned to his slimy face and I must admit that I had forgotten he was here.

Prichikit lifted a roll of tape and stuck several layers across Dougie's mouth. I gave her a nod of appreciation and turned back to watch the tracks of the remaining projectile clouds as they arced around the fourth planet after the Terrans' ship. There was an indication of weapons fire and another cloud disappeared, but it was far too late.

They would have received my reply moments before the closest cluster of missiles flew straight through their ship. A cone of debris sprayed out from the impact and it was a truly fitting epitaph for those dreadful people and their equally dreadful intentions. A brief cheer greeted the nine minutes old view of what we were seeing.

The two remaining projectile clouds were already manoeuvring to sling-shot around planet 4 and back towards us. A new set of blue predicted traces popped up, replacing the previous red nine minutes-behind courses and positions. The IFF then added a worrying extrapolation from the blue predicted real-time positions to the green dot which was us.

"What are these things?" I asked the main AI.

"Each group of projectiles consists of up to five self-propelled and self-directing objects," the IFF replied.

"Can we avoid them?" I asked.

"They are approximately three hours away based on our best estimate of their increasing speed. There is an approximate 80% probability of being able to destroy both clusters of missiles, but it is almost certain that some will get through."

I paused, before asking: "If they hit us, what will happen?"

"That is uncertain," it said. "Best case they will miss, although losing one or more rings is the more likely outcome. Worst case, the ship's main body will be hit and everything will be destroyed."

"But there must be something we can do, surely?" I asked, but the main armament was already charging and two pods were being readied for launch as directed projectiles. Maybe this was what Franky had meant when he asked me not to break anything?

The council had fallen silent as they watched what was happening.

"Ship," I called out, "start the wakeup process for all passengers in deep-sleep. Fully expedited wake up and I also want you to prepare enough pods to carry everyone away from the ship. I will stay on board to manage the evacuation."

The main AI confirmed, but added a warning that this would use up all of our pods. I turned to the council members.

"You must go to the sleep units and help people as they wake up. Every filled pod is part of the hive saved, so we need this done as quickly as possible. Also, put that filthy Terran somewhere safe. We can deal with him later."

My attention was jerked back to the main console as our ship's main armament fired, fired and then fired again, but we wouldn't know if it had hit anything until the nine-minute flight time to the missiles and then the nine-minutes back for any indications. The blue tracks of the missiles intersecting with our green blob were inexorable, and those magic three hours to impact were already slipping away.

Out of the corner of my eye I saw a feed of Prichikit manhandling Dougie into a pod, which was a very good idea. Any of the lockable storage containers would make an excellent prison cell. A pod door closure indication popped up but a flood of alerts sprayed across the console as the pod crash-disengaged under local control and powered away from the ship. It was accelerating at an indicated 3.5G when something was ejected into space. A red flag indicated that a living organic had been jettisoned. Our poor Prichikit.

There was nothing we could do as our protector was already beyond hope. The main AI indicated that the pod had disabled all remote control, but I dismissed the IFF's request to target the pod. No clear and present danger, so again, I could do nothing. I turned back to the consoles with an ever-growing anger at those Terrans, but I couldn't let that distract me from waking up the hive and getting them away safely.

The first indications of wakening sleepers started to come up. The wake-up process usually takes hours, but the ship was waking them as quickly as possible and soon there would be a lot of very sick people trying to make their way down to the pods. The Medlab and our council members would do what they could, but confusion was spreading and this would only get worse as more and more people woke up.

The IFF's countdown to impact seemed to be speeding up in front of my very eyes, but looking across the bank of consoles I was momentarily lost in awe. Franky had put me in charge of this massive construction that was more of an AI super-being than anything else. More information than I could ever understand was flooding across the screens, but the ship's AI collective had everything under control. I merely had to ask and it happened. Even if I didn't ask, the ship managed everything and we were but passengers in this marvellous construct. I again marvelled at Franky's understanding of how it all worked, but I still had to save my hive. I could only hope that I would be able to save the ship as well.

The IFF now had the tracks of our two outgoing pods converging nicely with the incoming projectile clouds. We also had a good stream of people wobbling down from the deep-sleep area to the pod bay, but time was not on our side.

Filling the first pod was proving to be a nightmare. The newly woken people got in the way, didn't listen, and all seemed to be trying to cram into the pod at once. The main AI's solution was to open the doors of three other pods, so at least the loading could now be expedited by everyone trying to cram into four pods at the same time.

Finally, the first fully packed pod launched. I also got a message from the Medlab saying that everyone had been woken, even if the ship seemed to be more full of the undead than the living. Current estimate for getting everyone into the pods was at least an hour and this was matched by the missiles' current estimated time to impact.

The second pod launched, closely followed by the third. After a worrying gap, the fourth pod launched, but the loading of our final pod was taking forever. The sick, the elderly and the creche could not be hurried, and they were all not helped by the ship's constant 1-2G evasive manoeuvring and the consequent ever-growing numbers of injured.

The two missile clouds were now only minutes away and their speeds were significantly relativistic. Even the IFF's best guesses were mostly speculation. A red flash said that the first of our projectile pods had been outmanoeuvred but that was matched by a launch indicator as our final pod blasted away. A bright green indicator quickly followed showing that a combination of main armament and our second projectile pod had managed to hit a missile cloud. Unfortunately, this came with an advisory that incoming crash debris would hit us at the same time as the remaining missiles.

Sirens wailed as an 'Unavoidable collision' warning flashed and there was another kick as the ship made a final desperate leap off to one side. Only my wings tucked down the back of the seat kept me in place and I hunched down as a hail of everything that was loose in the cabin flew past my ears.

The incoming missiles flew straight through Ring 1 and were thousands of klicks away before any alarms had time to sound. A ring segment had disappeared, vaporised, and indicators on every console blared out in a strident announcement of our imminent doom.

38
Franky, Alien, Subterranean

Franky

OK, so I didn't spend the night peering out into the hostile darkness while my alien pal got her well-deserved rest. She dropped off, I made myself nice and comfortable by the window, and all too soon my eyelids joined all three of hers and we drifted away with the native fairies.

Coming to in the wee small hours of dawn, I was presented with the embarrassing sight of the Alien standing on guard while yours truly lay flat out on the floor. I'd even been covered with an alien blanket, which was now keeping my rapidly awakening and very embarrassed carcass nice and warm.

"I thought I should keep watch in case we were surprised," crackled in my ear.

That was probably a lot more polite than I deserved and my abject apology was met with what I'd swear was a touch of sarcasm. Sarcasm from an Alien, and through a home-brewed translator? Pretty technically impressive and I'd have probably been a lot ruder.

I slipped out from under the blanket and was greeted by a chorus of complaints from yesterday's lumps and bumps. Outside, a lovely blue sky was in the process of banishing the red line lurking across the horizon and I guess it was the start of another shitty day in this particular paradise.

I tried another apology, but the Alien replied that she did not seem to need the amount of sleep that my species required. I'd forgotten how all three of her species' eyes constantly flicked about, with that single seemingly randomly selected eye stopping to nail me when she spoke. Rather unnerving, but I'll bet I looked pretty strange to her, especially this early in the morning.

To save myself further embarrassment I started tidying up the mess I'd left my gear in. I lifted the emergency pack to hang it on an odd-shaped metal hook sticking out of the wall, and the hook pivoted. A section of wall slid sideways to reveal a momentarily dark hole, with lights flicking on to reveal a plain-sided box with two buttons halfway up one side.

Both the Alien and I did each species' equivalent of an open mouth, eyes wide open and a mouthed "What the fff...?" It looked just like a lift and we both said "It's a lift," even if her follow up "I wonder if it still works?" showed that her compos was far in advance of my early morning mentis. She came across to have a look at it.

"Well I'm certainly not getting into that," I said.

The Alien's face gave its best version of "Really? No shit," and as if on cue, a large blue arm/tentacle flew in through the window. An all too familiar blue head blanked out the light and I dived for the PDW, my frantic fingers and thumbs just about managing to activate auto-target before I turned and gave our visitor a good long squirt. The face flopped back and the arm/tentacle jerked out after the rest of its mortal remains now plummeting earthward.

The Alien's mouth was moving but I couldn't hear a thing. There was a shadow at the window and another of those arm/tentacles came snaking in. I loosed off again and auto-targeting faithfully did its job. The arm/tentacle was severed, writhing across the floor as it violently distributed our bags all over the place.

The Alien was shouting but all I could hear was a dull tinkling from the PDW's cataclysmic noise. She obviously knew a lot more than I did about what was going to happen next as she started throwing our stuff hand over hand into the lift compartment, dodging another arm/tentacle as it came writhing in through the window.

I flipped around, pulled the PDW's trigger, but I'd run dry. I grabbed for the bag with my spare magazines but it was already flying through the air into the lift. Just as my oh-shit thoughts started to formulate, the Alien took a flying leap and tackled me off my feet to follow the bags. I lay there gasping as my bouncy friend slammed a hand/tentacle against the lower of the two buttons on the compartment wall.

The door snapped shut. Nothing else happened except that the button lit up. The Alien thumped the button again and my stomach was left behind as the floor dropped. She was still shouting and this time I could just about make out some of the words.

"Those animals aren't normally so aggressive. It was good you found this lift otherwise we would have been killed." Nice to know and no shit sherlock were my two immediate thoughts.

I eased myself into a more comfortable position and started ferreting around for a spare magazine. I eventually found one, clipped it in place, cocked the PDW and turned to the Alien in triumph.

"You really like shooting things, don't you?" she said. "Why does your weapon make so much noise?"

She was now looking at me with all three eyes at once, which I have to admit was even worse than the usual two random plus one laser-eyed gaze.

"Well, we wouldn't have got away if I hadn't shot those tentacles," I said, "and I don't like shooting things, only when they're after me."

I think we were both rather shaken by what had just happened and there was no more conversation as our downward plunge continued.

I was just beginning to wonder where the hell this thing went, when we were squashed down into the floor. A thump, all movement ceased and both buttons lit up.

The Alien lifted an arm and gingerly pressed the bottom button. The door slid open to reveal a long tunnel, extending away into the dim and barely lit distance. I didn't like the look of that, but I liked this lift even less.

"We need to get out," I said, "like asap," sliding out a pile of bags and following pretty smartish. The Alien came out with the rest of her gear, prudently kicking a box to chock the door open. Good thinking. That should stop the lift going back up again. I hoped.

The tunnel was old, cold and silent as the grave. The floor had that look saying no one had walked here for a very long time and the stale air prickled your nose with smells of dark underground places you didn't want to be in. I wanted to be here even less than when we'd got here.

"What do you reckon?" I asked the Alien.

Just one of her eyes looked at me, the other two keeping a good look down the tunnel.

"I think we should send your flyer to explore," was her answer, and all three of her eyes were now fixed on the dimness.

I disentangled the drone from the Alien's cobbled together translation-tech stew and, of course, all translation immediately disappeared. With her version of a sigh, she bent down and started fiddling with the collection of bits I'd just manhandled. I gave the drone a quick once over and off it went down the tunnel.

Eventually, a reflective end wall appeared out of the gloom, which was great, but surely someone hadn't built a tunnel going nowhere. And then I saw the fan of tunnels either side, with these splitting into others as they went further back. Something was being concentrated right where the drone was sitting, but a low power warning popped up from the drone. It did an abrupt flip and came back towards us.

I tapped the busy Alien on what was presumably her shoulder.

"The drone's found something," I said.

She looked at me, back at her pile of connections, had a quick fiddle and then gave me a gesture.

I repeated what I'd said and after another couple of twiddles, she turned back.

"See it," <85% xlate confidence> "Anything else...interest?" <90% xlate confidence> The translation was clunky but at least we were talking.

"That's it I'm afraid," I said. "We're about half a klick away but the drone's out of power. I think we should go and have a look."

The Alien considered. "Agree," she said. "I see...others...like. We look at."

"Works for me," I replied as the drone came whining in.

Getting our stuff together was really just waiting for the drone to land and the Alien to reconnect it to her pile of bits. She picked up the box that had been chocking the lift door open and it snapped shut. There were no controls on our side and I could only hope that it wasn't racing straight back up again to bring down one of those blue jobs.

39
And down they go

Soffee

Scylla's "Soffee, what are they doing?" followed the two mechanicals as they disappeared up the ramp.

"Those Smuts are just like Franky," I said. "Never happier than when they are playing with their toys," and at that moment my suit gave a low energy warning, echoed by Scylla's. We were just absorbing this worrying fact when a Smut called back, saying that they were confident they had full control of their machines but did not want to reverse back down. They would go to the top, then turn around in the courtyard and come straight back down again.

At the same time, Circe flicked me a quick message. She and Chary were bored. They were going to have a look further down the ramp while the Smuts were messing about upstairs.

"Don't go too far," I called back. "I want the Smuts back before we do anything too exciting, OK?"

The chittered reply did not exactly disagree, but it did not exactly agree either, and then a Smut interrupted to say that they had reached the top of the ramp. The weather was still dreadful and they would be down shortly.

Light from above reflected through the spray of raindrops falling down the open centre of the ramp and enough artificial lights were still working that I could turn off my suit's image intensification. The IFFs were all on high alert, but even with what had happened with the alien drop ship and then those missiles fired at Franky and the Smuts, we still hadn't seen any native sentients. It just didn't make sense, but I kept coming back to Dougie's story as well as the Smuts not being able to detect anyone. Maybe this planet really did not have any sentients living here anymore. But why? That was what we had to find out.

The Smuts were now spiralling down towards us, the spray of light from their mechanicals preceding them. They picked up Medea and Hecate before sweeping off again, the waiting flock of drones fanning out into the void as both mechanicals came to a halt at the bottom of the ramp.

It was a truly vast lozenge of empty space, delineated on all sides by perfectly set walls, floor and ceiling. Side walls slowly converged into the distance and everywhere was lit by the oddest of lights cast by a scattering of brilliant pinpricks embedded in the ceiling. All over the walls were cascades of designs, seemingly familiar out of one corner of your eye but entirely alien when you looked at them in detail. The drones' whining echoed around the dimly lit emptiness, almost like a challenge to this alien space that had been still and silent for so long.

A Smut's brain tickle interrupted my contemplation. They now had a good understanding of the mechanicals' systems. While it wasn't the most advanced technology they had ever seen, some of it was pretty cool. More importantly, they knew how the charging system worked and were pretty certain we could use the power banks to recharge our suits.

On hearing me repeat this to the girls, every suit immediately started shouting about how low its power levels were. Certainly, my suit was down below ten percent and we weren't very far away from them being dead on their feet. I just had this feeling about using the Smuts' mechanicals. Fair enough, power was power, and the Smuts were only talking about plugging our suits into the mechanicals' power packs, but every time we did something on this planet something bad happened.

Scylla was looking at me, her whole face a question, and it was clear that everyone else was thinking the same. We needed the suits, they needed power and I had to make a decision. The Smuts seemed convinced that this would be safe, and really, what other alternative did we have? I gave myself a mental sigh, then told the Smuts to go ahead.

One of them wrestled open a hatch in the nearest mechanical to expose an odd-shaped socket. Several minutes of fiddling later, interspersed with the Smut equivalent of mental swear words through mental clenched teeth, and the plug on the end of my suit's charging lead was connected.

The suit's charging monitor popped up, charging started, but suddenly there was a bright red intrusion alarm. All of the suit's systems went offline and swirls of colour appeared across the HUD, overlaying the alarm and changing to streams of random characters overwriting everything. Another suit waded in, brushing the Smut aside and yanking out the charging lead, but my suit was now locked. All I could do was sit and watch as its internal defences started to try and purge whatever it was that had just tried to get in.

The Smuts were sufficiently surprised that they did nothing, just standing there looking at my suit. I tried opening up a comm to the girls, but everything was shut down and it was some time before a Smut bothered to ask me if I was alright. The girls' suits had already taken a number of steps backward and there was some serious weaponry pointed in my direction. I very quickly confirmed that I was OK and that my suit had everything under control, even if I could only sit and watch.

After many cycles of purge, clean and reset, eventually the suit declared itself happy. It gave me back control, and as soon as I opened a comms channel I was deluged by a flood of communications from the girls.

"Hold on!" I called out. "One at a time please."

Circe quickly slipped in that it was she who had barged in to pull out the power connector, saving my suit and probably me as well. Over the continuing flood of worried questions, my suit also gave me its own report. As soon as the power line had been connected, a foreign AI had tried to get in through the power connector's data channel. My HUD had been scrambled by this AI flooding every channel with attempts to communicate, but that was all it seemed to be trying to do. The suit finished by saying it had run full diagnostics and a self-check. There was no longer any trace of what had tried to get in and it was confident that its power control sub-system could be fully isolated. This would allow any future recharge attempts to be carried out safely.

That was all very well, I replied, but what about this native AI? Also, to myself I wondered whether the suit wouldn't just say this anyway if the attacker was still in control? However, the other suits' reports of low power levels were becoming more and more insistent and every one of them was adamant that the charging process could be made safe, even if I remained unconvinced. Their universal confidence sounded just like an excuse, any excuse, to get a recharge, and a couple of wry asides from the Smuts only served to confirm my suspicions.

We had more back and forths, but eventually it came down to whether we still wanted our suits to be remain fully operational. That wasn't a question that even needed asking, so how could we recharge them safely? I knew what Franky would do. He would say let's have a go, what could possibly go wrong, then stand well back and see what happened. Not my preferred approach by any means, but we didn't seem to have an alternative.

"OK," I called out over the boundless enthusiasm now being displayed all around me, "we'll try it out with a single unmanned suit. I want the other suits ready to disable or destroy it if anything goes wrong, but only on my say so."

The suits came straight back that this was an excellent suggestion. I did try asking what would happen if they all got infected, but their power-hungry AIs just dismissed this as nonsense, not possible. I suppose we were going to find that out, weren't we?

I got out of my suit and everyone went back up the ramp. The suit closed up and I walked up alongside the clutch of expectant watchers. The girls' suits directed a collection of lethal weaponry at my suit, and I told it to proceed.

It duly plugged in the charge connector.

What happened next was a bit of an anti-climax. The suit's charging monitor showed the charge cycle starting. The charge indicator started creeping up and that was it. My suit reported nothing, none of the other suits saw anything and I started feeling rather foolish for having had all of my doubts. The charge indicator kept on creeping up, but then a massive burst of RF swept through the cavern, matched by an equally massive pulse on the mechanical's side of my suit's charging cable. The same swirling shapes and characters started slaving off the suit to my HUD, but stopped as abruptly as they'd started.

The suit jerked around to face us.

"Visitors to my planet," came its standard Terran voice, "I have commandeered this exoskeleton to communicate with you. I do not recognise you or your technology but you are very welcome. However, I must warn you that this level is dangerous and you must return to the surface."

Across the stunned silence I looked from my suit to the girls, and their shocked expressions mirrored mine. A Smut added its own version of shocked surprise and then we were flooded by threat assessments from the IFFs, all saying that an external agent had commandeered my suit. My only thought was that I'd better start by being nice and polite as we were, after all, uninvited guests and this was now the third demonstration of that since we'd got here.

"Thank you for your welcome," I said. "We are exploring this planet but you are the only sentient life we have found. Are you organic or tech?"

"I am the central control AI left in charge of this planet when its last inhabitants left one hundred and thirty-seven annuals ago," it replied. "I was instructed to assist any alien entities that might land, but my primary purpose is to guard the planet and ensure that what is held here cannot escape. You may go anywhere, but you must not approach the secure area."

That sounded ominous, and my reply: "So where is the secure area?" got no response.

I repeated my question but was again greeted by echoing silence.

"Can anyone see anything?" I called back to the girls. "I've got nothing."

"My suit is showing nothing anywhere," replied Scylla. "Maybe you could ask this AI to give you back your suit?"

That was a good idea.

"Could you please release my suit?" I asked.

My question echoed into the silence again, but this time the front of my suit opened out into its standard mount-up configuration. Charging resumed, and all of the standard data feeds came back as if nothing had happened. The IFFs reported no threats indicated, but I didn't believe any of it. My suit had previously checked out OK and yet this native AI had appeared out of nowhere. A glance flicked at the girls only got shrugs in return. I took a deep breath and started walking towards my suit, doing my best to ignore the deafening clang of mental alarm bells.

As I walked up, I asked myself what Franky would have done, but I already knew the answer to that. It sometimes amazed me how he'd managed to live this long, but that was Franky, this was me, and the growing calls for action from those sitting safely behind layers of weaponry didn't help one bit.

Every indication said that the suit was back in full working order. I knew that the only way to really find out was to get in and see. So, before better sense prevailed, I walked straight up and the suit wrapped itself around me. Everything came back online. There were no errors and no alarms. As far as I could tell it was a fully working suit.

The first thing I did was ask what had happened, but the AI could only recall a successful charging process. There was no indication of anything wrong, apart from a strange new icon in one corner of the HUD. I tried interrogating it but nothing happened, not even that 'Do not activate this function'-type popup you get when you press something you shouldn't. I asked the suit what this new icon was, but it did not know what I was talking about. It re-set the HUD and the display came back fully normal, with no odd icon. I did indeed seem to have my suit back, fully charged and ready to go.

"Everything looks OK," I called out and before I could say anything else the girls' suits' came striding in. Weapons packed themselves away, hands grasped for charging cables to plug into charging points and power started pouring into each of the ravenous suits just as it should do, no problems, everything as normal.

The girls' beady eyes were glued to what was going on, so I turned my attention to what the IFFs had found out about the cavern while we'd been messing about with that native AI. There was now a full-scale tactical mapping, although all it really showed was a massive triangle of empty space. The ramp and us were at its base, with just a single interrogative flagged up indicating a possible something out of the ordinary at the distant flattened tip. That was it, and the IFF was almost apologetic that it couldn't find anything more.

Disinterested agreement was the best I could get from the girls when I suggested we should probably go and have a look at this possible anomaly, but their concentration was still very much on the suits. Sitting here watching, I suddenly felt quite tired. It had been a busy day and this was only emphasised by the IFF's on-going mission timer. We had actually been on the go for well over half a day, and above us night had fallen. Maybe it was time for a break? We weren't in any hurry and if I was tired then I'd bet everyone else was as well. A visit to the little girl's room would certainly be very welcome.

I called this out and got back the expected chorus of jocular replies, followed by universal agreement. The Smuts were their usual selves, just being themselves, but I did get the faintest telepathic blowback of a chortle about three different species all about to do what we all needed to do, here in the heart of someone else's city and what that native AI was going to do about it. No wonder they got on so well with Franky.

So, decision made. We got out of our suits and with much muffled tittering us females retreated behind one of the mechanicals, this being matched by even more telepathic blowback from the Smuts sheltering behind the other. They really did seem to find this somewhat unusual utilisation of a different species' mechanicals and empty space quite amusing. From what I could hear all around me, I think there was general agreement on that.

A suit started dealing with the inevitable debris we'd left behind while the other three started to prepare some food. While now very much relieved, I think that we were all a lot more tired than we'd realised. The scratch dinner was quickly eaten before sleeping bags were retrieved and everyone started wrapping themselves up for the night.

My own bag beckoned, the underneath puffing up to lift me off the floor and the pillow inflating to support my head. I was tired, I was comfortable, but you know what it's like. You go to bed absolutely exhausted, but as soon as your head hits the pillow you're wide awake again.

Disjointed thoughts wouldn't stop racing around my head and I couldn't stop thinking about Franky, all of the way over there on that far distant alien continent. I suppose it was actually him being an Alien on that far distant native continent, but he was still on his own and I worried about him. I was sure the Smuts would tell me if anything happened, but they were several hundred klicks away from him. How would they know, really? All I knew was that he was there, we were here and whatever the Smuts might say about repairing their pod, there was no way back that didn't involve someone possibly shooting at them.

My thoughts wouldn't stop churning around as I lay there listening to my less troubled companions drift off to sleep. I dropped off eventually, but was suddenly jolted awake. I sat up in a panic, but it was silent, nothing moving, the suits positioned on all four corners like sentinels, their IFFs updating my HUD with nothing much at all. What had woken me up? I was used to living underground and there was nothing down here except that native AI. The suits couldn't see anything, we'd got my suit back, so what else could possibly be down here?

It took me a long time to get back to sleep.

The chittering of conversation and smell of breakfast woke me to an eager, if early, start. I was the last up and of course, the butt of everyone's jokes for sleeping in. A hot breakfast really revived the spirits, and getting back into our suits involved the usual laughing and joking, together with three flat refusals to go fully integrated. Medea and Hecate mounted up on the Smuts' mechanicals and we were off on our continued adventure to the top of the cavern.

It wasn't far, and sure enough, there in front of us was the outline of a door, traced out by a faint dust-filled crack. Off to one side was an equally dusty big red button. And of course, the next question was who should press that red button?

"Definitely your job, but wait until we're well away," said Scylla to muffled sniggers. The Smuts injected a more rational assessment, saying that it was unlikely that anything bad would happen. The native AI knew we were here and both the door and our two mechanicals were ultimately under its control. That left just me as the sole highly suspicious member of our party. However, we weren't going to get any further without someone, namely me, doing something. So, I waited until everyone had gone back as far as they needed to, then pressed the button.

It lit up as it sank into the wall, the door cracking open then swinging away leaving whorls of ancient dust spinning in its wake. It bumped flush against the inner wall and a cascade of lights flickered away from me to illuminate a tunnel going down to an end wall with symbols pointing left and right.

40
Flivver planetfall

Chitichca

Alarms proclaimed catastrophic damage, rotational imbalance, loss of atmosphere, and they were joined by other alarms as the doors on all of the elevators up to Ring 1 slammed shut. Pink sealant oozed from the door frames. A momentary pause, then a series of explosions as Ring 1 was detached from the main body and its rotation flung the disconnected parts into space.

The rotational imbalance alarms stopped shrieking and in fact, the sea of alarms was changing. Ring 1 was no longer part of the ship. As such, it was not being reported as part of the ship. Alarms were replaced by indicators showing the loss of the ring together with damage reports and endless inventories of what had been lost.

The IFF displays changed to no threats indicated and the ship's main armament went into standby mode. In front of me, the previously blazing rainbow had changed to ambers and greens, with just a single cluster of reds showing damage caused by the ring's explosive ejection. In fact, the ship seemed to be returning to normal operations, or as normal as you might expect after it had just lost an entire ring.

I, on the other hand, was not in such a good state. My nasty collection of cuts and bruises from the flying debris had attracted a Medbot, which started applying first aid over all of that pain. Swarms of auto-repair bots were also scurrying about and a full auto-repair status board snapped up showing what was being done.

Ring 1 was gone, never to return, and its debris would be orbiting this system long after we'd departed to the next tier of our lives. Unfortunately our hive's possessions stored in the ring had also gone with it. In between the Medbot's efforts, I asked the main AI if there was any chance of their retrieval, and it responded that suits were already out recovering essential equipment. It would make sure that our hive possessions were added to the retrieval inventory.

Rings 2 and 3 appeared to be largely untouched, although both were showing dangerous stresses from the violent use of our manoeuvring thrusters. It seemed amazing really that overall there were no indications of anything that immediately threatened the ship's operational integrity.

The ship's suits had now joined the auto-repair status board as they pursued the remains of Ring 1 and our possessions. The larger items would have to wait for the return of our pods and that, of course, raised a whole set of other questions. Ring 2 was already fully inhabited and that left just Ring 3 for everyone who had been living in Ring 1. The console was showing that Ring 3 was available for use, but I had no idea what that actually meant. I certainly needed to have a good think about where everyone was now going to live, and I needed to do that before people started coming back to the ship.

The next day was very busy. The main AI started bringing the pods back and that meant trying to find a way to get all of the injured through the Medlab. People were doubling up in Ring 2, but I was still waiting to hear back from the scouting parties we had sent to Ring 3.

Ring 3 turned out to be a real mess. It had clearly been used by a number of different species over reltime decades, and not even the ship's AIs could identify some of the more unpleasant remains they had left behind. Everyone working on the clean-up was now wearing protective clothing and the Medunits posted at the Ring 3 elevators had already started to get their first patients. If there was a bright side, it was that the hive was starting to realise that Terrans may smell odd, not understand anything, have very odd habits and be generally not us, but other species were far worse. From what we were finding in Ring 3, Terrans might actually be one of the nicer species to travel in space with.

A very late night was followed by an even earlier morning, and I awoke to pretty much the same state as I had left. At least retrieval of our possessions was now in progress, although the main AI was prioritising essential ship equipment over anything we had brought with us. Best estimate was that full retrieval would take at least another week. Major damage to the ship was now largely repaired but there were some remaining items that would require Franky's attention.

As for the remaining Terrans, we could now see the pod stolen by that vile Terran Dougie was orbiting Planet 4. It appeared to be trying to retrieve two suits which had somehow been left in orbit after the destruction of their ship, while at the same time trying very hard to stay out of our sight. Good riddance was my only thought. The body of Prichikit had been retrieved and was in the Medlab. She would be placed in stasis alongside her friend, ready for when we got to the planet.

"So, whatever do we do next?" I muttered to myself, which was answered by an amused snort from behind.

"A good question," said my ally on the council, for it was he. "People seem happy, but this will change if we stay out here doing nothing."

I nodded, but he continued: "We also have issues feeding three hundred people and you will have heard those idiots who are saying that we should take the ship for our own. I think we need to get to Planet 3 before anything else happens. Also," and here he smiled, "you will be pleased to know that a full council meeting has been called to discuss all of this."

He finished with an apologetic shrug, but I was not surprised. I had heard the whispers. People were worried about when they could get out of space and onto this planet, but maybe I could forestall any problems by getting the ship over there before this became a real issue? After all, it was up to Soffee and Franky to deal with any hive protocol matters, and they were currently on the Planet anyway.

"Alright then," I said, "good idea. Let's try and get over there and we can argue about anything later." To his nod, I called out: "Ship, I want to travel to Planet 3. Can you do this for me?"

"That is within your specified freedom of action," came the reply. "I will initiate immediately and adjust the Ring 1 retrieval schedules to compensate."

To my widening smile, my friend whispered: "I think we should keep this really quiet. If they know we can move the ship, they'll just shout even louder about how we should take it for our own."

"Ship," I called out, "please make our journey as gentle as possible. We do not want to worry anyone if they feel the ship moving."

There was a moment's hesitation before: "I will plan accordingly and only report to you," came back.

My friend smiled. "That AI is more intelligent than both of us."

"And that is certainly true," I agreed.

The consoles may still have been a riot of colour, but my time helping get the ship back working again had been a lovely break from the constant noise and general kerfuffle of the hive. They do say that a problem shelved is a problem doubled and I think I was about to find that out with the forthcoming council meeting.

My friend and I left the main control cabin and made our way up to Ring 2, walking straight into a lot more noise, trouble and argument than even I had expected. There was the usual interminable list of items relating to the hive and the ship, but we now also had loudly stated demands about taking over the ship. The original hard core of two disruptive members had now recruited other supporters to their cause. However hard I tried to make them understand that the ship would not hand over control without Soffee or Franky's agreement, they just would not listen.

Mention of Soffee and Franky then set off more arguments and I could only console myself with the fact that the longer this went on, the longer I could postpone telling them we were already on our way to Planet 3. At least when we were there, they couldn't keep arguing about getting there. Or so I hoped.

We eventually got to the end of this seemingly interminable meeting and I think that even the most outspoken people were relieved. I'd certainly had enough for one day. I managed to leave without anyone catching me for something and made my way back to the main control cabin, clutching something refreshing I had retrieved from the nearest food unit.

Unfortunately, I wasn't going to get away that easily. No sooner had I settled down to my steaming bowlful than both disruptive council members floated in through the doorway. They were obviously still upset, hunched forward, wings held slightly open and crests raised.

"Don't think we are blind to what you are doing," said the first, his companion standing there in an almost full-on threat display. "We all know you favour Soffee and Franky more than you do us and we aren't going to stand for it."

All of those years ago, Soffee had broken his leg when he'd tried to bully her. He had never forgotten the very public humiliation and, in fact, had never stopped trying to make the whole hive hate her despite all that she had done to save us. I sighed into my food.

"You know nothing about so very much," I said. "Both of you. I have been planning for this hive since before you were hatched, but so many things are just pure luck. I did not know that Franky would leave CS1. I did not know that he would find a ship and return for Soffee. I did not know that she would insist that he take both of our hives away with him and I certainly did not know that Soffee and Franky would grow to like each other. Everything has worked out very nicely but now you are doing your best to wreck it all."

"Hah!" he said. "You may say that, but that hybrid abomination and her dirty Terran are a joke, just like their so-called hive. They pollute the very air we breathe. We are the only hive on this ship and the ship should be ours, just like that planet. We should just take them now without any further talk."

"Well you should be careful what you wish for," I retorted. "Our protectors think she is a goddess and you can't go up against them. Also, how are you going to get hold of the ship? The main AI only answers to Franky and Soffee," and I paused, looking him straight in the eye.

"You would have to make a formal challenge for the ship and I can guess what would happen then." I smiled at them both. "You know what she is like when people try and take what is hers."

There was a silence as my suggestion and its inevitable consequences slowly sunk into their thick skulls. The shocked and outraged expressions slowly disappeared, to be replaced by something a lot more uncertain.

"I know that there has been bad blood between you ever since she broke your leg," I said, "but you'd better be careful she doesn't break your neck. You know what she is like," and I smiled again.

"She's a freak," he snapped back, "that's what she's like. She should never have been allowed into the hive and you..."

"...and you are a fool," I interrupted. "What do you think she will do if you threaten her hive? A broken leg will be the least of your worries."

More uncertainty chased across his face as he finally understood the inevitable results of what he was demanding. It was that life-long sense of entitlement. The spoiled brat who had always got others to do his dirty work for him finally being confronted with what would happen if he actually did something for himself.

He hesitated as if about to say something else then thought better of it, bumping into his now very uncertain companion as he turned to go. Their comical dance trying to get out of each other's way was a fitting conclusion to this idiocy.

I surveyed my now spoiled food and slumped back with a sigh. I shouldn't worry about this. Soffee would deal with it when she got back and if she couldn't deal with it then who could? I snuggled down into my chair and watched as the now not so distant Planet 3 grew larger and larger in the viewscreen.

I must have drifted away into the depths of sleep. A gentle ping, and then another, and I slowly swam awake to the ship informing me that we were approaching geostationary orbit above where Soffee's pod had landed. All available information was ready and could be presented on request.

I stretched out of my chair and blinked tired, scratchy eyes. I couldn't believe we were here so quickly, but no, it was actually six hours since I had fallen asleep. I sent out an urgent request for all council members to meet me in the main control cabin, before getting myself a drink to take away that awful taste in my mouth.

Half of the council stopped what they were doing and came straight down. The other half expressed outrage at being summoned in such a manner, before stopping what they were doing and coming straight down.

The only way to cut straight through the continued muttering was by jumping straight in and announcing that we were in orbit around Planet 3. There was a momentary shocked silence, followed by angry shouts and waving of arms. They were horrified, expressing loud opinions about their lack of trust in me, that I had done what everyone wanted but I had not asked them first, and so on, and so on, and so on.

Maybe the last few days had made me a lot less interested in listening to useless talk that went nowhere. We had come halfway across the galaxy, we were now where we wanted to be and it just wasn't worth arguing about. Even so, I let the shock and outrage run on until it dribbled away into a pointed silence. I presented the ship's status report and suggested that we send a landing party down to where Soffee and Franky had landed.

To my surprise, after all of the previous shouting and screaming this was received with some enthusiasm, even if there were yet more loudly stated opinions that I shouldn't have got us here, where we wanted to be, without having asked them first.

Eye crests were raised when I stated that as first hive down, Franky and Soffee had already granted us permission to land. I knew that Soffee would not mind me telling such a white lie and as for Franky? Well, I do not think he would have even seen that there was a problem.

The first thing we did was select a representative group of people to be first down on this new planet and I was particularly careful to ensure that we had the whole council with us. Just think what someone with council authority might do if they were left up here on their own.

Just making that selection took several hours and it was several hours more before we finally had people boarding the pods. Even so, they messed about, got in each other's way, kept changing seats because they couldn't possibly sit where they'd just been sitting, and the whole process looked like it would take forever. One of my less charitable thoughts was that maybe we needed some more Terrans chasing us to get them to hurry up and stop all this idiocy.

After all of that effort, the actual journey down was an anticlimax. We had a perfect descent track with a lovely view of the city which Soffee and Franky had selected, and our pods landed right next to theirs. Fifty thousand light-years to get here and finally, it looked like we were home.

The pod AI gave us its green light and the orderly exit I had been planning turned into a disorderly scramble for the pod's doorway, made worse by everyone having seen what was waiting outside. Most of us had never lived anywhere but CS1 and the blue sky, sunshine and matching warm breeze was more like a dream than reality. People were taking deep breaths of the lovely air, savouring each breath, bending down to touch the native vegetation as if only feeling was believing.

It was obvious that everyone felt that they owned the place, but that was a problem for later. The Grunt which Franky had left guarding their pods was standing off to one side, watching us but not coming any closer. I called over and he raised an arm in greeting, even if his gaze never left the sky. The large weapon slung over one shoulder no doubt told a story that we would need to hear.

A sonic boom echoed across people's conversations and my IFF flicked up an advisory. One of Soffee and Franky's pods was aiming to land near us, having taken off from over the sea. Its flight details were being sprayed into my left eye and there, almost at the limit of vision, a black dot was highlighted.

Several alarms popped up, and I could see that the attitude jets were struggling to keep it on track. Down it came on final approach and the main engines fired far too early, the pod corkscrewing as it dropped. A final bellow of flames and rocket exhaust and it crunched into the ground, leaning over as a landing leg subsided. Hah! Our hive gets it right and theirs doesn't was the general opinion.

The pod remained slumped onto its damaged landing leg and we could now see that there was a dent, almost a gouge, running all of the way down one side. The Grunt started trotting over as the secondary entry port jerked open and a Smut appeared, helping a second Smut out onto the emergency exit ladder that required several kicks to get it to open.

The first Smut climbed down and jumped off the bottom, but the second fell off the last step into the arms of the waiting Grunt. All three of them started making their way towards us and I could see that both Smuts' clothing was torn and grimy, their usually pristine fur smeared with dirt.

I was about to call out a greeting but one of them was already speaking. It welcomed us to the planet, then sent a high-speed telepathic squirt summarising everything that had happened. The Grunt's unceasing vigilance while supporting the second Smut was like an underline to the worrying details that the Smut was going through.

It finished by saying that they knew Franky and Soffee were still alive, but they had no idea where they were. If we wanted to go and explore, the best place would be the large central area where Soffee and her party had descended underground, but we should be careful. Someone or something on this planet was shooting at them, and it added a confirming wave back to the damaged pod for emphasis.

Worried conversations broke out as people's earlier enthusiasm started to be dampened by what the Smut had said, and I needed to get a hold of things. We had the facts, so let us take a look at all of them.

I called for people's attention. We had come here to explore and that was what we were going to do. Soffee and Franky had not seen any native inhabitants. Our IFFs could not see anything, regardless of what the Smut had said about being shot at. Its suggestion of going and looking where Soffee had gone underground was a good one, and then I played my trump card. We should fly over there, and we should do that right away.

Momentary silence, then a roar of agreement. Yes, we should fly. Flivvers fly and and we had been stuck on the ground for far too long. We should fly over to where Soffee was and we should do that right now.

The noise grew and our younger members in particular were very excited, even if some of our older people didn't seem too happy. No one had mentioned anything about flying, they weren't as young as they used to be... but really? You can keep giving people exactly what they want and they will never stop complaining. Sigh...

I caught a glance from my friend on the council and his muttered comment was a good reminder. The renewed and growing enthusiasm was all very welcome, but we were still on a new and dangerous planet. We couldn't have everyone just flying off on their own, especially after what had happened to Soffee's hive.

I called out over the tumult to council members, and we started marshalling people into groups. Control and management were our strengths and we would send those oh so eager youngsters off first. The older people, as well as those who seemed rather less than enthusiastic, could watch and see exactly how safe it was before having a go.

Eventually we managed to wave the first group off and away they went, laughing, joking and almost too excited to speak. A protector started spreading them out into a long line facing the wind.

With a shout of "Go!" they started running. Just a few steps and then they leapt into the air, strong wing beats pulling them upwards as they transformed into the flying creatures they really were.

The second group was already forming up, as it was obvious that no one wanted to wait and see what happened. This was just too much fun. I suppose that I would no doubt soon see about that as it was my turn next.

We did exactly what the first group had done. Our long line of people spread across the slope and I did feel a momentary panic join the existing complaints from my underused muscles and creaky frame. But it was too late now.

We started running. Unbidden, my body stretched out along the ground and we leapt into the air. Every muscle strained to keep my wings flapping, and my arms and legs tucked themselves away as my tail opened out behind. The kick of an updraft and I automatically adjusted, compensating, keeping everything in trim as the land dropped away below me.

Our collective shriek of delight pursued the first group of flyers as the exultant cries from those on the ground pursued us. My heart was so full of pride it might burst. Our hive belonged in the air. We were doing what we should have always been doing. We were flying off to help Soffee's hive claim this planet for all of us.

41
All roads lead to yesterday

Soffee

"Come on then, I've done the difficult bit," resulted in a chorus of grins. A Smut's "What have you done that was difficult? We didn't see anything," seemed perfectly serious as far as I could tell.

I didn't bother replying and two drones buzzed past me, quartering down the tunnel. They split at the T-junction, each going up a different tunnel arm. From the feeds we could see that after twenty metres or so each tunnel widened into a massive circular room, with the far walls being curved transparent barriers from floor to ceiling. Behind each barrier was a clear-sided vehicle, resting in a hole set into the side of a large pipe running left and right.

The suits' IFFs could see nothing dangerous and indeed, there were no indications of anything else down there apart from a thick layer of dust. The girls were clamouring to have a look, as were the Smuts, but I wasn't so sure.

For a start, why was there such a large and secure door? Doors like that were designed to keep things in, or maybe keep them out. We hadn't seen anything needing a door that large, but what if we went in and the door closed? The girls' response was that the suits could blow their way out, but did we know that they could?

Several less than helpful suggestions later, the Smuts suggested that we jam the door open with one of their mechanicals. This got a loud chorus of approval and it looked like I'd run out of excuses. Of course, like so many good ideas, achieving it was rather more difficult than describing it.

Our first attempt left a gap in the doorway so small that a suit couldn't get through. Then the door closed onto the mechanical and wouldn't re-open, leaving the mechanical clamped in its grasp. Much hammering at the red button later and the door opened, still leaving that too small gap. Time for another think.

Circe then suggested that we walk in first, then quickly slot in the mechanical before the door closed. The simplest solution is often the best and we duly followed her plan, leaving us in the tunnel and the door jammed nicely open.

When we got to the T-junction, people split left or right depending on how the mood took them. I followed Chary's suit, walking up the right-hand tunnel as the sides and ceiling opened out into that large circular room. My IFF highlighted the faintest line of footprints in the dust, large, clawed, and at least four feet involved.

There was no indication of how old they were and widening the search only saw our footprints trampling all over the rest of them. My suit bent over to have a closer look.

"A large animal made these, and a long time ago," was its response.

"Well I can see that," I said, "but actually this is really exciting. It's the first real evidence of what the people who built this city looked like and it must have been down here using this place, whatever it is."

The suit paused for a moment.

"The native AI says that this place is a travel waystation," it said, waving an arm at the diagram on the wall. "This animal might have been using it, but all we have is a line of footprints. The travel network extends over a lot of the planet although the AI cannot say how much of it still works."

It then changed to a direct person-to-person. "All indications are that this AI is only answering the questions it wants to. It has not said anything about this planet's inhabitants or what these footprints represent. We need to take the greatest care."

At this point Circe butted in. "My suit is saying this whole tunnel layout has been re-jigged. The back walls have been strongly reinforced to create a barrier between us and an area that extends away behind it."

"Danger! Danger! Evacuate the secure area immediately! Danger! Danger!" blared out at deafening volume.

Without another thought we spun around and raced back, charging up towards the tunnel entrance where the door was jammed up hard against the Smut's mechanical. There was just a sliver of space available and there was no way a suit was getting through that. We had no red button to press, the door was jammed hard against the mechanical and it looked like we were stuck.

A Smut managed to squeeze itself across the top of the mechanical and was closely followed by the other Smut, Medea and Hecate. That left just us four in suits on the wrong side of the door

The first Smut had now got into the mechanical's cockpit.

"Are you ready?" it broadcast. "I can move out of the way, but the door will then close. You're only going to have one chance."

A panel on the mechanical buckled inwards. The door jerked, following it, but then relaxed back, almost as if it was taking a breath before pushing again.

"Now," shouted the Smut, and the mechanical jerked out of the doorway, leaving a wide-open empty space

Chary's suit was already in the air over the front of the retreating mechanical and I followed, so close that my suit banged against hers. Scylla's suit pushed out after me and Circe came straight after, the door knocking her suit into the cavern as it shut with a thump.

"What the hell happened?" said Scylla, her suit spinning around to look at the closed door.

I had nothing on my IFF except the closed door. The suits did a quick sync but there really was nothing.

"We didn't do that," said one of the Smuts, "although I did momentarily pick up the presence of several sentient organics. The door seems to be shielding any further contact." It sounded quite surprised.

I tried calling up the native AI but there was no reply. Everyone else joined in but our calls just echoed into the grey emptiness. It was very frustrating, but if the native AI didn't want to talk, what could we do? The girls' expressions echoed mine, but at least we were safe. Quite what we were going to do next was, however, entirely another question.

My suit was still trying to contact the native AI, but was also sending out drones to scour the cavern for anything that might have changed. Slow, detailed scans came back but it was all the same. The walls were walls, the floor was the floor and the ceiling was the ceiling. This whole cavern was a massive empty underground space that looked like it had been deep-cleaned.

The faces around me were looking rather discouraged, but my suggestion of an early lunch put the smiles back. The suits started preparations, the drones came whining back and tendrils of mouth-watering smells started to disperse the cavern's ancient air. The door stayed shut, almost like it was taunting us. I couldn't stop myself going over to have another look.

I tried pressing the red button, then again and again. Nothing. My fallback plan of several kicks and thumps also didn't do anything. It was clear that nothing was going to happen until that native AI decided, and anyway, the delicious smell of the suits' food was making my stomach rumble. Definitely time for lunch.

That hot stew which the suits had almost magically conjured up rather curtailed any conversation, but unexpected seasoning was added by a metallic scraping that echoed across the cavern. As one, we turned to see the red door button lit up and the door swinging open once again.

Into the profound silence came a sound of distant footsteps walking up the tunnel. Closer and closer they came, until who should walk out of the doorway but Franky, clutching a collection of bags.

42
More tunnels, only different

Franky

It's a whole lot easier for two people to carry a pile of bags than it is for only one. I had bags across my shoulders, bags around my neck and the remainder clutched in both hands. I couldn't wait to get to that slowly growing square of grey at the end of the tunnel where I could put them all down again.

The grey square expanded into a large cavern and stone me! Standing there gawping were Soffee, the expanded girls, Smuts, suits and even a couple of unidentified mechanicals. I stood there with a stupid grin wrapped around my face as Soffee ran up and smothered me with her feathers.

"How you get here?" she said, her claws sinking into my back with an almost savage hug. "Every time you go it kill me and I kill you for almost not coming back," but my back was saved by the girls piling in for a group hug, asking me how I was, how did I get here, was I sure I was OK, etc, etc, all from very close up and at the tops of their voices.

"Hey, it's great to see you but what are you doing down here?" was my rather fatuous answer as I tried to disentangle myself from that all-enveloping feathery embrace, even if I wasn't trying too hard. My questions "How did you get here?" and "Where the hell are we?" didn't add much more, as everyone started telling me their own story, in their own different way and all at the same time. Soffee's arms around me weren't letting go and I relaxed back into her embrace, hugging right back as her Flivver scent overwhelmed me.

"It's really great to see you," I whispered into her ear and the hug tightened as more of the girls' chatter rattled around my ears.

"I just die when you in danger," she whispered, her claws slowly retracting as she pulled away to stare into my eyes, before re-applying that same savage hug and wrapping me in her wings. I was momentarily lost in that feathery embrace, but the girls weren't having any of it.

They grabbed ahold and started dragging me over to their little camp. I just couldn't stop smiling and my nose was also joining in the fun. Energy bars keep you alive but only just, and that appetising smell of hot food was just what the doctor ordered. One of the watching Smuts brought me a steaming container together with a matching sarcastic comment along the lines of us being halfway across the galaxy and some things never changed. Also, it added, they had informed the other Smuts that I'd found my way back, so I didn't have to. Distinct mental sarcasm, which is worse than spoken sarcasm, even if equally deserved.

That first spoonful of delicious stew was more than a sensual experience. It waltzed across my tongue, with the next spoonful becoming an entire dance troupe doing the same. The only problem was, in between watching me fill my fat face and listening to replies necessarily curtailed by the actions of my spoon, no one stopped asking questions. They wanted to hear my story, they wanted to hear it now, and I wasn't going to get away with anything else until I'd told them exactly what had happened.

So, placing my food down with an exaggerated sigh, I started with my pod's rather unconventional landing, but they knew all about that. I then went onto the Alien, moved to our troubles with the big blue creatures, followed on with our escape down the elevator and came to a refreshment halt with the end of the tunnel the drone had seen.

"And that was when it started to get a bit more interesting," I continued after several spoonfuls and a flood of questions about the Alien, why hadn't I mentioned it before, what were the blue creatures, etc, etc?

"We walked down towards where the drone had been up and found ourselves in the centre of a fan of tunnels, all going off to goodness knows where. In front of us was a roof high piece of Plexiglas, which slid up into the ceiling all by itself to reveal a funny little clear-walled capsule sitting in a large black pipe.

"A voice appeared out of nowhere, saying it was the AI in control of the planet's systems. Apparently, we were standing alongside a planet-wide transportation system and it could take us back to my companions, but the voice broke up before it could say anything else. I tried asking how it knew about you guys. No answer. I then tried asking why there weren't any natives here, but still no answer.

My initial thought was thank goodness for the travel offer, but the Alien wasn't happy. Fifty thousand lights from where I'd come from and this thing could speak my language? Also, no sentient organics, so who'd shot us down? Could only be an AI, and then up pops an IFF alert talking about movement where we'd got off the lift.

So, unidentified AI offering dodgy travel options, or face the blue jobs? No decision really, but safety first, right? I stuck my foot into the capsule and pulled it out again. Nothing happened, but the IFF movements were now halfway down the tunnel. I looked at her, she looked at me and I stepped into the capsule. She passed in our bags and followed close behind. A transparent door flipped down and sealed us in."

Everyone was now listening with rapt attention. However, the smell of food was still torture and I asked the Smut for another bowlful. Purely to satisfy the inner man and lubricate the tonsils you understand.

"But where is the Alien now?" someone asked. "She's not with you, so where is she?"

"Oh, it hasn't got weird yet," I said, through another appreciative slurp. "Just wait 'til you hear what happened next.

"The capsule was a clear envelope with some odd-looking chairs attached to the floor. We were just wondering how we made it go when a blue job appeared right alongside us on the platform. Momentary panic, but the capsule shot off like it had been fired out of a gun. We were caught by the seats coming up behind us which then rocked forward, gluing us in, their uneven contours and even odder shape making them more instruments of torture than seats. The acceleration kept on going and it really did feel like my nethers were about to be physically removed, when all of a sudden it stopped as abruptly as it had started.

"Several gasps and mumbled profanity were required from both of us as we eased ourselves out of the chairs and it looked like the Alien's shape had been as bad a fit as mine. The HUD informed us that we were now travelling close to four hundred klicks per hour and heading back under the sea towards you guys.

"Outside of the capsule was just a featureless blur, but the ride was smooth, like we were riding on air. We sat there in silence, rather stunned by what had just happened. The Alien flicked me an eye, but all I could think about were those blue jobs. Why did they want to eat us so much? Also, if some sort of native AI was in charge, why hadn't it stopped them chasing us if it was going to give us a ride anyway?

Thoughts to ponder, and nothing else to do. I dug into my pack for something to eat, had a couple of steps backwards and forwards, but we were stuck in this thing until we got to wherever we were going.

Actually, it was a bit of luck that the deceleration kicked in when I was sitting in my seat otherwise I'd be a thin layer of Terran all over the inside nose of the capsule. Pretty much a repeat performance of the acceleration, just with the seats swinging the other way, and I was only seconds away from becoming the first Terran with three buttocks when we finally lurched to a halt.

"The door flipped open and there we sat, gasping for breath and staring at an empty platform. Out of nowhere a bipedal mechanical appeared. It strode up and started spraying binder web all over the Alien. Let me tell you, transformation of friendly Alien to rapidly setting blob of gloop was quite a sight. The mechanical then grabbed the rapidly setting chair plus Alien globule and carried it out of the capsule, disappearing as quickly as it had appeared.

"I was still sitting there thinking wtf when the capsule door flipped down and off we went again. The acceleration was just as vicious as the last time except that thankfully it was only seconds before it reversed for the matching deceleration. Another wrenching halt, the door flipped open and there I was, more pain and another empty platform.

"I can tell you, I'd had more than enough of that whole high-G stop/start thing and I hurled our bags onto the platform before following pretty smartish. The capsule just sat there doing nothing, door wide open for the next unfortunate passenger. Just across from me was a tunnel entrance. I grabbed the bags, scooted along and here I am!"

The next couple of hours consisted of me finishing my bowl of stew, having a couple of refreshing drinks, re-telling the details of my crash, the Alien, the dangerous locals, our escape from the dangerous locals, the transport system, the Alien's disappearance and trying to answer a whole bunch of questions that I had no idea what the answer was.

As the discussions continued, a Smut dropped in a little telepathic bomblet.

"We have been examining the equipment in your bags. It is clear that the native AI is definitely hostile. The Alien's records have multiple references to an AI called Central Control and its distribution looks to be planet-wide. There are indications of a 'Secure area' close by where we are now and it seems that the AI has been catching and storing non-native species in this secure area," and with that they went back to whatever they were doing with the bags.

But hold on a moment. If all of that was true, then why hadn't this AI tried to capture us? Sure, the blue guys had tried to eat me and my companion, but that was hardly capturing. I tried the Smuts on this but they had no answer. Maybe I could just ask this native AI that Soffee and the girls had been talking about? Maybe it was Central Control.

"Central Control," I called out, "was it you that took my alien friend?"

My voice echoed into the cavern, the distant echoes rattling back to add to the eerie feel of the place. No response. I shouted louder, but the only response was no response. So much for that bright idea.

The Smuts, however, had obviously been working on something far more cunning than my feeble attempts. They'd started moving away from us, closely checking a piece of Alien equipment after each step. They weren't sharing what they were doing and on they went, step, check, step, check, step, check.

There was a loud "Crack." The edge of a panel jerked out of the wall close to them. Like lightening one of the Smuts leapt across and jammed a knife blade into the vertical slit that was already starting to close. Fingers were wriggled in, both gave a mighty heave and the slit groaned open as they really bent their backs into it. Collective telepathic shouts of success, until they stood by a gaping hole in the cavern wall.

"We found a map stored in this unit," said one, waving the piece of Alien kit. "There were indications of a door and we wondered if we could find it."

Everyone had now crowded around the dark hole. A torch lit up smooth white walls, floor and ceiling that stretched away to a distant and very dimly lit vanishing point. Great! Another underground hole going F-knows where, and this one didn't even have any lights.

"Your Alien has rigorously mapped most of the planet," a Smut continued. "This tunnel was indicated."

"Well, OK," I said. "All very interesting, but am I the only person worrying about where this goes and why there aren't any lights?" but no one was listening. Soffee and the girls were running back to their suits and obviously knew what they were going to do. I knew exactly what that was going to be.

"Can you see where it goes?" I said to the Smuts. "Another hole disappearing into the darkness doesn't sound too good to me."

"As far as we can see, this leads to a large underground anomaly that the Alien detected from orbit," it replied. "We have no other information, so would recommend the greatest caution."

"Well it looks like we're going down that hole whatever," was my response, but both of the Smuts were looking at me, a sort of telepathic question mark hanging over their heads.

"What?" I said.

There was a pause. "We have found a way to go and find your alien friend. Isn't that a good thing? Soffee and the girls certainly think so."

"Hey," I replied, "I didn't say I didn't want to go," but the Smuts were still looking at me in that way they have of peeling back the layers of your soul, as well as no doubt reading exactly what I was thinking. They didn't look impressed.

"Look," I said, "of course we have to go but I can't help feeling we might be getting into something we can't get out of."

Still not a word from either of them. They just stood there looking at me before turning back to their alien technology. Bit of a bastard really, talking to people who can read your mind.

Still, everyone was getting themselves ready and whatever I might think, I needed to do the same. I went off to grab a couple of bags, before walking back to the group now clustered around the entrance. Soffee turned away from my wave. She was definitely not impressed.

A quick warning to us pedestrians and the suits' light flicked on. They formed up in line ahead and started straight off down that now brightly lit tunnel, leaving a little black cloud hanging over me.

You know what? It was the end of a long, tiring day. Soffee was in charge and whatever they might think, I did want to do this. It was just that feeling I had. There were things waiting down there and they'd be a lot worse than the blue jobs, and that was a fact.

I really hoped that Soffee and girls knew what they were doing.

43
Another planet, another junkyard

Franky

That long white tunnel turned out to be very long indeed. I started off walking alongside one of the Smuts for an update on anything else they'd found on the Alien's equipment. However, it seemed like I already knew everything, even if "it is clear that the Central Control AI is very advanced, with a persona mimicking what we assume is the sentient species that built it."

So, sort of interesting, not entirely unexpected and annoyingly unilluminating, just like so much of what the Smuts said. After that my companion remained silent, so I left it to its own thoughts as we just kept tramping along.

On CS1 the tunnels followed the rock strata and undulated all over the place, but this tunnel was dead straight. White walls, white ceiling and white floor, all extending out to a distant, unmoving pinprick in front and behind. Suspicious old me kept on flicking an eye just in case, and I know, pretty silly what with the suits monitoring everything. Trouble was, my worries kept growing and I had no way of scratching them.

Every couple of minutes I'd have another look behind and you know what? My experience of distant vanishing points is that they generally stay distant and don't move. Still, eyes do play tricks, especially when artificial lights and a planet-sized worry wart are involved so I figured it was just me. However, the next time I looked, that distant vanishing point was definitely not distant and certainly not vanishing.

I called this out to Soffee.

"I know," came straight back. "It look like walls behind us closing together and closing bit move towards us."

The suits bent to scoop up those on foot. They then clicked up several gears, with our previous brisk walk changing to a run away from those now very obviously approaching converging walls. As we ran, the visor on the suit carrying me momentarily cleared and there was Chary's smiling face. A tongue momentarily stuck out before the screen went opaque and the suits really started legging it. Above the whirring mechanics and clump of running feet there was an ominous graunching noise which kept getting closer in spite of us running away as fast as we could.

We were now moving at approx. fifty kph, but the walls alongside were starting to craze and distort as they chased us along the tunnel. The suits jerked forward and we were now running at top speed, but those cracking walls wouldn't stop getting closer. A quick IFF popup dragged my eyes away from our impending doom, and thank goodness. There in front of us was a small but growing square of bright light.

The bright square expanded rapidly and my suit burst out into a wide-open space, scrabbling and skidding across the floor as it tried to stop itself running into a vast pile of bent and twisted metal. The last suit popped out after us and there was an enormous grinding crunch as the tunnel entrance became a vertical crack.

All of us rather shaken passengers dropped off to the floor and stood there gaping. We were in a vast, brightly lit space, surrounded by untold multitudes of very much the worse for wear mechanicals of all shapes and sizes. It was a massive alien breakers yard, but how, why and where the hell were we? As if on cue, that all too familiar voice blared out.

"Visitors to my planet, you are most welcome to the technical maintenance area of the city above. However, this is a secure part of this facility and you must leave immediately. I will provide escorts."

Two bipedal mechanicals appeared out of the junkyard and actually, I can't blame anyone for what happened next. We'd nearly been squashed flat and I think that everyone was getting rather tired of Central Control. Soffee's suit mounted up two RPGs and without a pause, fired them at the approaching mechanicals.

Each was bang on target and I have to admit that the resulting detonations plus clouds of fragments were very satisfying. However, what happened next was totally unexpected. Soffee's suit initiated an emergency exit and catapulted her out onto the ground before closing back up again and deploying all of its main weaponry.

Each of the weapons came online and started firing at the girls' suits. However, those crafty girls had their eyes wide open and were already leaping up into a free-form gymnastics display entitled 'Get the hell out of the way as quickly as possible.'

Each flew away in the graceful arcs that the suits' designers had obviously decided was the best way of staying alive, while at the same time mounting their own weapons and firing back. Of course, while laying down a continuous stream of fire, Soffee's suit was also doing its own version of this battle ballet, but the element of surprise had been lost.

It got off two more shots before an incoming torrent of energy beams, solids and explosive projectiles resulted in immediate transformation from a suit to pile of scrap with a side order of bits flying everywhere. Two of the still-pirouetting girls' suits were also caught, one having an arm blown off and the other being drilled dead centre.

Both dropped to the ground with a monumental crash. The remaining suit landed in a defensive crouch and stood there, scanning around every which way.

This whole crazy dance had taken but a handful of seconds and those standing watching were left deafened, mouths open and brains scrambled. The Smuts snapped out of it first and started running across to the nearest suit's remains. I raced over to the other one, keeping everything crossed that armour and anti-G protection had saved the occupant.

As I approached, Circe emergency-exited, standing there with feathers everywhere but looking OK. The Smuts called out that they had managed to extract Chary, so it looked like we'd got away with it.

"I always worried about that disappearing HUD icon," said Circe as Soffee patted down her wings and arms.

Seeing my quizzical expression, Circe continued: "After Soffee's suit was taken over, we always suspected that it hadn't been purged properly, so we activated full covert monitoring. Sorry we didn't tell you Soffee, but we didn't want to warn the native AI."

Chary was now walking in our direction. She waved a greeting which turned into a complex hand gesture and a stream of chittering. Circe gave the same straight back.

"Those girls," Soffee muttered under her breath, "this isn't game. Someone get hurt if they not careful." To my raised eyebrow she continued: "They running competition to see how many times they protect us from danger. Chary happy she now two-up, although is mystery how they measure."

"Well, Central Control definitely knows we're here," I said. "That's the second time it's tried and it won't stop now." Sure enough, the remaining suit was already flashing up warnings.

"There's lots of movement coming our way," said Scylla. "We need to get out of here or at least take cover," and with that her suit popped up a drone and leapt behind one of the larger junk piles. No need for further encouragement and we all rapidly leapt likewise.

"I think we close to what Central Control trying to hide," said Soffee and without waiting for a reply, she chittered something across to Circe and Chary.

They and the other two Flivvers nodded then ran out and took off, flapping hard until they were soaring across the cavern in large overlapping circles. Circe called down that they would push out a bit to see what was there.

"The drone is showing steps running up the far wall," a Smut piped up. "We will investigate."

A group of bipedal mechanicals burst out from behind a pile of junk and started running straight for us. They didn't appear to be armed but Scylla wasn't taking any chances. Crack, crack, crack and pieces flew everywhere.

Red alerts were popping up all over the place as more and more mechanicals flowed out of tunnels in the walls. It looked like Central Control was trying to squash us flat by sheer weight of mechanical numbers and we needed to get out of here. But where? Those stairs on the distant wall looked like the only option but where the hell did they go? I ducked back into cover as Scylla's suit dealt out more death and destruction. Those bloody mechanicals were everywhere.

Her suit raced past and I followed Soffee as she ran after it. Everywhere I looked, streams of mechanicals were coming for us. We could probably outpace them in a straight line but those dead mechanicals and piles of junk didn't give us one. Central Control's floods of pursuers were going to engulf us pretty quick if we didn't shake a leg.

44
Secure area

Franky

Sprays of debris rattled past as more explosions cracked around my tortured ears. Scylla was doing a great job clearing out our pursuers but her suit's power and ammo levels were dropping fast. The continual dodging around piles of mechanical junk wasn't actually doing Soffee or I any good either, although thankfully that stairway up the wall was now just a couple of junk piles away.

I called out to Scylla and her suit bounded past, going up the stairs six at a time. A much slower Soffee and I followed, each step an agony of aching legs and gasping lungs as the rivers of Central Control's minions never stopped flooding in towards us.

The mass of pursuing mechanicals smashed into the wall with an earth-shaking crunch. A wave of stillness flowed outwards, everything continuing to pile into the widening log jam. Across this now stationary obstacle-course the Smuts came a-hopping, twisting and turning to avoid the madly waving forest of manipulators, but each was a natural at this lethal game of hopscotch.

A final leap and they bounded up the stairs, our flock of flying Flivvers following right behind. One after the other they dived across the stationary sheet of crushed mechanicals before zooming up the stairwell, each landing in a graceful flare-out.

Once their tail end Charlie was down and clear, Scylla's suit started applying the maximum of brute force to make sure that nothing else came up those stairs. It first pounded down the metal bannisters into a fretwork plug. It then hammered in a couple of ripped out wall panels. Finally, it jumped up and down on everything to ram it all in just that little bit tighter, before standing back to regard its handiwork with some satisfaction.

Finally, we had some breathing space, but it wouldn't last long. Looking around, we'd managed to get ourselves up onto a long thin platform. On one side was a rock wall and on the other a waist high barrier. There was nothing else, and thank bloody goodness for that, even if an empty platform wasn't going to stay empty for long.

A handful of tottering steps took me across to where everyone else was standing at the barrier, just in time to join their collective gasp. Our platform was actually a balcony halfway up an enormous retaining wall. We were looking out over a vast artificial chasm, carpeted with a chessboard of square areas that spread into the distance. It was the oddest thing I'd ever seen in my life.

Scylla's drone was already scanning out into the void and its feed showed that the squares were laid out as self-contained habitats. Each one was different to the others and an occasional empty space gave strangely incongruous gaps amongst this oddest collection of artificial micro-worlds. High walls bounded each square, with the tops curving inward and multiple layers of barbed wire and other lethal-looking devices spread about. It was one hell of an investment to do what I was just beginning to realise this whole place was for.

And, just when you thought it couldn't get any worse, it did.

"This is the central secure area and you are welcome," blared out that all too annoyingly familiar voice.

I wondered where you'd got to, you irritating bastard. Central Control really was starting to get up my nose.

"My creators put me in charge of planetary maintenance and security. I use this secure area to store all of the alien organisms that land here."

"But it's deserted." I shouted back.

"Aliens have been landing here uninvited for hundreds of annuals," Central Control continued like it hadn't heard me. "You are just the latest of many. Whatever I did, I could not stop these landings, or the danger. I therefore looked for, and found, somewhere far away where my masters would be safe from..." and it crackled into silence. More silence, more crackling, before "...ave been travelling for 137 annuals. I confidently expect them to make their remote planetfall in another hundred..." before there was another deafening crackle, then silence.

"That was strange," said a Smut.

"Err, Central Control," I called out, "are you still there?"

My answer was a spray of sounds, the like of which I'd never heard. The best my translator could give was <Language? Unknown stem – no translation>.

There was another crackle and the sounds transitioned into "...many of my makers were killed during the exercise to take them off-planet."

"What's going on?" I mouthed to Soffee. "This AI's got a screw loose," making the obligatory twirling finger gesture around my ear.

Another crackle, then "...seen the organics I use to round up Aliens who land here. Also, I know Aliens. Tell them not to do something and that is exactly what they do. I have told you many times to stay out of the secure area and yet you are he-" and it broke into more of those strange sounds.

A Smut came in to say that there was a definite possibility this AI was not entirely stable, to which my mental "D'you think?" was answered by their equivalent of a shrug and "Just saying..."

"This really is weird," I whispered to Soffee. "We need to get out of here."

Soffee smiled. "Why you whisper?" she said. "I sure Central Control hear everything, even if is crazy as moon."

"Smartarse," I replied, kissing the end of my finger and pressing it to her nose, "even if you are my lovely smartarse." The look I got back was rather too appraising for comfort.

I flicked a quick thought to the Smuts: "Any ideas, guys?"

They came back agreeing with us both and saying that they would have a look around. They also warned me not to trust anything that this AI said. I didn't bother replying to that.

I turned back to Soffee. "It can't hear telepathy," I said, putting my thumb to my nose and wiggling my fingers. She smiled and started chittering to the girls.

"It also not speak Flivver," she said.

"You hope," I said, "but hold on a minute, I've got an idea. Central Control, do you have any Aliens that are still alive?"

Silence, and then a crackly "...Alien that came with you...they die so quickly... how carefully I make their habitats," and with almost perfect timing, an IFF advisory popped up.

Our drone was hovering over a habitat, looking down. Looking up at it was my alien friend. She raised an arm/tentacle and waved.

45
Insecure area

Franky

Soffee's smile as I called out "It's her!" was added to by eyes raised to the ceiling as my arm involuntarily lifted into half a wave. Idiot. She was a least a klick away, but she was stuck in one of Central Control's little cells. How the hell were we going to get her out?

A Smut interrupted: "We have found Central Control's physical network. There is a lot of historic damage but it connects back to a highly active computing resource. We think that the Central Control AI may no longer be as distributed across the planet as it says. We will continue to investigate."

I looked around but they'd disappeared.

"Where've you got to?" I thought, and my eye caught a distant wave at the top of a set of caged steps running up the side wall. "Blimey, you be careful," but this stating of the completely obvious just got back the quickest of eyes-raised affirmatives.

There was a large thump and the platform shook. What with Central Control, the Alien and now the Smuts, I'd been distracted from what we'd just escaped from. However, whatever was stuck down the stairwell obviously still wanted to get up here. The hammered-in metal stopper jerked upwards, and a second thump shook the platform as it jerked up some more. Everyone shuffled away, their worried eyes following the suit as it strode in to try and stop the plug's peculiar upward dance.

"Right," I said, "we need to get out of here. Any thoughts?" but while everyone pitched in with broad agreement to the former, no one had anything useful for the latter. Also, those two thumps had been merely an overture for the regular drum beat that was now rattling the underside of the stairway plug. The suit wasn't going to win that game for very long.

"OK…" I said, but Soffee was already there.

"Is time protectors stop running," she said. "We cannot stop mechanicals but we protect hive and Alien is allied to hive." The Flivvers were listening to every word and this was obviously exactly what they wanted to hear. Short, sharp and no doubt violence applied to the bad guys. Everything a protector could possibly want.

"We fly over and rescue alien friend," she continued. "Girls, you go. Medea and Hecate stay in case help needed here."

Scylla's suit was now doing the oddest of dances as she tried to get out of it while it never stopped thumping down that metal plug. It was the oddest birth from a leaping mechanical biped, but she was out, running over as the unburdened suit applied even more violence to the problem.

"I go and help Smuts," Soffee finished, "but we need make sure protectors properly ready," and she walked over to them, chittering as she went.

Weapons and ammunition appeared as if by magic. I was amazed, but shouldn't have been. Soffee had already demonstrated how useful wings and feathers are for keeping things concealed and these Flivvers were past masters.

Soffee shared it out, helping with fittings, checking everything and pretty soon we had five fully armed organic fighter aircraft standing there. They clustered into a circle and clasped hands, raising them into the air with a deafening screech before turning and jumping onto the wall. A final chirrup from Soffee and they leapt into space, the cavern ringing with exultant shrieks of their ownership and dominance. I suppose we'd just have to hope so. Central Control hadn't finished with us yet.

"I go see Smuts," said Soffee. "Look after yourself," and with a quick peck on my cheek she ran over to the caged steps, carefully fitting her wings in before starting to climb.

The suit had a close IFF-eye on our air force and I could see that they were being tracked but no targeting was indicated. It ripped off another wall plate and rammed it down, adding its own accompaniment to the thundering beat from below.

A Smut's interruption was a welcome relief.

"We have found secure networking and power going into a secure server area. We do not understand the technology but it looks like any physical security is highly compromised. There are clear indications that this is where Central Control's computing resources are located."

They were standing high on a metal platform in the angle of the roof. I waved at them and their sardonic response was all that needed to be said, really.

"We have a way in," one of them continued. "Also, there are controls on this platform to move the roof gantries. We will continue to investiga..."

"Movement," Circe broke in, "I see movement, but I don't think I'm reading it right. There's movement all over the place." She was answered by a crashing bang out in the cavern.

"You sure you're not just reading us?" Scylla called back but there was no immediate response.

"Central Control is up to something," I called out. "I've got a really bad feeling about this," but my IFF couldn't give me anything about what Circe had seen.

The girls were now a long way over the habitats. The drone feed popped up a red movement indicator several sections away from where they were headed, but that was it, just movement, no definition. What the hell was going on out there?

I thought this up to the Smuts, but they were busy and didn't respond. At the same time, my HUD popped up another alert and changed its drone's eye view to an outline of the habitat sections surrounding the Alien.

And there we were. Absolutely bloody amazing. A whole area of habitat sections was slowly changing shape, with the movements matched by thumping crashes and clouds of dust.

"Circe," I called out, "can you see this? Something really strange is happening," but they were obviously far too busy swooping down towards the Alien's habitat to answer.

Now, I've always said that you can judge a species by how it reacts after it's been imprisoned by unidentified mechanicals and then three, blue, winged, bipedal sentient beings you've never seen before, all armed to the teeth, land in front of you. My split feed from the girls and the drone showed them walking up to my erstwhile companion and yet again, I was impressed. Rather than your typical Terran re-action of jumping back with every expression of shock/OMG/WTF and grabbing for a weapon to defend herself, the Alien just asked the girls if they knew me.

Of course, when I say asked, what actually happened was the girls' translators did their best to translate the Terran speech-type noises that the Alien was making. There were then a few moments of blank incomprehension while the technology did its best, failed, tried again, failed and then eventually came up with something understandable. At that point everything got a lot more convivial and the Alien waved the girls over to where she'd been doing something by the wall.

My HUD popped up an updated mapping display and finally, there it was, Central Control's little game. You must know the children's game having a three-by-three board, eight counters and a blank space. You move the counters around using that blank space, but Central Control was cutting out the middle man. Those spectacular crashes and bangs were habitat walls moving and grinding up each other's contents. The HUD's best prediction was that two of the opposing walls of the Alien's habitat would soon start moving together and she'd be squashed flat. I called this out to the girls, but all I got back was that they were trying to jigger open the habitat's door.

I was about to call out to hurry up, but instead had a much more useful idea. Maybe our two Flivvers on lookout could help? Highly dubious responses were the result of that suggestion but off they swooped, flying hard for the now very obvious crashing, banging and clouds of dust.

"We think we have a solution to Central Control," piped a Smut into this madness. "We also have a way of moving the gantries. Soffee says give us two minutes then take cover."

Take cover? What did that mean on a long thin empty platform but a platform-shaking double thump with matching metallic screeches took that straight out of my mind. The metal plug plus our suit cartwheeled into the air as the front of a large mechanical squeezed itself up through the straining staircase hole. The metal plug sailed over into the habitats below but the suit's frantically firing thrusters just managed to bring it back onto the platform as more and more of the mechanical appeared.

Large splits cracked away from the previously immovable hole through which the large and irresistible mechanical was now thrusting itself. One whizzed past and I danced away, dodging another that opened up right under my feet. However, and as if on cue, a window in the side of the mechanical slid into view and the suit duly did its duty. An RPG flashed across, there was a thunderous explosion and the flower-petalled metal edifice dropped back down through the much-enlarged staircase hole.

A hailstorm of debris flew past and I was just checking some of my more spectacular ouches when a roof gantry dropped from the ceiling. One end smashed onto the balcony wall and shards of concrete sprayed everywhere. A cascade of gantries was now disengaging from the roof, each section crashing together as they formed a suspended jungle gym-type path extending away towards the Alien's distant habitat.

Next moment, the suit ran over and shoved me behind itself. A metallic spring of small mechanicals was bubbling up through the burst-open stair hole and flooding across the platform. The suit started picking them off but there were so many it was hit one, miss three at best. Central Control must be pretty desperate to lose all those mechanicals, but the suit's ammo and power levels were approaching critical. Maybe its plan wasn't so stupid after all.

My eyes were dragged away from that moving wall of metal by a burst of telepathic blowback from the Smuts, but they weren't talking to me. Soffee had disappeared and up there in the angle of the roof something was happening. The suit squawked a warning that it was down to its last twenty.

"Girls," I called out, "I could do with some help over here."

My reply was a flood of untranslatable Flivver bad language but I tried again. "Look, you lot have all the weapons. The suit's nearly dry and then we're screwed."

Circe popped up, her face framed by roiling dust and dirt. She chittered that they were still trying to get the Alien out but she would try and send some help. I caught another squirt of mental blowback from the Smuts and with it came a flicker of movement high up on the wall. Almost from nowhere there was a hole, and out of it were sticking Soffee's head and shoulders.

She struggled an arm out, then another, and I heard/felt a muffled thump. A spray of dust flew out around her and she popped out of the hole like a cork from a bottle.

46
No Central Control

Franky

An untidy ball of limbs and wings tumbled out of the dust cloud and dropped like a stone towards the habitats below.

"Come on, come on, come on...," and the plummeting confusion stiffened into a flying wedge, which with one mighty flap turned into a swooping, flying Soffee.

A second massive flap and she zoomed upwards, even if now far below me and well out from the wall. Another flap, and then another, each one bringing her a little higher, but she wasn't a Flivver and she didn't know how to fly. My eyes were locked on that gasping, straining face as each desperate wing beat brought her closer, clutching for height, straining desperately to stay in the air. Scylla's suit rushing straight at the surging sea of mechanicals was the briefest flash in the corner of my eye, but Soffee's agonised face was all I could see.

Her powerful wing beats were starting to falter, muscles exhausted from moving those massive wings that were only just keeping that non-Flivver bulk in the air. She wouldn't stop flapping until she'd used up every scrap of energy, but the tank was empty and she was dropping out of the air.

I leaned over the balcony wall as far as I could, holding out my arms, willing her to keep going, shouting her on. She was ten metres out, then five, then three but her strength failed, a last feeble flap driving her straight into the wall as she grabbed hold of my hands, nearly jerking me over the edge.

"Got you," I shouted but actually, I wasn't that sure. The balcony was cutting into my stomach and Soffee's slumped, exhausted weight was inexorably dragging me over the edge.

It was going to be first time or nothing, and with a jerk that nearly dislocated my shoulders I yanked her up. We wobbled back into balance but those feathered fingers were slipping. She dug in her claws and the spike of agony was just what I needed. One final heave and her arms and shoulders slid over the balcony edge with the rest of her tumbling over as I slumped back exhausted.

"I thought you couldn't fly," I said into her feathers, holding on like I was never going let her go.

"I also not know," she said in between her heaving gasps for air and hugging me back, but she stiffened. I lifted my eyes to the solid wall of approaching mechanicals.

"Can't you do what you did on CS1?" I asked, my eyes glued still to those ranks of malevolent metal.

"I sorry," she said, "it happen if it happen and I so tired."

She sagged into my arms, but our lovely moment was destroyed by Medea and Hecate's ear-splitting screeches as they swooped in, opening up with everything they had.

A sea of explosions knocked us back against the wall, our two saviours flaring in as they opened up yet again at the scurrying mechanicals. A brief shout from Medea that we needed to get back to the gantry before their rods of fire again lanced across the platform.

A few last shots, but they'd done what they could, were out of ammo and needed to get out of here. They ran to the balcony wall and leapt off, leaving me deafened, peppered with debris and still struggling to heave a very floppy Soffee onto her feet. A renewed spring of mechanicals had started bubbling up through the twisted hole in the platform and it didn't seem like it was ever going to stop.

We just about managed to stagger off through the haze, and I walked straight into the end of the gantry. That almost finished me off and I could barely stand as I gasped and coughed. There was certainly no way Soffee was going to get onto that gantry. In fact, both of us staying on our feet was about the best we could manage as that crunching, grinding mechanical mass just kept on getting closer.

It was inexorable, a wave of charging machines grinding its way through the Medea and Hecate's debris and there really was nowhere left to hide even if Soffee and I could have moved. I wrapped her up in my arms and closed my eyes, but suddenly, magically, the noise faded away. There was no more vibration. An almost physical silence surrounded us.

Hoping against hope I very cautiously opened one eye. Almost close enough to touch, a stationary sea of metalwork stretched away from me. There was just the odd click or creak scattering across the expanse, with curling tendrils of smoke being the only movement.

"Everything's stopped moving," dropped into the silence courtesy of Circe.

"We concur," said a Smut. "We can see no movement from up here."

Soffee was still sagged inside my arms but her face creased into a smile.

"I think I get Central Control," she said. "Smuts find server room. Is very strange, all sludgy organics and very smelly. I use special just like Dane's and he be so proud. He always say not leave home without one and I blow everything to pieces."

"My beautiful destructive genius," but my arms were almost too tired to hug her.

I tried to get more of a grip, but she struggled out of my arms. A cascade of dust as she opened her wings then billowing clouds as she gave them a good shake. A quick check all over, the odd mis-placed feather preened back into place and she suddenly looked a whole lot better.

"I think we go find your friend," she said, "then we get hell out of this craphole piece of shit place and soon as bloody possible."

My "Wherever did you learn such dreadful language?" got both a very well-deserved prod and a lingering hug.

47
Up and out

Franky

Soffee waved to the Smuts, who were now standing high up on their metal platform looking down.

"There are no indications that the Central Control AI entity still exists," said one. "Also, we have made a route to the Alien's enclosure using the roof gantry-ways," and without another word they started walking along their suspended metal pathway, terse to the last.

"We're going to have to walk," I said to Soffee. "Are you OK with that?"

"I fine now I back on ground," she said, dusting the remaining grains of dust off her feathers. "Ground much safer than air."

"You reckon?" I said, glancing around. "All far too exciting for me. Also, you know these things aren't dead? They're just waiting for something to tell them what to do and we need to get out of here before something does just that."

She brushed past me and made a beeline for the suit's remains, dipping in and out of the herd of stationary mechanicals. It felt like a thousand eyes were watching and I tried to follow along as close behind her as I could.

The suit was easy to find, but it was no longer suit-shaped. Its final act had been to lay about itself with mis-shapen chunks of metal clasped in both hands, whilst various mechanicals had done their best to return the compliment. Definitely exceeded the manufacturer's specifications on that, but it wasn't going anywhere, anymore, anytime soon.

I had another quick look around, but Soffee was busy with the suit, just finishing off a quick Mediscan.

"You OK?" I asked. "Really?"

"I think I strain every muscle," she said, "but scan show no problems so I fine." She finished with an enigmatic smile.

"You must have been worried about something," I said, but got just a quick squeeze of the hand before she started ferreting around, adding bits and pieces from the suit to a growing pile of scavenged essentials. The whole place was still deathly quiet, but it felt like every one of my hairs was standing on end. We really did need to get out of here.

"I finished," said Soffee, shouldering her small pack bulging with goodies. "I make suit do destructive firmware format so no one can use against us. We ready?" and with that she strode off towards the gantry.

Every step felt like something was about to grab me, but up we jumped onto the metal gantry way and I felt my whole body relax. Safe at last. Assuming, of course, the little bastards didn't start coming after us on the gantry.

The thin latticework between us and eternity was a bit of a stomach clencher, but I was so relieved to get away from those mechanicals that I could almost forget how high up we were. Habitat after habitat passed below and we were almost floating along over this mad wonderland. All of that time and effort just to capture and hold any Aliens that had come here. All of those people, kept here over the decades. Central Control was gone but so had they.

It seemed somehow worse that a technical entity had done all this, but maybe that was the problem. Xenophobia was xenophobia, and if you were an AI then everything organic was going to be different to you. Central Control had just taken it to its logical conclusion. It was just difficult to contemplate, as the whole thing was so far outside of my experience and made no sense. I mean, I'd lived my whole life with other people, species, whatever. The whole was always greater than the sum of its parts, even if you didn't have to like everyone.

I was jolted out of my reverie by Circe who came swishing into the side of the gantry. She clung, bursting into a chittering stream so fast that any translation was several steps behind.

She'd come to see if we were alright, and as we were, we needed to get over to the Alien's habitat as quickly as possible. They hadn't been able to get her out before the habitat's walls started crushing together. She'd managed to leap between pieces of wreckage, but just as Soffee's bomb had gone off she'd lost her footing and fallen between two large sections of floor. She was badly injured and they could no longer see where she was.

Circe sprang away from the gantry and started flying back. We broke into a jog, but with the gantries criss-crossing their way across the cavern roof we had a constant succession of angles and corners. It seemed like having to run twice the actual distance, but eventually we made it, standing above the scrunched up remains of my alien friend's habitat. A fifteen-metre-wide slot was all that remained of the original hundred metres square and quite clearly a hundred didn't go into fifteen.

I could see the two sections of floor she'd slipped between, but she was so far down that there was no sign of her. As I watched, one of the sections jerked and the surrounding area settled.

A Smut called in: "We have communicated with the Alien. She is badly hurt and says that no one should risk themselves to save her. It was a pleasure to meet Franky and a privilege to meet all of the other entities. She is sorry that she cannot continue to be a member of our group."

There was another movement, several pieces of rubble settled and the two pieces of floor slowly squeezed together.

"I can get no further communication," the Smut dropped into the silence.

We stood there staring. There must have been something we could do to save her, but what? The depths of my sadness were only emphasised by the cracking, crunching and settling of the habitat as my friend was buried. All of those other Aliens that had died here and there really was no one left. Bloody Central Control on its mission to capture everyone who ever landed here and it wasn't even here anymore, just the remains of what it had done. What a complete waste.

Soffee nudged up against me and her feathered hand slipped into mine. It didn't make me feel any better. In fact, I just wanted to shout at the sky, but, just, well, eh? I looked at Soffee who was looking at me. We'd come all of this way, we now knew what had happened to the planet's inhabitants and we were the only organic sentients left. It should have felt good, but it actually felt pretty crap.

A Smut interrupted my ruminations with news that they may have found a way out of the cavern.

"If there's a tunnel involved, I hope it's not like last time," was Scylla's comment to much Flivver mirth.

The Smut followed up that they would keep working on it and let me know. All of that seemed to raise the spirits of our Flivvers, including Soffee, and it was interesting to see how quickly they'd cheered up.

Flivvers are pretty binary in their view of the world, and especially protectors. Soffee had dealt with Central Control. It was sad that the Alien had died, but she hadn't really been part of the hive and they'd done their best. There were no more threats, so everything was just great. Simple as that.

The Smuts were keeping any views they might have very much to the themselves, and that came back to me. I'd met an Alien who, I'd like to think, had become a friend. This mad alien AI had killed her, and added yet another person to the growing list of people who'd made the ultimate sacrifice keeping me alive. Now don't get me wrong, I was very grateful. It was just that why did everyone have to keep on dying?

These dark thoughts just wouldn't stop rumbling around, and it took another telepathic flash from one of the Smuts to drag me back at least some way towards the light. It seemed that they'd now found a route all of the way back to the cavern we'd originally left. It looked like an easy route, although it was going to be the best part of two day's walk.

I called over to Soffee, but her amused comment was that our next problem was going to be getting everyone out of the air. All the time that I'd been moping and the Smuts had been working, our Flivvers friends had been making use of the cavern to get in a bit more flying practise. They were now cavorting about all over the place and having far too much fun to listen to anything we said.

Soffee tried shouting up at them but was rewarded by a chorus of laughter and mockery along the lines of "Come on then if you think you can catch us." She shouted up again, and then again, but all she got was more friendly insults and a cascade of swooping down closer and closer, like they were playing chicken.

This went on for some time, but eventually Soffee started getting bored, we really did need to get going and, after all, Soffee was head protector so they did need to listen. Each came swooping in for an extravagant landing and even loud whoops of joy, with group hugs and much excited chittering about how good it was to be flying again.

We finally managed to chivvy them into some sort of order and it looked like we might actually go somewhere. The Smuts led the way, both of their noses staying buried in the Alien's tech as we passed out of the cavern into a network of dimly lit unmarked tunnels. It was definitely only for those people who had a map and, as Soffee said, just like being back on CS1 except that we could only hope the Smuts knew where we were going.

Four hours later and both our day and our legs were pretty much done, especially as we'd been on the go since before the squashing tunnel incident. Everyone was looking forward to whatever meagre rations Soffee and I had managed to salvage, but pretty meagre it turned out to be. A lucky dip into Soffee's bag was as good as it got and from the various comments, everyone couldn't wait to get outside. Soffee set a watch rotation, just in case, and everyone got themselves ready for sleep.

I fell asleep pretty quickly and didn't manage to disgrace myself doing exactly the same thing when it was my turn for watch. I finally awoke to laughing discussions about finding places for people to, as you might say, take care of Smut, Flivver and Terran business. Another lesson learned by all and sundry. Last night had been rather ad hoc, and much longer trips were now required to avoid the results of those previous less well-planned activities.

Much tittering in darkened corners later, we shared out the remaining food and drink and started off on what was hopefully our last day down here.

The tunnels were exactly the same as yesterday, with the Smuts' noses staying buried in their map at every bend or junction, followed by more dimly lit tunnels and then more of the same. A long morning started to wear into the afternoon and it was a real relief when finally, a Smut's mental exclamation said that we were here.

"Where?" was my immediate thought, but sure enough, at the end of our current piece of tunnel was a dimly outlined door. Up we walked and there was a nice red button, all ready to be pressed.

Scylla did the honours, and with a metallic clank and groan of old machinery the door creaked open. I don't know what we'd expected to see, but there in front of us was the same cavern we'd left several days ago. Those clever Smuts had done exactly what they'd said they would.

One of them took that moment to make a somewhat cryptic comment.

"Now that we are outside the secure area, we are in communication with our party. They are safe and others have joined."

Without another word they went straight over to the mechanicals and started opening and closing panels, kicking tyres and generally showing every evidence of telepathic satisfaction.

Those wanting a ride mounted up behind and we headed off to the ramp. Previously weary steps started to regain their spring as we started circling upwards, eager conversations bouncing around as we got to the first shaft of golden sun splitting the ramp. None of us could wait for that first breath of freshest air and a face full of sunshine.

48
Straight back down again

Franky

A crescent of brightest blue opened up above us as we came out of the depths, flutters of breeze providing tempting smells of the outside. A slightly strange IFF alert also came up, but you know what? We were here, who cared?

We walked off the top of the ramp and the sun's warmth caressed my face, fresh air filling my nostrils and clearing out the smell of underground places. Aaaah, nothing like it in the known Universe.

"Well, well, well," came a voice from behind me. "Look who's finally come out to play."

Standing against the courtyard wall was our old friend Ms Black-suit from Servcon. Alongside her was a suitably bulky black-clad minion, with someone else on the other side. I must be dreaming. In all the places in all of the galaxy, who should find his way here but that scumbag Dougie.

Ms Black-suit raised a pistol and pointed it at me.

"Just you stay right where you are," she said. "We wouldn't want to spoil anything now would we."

They started walking towards us, Ms Black-suit's weapon never leaving the centre of my chest.

"Have you got anything?" I whispered.

Soffee and the girls whispered back that they had nothing they could get to quickly enough. Amazing really. I'd asked them what they had and they were more concerned about getting to it quickly enough than what it was.

"Finally got here then?" Dougie's shit-eating grin called over. "Shame it took you so long," but a contemptuous glance from Ms Black-suit shut him right back up.

Ms Black-suit came to a halt right in front of us, the other two spreading out on either side.

"Shan't keep you long," she said with a grin. "We just want a permanent loan of your Harpy," a mock bow in Soffee's direction, "and we'll leave you in peace."

All five Flivvers moved up to stand alongside Soffee.

"Come on missy," said Ms Black-suit, "we haven't got all day. Come over here and no one'll get hurt."

No one moved and I couldn't see Soffee going anywhere.

There was an exaggerated sigh from Ms Black-suit: "You make things so difficult."

She flicked her pistol across and fired at Circe. There was a bright flash and a hole appeared in the feathers of one wing, a matching puff of smoke blowing away in the breeze. Circe glanced down at the charred hole and made a very rude gesture back.

Ms Black-suit grinned as she raised her weapon again but the girls leapt into the air, strong wing beats pulling them upwards as Soffee, Hecate and Medea ran straight for the ramp.

If she's got auto-targeting this isn't gonna end well, but Ms Black-suit and Dougie jumped towards me, and I was an idiot. They were following the first rule of how you get something you want, namely, grab hold of something the other side wants. They nearly had me when Circe came swooping down and threw a large flechette at Ms Black-suit.

There was a shriek of pain as it sank into her right thigh. She staggered, firing as Circe went jinking past. Another flash, more smell of burning feathers and Circe's zoom turned into a corkscrew. She just about managed to flop over the edge of the roof and disappear out of sight.

Dougie gave a triumphant shout and bent to help Ms Black-suit, who was crawling towards me with murder in her eyes. An object came spinning up from the ramp and there was an ear-splitting bang as everything disappeared into a cloud of smoke.

Scylla swooped in and grabbed my arm, unceremoniously bundling me away. We stumbled down the ramp, my eyes adjusting as the sunlight disappeared, but my ears still deciding whether or not they were going to start working again. Soffee came up and high-fived Scylla, both of them bursting into rapid chittering as Scylla kept on dragging me down the ramp.

The summary my translator managed was that Circe had another hole in her wing and couldn't fly. She wasn't in any immediate danger but was staying up on the roof out of sight. Chary was high in the sky keeping watch, but also staying well out of Ms Black-suit and Co's way. Medea and Hecate were further down the ramp with the Smuts.

We continued walking, plans chittering back and forth as we carried on down. The Smuts pitched in that the mechanicals' power packs were dead, so great, more good news. Several more rotations later and we walked off the end of the ramp into the cavern that we'd left just a short time ago.

And where did that leave us? Ms Black-suit was obviously a lady on a mission and she wasn't going to stop. The bad guys were in the right place and we were very definitely in the wrong place, with the only bright side being Circe's bullseye with that flechette.

"What was that thing you threw?" I asked Soffee.

She smiled. "Dane tell me always have flash-bang handy. He say never leave home without one."

"This 'never leave home without one' is a bit of a recurring theme isn't it?" I said. "I'm gonna have to have a word with that Dane."

Scylla sniggered and I probably hadn't seen the half of it. Still, as far as Dane was concerned the regular carrying of lethal weaponry was perfectly normal, so why was I even vaguely surprised by his eager pupils?

"Anyway," I said, "what have we got for when they come down here?"

A quick huddle and it transpired that Soffee and Scylla had swords, knives, flechettes plus diverse explosive devices secreted about their persons. Hecate and Medea had much the same, but the only firearm was my PDW and that had just two mags left. So, we weren't going to be able to fight our way out, but our defences were also pretty crap. We didn't have any hiding places except for the tunnels, and no one wanted to go back in them.

As for Ms Black-suit and her mates? Who knew?

We were just digesting all of this when "Hey Franky," came echoing down the ramp. "You can pass on my thanks to your little friend, but we've got full Regenmed up here so she can go screw herself."

Both Scylla and Soffee smiled.

"Look, come on," continued Ms Black-suit, "let's be civilised about this. You can't stay down there, so why don't you come up and have a chat? Your mate Dougie's got a drink with your name on it and I'll bet you could do with one of those, eh?"

Before I could reply, Soffee shouted back, explaining precisely what Ms Black-suit could do with herself, her drink and her Regenmed, using full anatomical details and liberal use of bad language. There was a brief pause while those above digested her choice suggestions.

"Really?" the voice eventually continued. "That's it? You know we're gonna come down, and if the easiest way is scraping bits off the floor for the cloning tank then that's how it's gonna be. It's your choice."

There was another pause, which went on and on. I was about to break the silence with something suitably abusive when she said: "Ok then, tell you what. While you think about that, here's something else to think about."

An odd, metallic rattle started, coming and going but getting closer and closer, louder and louder.

"Get away from the ramp!" I shouted and dived to the side, grabbing Soffee as I went past. We hit the ground and I rolled, wrapping her up in my arms as a silvery sphere bounced off the end of the ramp.

A deafening "Crack!" hit me in the ears and fragments whined overhead. Several sharp thumps rewarded my best shielding efforts, but as far as I could tell Soffee was OK. I tried rolling off but an agonising spasm of pain told me that wasn't such a good idea. She started sliding out from under me, and my "Shhhh..." plus agonised expression got her oddest expression right back.

I just couldn't move, or at least not without feeling like I'd broken in half. Soffee's face was still wearing that odd expression as she gave her wing a yank to get it out, being greeted by my shout of pain. I tried wriggling my hand around, but immediately wished I hadn't. It just hurt even more and my hand came back covered in blood.

Soffee stood there looking at me while I tried to move again, but nope, that really wasn't happening. She bent to have a look before straightening back up again with new odd expressions on her face.

"There blood everywhere," she said. "Is all red."

I must admit that what with my agonising pain, my "Yeah well, you should see the other guy and anyway, what the hell colour should blood be?" came out rather more crossly than I'd intended.

Her shocked reply of "But is wrong colour," followed by "and who is other guy?" turned my irritation into a momentary smile, even if new stabs of pain made it difficult to reply.

"I really can't move," I said. "Can you see what's wrong?"

By now Scylla had come over and was taking a great deal of interest. She even tried a quick prod which, after more bad language from me, seemed to answer her unspoken question. They stood back up again and had a jolly good whisper, their eyes flicking back and forth and hands held across their mouths to hide what they were saying. I mean, really? They didn't have to tell me it hurt and that was for sure. Soffee squatted down again.

"OK..." she said, putting on her most encouraging face. "There many holes with blood coming out and piece of metal sticking out of leg."

She stopped and glanced up at Scylla.

"We have Medikit," she continued, "and Scylla know some medicine but only for Flivvers. She not know Terrans and your red blood make her feel bit funny."

"Well, it's not great for me," I said, "but if you don't stop it leaking out I'm in a lot of trouble."

I was actually starting to worry, especially with what my HUD was now saying. Sure, the nanos would deal with any infections, but they couldn't put blood back in. With the amount that seemed to be leaking out, someone needed to stop that happening, and fast.

Soffee and Scylla had another quickly chittered conflab, after which Soffee flicked me a quick smile and bent to stroke my cheek. Scylla knelt down wearing a very worried expression and muttered something about doing her best. I replied that I had total confidence and sorry for the red blood everywhere. I'm not sure that helped.

Having someone from another species, who's not familiar with Terran physiology, look you over, was a challenging experience and not least because she was trying to be gentle, but gentle to a Flivver. It also didn't help that Flivvers have claws. The next couple of minutes consisted of her having a prod, me howling "Aaagh!", she trying somewhere else and me having another shout.

Still, a modern Medikit is a wonderful thing and this, together with her paramedic skills and a bit of inspired guesswork, seemed to plug the holes. She then helped me to my feet for a stagger across to the cavern wall where hopefully I'd be well away from any other little exploding surprises.

I subsided against the wall as Hecate came running down the ramp with some very unwelcome news, or maybe it was just more unwelcome news. We now knew exactly what the bad guys were doing as she'd just seen three people making a slow and very careful way down the ramp towards us.

Soffee came over, bent down and ran her hand across my forehead. She kissed a finger, pressed it to my brow and with a rather purposeful expression picked up the PDW.

"What're you doing?" I asked.

"I do what protectors do," she said. "I go find other guy," and I do believe she smiled.

"Well, at least we're sort of even now," I said, gesturing at my sodden bandages.

"You so funny," she said. "Bad as girls," kissing her finger and pressing it to my lips. I couldn't blame her for not wanting to get her feathers messy and let's face it, a kiss was a kiss anywhere, and especially down here.

She called over Scylla and the two of them made their way to the bottom of the ramp. They'd obviously been raiding Dane's haute couture collection for the well-dressed protector, and Soffee had so much weaponry strapped to her that she clanked.

That bloody voice came echoing down the ramp.

"Hope you liked my little present. Anyway, last chance. Send up the Harpy and we're out of here, otherwise we're coming down to get her."

Soffee and Scylla moved in towards the wall, but I was distracted by a flicker of movement out in the cavern. An IFF alert also popped up but my eyes were so full of gunge I couldn't see what it was complaining about. A convenient sleeve judiciously applied and I almost wished I hadn't.

Two of those oh so well remembered blue creatures were running across the cavern and heading straight for us.

49
The operation was a success, but the patient?

Franky

Flippin' 'eck, those guys were shifting but where in hell's name had they come from? Some sort of weird Central Control endgame no doubt, but Soffee was well ahead of me. She had the PDW stuck into her shoulder and red dots were bouncing across each of the running figures as they approached.

They slowed, eyes glued to Soffee as she stood there like a feathered sentinel in the cavern's greyness. Their paths gradually diverged as the running changed to a pattering trot, then a walk, before coming to a very deliberate stop, them looking at Soffee looking at them. A chitter from one of the girls and each animal flattened to the ground, eyes flicking from side to side.

They took a stealthy step, then a second and a third, but stiffened to a halt as Scylla stepped away from the wall. Medea and Hecate followed, drawing their swords as they walked into the cavern, out-flanking both creatures.

The blue guys took a good look around and coughs flew between them as they contemplated what they were seeing. Soffee started edging forward, and Medea and Hecate were now arcing in behind, a Flivver fishing net slowly gathering up our two blue fish. Soffee stopped, kneeling as she lay her head along the PDW's stock, the bilious green light from the auto-targeting lighting her face. The blue guys looked left and right, then at each other. A nod, and they started walking towards Soffee.

"BBBRRRRRTTT!"

The air was ripped by the banshee snarl of Soffee's PDW as it carved a line of holes across their noses, the ricochets whining into the cavern and a cascade of cartridge cases tinkling to the ground. They stopped, shocked, eyes wide open. Medea's sword brushed the cavern floor and they spun around, gathering themselves in an instant before leaping at our two corralling protectors.

Medea and Hecate sprang back, wings flapping as they evaded the wildly swiping paws. Snarls of pain greeted protector sword slashes and both blue creatures dropped back, licking their wounds as hooded eyes never left the feathered whirlwinds blocking their way.

Our two Flivvers dropped into classic fighting crouches, swords held high, wings wide open, dwarfed by their adversaries. A still, unreal tableaux. Lions stopped by bluebirds. The lions glanced at each other. They hadn't expected that. More coughs and grunts. They took a step back, glances flicking around as they kept on moving, heads flicking this way and that, choruses of coughs as Soffee and Scylla tightened the contracting ring of blue that was pushing the creatures in towards the ramp.

A creature stopped, its head flicking round. Several large sniffs. Easier prey perhaps? Another cough and they were off, leaping up the ramp and disappearing as if by magic.

A crescendo of animal roars, human screams, bursts of firing, then silence. Nothing more. Nothing at all. I looked at Soffee and she looked at me, one of her eye crests slowly rising into a question mark.

"Nearly got us there, you bastards," echoed weakly down the ramp, "but your friends are spread all over the floor, so screw you." Choking coughs, then silence.

I knew what those hell hounds were capable of and they'd obviously done at least some of that up the ramp. Trouble was, who or what was left? At least one black-suit guy for sure. Now they'd creamed the blue guys they'd be coming down here.

But you know what? Everything was hurting so much I didn't care. Soffee could sort it out and if she couldn't then who could?

We waited, and then we waited some more. I shifted to find myself a less painful position, but each of Scylla's carefully bandaged holes was still very much alive, well and making its presence felt. And then my day was made totally complete by a HUD alert saying that I needed urgent medical attention, and now. So great, thanks a lot for absolutely nothing.

I called to Scylla and she came over to take another look. She lifted things, she prodded things before emerging wearing her even-more-worried look. She called to Soffee, and from the muffled chitterings, I made out that Scylla was (a) very proud of the hive chief who'd been so heroically injured and (b) very worried about the hive chief who'd been so heroically injured but was now bleeding so badly she couldn't stop the bleeding however hard she tried.

The chittering continued before Soffee very obviously came to a decision. Somehow, she managed to strap on even more weaponry handed to her by Scylla and they hugged, or rather, they hugged and clanked. She then stepped over to the ramp and very slowly disappeared upwards. In the meanwhile, Scylla started digging around in the Medikit. She emerged holding handfuls of bandages and a collection of sachets all rather worryingly labelled 'Permanent Cellular Adhesive – Use only in case of risk to life.' Then, with the Flivver equivalent of a smile that said this isn't going to hurt a bit, she looked into my eyes, stroked down my arms with both wings and started unpacking the red soggy laundry.

I rather zoned out for a bit, what with the pulling, prodding and stabs of agony, but zoned back in to see Soffee's face rather magically floating there in front of me. She had to try several times, but eventually I got what she was saying. She'd seen where the black-clad guys had met the blue guys and it was a mess. There were two tracks leading upwards. She reckoned we should follow those tracks.

Well, anything that got us out of this hideous tomb was OK by me, but first there were a couple of problems to solve. Numero uno? How the hell was I going to move? No idea on that one, but while Soffee rounded up the troops, I did my best to round up my most positive thoughts. We then tried various ways of getting me onto my feet, and me then staying there. A bit of a game really, what with everyone trying to help, grabbing bits they shouldn't and much associated shouting and swearing by yours truly.

Whatever that grenade had done, my back and right leg were totally knackered. Hoisting me up turned out to be the easy bit, but then we had to work out how an eighty kg Terran was going to be supported by two forty kg Flivvers. For some reason the two Smuts only stood back and watched while I smeared lots of blood all over Medea and Hecate.

Several attempts later and off we went, Soffee and Scylla leading the way and me doing my best not to collapse all over the place. Three rotations of the ramp later, and believe me, I was counting every step, a dark, dribbly rivulet was just in the right place for my foot to tread in. Another half rotation and there were more streams to dodge, as well as the bodies, body parts and other pieces of nastiness spread all over the place. The top half of a black-suit guy was poking out from under a blue body and his other half was wedged under the other one.

So much blood and so much mess. Just like 'Wazzap???' back on Servcon.

We edged past this horror show and continued upwards, following trails of sticky footprints. I now needed regular pauses for breath and my two supportive companions were also pretty glad of the breaks. My body felt like it was breaking in half, and you know what? Maybe it was. I just couldn't tell any more.

An aeon of pain later and splashes of sunlight shivered down, reflecting off the floor and the walls. Soffee stopped, turning to me with an expression of wonder.

"They here," she said.

I was having the greatest difficulty concentrating on anything other than putting one foot in front of another so my response was somewhat short and summarised. However, she repeated herself.

"But they here," she said. "CS1 hive. How is possible?"

"Don't ask me," I grunted. "I only work here," but she wasn't listening, her eager gaze looking upward as she bounded away up the ramp.

The sun got brighter and brighter with every step, and in spite of the pain I could now catch what Soffee had been talking about. Echoing down to us was the sound of a flock of birds, an out of time memory from my Old-Earth childhood, even if louder, deeper and more solid than I ever remembered. In fact, it was just like that Flivver hive on CS1.

Another half circuit and my eyes lifted up to lovely blue sky, but also Flivvers, Flivvers, everywhere. They were flying, they were sitting on the courtyard wall or just standing looking at us. Chitichca gave me a wave, but oddly, no one came any closer.

A final few steps and I just about managed to stagger off the top of the ramp into the open air.

"Well, well, well," broke through the sea of chittering. "And look what we've got here."

'Wha..the..fff..?' was the best I could manage as me and my Flivver walking frame ground to a halt. A trail of blood running from the top of the ramp stopped at Ms Black-suit, who was lying there wrapped in bandages and pointing a pistol at us. She was definitely not a well person, but Dougie, of course and as per usual, was unblemished. Our eyes met. He raised a finger to his forehead in that customary greeting before nodding over to a dead Flivver lying on the ground, the customary smirk and shrug saying it all.

"Happy-family time," grated Ms Black-suit. "Bloody charming. Well, I'm still here and so's that Harpy. Hand her over or you're dead."

"But there's a whole Flivver hive up here," I gasped back. "You've no chance."

"You just don't get it, do you?" she said. "That Harpy's one of only three ever made. The people who made her, hell, even the whole planet's gone. She's a biological marvel and worth a galaxy's ransom. Which I want."

"No one owns anyone," I gasped, sagging against my Flivver supports. "You can just piss off."

"Well, you said it," she said. "If I don't get her, no one does," and her weapon flicked across to Soffee.

My agonized lunge tackled Soffee out of the way, the mental "Gotcha!" as we went over only matched by the searing pain of Ms Black-suit's shot. Scylla, of course, was well ahead of everyone. Even before the shot, her right hand was sweeping behind a wing where she pulled out a spiked object and threw it at Ms Black-suit. Whatever it was sailed through the air and stuck into that black-clad chest. A red light flicked, before it and Ms Black-suit exploded.

By this time, I was lying on the ground feeling most peculiar. I could also smell burned dinner, but what was that all about? Whatever. Wasn't important. Dougie was running and the mass of Flivvers circling overhead squeezed into a sharp point as they came diving down after him. He managed a couple of wild shots before the blue arrowhead splashed all over his running figure, final screams disappearing into their deafening screeches.

I couldn't move. Soffee was kneeling in front of me with a horrified expression on her face which blurred as my head involuntarily thumped to the ground. Everyone else was standing there staring, and if it's possible for feather-covered faces to blench and go white, that's exactly what they did.

Soffee reached out to scoop up my very floppy head.

"Hey beautiful," I said, looking into those deepest, blackest eyes. "I do exactly what protectors do. I protect."

"Yes," she said, her lips trembling. "You always protect me."

"Oh c'mon, don't be sad," I said. "No more of those bloody Black-suits and you've finally got your Treasure planet."

"You always give me what I want," she said, a tear rolling down her cheek. "Always."

"I'm so cold," I said. "Can you hold me? I'm as cold as ice."

Her "I never let go, dearest man," blended into the Flivvers' screeches, everything floating away behind a growing mist as Soffee's feathery warmth and soft kiss disappeared into the silent depths of darkest night.

***

Soffee

Franky flopped, limp and unmoving. Scylla pushed in, hands full of bandages. Medea eased Franky's body out of my arms.

"We have him," said Medea. "Keep watch. We've got this," but I couldn't move. This can't be happening.

Medea shouted across to Hecate and she started digging into my pack. Scylla was also shouting as packet after packet flew across, to be ripped open, their contents pressed into the floods of red blood. Mother's wings wrapped me in her protective bundle.

"Do not worry," she said. "Your protectors can save him. Just give them space."

She shrieked across to the other-hive people who were standing there, watching. Medea and Hecate's voices joined Mother's, their voices blending with Circe's and Chary's as our hive cry echoed around the courtyard.

A blue wave streamed across and Smut brain tickles told me they were preparing a pod to get Franky up to the ship. Scylla and Medea had started wrapping him up in a blanket and a flood of other-hive people clustered around, each grabbing one of the many lines that Hecate was attaching to the Franky-bundle. They walked outwards, tying the ends around their waists, the rope spokes snapping tight with Franky now at the centre of their wheel of blue.

The wheel rim leaned outwards and with a shriek of "Now!" everyone leapt into the air. A whirlwind exploded around the courtyard, the ring of flapping people constricting as they rose with Franky's blanket parcel in the centre. The blue rimmed rope cone lifted up and out of the courtyard, one moment there and the next moment gone with just a maelstrom of sand and dust to mark its passage.

I looked across to see another ring of people forming up, the wrapped-up body of the person that Dougie had killed in its centre. With a shriek they leapt into the air, and another windstorm thrashed around as they lifted up and out to follow Franky.

The tempest died, leaving a sudden silence which underpinned the falling whorls of sand. I was the only one left. The person who couldn't fly. Left here on my own while everyone else flew off to save Franky.

But wait, I wasn't alone. The remains of that dreadful Terran women hadn't moved and Dougie was lying sprawled against the wall. Their outlines were slowly smudging under the dust's gentle haze, but they weren't going anywhere.

Seconds ago we had been fighting for our lives, but it was now just an empty courtyard, in a city, on a planet fifty thousand light-years from where we'd started. Both hives had gone to look after Franky and I really needed to get after them.

"Soffee..." A croak from Dougie jolted me out of my thoughts.

I turned, and very much against my better judgement started walking towards him. As I went past the body of the Terran woman I paused. No, surely not. She was moving, but no, it wasn't her. A minute head framed by legs appeared in the leg opening of her jumpsuit before popping back in again.

I was now getting movement indications all over the place, but the IFF's assessment was that there was no danger to me. It was just small native animals enjoying the alien bounty that had landed in front of them.

Dougie was struggling to sit up, moving awkwardly and obviously in a lot of pain. Lying next to him was a knife with his implants spiked onto it. Serves you right, you vile creature.

"Hey Soffee," he said, his voice breaking as he shifted position. "What's 'appening?"

"What is happening is that girls and other hive take Franky back to ship. Your friend shoot Franky and you lucky other hive not kill you."

"Whoa, hold on a minute," he said, shifting once again. "Franky was nothing to do with me. I mean come on, he's a mate."

A dribble of his odd-coloured blood was oozing out onto the stones and it didn't look like he could move. He lied like he breathed, but he was no longer any threat to me or my hive.

"OK," I said. "I have things to do and is time I go I think."

"But you can't just leave me here," he said, raising a hand and immediately wishing he hadn't. "I mean, I can't hardly move."

"On CS1," I said, "is dirty deeds done dirt cheap I think? Well I not care about you or your dirty deeds. I go find Franky and hope I never see you again."

"But you can't just leave me here," he called out as I walked away. "What am I going to do?"

"You do what you want," I called over my shoulder. "Is your choice."

My IFF popped up a quick update showing that the general movement was now contracting all around him.

"Soffee!" Dougie screamed as I walked into the tunnel through the wall. "You've gotta help me. I can't move. You can't just leave me here. Soffee, please...," but his words were snatched away by the breeze as I walked out onto the vast sunlit plaza.

A distant rumble of thunder rattled around the vast circle of buildings, and there on the horizon a twinkling dot thrust itself into the sky. It was Franky's pod, and I got a brief message confirming he was alive and that Scylla was looking after him.

Some sort of comfort I suppose, but I wasn't with him. I hadn't been able to protect him, just like I hadn't been able to protect him from those pirates on CS1. I could only watch as that fine white line split the sky, taking every one of my hopes and dreams with it.

The thunder died away as the sparkling dot at the tip of the line merged into the sea of blue. I was alone, again.

The deserted city stretched away from me, still, silent, a memorial to the lost people that had built it. The breeze blowing past was an almost tangible echo of their presence, but they were gone and our hives were here. We had travelled halfway across the galaxy and this lovely planet was finally ours.

I lifted my face to the sky, my wings loosening in the sun's warmth. All around me the silent buildings looked in, asking me who I was and what I was doing.

It could have been a warning, but it didn't feel like one. It felt more like a welcome. My dreams were up there with Franky, but dreams do not disappear. We hold them safe in our hearts until the time is right, and this planet felt like the right time and the right place for every one of them.

50
Hestia

Soffee

No one was up as I made my way through our new hive space, the early morning sun scattering across its ever-changing sculpture of half-built angles and edges. Living on the surface of this planet still had an edge of unreality about it, but every morning's blue sky and fresh air was truly a balm to the soul.

The wide plaza at the front of our building greeted me with a view of the native city that stretched away to the horizon. Even without Central Control guiding them, native mechanicals continued with their never-ending cleaning and repairs, keeping it exactly as it had been for decades or even centuries. But it was nothing more than a vacant mausoleum. Up here on this massive hillside, we were building our own hive spaces for two hives that had travelled half way across the galaxy to claim this planet. Franky being here would have been perfect, but I knew that was still many weeks away.

A chittered greeting and Hecate walked out into the sun. She spread her wings and took off straight into the smooth elevator of morning breeze blowing up the hillside. And that, of course, was why we had built our hive spaces here. Anyone could open their wings and fly, or at least they could if they were a Flivver. I could just about stay up if the wind was strong enough, but even my best efforts only attracted pitying looks from the other hive.

Mechanicals were growling into life, getting ready for the day's work ahead. Their attendant Smut sent me a briefest good morning brain tickle. We were so lucky that all four of them were never happier than when playing with their bounteous alien toy box. Our marvellous new hive spaces weren't going to build themselves and the demands for more and more mechanical servants never stopped.

Looking up, Hecate had now receded to a distant dot in that vast expanse of blue, and I gasped as an icy hand settled around my heart. Every time I looked up I saw it, the white line of Franky's pod flying away up into the sky. I took a deep breath, and then another, a lonely tear joining to trickle down my cheek. Franky was OK, I knew he was, but he was up there while I was down here. However much I wanted to be with him, we had troubles down here that just wouldn't go away.

It was the other hive, always the other hive. Three hundred of them versus seven of us and they thought they owned everything. No one cared that my hive had brought them here. No one cared that my hive had been first down on the planet and secured it. They wanted every single thing they saw, as well as everything they didn't see, and it was constant demands, agreements made and broken plus daily confrontations that never stopped.

I could only hope that when Franky was well enough to come down, our hive chief talking to their hive chief would manage to solve these problems. And that was two nice thoughts to contemplate as I placed both hands around my baby bump to watch the dots that were Scylla and Circe cavort around Hecate.

They were obviously having a marvellous time and I felt a quick stab of jealousy as I watched them. Of course, they weren't up there just for fun. More and more native creatures had started sniffing around these new people who had invaded their planet. Those two blue creatures were just the start, and after several more close encounters we now had unceasing aerial patrols up on watch. Forewarned was definitely forearmed and even the other hive agreed with that.

And talking of which, there was still that oddness of Dougie and the other Terrans. When the Smuts had gone off to retrieve their mechanicals from the ramp, they didn't find a trace of any bodies.

Scatterings of clothing were strewn about but there was nothing else, not even the knife which had been stuck through Dougie's implants. The girls had joined the Smuts' search, but there was nothing anywhere. I just hoped that this truly marked the end of Dougie's and the other Terrans' dirty deeds, wherever their remains had got to.

Scylla and Circe's dots had now peeled away from Hecate, twisting and turning as they cavorted across the sky. Right above me they tucked in their wings and dropped like two blue arrows. Down and down they came, blue slivers turning into feathered missiles that whipped overhead before pulling up into massive loops. Each cascaded down across the hive space, massive wing flaps killing their speed as they dropped into land right in front of me. Big show-offs!

"Nothing to see," said Scylla as she folded her wings. "Nothing from anyone else either so it looks like we're clear. Also, did you see the Medlab's latest? Franky is so much better now that all of those stem cells you donated are finally growing, even if," and she sniggered, "he's got blue patches growing all over his body. He never stops moaning about what it's doing to his lovely black skin, but the Medlab thinks he must be feeling better if he's started to complain. Also, some of the bigger patches have started to grow feathers. Feathers on a Terran. It's just so funny."

She leant in and squeezed my arm. "You must stop worrying. He really is getting better and he's also turning half Flivver, half Terran, just like you,' and she smiled as she stroked her wing down mine. "And oh yes, the Medlab said you need to get up to the ship for your next checkup."

"Well, I thought it said that I shouldn't try getting into a pod in my condition, whatever that might mean," I said. "My implants will tell me if there's anything wrong and it only wants me up there to do more tests, wretched thing. Anyway, I can't possibly go up and leave the other hive down here on their own. Whatever would they get up to?"

"Well, no one is expecting you to do much in that state," said Circe pointing at my beautiful bump. "Soon you won't be able to walk," and both of them sniggered.

Every Flivver on the planet thought it was the funniest thing ever that Terran mothers grew babies inside themselves. Flivvers laid eggs, which were hatched in the hive crèche, and that was the way it should be. This growing of babies inside a mother's ever-growing bulge was something they couldn't take their eyes off, almost like it was too awful to watch but they just couldn't help themselves.

"Well, these are our hive's first babies, going to be born in our lovely new hive space, on this new planet, and it's all ours," I said, stroking the bump in which two little people seemed to be trying out their wings, legs and arms, all at the same time.

The thought of our growing hive made for a companionable silence as we looked up at the hive crest rising from the top of the hill, that intertwined Terran and winged Terran/Flivver overlooking everything. I did wonder what those stall-holders on CS1 would have made of the pins they'd made for Franky all of those decades ago, now raised up for our hive, on our new planet, on the other side of the galaxy?

51
Acknowledgements

Many thanks for taking the time to read **Soffee**. I hope that you enjoyed it. If you did, please post a review and tell all of your friends. It really does help the struggling author.

The second book in the series will follow shortly and I hope that you enjoyed **Soffee** enough to give this one a try as well.

There are far too many people who have offered me their various assistances to thank everyone. However, particular thanks go to the following for their constructive suggestions and razor-sharp critiques: Andrew Cull, Chris Wortley, Dave Trew, Helen Leask, Helen Hawker, Mary-Ann Kruger, Patricia Morris, Steven Watson, Stuart Leask and Tim Payne. Also, many thanks to Charlie Christian for his superb job with the graphics.

Printed in Great Britain
by Amazon